JULIAN

Anna Katmore

JULIAN

Copyright © 2012 by Anna Katmore

Edited by Annie Cosby,

www.anniecosby.com

Cover design © 2018 by Anna Katmore

All rights reserved

www.annakatmore.com

To my wonderful parents.
I could never break my wings as fast
as you gave me a new pair.

*

And to my grandmother, Katharina.
May your angels take care of you. Always.

In the wrong direction

I faced a moral dilemma.

Take it…don't take it…take it…don't take it?

The soft cotton of the purple sweatshirt in my hand tempted me sorely. It wasn't covered with holes or stains, but perfectly intact, like nothing I'd worn since I was five years old. I could even rub the hoodie on my cheek, and the threads wouldn't scratch my skin like the nasty gray hand-me-down pullover I wore today.

Only the price tag stood between this perfect sweatshirt and me.

I searched the Friday afternoon crowd at Camden Market. The place brimmed with people. Everyone was busy scanning clothes, jewelry, shiny little knickknacks, or small toys. The stand-owner had her back to me as she talked to a customer. If I wanted to nick the sweatshirt, then it had to be now or never.

Take it?

"What are you waiting for, Montiniere?" Debby purred in my ear. "Take it or leave it. But make it fast, because I just had my hand in her till." Her blonde brows waggled.

Debby Westwood was not my friend. At least, not in the sense of *Hey girl, let's have a pajama party and tell each other our weirdest secrets*. I used to hang out with her. Debby's *the-entire-world-can-kiss-my-arse* attitude totally impressed me. She'd become my idol from the moment she rammed into me on Earls Court a few months ago. If I remember it right, she'd been on the run from the fuzz for the theft of a pair of crocodile stilettos. Jeez, I should have known consorting with a criminal would only get me into shit.

Debby wasn't a resident of London's youth center like me but spent her life on the streets. As for me, my warden, Miss Mulligan, allowed outings from the Lorna Monroe Children's Home only on Tuesdays and Fridays. And I was lucky, because anyone under the age of seventeen wasn't granted even that.

Praise my seventeenth birthday! I'd been ecstatic when I no longer had to attend group excursions. London was way more fun alone. No teachers, no rules, no nothing.

Just me. And this pretty purple sweatshirt.

My fist tightened around the fabric. *Thump-thump-thump.* The sound of my heartbeat boomed in my ear, faster and faster as I got closer to taking what I wanted. I knew it was wrong. My throat went dry. I had difficulty swallowing.

Suddenly, my backpack was unzipped, and the sound raised the small hairs on my arms.

"What are you doing?" I hissed as I swung around to face Debby.

She flashed a mischievous grin. "Helping you." Covering me from the view of the stand-owner, she stuffed the sweatshirt halfway into my bag. "Look at you. Your rags even scare the dogs away. You're lucky I spend time with you."

I glanced down at my ripped jeans and tattered boots. Heat flooded my face. Even though Debby didn't have a permanent roof over her head, she dressed like the queen of Oxford Street. If her slacks or shirts got dirty, she discarded them and stole new, brand-name ones. Simple as that.

When I first met her, it hadn't taken the girl long to convince me that there was more than enough stuff for everyone. Debby's *Shoplifting 101* philosophy: The exaggerated prices people paid for high heels and leather jackets made good on the few pieces we nicked from time to time.

Like this sweatshirt.

I kept my eyes on the freaky-looking stand-owner, dressed in striped tights and a straw hat, and waited another heartbeat before I shoved the sweatshirt all the way into my backpack. She must have heard my heart pounding, because she turned around at that moment.

After staring for a second, she glanced down at my backpack. "What the hell—"

My gaze snapped to my bag. *Crap!* A sleeve peeked out.

An instant later, she pulled a whistle on a chain from underneath her collar, and her cheeks bloated like two tomatoes on a vine, setting London's entire South End on alarm.

"Go! Go! Go!" I pushed Debby forward as I dashed away from the clothes stand.

"Thief! Stop!" The shrill voice echoed down the street followed by another alarming whistle. Heads turned our way. From the corner of my eye, I spotted two men in uniform stepping away from a kiosk and scanning the crowd. They were searching for us. My adrenaline kicked in, tensing each of my muscles like an over-stretched rubber band.

"This way!" Debby tugged on my backpack, almost tipping me sideways. She pulled me behind another stand with yellowed books and silver cutlery. There were more stands ahead. Shoppers turned annoyed eyes on us as we pushed through the crowd.

"Jona," Debby panted. "We need to split up. They can't catch us both. You go left, and I'll keep straight."

I turned to the left. A bloody dead end.

"You want me to play bait for the cops? Are you nuts? They'll get me!"

"You're not eighteen yet. They can't nail you for anything." Her hand curled around my upper arm. She shoved me forward as she scanned for the policemen. "Your teacher will save your arse. She does every time."

"No! She threatened to let me rot in prison if I ever steal again."

"Don't be such a wimp." Debby's shoulder collided with mine, shoving me sharply to the side. My lungs stopped sucking in air. Mouth open, I pivoted to face Debby. Her evil grin was the last thing I saw as she vanished into the crowd.

"The brats ran this way," a gravelly voice reached me.

I peeked over my shoulder. *Bloody hell!* The cops were fast on my heels. Their blue caps bobbed out from the crowd and moved steadily forward. I was an easy target for them.

No, not today.

Debby had gone straight on, so I angled to the right. There had to be a way out of this open market. The pounding in my ears shut out the murmur of the shoppers. My gaze darted over the crowd. Bobbing heads moved like waves. *Dammit!* Which way would get me out of here?

I stopped, trying to catch my breath, then I twisted. There was no thinning of the crowd, but the blue police caps came on, angling my way at a speed that should have been impossible in the packed market.

Beads of sweat dotted my face and the back of my neck. Miss Mulligan would kill me if I got involved with the police again.

I used my hand as a shield against the gleaming afternoon sun. A dowdy overweight man with a green hat shoved me aside. I lost my balance and nearly knocked over a toddler sucking on a lollipop with huge brown eyes gaping up at me. Instead, I collided with an old lady whose shrill cry not only pained my ears but also gave me away.

"Sorry, ma'am," I muttered, noticing her hunched back and the scarf wrapped around her gray hair. Her glasses sat askew across her nose, and one of her crutches had dropped to the ground. I bent to pick it up for her.

"Are you all right? I didn't mean to hurt you." I ducked my head and adjusted the glasses with shaking fingers. My feet were already bouncing in the direction of escape.

"Get off, you nasty child!" The lady dropped the crutch to swat my hands away from her face. "Don't any of you kids have eyes in your useless heads?"

That got me moving. I dropped to my hands and knees and crawled away, doing my best to dodge the oncoming pedestrians. A heavy boot landed on my fingers. I bit my tongue to keep from screaming. Maybe crawling wasn't the best way to move through a crowd as thick as Miss Weatherby's vanilla pudding. I jumped to my feet.

"Move!" The same gravelly voice I'd heard earlier parted the crowd like the Red Sea.

"Riley, I got her!" called a very angry cop.

The man leaped forward, lunging for my arm. I spun on my heel, ready to dash away to safety, but instead I bounced right into the solid, uniform-clad chest of my captor's partner. He was smaller, and stout, but his grip on my shoulder was iron.

Ice-cold fear settled in my veins. "Let go!" I kicked his shin and wrenched free from his grip.

The man yelped and hobbled on his good leg. People surrounded us like this was a stupid carnival, only they all had the same judging look in their eyes. They'd caged me in. My stomach slid to my feet. No chance of escape.

Oh dear Lord, I was in deep shit.

The tall cop ripped my raggedy backpack from my shoulders before he shoved me to the pavement. His knee dug into my spine.

Brilliant. Just the position I wanted to be in.

My shoulders felt as if they popped out of their sockets when he wrenched my hands behind my back. Cold metal closed around my wrists. The ominous click of the cuffs resonated in my ears, sending a red haze of hysteria through my head. *Oh please, not again.*

Debby's first rule when caught shoplifting: Deny everything.

Swallowing hard, I gathered what was left of my courage. "Leave me alone!" The words were muffled with my cheek grinding painfully against the pavement. "I did nothing wrong!"

My long hair caught in the officer's hand as he yanked me up. I groaned. This was going to end nastily. I needed a plan B. Fast.

"Of course you didn't do anything, kid." The cop named Riley laughed harshly as he rummaged through my backpack. "Let me guess, you're a kleptomaniac, and you have a medical certificate for legal pilfering in London?"

Making fun of me?

Debby had also taught me not to show fear in those moments. And she'd taught me well. I stuck out my chin. These jerks wouldn't get the best of me. "Take off the cuffs, and I'll fucking *klepto* your balls!"

"Watch your tongue, missy. You're in no position to threaten a police officer." Riley gave me a hard stare. "Is this your backpack?"

I glowered back. "Nope. Never seen it before."

"Ah, that's funny. Because here is an identification card from the Lorna Monroe Children's Home, which coincidentally holds your picture." He held up the ID and flashed an ugly grin. If he'd moved his hand an inch closer, he could have shoved the small white card up my nose.

"I lost my wallet last week. Seems like someone found it." I fought to keep my expression blank.

"Of course. And that person forced this bag on you then. Oh, and the sales lady stuffed this"—he pulled out the purple sweatshirt and dangled it in front of me—"into the backpack while you walked by her shop, right?"

I stared him straight in the eye and cocked a brow. "Shit happens."

The tall man behind me grabbed my shoulder and shook me. "That's enough. You're coming with us."

I cast a sneer over my shoulder as he pushed me forward. "How could I ever resist when you beg so nicely, Officer?"

The muscle in his jaw ticked, but he restrained from speaking. His grip on my arm tightened as he led me out of the market. Shaken, I walked alongside the cops with my gaze on the ground to avoid the curious looks of witnesses. Their stares tormented me more than the steel cuffs cutting into my wrists.

When we reached the patrol car, I finally lifted my gaze. Across the street, Debby-*the-bitch*-Westwood lurked in the doorway of a dirty gray house with a snide gleam in her eyes. I stopped short, my anger heating my blood, then I jerked my arm free from the tall cop and marched forward. "I hope you're happy now!"

Debby disappeared even before he could grab me again and pull me back to the car. "This one's mental," he whispered to Riley.

Bearing down on my molars until my jaw hurt, I scowled at the two men.

The taller officer shoved me into the backseat and slammed the door shut. My body shook as the truth of my dire situation washed over me.

The cops climbed into the front seats. My gaze hardened once more as Riley inched the car into London's traffic.

The tall one curled his lips as he looked at me through the cage partition. "I always wonder what drives kids like you to steal. Doesn't the system provide you with all the luxury you need?"

I gathered my saliva to make a good spit at him. But that wouldn't exactly help my situation, so I struggled to swallow my anger along with the phlegm. He wasn't the only one in London who rated homeless children as lower than dirt.

"I get a kick out of riding in police cars," I replied, my tone dripping saccharin sweetness. "It's always the highlight of my week." The steel around my wrists dug uncomfortably into my back. I shifted a few times, ending up propped against the door with my legs pulled to my chest and my dirty boots resting on the worn-out beige cushions of the backseat. The heat of early August had warmed the cabin like a sauna. In the stuffy air, tickles of sweat rolled down the valley between my breasts.

At a traffic light, my gaze drifted upon a bus and skated over a young woman inside it. She carried a baby, trying to cool the kid down with puffs of her breath. A sigh escaped me. She would never let her child down or send it off to an orphanage to fend for itself. Her baby would grow up in a cozy home, with a loving mother, far away from the kind of mess I was stuck in. *Always falling into a pile of crap.* I cleared my throat to stop it from constricting.

Riley pulled up in front of a narrow, familiar brick building. Seconds later, he opened the car door for me. I decided my butt had grown roots as I scowled at his blotchy face. It seemed the heat troubled him even more than me.

"What? Does the *Skillful Dodger* need an invitation to get out of the car?"

"What? Is Mr. Donut actually referring to Dickens?" I pulled a wry face then scooted over to climb out. "You better read the book again, moron."

With the damn cuffs on, getting out was a bitch. I bumped my head against the doorframe. Pain exploded in my skull, followed by a shower of stars dancing behind my eyelids.

Just another bright spot in my crappy day.

"That serves you right," Riley snorted between hiccups of laughter.

"Lord, let him choke on his giggles," I mumbled with my gaze raised skyward. With my wrists crossed in the small of my back, I tugged up my hand-me-down jeans that always sat loosely on my hips.

The taller officer marched into the building, holding the door open like a gentleman. If only I'd had my hands free to open the door on my own and then slam it in his goddamn face.

Riley fought to keep up with my quick stride, but I beat him to the stairs.

"Don't worry, I know the way." I climbed the steps to the first floor where the main office was. Unfortunately, I had to wait for one of the oafs to open the door.

As Riley and his partner arrived on the first floor, my exaggerated sigh drew their attention. One flight of stairs had Riley panting like a dog.

The tall cop planted a hand on my shoulder. "No need to hurry, lass. You'll meet justice soon enough."

I shrugged his hand off. "I've got news for you, Riley and Riley's partner. I'm only seventeen. That means I'm not old enough to face legal punishment for a minor crime like...borrowing a sweatshirt." I gave them a wide grin, which didn't come as easily as I had hoped when Miss Mulligan's warning rang in my head.

"Borrow?" Riley puffed. Amusement edged his tone, but his angry face confirmed I would be walking out of here—without cuffs. I turned my face away and exhaled, relieved.

Riley twisted the doorknob then walked into the office first. Shoulders squared and back straight, I followed him into the room with the high, arched ceiling. The sun shining through the narrow, tall windows blinded my eyes for a second, while the stench of sweat and the smell of police dogs hit my nose.

A handful of cops lingered behind wide desks, sipping from coffee mugs and chatting to each other. No one glanced at us, so I avoided the German shepherd sprawled out on the floor and strode down the aisle between two straight lines of desks, directly to reception.

Hip against the counter, I gazed down at the black-haired guy with designer stubble. His bright eyes stood out against the dark blue of his uniform.

"Hi, Quinn. How you doing? Sorry, I'd shake your hand, but I'm afraid that right now—" I twisted and raised one shoulder, displaying my shackled wrists. "I'm slightly indisposed."

Quinn rubbed his hands over his suntanned face. The moan came through muffled and somewhat choked. "Shit, Jona! Tell me you were part of a sick party gag and now you're here to get trick cuffs removed." He peeked through the slits between his fingers.

A sheepish smile crept to my face. "You might want to take a second guess."

He lowered his hands and folded them on the desk. "Why can't you keep your butt out of trouble? Kids your age are supposed to hang out in parks, not at police stations."

Quinn was a nice guy. Big eyes, styled hair, and a muscular body. He was hardly ten years older than me. Once, I had asked him for his real age, but he just told me he was "old enough to know better."

Unlike my relationship with Debby, I did consider Quinn a real friend, even though he worked for the police. And not just because he used to make a stop at McDonald's to buy me a sandwich when he volunteered to take me back to the orphanage so often. He was someone who saw me, the teenager, and not the criminal.

During the one year we had known each other, he had never passed on a chance to try to talk sense into my rebellious head. And today was no different. His nostrils flared as he heaved a hopeless sigh. "What did you do this time?"

Riley punched his fist on the countertop, the purple sweatshirt clenched between his chunky fingers. "*Jim Dawkins* here went fishing at Camden Market."

I rolled my eyes. "Jack. It's *Jack* Dawkins. Someone should smack a copy of *Oliver Twist* over your head." I'd have done it myself if I had a book within reach that was thick enough to leave a dent in this bonehead. And, of course, if currently my hands weren't cuffed. I cast Quinn a meaningful glance. "Why do you surround yourself with idiots?"

Riley started forward with fire in his eyes, but Quinn held him back by his arm. "Thanks for bringing her in. I'll deal with her from here."

The stout officer snarled but finally trudged away, throwing off steam that would make Thomas the Tank Engine proud.

Once Riley and his partner disappeared, Quinn regarded me with wry sympathy. "You know, Abe will have your head for this." He paused as I gulped.

Stealing a Nintendo from Stanton Electronics eleven months ago had gotten me the first chance to see a courtroom from the inside and make the acquaintance of Judge Abraham C. Smith. I liked to call the balding judge a special friend, even though *a plague* had become his choice description for me.

Minor offenses had cultivated our *friendship extraordinaire* ever since. Although Miss Mulligan continuously saved my butt, the last time I'd seen Abe, he had sworn he would lock me away for the next five hundred years if I showed up in his office again. I had half-expected steam to come out of his ears. He'd sent me out of his office with a glare as sharp as Superman's laser vision. I wasn't too keen on meeting him again anytime soon.

Quinn stood up and placed his palm on my shoulder. Unlike the other cop's hand, I allowed Quinn's to stay. "Let's fill out the forms, kiddo, and then we'll call Miss Mulligan. I can't get off right now, so your warden needs to come here and pick you up."

My stomach dropped. I could picture the freckled beanpole freaking out when she heard I was at the police station—again. My eighteenth birthday was only seven weeks away. Six weeks and five days to be exact. She wouldn't make her threat real and turn me over to the law so close to my release from the orphanage. Would she?

*

A couple of hours later, Miss Mulligan led me through the wide double doors of the institution. My eyes were focused on the gray linoleum floor, but the whispers and contemptuous stares of the others in the hall didn't escape me.

"Go to your room," Miss Mulligan ordered. The effort it took for her to control her temper reflected on her red face. "I'll make a call to Judge Smith now and deal with you later."

Calling Abe? Thank goodness, she was on my side after all. I knew her tactics from the past. First, she would call the court and try to reason with the officials, promising to make up for the damage, or in this particular case, the stolen sweatshirt. Then she'd take me to a hearing where I would show my good will and act very, very sorry. In the end, I might get away with being locked in my room for a couple of weeks and probably no TV.

Acceptable.

That evening, the warden came to my room on the third floor to inform me the dreaded audience with my friend Abe was set for Tuesday—and to tell me she would be the happiest person in the world the day that I turned eighteen and left the orphanage for good.

There was no reason not to believe her.

The four days between my capture and the meeting at court I spent in my sparsely furnished room with dirty white walls. Curled up on the worn metal cot, I stuck my nose deep in a book, my feet shoved under the thin blanket. The lamp placed on the stool that served as my nightstand had a weak bulb that hardly provided enough light to decipher the letters on the pages at night, but that didn't stop me.

I read the story of Peter Pan and how he taught Wendy to fly above a sleeping London. Bloody hell, I should have left my window open and begged for someone like him to come through and carry me out in his arms. Then again, with my problem of vertigo, I wouldn't have made it past the windowsill.

On Tuesday morning, I dressed in the best pair of black jeans I owned, fixed the hole over the right knee with a safety pin, and scrubbed my scuffed boots. A dark gray hoodie with ragged cuffs that constantly slid over my hands had to do on top.

Miss Mulligan, wrapped in an abominable pink suit, escorted me to the courthouse in a taxi. I was to meet Abe in the smaller, almost private office behind the big hall, where minor cases were handled.

As we strolled down the hallway, the distinct scent of lavender and cherry blossom floated in the air. The smell set off an ice-cold trickle at the back of my neck, waking memories of painful days long ago. I knew only one person who used to wear this particular perfume.

I stopped dead and whirled around. Miss Mulligan sent me a puzzled glance. Breathing deep, I inspected the hallway up and down, but the one person I searched for was nowhere in sight.

A long breath wheezed from my lungs. Good, it was only a mistake.

In front of Judge Smith's office, a guard stood watch. He let us in when we showed him my nice official invitation. He frowned at my hands shoved deep into my pockets, but I ignored him and followed Miss Mulligan through the door.

Wide windows on two walls brightened the beige-carpeted office. A small number of people gathered on one side of the room close to the door, some sat next to the judge's big desk. I caught a glimpse of Quinn's encouraging eyes and felt a cloud of calm settle in my chest for a moment. Then my gaze zeroed in on Abe.

He looked up from a stack of papers as soon as I crossed the threshold. His disapproving eyes sent shivers down my back, but even as my warden slowed her pace, I walked straight up to him.

"Never show weakness or fear," Debby's advice rang in my ears.

"Jona Montiniere." Abe adjusted his small round spectacles and gave me a quick once over.

Squaring my shoulders, I lifted my chin and displayed my best let's-talk-shop grin. "Hello, Abe. Is business doing well?"

The judge ground his teeth. "You keep me busy enough," he grumbled through his beard.

I always wondered how it could be that men lost the luxury of hair on their heads, while stubble still sprouted wildly on their faces. This was not the best moment to bring up the prickly topic, though. Not with Abe already gathering momentum.

He scanned his papers again, shoving the glasses farther up his nose. "This is the twenty-third time in less than one year that I have you standing here."

At the word *twenty-third* an awed whistle came from the seats. I cut a quick glance to Quinn, who cocked a brow.

"Is there anything you can say in your defense?" the judge

demanded.

I pouted, Quinn only shrugged.

Next to him sat Riley, who stuffed the last bite of a doughnut with pink icing into his mouth. It brought a grin to my lips, and I turned back to Abe.

"I'm a kleptomaniac and have a medical certificate for legal pilfering in London."

Riley coughed, slamming a hand to his chest, but it was the deep chuckle from the back of the room that drew my full attention. First, I only glanced over my shoulder. But glistening sunlight blinded me, and I spun around.

For an immeasurable moment, nothing but bright white fog absorbed and swallowed everything within reach. Awestruck, I didn't even squint. Then a tall figure emerged from this glowing mist. A long, white cloak floated around the person's legs while the sleeves, long and wide, covered the masculine hands almost completely. Fathomless blue eyes appeared next, followed by a smile that could have melted glaciers in the Arctic.

It had to be a reflection of light streaming through the south window. An illusion caused by today's stress and tension. But it didn't disappear.

Every single pair of eyes in the room locked onto me with confused stares. Their gawks prickled my skin all over. Only the illuminated person lowered his gaze. He retreated a couple of steps to the shadowed line along the back wall. Instantly, the fog around him disappeared, and I could make out the fine features of a young man. A casual pair of blue jeans and a black leather jacket replaced what I was sure had been a white cloak.

Obviously, they had to add *delusional* to my medical certificate.

His clean-shaven face revealed a strong jaw topped by a sensual mouth. When the corners slightly lifted, my heart banged against my ribcage, fluttering like a sparrow caught in a cage. Strands of tousled golden hair fell over his forehead, reminding me of warm honey. Even with the mystic light gone, the guy who remained was godlike.

Bloody hell, what had brought a god to my hearing? It was just a freaking sweatshirt!

As he arched one delicate eyebrow, I snapped my mouth shut before drool could drip from the corners. Heat rushed through my veins and filled my face.

"Miss Montiniere, will you please pay attention?" Abe's words sounded far away.

Those sapphire eyes held me captive. I never wanted to leave this personal prison of ours.

Slowly, a bony arm looped around the god's bent elbow.

Cherry blossoms? Why did the room suddenly smell of lavender and this distinctive note of spring in bloom? The mix of floral scents pulled me back to the present. How long since I had smelled it the last time? That must have been something close to five years. I let my gaze trace the skinny arm and wander farther up.

Horrorstruck, I gaped at the face of the one person I never wanted to see again.

A minor problem

Judge Abe's square office, with all the people shoved inside, started to spin around me. I felt like someone had stuffed me into a too-small box and now tried to push the top closed against my head.

"Who let that bitch in?" Muscles quivering, I glowered at Charlene Montiniere.

"Watch your tongue," the judge warned. "This is a court of law."

"The fuck I will," I spat. My eyes staked her. "This woman dumped me at an orphanage when I was a kid. She never even looked back." Fear tightened my throat. How was the hag going to ruin my life this time?

Charlene gaped at me. The skin sagged into bags beneath her sunken eyes. Her matted red-orange tresses had once been the exact match to my own long auburn hair. She wore a stark shade of red lipstick that clashed with her pale, bony face. In short, she looked like she'd been through hell.

Good, I hoped the bitch had suffered just as much as I had. She could crawl right back into whatever rat hole she'd emerged from. And she'd better not even think about saying anything to me. She'd lost that right when I was five.

My hatred-filled glare silenced her. One of her shaky hands rose slowly, as if she wanted to touch me from the ten feet distance that stretched between us.

"Drop dead, Charlene," I growled.

"Jona Montiniere, I insist on you behaving in an appropriate manner, so we can continue this hearing," Abe Smith roared. "I understand your mistrust against your mother, but once you listen to the reasons, you might change your mind."

No way in hell.

The alarm signal in my head flashed bright red. Another minute in the same room with my mother would have been an eternity too long. I spun around to face the old man behind his monstrous desk and gave him a mocking military salute. "Goodbye, Abe. I'm outta here."

The roar to call me to order was futile. Consequences? Not my concern. I strode toward the door, my only goal fresh air and a good deal of distance between me and that bitch.

People shouted my name, some addressing me as Miss Montiniere, others using only my first name as if we were friends.

"Kiddo, don't be ridiculous. Stay where you are!" Quinn called out.

Not happening.

His desperation wouldn't stop me from leaving. But a set of chunky arms around my waist could. Riley was the first to capture me. The delight of victory shone in his eyes as he pressed my back against the wall. "You're not going anywhere, little miss, apart from jail."

Don't panic. Hysteria never got me anywhere, and there was a very real place I needed to get right now. Out of this room.

Fists clenched, my nails bit into my palms. "Take your bloody paws off me!"

The high-pitched squeak Riley gave nearly shattered my eardrums when I bit into the hand he'd clasped on my left shoulder. The donut residue I could taste on it made my stomach roll.

He jerked his arm back. "Damn brat, you're gonna pay for this!"

Over his shoulder, I spotted both Quinn and Riley's partner rushing toward me, but the stumbling Riley bounced into Quinn, and my only friend at the police station staggered sideways. He caught his balance by grabbing Miss Mulligan's arm. The warden squealed hysterically and slapped his hands away.

All the confusion in the room was my chance of escape. However, my freedom was short lived. The moment I started for the exit, Riley's tall partner caught my wrist and swung me around. The momentum tossed me against the edge of a small, dark brown desk in the back corner of the room.

In self-defense, I leaned back on the top and pulled my legs to my chest as the policeman came for me. My hard kick hit his chest, and the soles of my boots popped a wheeze out of the cop. The deputy careened backward, doubled over. When he caught his breath, he cursed in a tongue that would have made Debby

Westwood, the uncrowned queen of swearing, go green with envy.

I shoved away from the desk, but my chance of flight was gone as the door flung open and two guards stormed in. Whether it was Riley's screams, Miss Mulligan's screeches, or a secret button under Abe's desk that alerted the guards, I never knew. But they had my shoulders pinned to the floor before my next breath. All air escaped from my lungs. A flash of pain soared through my upper body.

"No!" two men in the room shouted at once. One of them was Quinn. His voice was edged with sheer horror. In that moment, I was grateful he didn't just abandon me like so many others had.

Who the other worried guy was, I couldn't tell.

One guard pulled handcuffs from his belt. He fastened them around my wrists in front of me. Neither my kicking nor shrieking could prevent the awful click when the locks snapped into place.

"Get off her, you idiots. She's only a kid." Quinn elbowed his way through to me. "Are you all right, kiddo?"

The pain in my chest and back eased. I could finally draw in air. "Wow, what a fight!" It didn't feel like anything was seriously injured or broken, so I pressed my lips together and gave Quinn a halfhearted not. "I'm fine."

I had to be. *No weakness. Ever.*

He wrapped his fingers around my upper arms, pulling me to a wobbly stand. "In God's name, Jona," he whispered. "I beg you, behave."

A deep growl preceded my answer. "As you wish, *sir.*" What other choice did I have with the cuffs on?

From the corner of my eye, I caught a glimpse of my mother's companion. The fair-haired god studied me with narrowed eyes. *Trying to figure me out?* That made me very uncomfortable.

With a gentle tug, Quinn led me up to Abe's desk. I turned my head to hold the blond stranger's stare for another moment. His arm was wrapped in a supporting way around my mother's shoulders. *A god in his early twenties with Charlene?* In what universe would a bony bitch like her find a lover so close to my age—and that gorgeous to boot?

"Jona Montiniere!"

The murmurs in the room ebbed with Abe's thundering. My head snapped toward him. Nerves steeling for what was to follow, I quickly rebuilt my mental wall of protection.

He had risen from his chair and braced himself on the desk, glaring at me over the rims of his spectacles. "This time, you stepped over the line. Contempt of court. Assaulting an officer."

"What? They assaulted me first!" My shout echoed in the room, no less angry than his. "Riley here should be sued for child abuse."

"Enough!" Abe roared. "Shut your mouth and sit down."

Sit down? My dramatic glance behind me was enough to point out there was nothing but the floor to sit on.

Abe rubbed his temples. "For heaven's sake, someone fetch a chair for the girl."

One of the guards hurried to shove a chair into the back of my knees, and I plopped down on the uncomfortable wooden seat. Quinn stood beside me, arms folded over his chest like the bouncer of a night club. *Ooh, my personal pit bull.* This eased at least some of my fear. I could lift my chin again. The move always ignited the pig-rude manners I'd gleaned from Debby.

The judge calmed himself with a few heavy breaths and sat down, too. His black robe with puffy sleeves made him look more like a watchful owl than a person of authority. When he lowered his gaze to the papers in front of him, I took the chance to poke

Quinn's thigh with my elbow.

"What?" he hissed.

Hands lifted, I displayed the torturing shackles and grinned sweetly. "Remove these?"

Quinn cut a glance to the exit then studied me for a second, his brows furrowing into a line. "I don't think so."

Huh? And I thought he was my friend. My *you-evil-bastard* scowl only coaxed his grin, and he tousled my hair.

When Judge Abe cleared his throat, all eyes returned to him. "Miss Montiniere, I've followed your criminal progress for nearly a year now. As I was informed, you will be released from the Lorna Monroe Children's Home in less than seven weeks." He pulled his glasses off his nose and placed them carefully on the stack of papers. "This gives rise to serious concern. With a criminal past like yours, I don't doubt for a second that you'll be out on a robbing tour of London as soon as you turn eighteen."

Criminal past? *Hello?* "I only nick from the rich to give it to the poor." In this particular case, the poor was me. "Shouldn't a person in your position exercise his office without prejudice?" I had hardly spoken the words when Quinn's fingers dug painfully into my shoulder.

The judge let my statement go by unnoticed. He only drew a deep, slow breath. "To prevent the worst, I should let you stay under house arrest in the orphanage and delay an official accusation for your latest theft until you turn eighteen. In that case, I would have full authority to send you to prison."

Holy shit.

He paused to smile, and I wished the watchdog at my side would unshackle my hands so I could scratch the judge's glassy eyes out. "But as it is, I'm pleased to welcome your mother into this room today. We had an unofficial meeting this morning, and I'm glad—"

I jumped from my seat, cutting his sentence short. "You were the traitor who called her to this meeting?" A siren went off in my head, tuning out common sense.

"Sit, Jona," Quinn barked through clenched teeth. His palm on my shoulder pushed down hard. I whined, but gave in to his strength.

"And I'm glad," Abe continued, as if no one had interrupted him in the first place, "she told me about relatives of yours in France, who offered to give you a home and a place to stay for as long as you wish. Your aunt and her husband own vineyards there, and you will do charity hours on the grounds every day until you come of age."

The judge had gone nuts. This was the only reasonable explanation for such nonsense coming out of his mouth. "You're going to ship me off to the continent? Like a slave? You can't do that! It's illegal." It had to be. *Right?*

Abe quirked one brow, dismissing my assumption. "Since serious health issues made your mother dependent on other people's help, she currently lives with her sister in France. We see this as a great opportunity for you to get to know your biological family and maybe tighten the bonds anew."

"How can something be tightened that didn't exist in the first place?" I muttered. There was nothing in this world that could form or tighten anything between me and my mother. Let alone a bond. *No contact with that bitch and her pet, thanks.* And where the hell did this said aunt come from? I'd never heard of any relatives in Britain, France, or anywhere else.

If I'd jumped up to protest again, Quinn would only have pushed me back into my seat. Instead, I raised my right arm, like a good little girl, to draw the judge's attention. Annoyingly, with the cuffs on, my left hand lifted, too.

"Please, take me to prison instead." My request came out dry and emotionless. Dead earnest.

From above, Quinn glared daggers at me. I cut a glance at him, but then studied Abe's old eyes again, awaiting his final adjudication with an empty pit in my stomach growing fast.

"I do believe you graduated from high school last spring?"

Not knowing what Abe's question could have to do with my punishment, I nodded. My marks in math had been lousy, but at least I did it.

"And currently you aren't taking any summer classes in Miss Mulligan's Children's Home?"

"No."

"Then you are going to live with your family." The bang of his little wooden hammer on the small round plate sealed the matter. "Now get out of my courtroom and never come back."

Shit, I was screwed.

When they started making plans over my head, and voices mixed to a painful blur, Quinn let me wait outside the room. I had to promise not to run off or pick a fight with another officer before he would even open the door for me. I restrained myself from giving him the finger and slipped out.

Elbows propped on my bent knees, I sat on the floor in the hallway with my back resting against the windowed wall. The chain of the cuffs rattled mockingly. With them on, I wouldn't get far on an escape for fresh air. I might as well surrender to my horrendous fate.

Utterly miserable and confused about my new future—and no less annoyed by the glances of passing officials—my head dipped back, my gaze focusing on the blank ceiling. Out of habit, when I was by myself, I started humming a song I didn't know the name of. It always had a strangely soothing effect on me. Odds were I had made up the melody myself over the years. But I'd hummed, whistled, or tapped the rhythm with my fingers so often that the tune wouldn't get out of my head.

The door opening opposite me didn't disrupt my low singing. But when my mother's blond friend came out and leaned one shoulder casually against the column in the middle of the hallway, the hum died in my throat.

"Hi," he said with a compassionate look that made me once again wish the traitor, Quinn, had taken off those damn handcuffs so I wouldn't look like a complete idiot.

Lips pressed together, my fingers waggled in a feeble greeting. The mere sight of this man sent goosebumps over my skin.

"That was quite an interesting...*situation* in there."

With an evil grin, I hoped to send the message *Mind your own crap, buddy*. Out loud, I said sweetly, "Glad you enjoyed the show."

"I didn't really." He wrinkled his nose. "Getting into a fight with a group of cops wasn't your best idea. Even a smart girl like you might get hurt at some point."

Yeah, sure. My eyes narrowed to slits. But his words warmed my heart in an unfamiliar way.

The young man nodded his chin at my tied hands. "They look a little uncomfortable."

And they bloody well were, but I shrugged it off like it was nothing unusual. "The latest fashion. You heard the judge, I wear them quite often."

A teasing smile that spiked my blood pressure played around his lips. "Shall we take them off?"

He had to be kidding. "Unless you've got teeth like a hacksaw, I don't see how that would work."

The guy crossed the hall to me, pulling a key-ring from his pocket. He squatted, leveled his eyes with mine, and shook the keys in front of my face. The friendly jingle of metal filled the high hallway.

My mouth fell open. "Where did you get those from?"

"Officer Madison."

"You stole them from Quinn?" I pulled my hands out of his reach.

"Of course not." The blond god gave me a pointed look. "I asked for them."

Why would this guy ask my police friend to release me? Frowning, I concentrated on the safety pin in my jeans. "Quinn wouldn't free me when I asked him to."

His intense blue eyes locked with mine. "I had to solemnly swear to keep an eye on you. Now hold still." Cool fingers curled around my wrist to steady my hand while he unlocked the first cuff. My skin warmed under his fingers.

Why would he give his word to an officer, just to free me? Why even care? He'd do well to stay behind that door, holding my horrible mother's hand instead of setting mine free. With a click, the other cuff came off. I flexed my hands and rubbed my burning wrists. The shackles had left crimson red marks on my skin.

"Better?" He tilted his head and arched one beautiful brow.

My head bobbed, but I found no breath to answer.

"Okay then." He used my knees to push himself up and stretched to his full height.

Now, he probably expected my gratitude following his selflessness. My gaze focused on the ripped hems of his jeans, my lips remained sealed.

When he turned on his heel and marched off to the left, I glanced up. "And now you're going where?" The words shot out before I could stop myself.

"Bathroom break." His arched brows dared me to object.

My lower lip threatened to pop from between my teeth as I chewed on it. *Don't speak!* "But you're supposed to keep an eye on me."

After studying me for a couple of seconds, his expression softened even more. "You're not going to get me into trouble."

A balloon of warmth exploded in my chest. I let him take another stride away from me. Two. Three. Four. "How can you be so sure?" *Shut the hell up, Jona.* "According to everything you know about me, I'll probably be gone when you get back."

A shrug of one shoulder and his beguiling smile struck me silent. "I trust you." A moment later he disappeared around the corner.

My chin hit my chest.

Trust me, my arse! He must be nuts if he thought I could be trusted. With a snort, I rose from the linoleum floor and strode toward the exit. But I bounced into a solid wall of bad conscience.

"Dammit." I kicked the real wall to my right. The rubber sole of my boot left a black mark on the white surface. I shouldn't even have had to think about it, so why in the world did I hesitate? And for a stranger?

The exit had never looked better, and yet invisible shackles prevented any further step in its direction. Breathing became increasingly harder, and anger burned like a flame through me. What was this stranger's hold over me? I shouldn't have wasted another thought on him. After all, I hadn't asked him to remove the handcuffs.

But he took them off anyway. And he trusted me.

A growl rumbled out of my throat. I shot an angry glance heavenward and raked my clawed fingers through my hair. With a helpless sigh, I returned to the spot where he'd found me. Standing with my back against the column and arms crossed tightly over my chest, I awaited his return.

Only seconds later, footfalls announced his approach in the hall behind my back. The steps slowed, and a hardly audible sigh of dismay drifted around the column to me. I grinned to myself, savoring this sweet, however short moment of victory. Then I shoved away from the post.

Relief washed over his face at the sight of me, the corners of his mouth tilting up. "It's good to see you again."

I steeled my expression and ground my teeth then spun on my heel and trudged back toward Abe's office, intending to hire Quinn as my bodyguard to keep this goddamn Good Samaritan at arm's length.

"Damn you to hell," I muttered on the way.

He laughed behind me. "Oh joy."

*

I zipped my backpack shut over my three t-shirts, my only other pair of jeans, and the few precious books I owned. The sun was setting over the low rooftops outside my window. This would be my last night in an institution I had called home for over twelve years.

Damn old Abe should have sent me to prison. Could hardly be worse than the orphanage. But, to banish me from the country and condemn me to live in the same house with my mother was unspeakably cruel.

"It's not even two months," Quinn had said after the hearing. "You're a tough girl, you'll survive."

Actually, he was the only person I was going to miss.

A knock rattled the door. That should be him. The judge and Miss Mulligan had thought it a good idea for me to spend an evening with my mother and her companion before attempting a journey to a foreign country with them. Charlene had beamed while her friend covered his smirk with a cough. Quinn accompanying me tonight was the one condition on which I had agreed to go.

I pulled the door open and stared. For at least three whole seconds. Quinn in casual wear. Without his uniform, he looked even younger, and his dark gray t-shirt and bleached jeans fit him perfectly.

My black zip-up sweatshirt and ripped jeans suddenly didn't seem like such a nice thing to wear anymore. Maybe I shouldn't have removed the safety pin from the hole in the knee.

Quinn offered me his elbow. "Are you ready, kiddo?"

"Ready to face the dragon and get roasted? Never. Let's go." I looped my arm through his and pulled the door closed behind me.

"It can't be all bad."

"You have no idea."

Downstairs, Quinn held the door open for me and led me to his black BMW parked around the block. We both climbed in, and he pulled away from the curb. After a while of staring silently out the window, my train of thought broke with Quinn's not-so-subtle cough. I tilted my head his way.

He briefly glanced at me then faced forward again. "You know, I was quite surprised to see your mother today."

When I remained silent, he added, "Probably because you told me she was dead."

"If only." Arms folded over my chest, I concentrated on the car in front of us, wishing Quinn would crash into it at the next intersection. That would give us an excuse not to show up.

We passed the intersection without incident. Damn Quinn for being a safe driver.

I needed to come up with a strategy. Fast. Before we arrived at the pub and there was no way for me to escape confronting Charlene. When the uncomfortable buzz in my stomach increased, I cleared my throat and gave Quinn a sweet smile.

His eyes darted back and forth between me and the windshield. "What is it, Jona?"

I leveraged my best sad puppy look. "Is there a chance you don't know the way and we end up in the city watching a film instead of meeting them?"

He laughed. "Shit, no. Abe would have my arse for kidnapping you."

Okay, that was a major fail. Plan B. "Do you like me, Quinn?"

Head tilted, he placed his palm on my forearm, squeezing slightly while he steered the car with one hand for a moment. "Sure, I do."

"Would you marry me?"

"What?" The car jerked a bit, because he yanked his hand back so fast it bumped against the steering wheel.

"If you married me, no one could force me to go back to this morally corrupt woman they call my mother." I lifted my chin. "I would be an independent adult then." *Sort of.*

"Oh, is that so?" A relaxed chuckle rocked his chest while he steered the car around Kings Cross. "Well, I'm afraid that would bring along trouble with Bethany."

I frowned, running my fingers up and down the smooth seatbelt across my chest. "What's a Bethany?"

"My girlfriend."

"You never told me you had a girlfriend."

He looked at me. "You never told me your mother was still alive."

Touché. But it was a shame my brilliant plan B went down the gutter.

Lips pouted, I craved his attention again.

His eyebrow arched. "What are you thinking about *now?*" The question sounded damn close to a warning. Amazing thing, his intuition, when it came to me.

"You and Beth could adopt me." Sickly sweet innocence dripped from my voice.

Quinn waited a second before he covered my hand with his. "You're too old to be adopted, sweetie."

"Yeah. And Bethany wouldn't be happy with a brat like me, would she?"

His fingers closed around mine. "You know that I've never seen you that way."

My gaze dropped to our joined hands. "Yeah, I know. Guess that's why I like you so much. You're the only one who ever cared."

This was the first time in years I'd had an open conversation with anyone. Honesty usually stood locked somewhere deep down in the dungeons of my heart. But with Quinn being close like a brother, that door cracked open from time to time. If only a little.

"Soon you'll have an entire family to care for you. And that boy seemed really worried today as well."

"I don't see what's positive about living with a dragon and her child-lover."

Because he needed to shift gears, Quinn withdrew his hand. "Oh, he's not her lover."

"How do you know?"

"I had a chat with him. Apparently, he's some sort of caretaker. Very nice guy."

If Quinn said so, I had no reason to doubt it. But the sudden excitement in my stomach when he spoke of the guy was a riddle to me.

"Don't worry," he added with a grin. "I only told him good things about you."

As if there was anything good to say about me. That would include my name, and...yeah, that was about it. But speaking of which. "Did he tell you his name?"

"Yes."

I waited. Nothing. "And?"

Quinn smirked. "Are you interested in the lad?"

I poked my elbow into his ribs, which made him laugh out loud.

"Careful, kiddo. I'm driving."

"I'm not interested in *him*," I snapped. "I'd just like to know who I'll have to deal with for the next six weeks."

"Ah, right. Must be exciting to meet relatives in France. What's your aunt's name, anyway?"

"No idea. I've never met her. And who cares?"

"Hah! I thought you would like to know *anyone* you'll have to *deal* with." He chuckled, and I didn't like it. "You know the guy's only a few years older than you. If you're nice to him, who knows, maybe *he'll* want to marry you one day."

Quinn deserved a slap for his teasing. Scowling at him, I

ground my teeth. "Did he tell you that he left me alone in the hallway today after he freed me from the handcuffs?"

Quinn frowned at the red light stopping us for a moment. "Did he? Really?"

"Yes, he went to the bathroom. So what does that tell us about him?"

"That he trusts you?"

"No!" Interesting that Quinn came up with the same words as the blond guy. "It only shows how irresponsible he is. Leaving a criminal alone."

"And what an evil criminal you are."

Damn the playful glint in his eyes.

Two minutes later, my heart sank to my gut as Quinn parked the car in front of a pub called *Antonio's* and cut the engine. A few deep breaths couldn't ease my tension. Quinn studied my face for a moment then opened his mouth.

I cut him off, pointing my finger at his face. "If you're going to say, *Just grin and bear it!* I'll punch your nose."

His laugh echoed inside the car. He ruffled my hair and brushed my cheek. "Keep the fight up, tiger. I know you can do this." Then he opened the door and climbed out.

Finger at the ready, I waited to push the button to lock the car from the inside as soon as he would slam the door shut. Heck, I shouldn't have declined when Debby offered to show me how to short-circuit a car.

The car door still open, Quinn looked back at me. "Are you coming?"

"Yeah, don't worry, policeman. I'm hot on your heels."

He waited until I was out of the BMW before he shut his door. The man knew me too damn well. He pushed a button on his key.

The turn signals flashed twice while the car doors locked automatically. I waited for him to circle the car then hung on to his arm.

"Did you bring your gun?" I whispered with my head turned to his shoulder as pedestrians walked by.

"What do you need a gun for?"

"You never know. They come in handy at times. Have you ever shot a dragon?"

"Jona!" His growl came with a playful bump of his hip against mine.

I tripped over my untied laces and stumbled. When Quinn grabbed me, giggles erupted from my chest.

"By the way," he said under his breath. "His name is Julian."

"Julian…" The name rolled off my tongue.

I glanced up from my boots to the pub entrance and found myself staring into the angelic blue eyes of a French god.

Kicks under the Table

𝒟amn! I had to say Julian's name at entirely the wrong moment, didn't I? The hem of my hoodie caught in my death grip as I bit my wayward tongue, facing his knowing look. It surely lifted his ego above London's roofs.

Even in the dimly lit street, I must have glowed like an overripe strawberry with the heat shooting across my face. Quinn got the full blast of my scowl for steering me into this embarrassing situation.

Julian stood right beside my mother and slung his leather jacket over his shoulder, hooking it with one finger. The white shirt he wore accentuated his deep blue eyes. He stared at me with a smile. A crooked one. It was cute, somehow...

I mentally slapped myself. What was wrong with me? So far a smile had never made me lose control and forget myself. Usually, I was quite immune to any boy's charm. I clearly wasn't myself today.

After Quinn had shaken hands with the dragon, he nudged me in the back and held his hand out to Julian. "Jules. How're you doing?"

Jules? Did I miss something?

Julian knocked his hand into Quinn's. Memories of his warm fingers around my wrist mocked me from the back of my mind. Suddenly, all I could think of was to hold out my hand to this stranger and beg for the pleasure of his touch once more. His fingers, long and masculine, seemed as if they could coax a soft purr of surrender from even the most terrifying of lions.

Bloody hell, what was I thinking?

Hand stretched toward me, Julian tilted his head. "Hi, Jona. Everything all right?"

Not given to sympathize with the enemy, I shoved my hands deep into the pockets of my torn jeans. "Save your pleasantries. Just because you freed me this morning doesn't make us friends."

He leaned a little closer. "Still pissed you couldn't bring yourself to run off because of me?" he whispered.

Pardon? I fisted my hands to my hips and took a step backward. "I'll have you know that I didn't leave the court for Quinn's sake. He trusted you with watching me. And you...failed. I wouldn't cause my friend trouble because of *your* carelessness."

Those warm blue eyes leveled with mine. Damn, they kicked me off my train of thought.

"At least you care for *someone.*"

Hands clapped behind us, Quinn's voice carried to my ears, but his words made no sense to me. Julian's intense stare held me captured. His gorgeous eyes knew no barrier. They penetrated my steeled core until I felt naked before him, with all the dark bits of my soul spread out for him to see.

I so hated it.

Neither of us broke the stare. Then slowly, on his left cheek, a sweet dimple appeared. A lopsided grin followed. "What do you say, shall we go in?"

I watched his lips part as he spoke and soaked in the chime of his voice. But it took a moment for me to understand. We were alone. Quinn and the dragon had already gone inside. Lips pressed together, I tore my gaze from him and stalked through the door of the restaurant. A low chuckle drifted to me as he followed on my heels. The fiend knew he had distracted me.

The smell of spicy food hung in the low vault-like restaurant. One foot placed on the iron bar under the counter, Quinn was talking to the waiter. My mother flanked his left side, her elbow resting on the countertop, and I caught the first real glimpse of her this evening.

A claw fixed her limp hair at the back of her head, the faded red contrasting with the black of her silk blouse. A mud brown skirt that didn't quite reach her knees enhanced her narrow hips, and high heels brought the top of her head level with Quinn's eyes. Her left foot slipped out of its shoe at the heel, suggesting she felt anything but comfortable in them. So who the hell was she trying to impress?

Shaking my head, I joined Quinn on his right. He leaned slightly my way. "Glad you made it in. For a moment there, I thought you wouldn't be coming."

"Oh, and miss out on all the fun? How could I?" I rolled my eyes, but the bartender was the only one who noticed it, and the corners of his mouth twitched.

I moved my gaze to Quinn. "Why are we standing here?"

"Waiting to get a table."

I pivoted and glanced around. "Why, there's a nice table over there. We can take that one."

Quinn followed the direction of my pointed finger then gave me a hard stare. "That's a table for twelve. I'm sure we can get something more private."

"You want privacy?" My intentionally loud tone caught my mother's and Julian's attention. "I'd say we better get rid of the annoying company then."

The off-duty officer slipped his hand under my hair and placed warm fingers on my neck. His squeeze was none too gentle. "You're too sweet today, little witch," he said through a wide grin and gritted teeth.

"I'm doing my best."

"I don't doubt it for a second."

A waiter came from the back of the pub and led us to a niche with a small table. Square. Quinn and my mother lowered at opposite sides. Julian went around the table, giving me a suggestive glance over the candle-lit top before he eased down. This left me to sit between my mother and Quinn.

Just great. I coughed innocently and shoved my chair toward Quinn's side as far as possible.

He waited until I had made myself comfortable, then he leaned in with a puzzled frown. "Maybe you'd like to sit on my lap?"

Yeah, too funny.

My mother's continued silence didn't bother me, but her focused way of watching me got my goat. Her profile loomed in the corner of my eye at all times. Disgusted, I propped one elbow on the table, my chin cupped in my hand. A perfect girly grin displayed on my face in spite of the annoyance that slung its noose around my neck. I turned toward Quinn to avoid the dragon's stare.

"So, you two are really close friends, right?" That was Julian's attempt to break the ice.

I would have much rather reached out to *break* my mother's neck.

Quinn bobbed his head, but I was equally quick with a reply. "He's my lover." I jerked my chin in Charlene's direction. "She yours?"

My mother sucked in a sharp breath and clapped her hands to her mouth. Very amusing. Not quite so funny was the kick against my shin coming from Quinn's end.

"Ah, fuck." My startled laugh tore my unholy curse to shreds.

Julian was the only one who seemed utterly untroubled by my assumption. He folded his arms on the table, slowly leaning most of the weight of his upper body on his elbows. His hard gaze pinned me. "You'd never believe just how close we are."

Holy crap, why did everything he said sound like the alluring purr of a leopard?

I opened my mouth for a snappy retort, but nothing whatsoever came out. For the first time in years, I was dumbstruck.

The waiter coming for our order was my rescue. The dragon asked for water. That fit, maybe she could extinguish the fire in her throat with it. Julian took a glass of O.J., and Quinn ordered alcohol-free beer.

"And what'll it be for you, Miss?"

I lifted my gaze to the man dressed in a white shirt and black pants. "Hm, I think I'll take a tequila for starters. Better make it a double. The night is long. There's still a lot to endure."

The cutlery on the table shook when Quinn kicked my shin under the long cloth again. I yelped and cussed.

He ordered a glass of Coke on my behalf, and the waiter hurried off, shaking his head.

"Are you all right?" Julian sounded worried.

"Perfectly fine," I said through gritted teeth, casting Quinn a sideways scowl. And here I'd thought he was my friend. He probably couldn't wait until I had to leave the country.

When everyone was set with their drinks, Quinn leaned forward, addressing my mother. "So, France it is—where exactly are you going to take our little princess?" His soft tone held a hint of regret, and he cut a brief glance my way.

My heart warmed. Clearly, he was going to miss me as much as I was going to miss him.

"My sister lives in the South. Provence. In a place called Fontvieille."

I'd heard the word Provence before, but the last bit was a cryptic lull to me. Anyway, Charlene's rambling didn't interest me at all. The folding of my napkin into a neat fan distracted me easily enough. Squeezed in the middle, it looked like a pleated bow. And when bent, it was the perfect resemblance of a white cloak reflecting the light from above. Such as I had seen in the courtroom this morning.

The memory made me suck in a lungful of air. I swallowed. My gaze wandered across the table and over the edge to where Julian was leaning back in his chair with his fingers laced over his stomach. My eyes traced the line of buttons on his white shirt up to the collar. His jaw line came into view, followed by the sensual shape of his upper lip. Before I knew it, I was staring into his midnight-blue eyes.

And he stared straight back at me.

A jolt of surprise straightened my spine, but he remained in his relaxed position, not moving a muscle. Was he reading me? The unnerving tension between us grew quickly, though he didn't seem affected at all.

"...The wine they produce earns them enough to fund a high standard of life," my mother's ramblings drifted to me. "My sister and her husband don't have children, though they would have loved to have a baby. They're delighted by the idea of having their niece in the house for a while."

Quinn folded his hands on the table. "I was wondering, Miss Montiniere—"

"Oh, but please, call me Charlene." She gave him a quick smile.

"Yes, Quinn, please. You *must* call her Charlene." Sugar dusted my voice. "A fitting name for a merciless dragon, don't you think?"

Pain shot through my right leg. If Quinn kept kicking me like this, my shin would be all shades of green and blue before the evening was over. This time I returned the kick, but missed his leg by an inch. My boot only scraped his jeans. "I can't believe how annoying the rats are in this restaurant."

"And I really can't believe that you left all your manners back home," he replied, like me, speaking through clenched teeth.

"I beg you, Quinn, don't be mad at my daughter. I deserve her wrath and distrust." My mother's gaze moved to mine. "Don't I, Jona?"

Sick to my stomach, I glowered at her. "I'd rather you didn't speak to me at all, *Charlene*."

Her glossed lips thinned to a line, and the corners subtly pointed south. She couldn't honestly have expected I'd call her *Mom* after she messed up my childhood so royally?

The dim bulbs in the restaurant dipped her bony face in a

mystic light. For an instant, I thought a ghost of the past stared at me through her deep brown eyes, the only color about her face that had remained as intense as I remembered it over the years. Distracted by her longing stare, I almost failed to notice the forward movement of her hand. Just before it could land on mine, I jerked my arm back and tucked both hands in my lap. The tablecloth hid them from her touch.

She reached for her glass of water, traced the brim with her slim finger, and then took a sip. "I'll be honest with you. There won't be an endless chance for us to talk. I'm ill. Seriously ill. It's cancer. With no hope for a cure. Julian sa—" She cleared her throat, stroking the stem of her glass. "The doctors don't even give me until the end of the year."

"Alas, this is the first good news of the evening," I exclaimed.

From across the table, strong legs circled around my crossed ankles, lifting my legs off the ground. The quick move dragged me lower into my chair, and I clasped the table with a startled hold. Quinn's subsequent kick missed my shin.

"That one was predictable," Julian said, his eyes as dark as shards of obsidian. He lowered my feet to the floor, then withdrew his legs, and left me wondering whether he was referring to the kick from my friend or my cold retort.

Everyone fell silent. Shooting a glance at Quinn, I realized my mother's illness wasn't a surprise to him. She must have talked to him this morning in the courthouse after my spectacular failure at fleeing her presence. Probably twirling him around her little finger with his pity for the helpless. And he totally fell for it. *Stupid policeman.*

Her days were numbered, so what? All the better, I'd say.

"You see, Jona." With her mentioning my name, my mother

drew my eyes away from Quinn. "I don't want to *leave* without taking the chance of making up for the hard life you've had."

"You want my forgiveness?" That was ridiculous. A tight laugh escaped me.

"I beg you to accept your aunt's offer to live in her house. She can provide you with all the decent comforts of life that I never could. She'll see to you having a good start in your adult future." Her lower lip trembled. "And for me, I only wish you could forgive my weakness in the past."

"Then I'm afraid you'll go down with your only wish denied." A growl of menace made it up my throat. "I'll do as the judge ordered and spend the remaining six weeks till my birthday in shackles on the vineyards of an aunt I don't know. Not quite the time to form a suitable future. As soon as the punishment is over, I'll return to London and make my living here. Without you. As I've done during the past twelve years."

"With the police fast on your heels and Abe Smith holding a cell free for you?"

It wasn't so much Quinn's bantering that bothered me at this moment as it was Julian's low chuckle when his eyes met mine.

"I'm not a half-wit as you all seem to think." I squared my shoulders, clenching the table cloth in my fists. "And if it means I'll have to wash dishes in a pub like this ten hours a day to fund my future, then I dare say it's the lesser evil compared to the hell I'm going to be sent to tomorrow."

Tears stung my eyes. Finally coming after being suppressed for half a lifetime, they couldn't simply be blinked away. My abrupt rise from the table knocked the chair backward, and it landed on the floor with the piercing sound of wood clattering to stone tiles. If the dragon and her friend decided to finish their drinks of victory-over-

Jona, I needn't be part of their celebration.

I made a dash for the exit. The curious faces that followed me from every table in the room lanced my heart.

Cool air outside slapped me in the face. The door slowly closed behind me.

Run, my mind screamed. But where would I go? The brave speech inside was nothing but a betrayal to myself. Hardly able to do the math of a senior high school student, I didn't think London had much to offer me. No one would hire me for a real job just because I was able to recite Jane Austen by heart.

The sleeves of my hoodie soaked up my tears before they could roll down my cheeks. The solid wall at my back provided mild comfort. I tilted my head back and studied the night sky. It couldn't possibly be my destiny to end up in one of Abe's iron-curtained cells one day.

The door of the pub opened, and out stepped a tall figure. Through the mist of moisture pooling in my eyes, it took me a second to recognize Quinn.

"Oh, there you are," he said softly, as he leaned against the wall the same way I did. "I almost feared I'd have to spend the night on the streets searching for you."

After a few blinks, my gaze moved to his face and back to the sky. "There's no place for me to go. No one wants to have me."

He took my hand. "I just met someone who does. And I've heard of a handful more people who'd be delighted to welcome you to their home. Kiddo, look past your pride for once and see the great chance they're offering."

"Why are you so willing to shove me down the lion's gorge? You heard all her false words," I spat. "The only thing this woman wants is peace for her soul before she kicks the bucket."

"And is that really such a bad thing?"

I jerked my hand out of his. "Damnit, Quinn, whose side are you on?"

"Yours, Jona. Can't you see?" Without warning he pulled me into an embrace that knocked the air out of my lungs. "I've hoped for a twist like this ever since you first strode up to my desk at the office and planted your butt on my stack of case files. You were the cheekiest brat I'd ever come across, but I saw the hurt in your frightened eyes when you tried to mock us both with your snappy talk."

He brushed strands of my hair out of my face. "Why don't you give your mother and her family a chance to meet the great girl I know must be hiding somewhere deep in there?" The hint of a grin appeared on his lips while his finger stabbed the spot between my collarbones.

If there was any great bit of me, then I would make a double effort not to let my goddamn mother get within reach of it. "Want to know why I told everyone my mother died in a car crash?" I sniffed.

Quinn's eyes held mine as he nodded.

"Because I was too ashamed for them to know the truth. That she abandoned me for the sake of her violent lover who whacked the shit out of me anew every night. She gave me away. She chose her sick boyfriend over her own child." My throat constricted as the words wrenched out. "I couldn't bear people's disdainful glances any longer. Their whispered taunts behind cupped hands about what a miserable daughter I must have been that my own mother refused to keep me." With the back of my hand, I wiped my nose and twisted away from Quinn's hold. A moth circled around the beam of light from the streetlamp. I watched it land on the bulb then flutter away. "So I invented her honorable death."

Strong arms closed around my shoulders and turned me back. Quinn pressed me to his chest. "I didn't know."

"Of course you didn't." The cotton of his t-shirt muffled my words. "Your disgust would have been the least bearable of all."

Off to the continent

The last night in the orphanage seemed like the longest in my life. After Quinn had returned to the pub to give our excuses to my mother and her weird attendant, he drove me back to the place I still called home. Not until he promised to come see me off at the airport the next morning did I let go of my only friend's arm.

Fear of the coming weeks clamped like a fist in my stomach and kept me from falling asleep till the early morning hours.

I had seen all kinds of emotional farewells on the small TV in the common room, but none of those applied to my leave-taking that day. Apart from Quinn, Debby would have been the only person worth a goodbye—if she hadn't sold me to the devil the other day and brought about my unholy punishment.

At seven forty-five, I returned to my room after my last shower in the common bathing area. Pulling back my wet hair, I fixed it with an old rubber band I'd found in the pocket of my jeans when they had been handed down to me. As I slipped through the door, I yelped, and my heart shot to my throat at the sight of Julian sitting on my bed.

Elbows braced on his knees, he leaned forward. His blond hair gleamed like minted gold in the sun streaming in through the window. "Not quite the welcome I had hoped for."

Frantically, I scanned the room for the other intruder, but the dragon was nowhere to be found. "What are you doing here?"

"Summoning you. Your mother is settling your check-out with the headmistress." The bedsprings squeaked when he rose from my cot, then he glanced around the room.

Crap, not what I wanted him to do, especially when he focused on the cobwebs in the corner above his head.

"Isn't this a lovely place?" he murmured.

I let a casual shrug roll off my shoulders to cover how much his words offended me. "Cobwebs, dust, it's still home."

"After the dramatic end of last evening, I wasn't sure if you'd still be here today."

"What a terrible shock for you to find my room empty then. Especially after all the trust you put in me at the courthouse." I picked up the book I had been reading last night from my nightstand and withdrew my only pen, which had served as a bookmark last night. I dropped the pen into my backpack. "I'm sure you and the dragon wouldn't have hesitated a minute to search the city for me."

Quite nonchalantly, Julian stepped into my space. Biting the inside of my lip, I remained where I stood when he lowered his lips to my ear. "With that tongue of yours, we wouldn't have had any trouble finding you." His warm breath brushed my hair as he spoke.

I sighed, inhaling his scent. His skin smelled of wild wind and ocean, and that melted my armor. A memory surfaced in my mind of the one day last spring when Miss Mulligan had taken us to the sea and I had waded through the gentle waves rolling to the shore. Closing my eyes, I could still feel the wet sand between my toes.

"Are you ready to go?" Julian's question came from behind me.

I opened my eyes, blinking against the bright light from outside. It seemed even the sun chided me for the moment where I'd let down my guard. I straightened and turned. "As ready as one in this sick situation can be."

"Good." His impudent grin mocked me from three feet away. "Let's not waste any more time in this nasty place then."

He bent, picked up my bursting backpack from the floor, and headed out. It was nice that he carried my heavy bag. Although, compared to my mother's inescapable presence, it was only a small burden.

My gaze swept over my small room a final time. It felt as if I was leaving a part of me behind. After all, this had been my home for so long. Listlessly, I closed the door.

"The lift seems to be out of order today. We have to take the stairs," Julian informed me when I caught up with his long strides.

"That lift has been out of order ever since I moved in."

He looked at me, his gaze filled with sudden irritation.

"What did you expect to find here?" I sneered. "The Grand Plaza?"

Julian shook his head and walked a little faster. Even though I didn't see his face, I could just picture him rolling his eyes.

Three flights of stairs gave me plenty of opportunity to study his backside. The muscles flexed with every step he took. Never being one to stare at a boy's butt, it surprised me how hard I found it to tear my eyes away from the stunning view.

Between the first and second landing, he shot me a suspicious glance over his shoulder. Throughout the years, I'd become an expert at muffling the sound of my footfalls while wandering through the building at night to find a book in the library.

"Thought I was going to run?"

"Just checking," he murmured, facing the steps again.

Downstairs, my backpack landed with a dull thud on the floor. Julian planted his nice bottom on the second step, his elbows propped on his knees. A spider made its busy way past his shoes and disappeared into a crack in the brittle wall.

Julian angled his head to gaze at me. "Don't tell me you're going to miss this place."

I shrugged and folded my arms over my chest. "You should come here in the winter when the mice move in for a warmer place to stay and a nice meal in the cafeteria."

His brows arched and seemed to plead with me to confess I was only joking. I didn't bother, but shifted my weight to my other foot, mimicked his raised brow, and dared him to call me a liar. He didn't take the bait.

"Well, in your new home you will have to do without your speedy companions. The only furry thing there will be the giant hound."

A dog? A giant dog? "No one said I'd have to share a house with a monster other than my mother." The image of Rusty the Rottweiler ran screaming through my head. When I still lived with the dragon, that stupid dog had flashed his fangs at me whenever I walked by our neighbor's garden. A hint of wariness crept into my voice. "And just how big would that dog be?"

Julian waited a second before he answered. "I know people who mistook it for a horse." His quiet tone released a shudder down my spine. "But don't worry. They keep the dog well fed, so it should restrain from eating a snotty brat like you."

The door behind me squeaked open, and I nearly jumped out of my skin, half expecting to find myself staring into the open maw of a giant ogre. The beaming face of my mother was just as shocking.

"Oh, you're already here." She reached out with one hand, but apparently thought better of it and pulled back before her fingers made contact with my cheek. "I've got all the papers for your departure. The taxi is waiting outside. I suppose we can start our journey."

Miss Mulligan shook my hand, mumbled some crap I didn't listen to, and then saw us off to the front door. Julian stuffed my belongings into the boot of the black car next to two other suitcases. He climbed into the backseat after me while the dragon sat in front.

"Now put on a nice smile and enjoy the trip," Julian whispered as he leaned over to my side. "You'll like the flight. I guess you've never been in an airplane before?"

"Airplane?" *Oh shit!* I hadn't even thought about that part of the voyage! My knees started to tremble. "Isn't there a way to go by car or train? Or even a ship?"

His forehead creased into a frown. "What's the problem? Are you afraid of flying?"

"I wouldn't say that exactly." Because I'd never been up so high. Actually, just climbing the first few rungs of a ladder scared the wits out of me. Not to mention the horror when I had dared to lean out the window in my room. That dare had won me a brand new pullover Debby nicked from H&M, but the prize was hard-earned. "I just have a little issue with heights."

Julian pursed his lips. "We best not give you a window seat."

Within forty minutes we arrived at Heathrow Airport. I followed on Charlene's heels, frightened I might get lost among so many people. But then again, what was I worrying for? This would be my last chance of escape. Maybe drop back, then take a wrong turn, and dash for freedom? My strides getting slower, the distance between me and my mishap of a mother grew steadily.

People wheeling their suitcases filled the space between us. Anticipation grew inside me. I stopped and peeked around, searching for a good place to hide until the dragon was out of sight.

From behind, someone slipped fingers under the straps of my backpack and pulled it down. "Let me carry this for you. We don't want you to miss your flight for the sake of the heavy baggage."

"Quinn!" I spun around and flung my arms around his firm body. My nose buried into the fresh smell of his dark uniform.

He laughed, staggering back a couple steps at my enthusiastic embrace. "All right, kiddo. I get it. You're happy to see me."

"I thought you wouldn't come after all."

He grabbed my shoulders and held me away from him to look me sternly in my eyes. "When did I ever break a promise to you?"

The chance at escape might be gone, but his showing up filled me with happiness. I smiled, knowing he'd never go back on his word.

Julian approached us. "Morning."

"Hey, Jules." Quinn planted a heavy hand on Julian's shoulder. "I hope you had no trouble bringing the princess to her carriage."

One corner of Julian's mouth lifted. "So far she's heeled like a nice puppy."

I glared at both of them. "Would the two of you stop making fun of me?"

Julian took a small step backward, hands lifted in defense. "Your mother is at the check-in desk. Do you want to take your backpack with you into the cabin? Otherwise I'll take it to her now."

"No, just take it." I picked up my bag and shoved it at his chest.

He didn't budge at my hard push. One strap over his shoulder, he trudged toward my mother, who stood in a snake-like queue at the luggage drop-off. With him gone, I had a moment to say farewell to my friend.

Quinn pulled me aside. "Listen, kiddo. I'm sure your aunt and uncle will provide you with anything necessary. Food, clothes, a room. So no stealing in the foreign country, is that clear? Especially not from their house." He pointed a warning finger in my face, and I restrained the impulse to snap my teeth at it.

"I'll be nice."

"Jona, I mean it."

"Okay. Got it. No stealing." I blew a strand of hair out of my eyes. "What about gambling and selling my body for money?"

His eyes grew wide, and his jaw dropped to his chest.

I fought back a laugh. "Close your mouth, buddy, I was only jesting."

His dark brows furrowed.

"Honestly!" I lifted my palms in surrender.

"Very funny." If he'd been a little bit more like me, he'd have stuck his tongue out with the words. But he didn't. Instead he heaved a sigh and slipped his hand between my hair and my neck. "You just be a nice girl, do you hear? Don't do anything reckless.

And in God's name, don't even think about running off on your own once you're in France."

I raised one innocent brow. "Anything else?"

Scratching the stubble on his chin, he pursed his lips. "Beware, cars hit from the right side in mainland Europe."

"You mean from the wrong side?" I offered.

Long wisps slipped through his fingers as he ruffled my hair. "Exactly." His low chuckle reminded me of how much I was going to miss this man. He was more like family than my mother could ever be.

A moment later, Julian approached us again, this time with the dragon in tow. "We're boarding in twenty minutes. Better get through passport control now."

Bile rose in my throat the moment he announced our short departure.

Quinn didn't miss the tremble of my lower lip. He dipped his head, brushing his thumb over my cheek. "You'll be okay, kiddo." Then he turned to Julian. "You'll take good care of the princess, won't you?"

"I promise." Julian's eyes fixed on mine as he spoke.

My mother said goodbye to Quinn and shook his hand. "Thanks for watching over my baby. I hope we'll get a chance to meet again."

Her baby? Which one? The one she would have drowned in the river with a happy laugh? I had to look elsewhere to restrain from making this woman eat her teeth.

She and her pet started for passport control with me following at a reluctant pace.

"Julian!" Quinn's shout had us all turning around once more. He retrieved a set of silver handcuffs from the back of his belt and tossed them at Julian, who caught the glinting object with one hand. "You might want to make use of those. And better keep an eye on the exit."

Julian's chuckle didn't bother me half as much as it should have. Neither did Quinn's final banter. Before I knew it, I broke into a run and slammed hard against Quinn's chest. His arms enveloped me with the strength of a best friend, and I wished there was a way to stay in this protective cage.

"Cheer up, kiddo. It's only for six weeks," he said into my ear. "If, after that time, you still want to return to England, I'll come and pick you up myself." He pressed a kiss to my temple. The first and the last. Then he cupped my chin. "Now go meet your family. They're waiting for you."

There was no way to delay the walk into the lion's den any longer. Slipping away from Quinn's hug, I dragged my feet over to the sliding glass doors where the dragon waited for me. Every so often I cast a glance over my shoulder to ensure Quinn was still there. He waved, then shoved his hands into his pockets, but didn't move. We rounded the corner and he was out of sight.

After we passed passport control and security, my suddenly lethargic body slumped into one of the many red vinyl chairs lining the wall. Arms crossed and jaw set, I waited for the time to board the plane.

It took not a minute for Julian to sit down next to me. "You know, six weeks isn't an eternity. Give yourself a push. You might even enjoy the stay."

"Yeah, right. Like pulling a tooth."

Resignation filled his sigh. He brought his hand down on my thigh for a second. The move caught me unaware, and I completely forgot to jerk my leg out from under his touch. Instead, I stared at his fingers for as long as they lay on my jeans.

Then he rose from the seat and crossed the hall to the huge windowpane where Charlene stood and paid attention to the traffic on the runway.

Even with his gentle caress gone from my leg, the spot where he'd touched me remained prickling with heat. An odd sensation raced over my skin. I rubbed my hand over my thigh; my heart pounded as warmth filled me.

Whether there was magic in his touch or I'd lost my mind, I couldn't tell. Either way, his unexpected caress distracted me long enough to ease the pain over the departure from my hometown and my only friend.

Over the loud speaker, a stewardess announced the plane was ready for boarding. I rose from my chair and followed Julian and Charlene through the final ticket control. The noise of the plane engines grew louder with every step down the narrow gate. A slight chill wafted into my face as I stepped over the small gap and entered the plane.

Two captains and another hostess greeted us at the entrance and wished us a pleasant journey.

"Pleasant, my arse," I mumbled and trudged down the narrow aisle behind Charlene until she found the row with our seat numbers inscribed overhead.

She turned to me with an expectant smile. "Would you like to sit by the window?"

Julian uttered a few words in French to her. Her expression fell, then she slid into the window seat. Did he just reveal my little problem with big heights to her? I wished he'd chosen English to sell me out.

Damn! Shock weakened my knees as I realized in France no

one would speak my language at all. Julian planted himself next to the dragon which left the aisle seat for me. I collapsed into the navy blue seat, my mind racing.

The flight attendant had the passengers buckle their seatbelts. I slid the metal slots together, but the belt was long enough for me to fit in there three times. I opened the buckle and searched for a second, shorter belt around my seat, but there was none.

"Let me do it for you." Julian's fingers were on the seatbelt before I could refuse his help.

Hands lifted to my shoulders, I watched as he buckled me in then pulled at the loose end to tighten the belt around my waist. His alluring, sweet scent filled my head when he leaned toward me. I licked my lips.

His hand rested on my belly. "Too tight?"

Slowly, I shook my head. He stared into my eyes for an infinitesimal second longer, then he leaned back. I had to forcefully take in a breath. "Thanks."

On the small screens attached to the overhead compartments, an animated hostess had started to give instructions for what to do in case of emergency. I strained to listen and memorize the appropriate conduct in the unlikely event of the aircraft performing a landing on water. The short movie of people gliding down on a giant slide and then initiating their life-vests in the water freaked me out.

"If it's so unlikely, then why show this movie?" I clenched my teeth and prayed that Julian wouldn't notice my trembles. *Crap.* No such luck.

"Relax. Nothing's going to happen," he whispered in my ear.

The plane taxied back then rolled to the runway. I stared straight ahead, focusing on the headrest in front of me.

The captain announced the time in France would be one hour

ahead of British time and the weather on the mainland was supposed to be sunny and close to thirty degrees centigrade. He expected the flight to take sixty minutes. There shouldn't be turbulence, just a slight rattle when the aircraft crossed the border of the island to the sea.

Bloody brilliant. This was going to be one hell of an hour.

A happy thought

Sitting with my back pressed to the seat, I really didn't want to look through the small porthole window, but I couldn't help myself. Outside, parts of the wing moved up and down with an eerie creak as the aircraft came to a standstill at the start of the runway. My stomach churned.

"Don't be afraid." Julian leaned toward me, and the warmth of his breath slowed the rollercoaster in my belly. "They are not loose parts. It's standard procedure. The captain's testing everything before takeoff."

"Isn't *now* a bit late to be testing everything?"

"That's routine, believe me."

I hoped he wasn't bullshitting me. Tipping my head back to my seat, I focused toward the front.

Seconds passed, the sound of the revving engine dotted my forehead with beads of cold sweat.

The instant the airplane shot forward with break-neck speed, my back plastered into the seat. My knuckles turned white with the strength of my grip on the armrests.

Dear God, I'm too young to die. I had yet to get my driver's license!

If only Peter Pan was here. He would know what to do. *Think a happy thought. Think a happy thought.* My lips moved as I repeated the mantra in my mind like a prayer. But, alas, no happy thought came to me.

The craft flew down the runway like a rocket, the world outside zoomed past in a blur. If I could have moved a single muscle, I might have made the sign of the cross. Instead I begged the Lord for a painless end.

All of a sudden, a feather brushed the back of my clenched fist. No, not a feather. Julian's fingers were as soft as a whisper. I sneaked a glance to my right and fell into gorgeous sapphire eyes.

Slowly he unclenched my fingers and laced his through mine. "Everything's all right."

His light tone tempted me to believe him. His touch filled me with trust and comfort and left no doubt I'd be safe as long as he held me. He squeezed my hand. A beautiful, crooked smile appeared on his face.

Gee, here was my happy thought.

Then I went deaf. Something got stuck in my ear. But my breaths became calmer, and inside my boots, my toes uncurled.

The plane climbed the sky with an ease I would have never

thought possible. I dragged in a deep breath and my ears unplugged. Julian's gentle hold kept me grounded. And when I could tear my gaze from our joined hands, I dared a look out of the oval window.

London from above was a marvelous sight. But seeing the metropolis shrinking underneath the plane's belly also confirmed the end of life as I had known it for years. Ripped from my island, I was being exported to slavery for an endless six weeks.

Julian's hand was still covering mine. Slowly, my fingers withdrew from his. This was the second time he'd touched me that day, and similar to the first, my entire body had calmed and warmed from the inside. It was unlikely he even realized how I reacted to him. How much I appreciated his caress and the soothing effect it had on me. *All the better.* I'd die of shame if he found out.

Avoiding his stare, I focused on the attention-consuming task of wiping my sweaty palms on my jeans.

"I guess you're feeling better." He leaned forward to retrieve a book from his backpack underneath the seat in front of him and stuck his nose in the pages.

I cleared my throat, turning my gaze anywhere but toward him.

In front of me, a man stood and rummaged in the overhead compartment. He lowered to his seat with a white pillow in his hand and stuffed it behind his neck. My eyes squeezed shut for a second. But this only made me all the more aware of the unfamiliar, pleasant sensation still surging through me. My heart felt warm, like someone was pointing the heated stream of a hairdryer straight at it.

I hugged my arms around my waist and pulled my legs to my chest, my feet resting on the seat. Positioned like this, I felt a little more protected...from the eerie effect Julian had on me without his knowing.

Like the captain had foreseen, the crossing of the border

between land and sea didn't go so smooth. A series of rattles shook the aircraft and threatened to shatter it at any moment. Panic grabbed hold of me anew, but this time I took care to keep my trembling hands in my lap and out of Julian's reach. The book was still held up to his eyes as if he was deeply emerged in the story, but he glanced at me every so often.

For as long as the rattle went on, I doubled my effort to even my breathing. "No need to touch me again," I muttered, frowning at him sideways.

Julian closed his eyes, his lips compressed, and a dimple appeared in his cheek. "As you wish."

I wish to hell you'd stop laughing at me, you oaf! Argh, why did I even care what he thought of me?

I shot a glare at the dozing bundle in the window seat. "And the dragon sleeps like a stone while the world is falling apart around us. That fits. Always oblivious to the rest of the world."

Just then, I caught Julian's free hand gently stroking her forearm. *What the bloody hell—?* So he was her lover after all. A balloon of jealousy exploded in my chest. It was unthinkable what his tender caress would do to her when I was so deeply affected by his slightest touch.

The stroking stopped.

A frown creased my brow. His lips thinned to a line as his hand slid away from my mother's arm and clasped the book again. Long lashes shielding the blue of his eyes, he kept his gaze on the pages.

A moan rose from my mother as she stirred, but Julian didn't move. On purpose I assumed. Trying to hide from me his deep concern for her.

With the absence of his touch, my mother became fitful. She

awoke, her face contorted with lines of pain. A minute later, she sat up straight, gazing out through the tiny window. And all that just because he wasn't touching her any longer.

My eyes locked with Julian's as my blood ran cold.

*

Though the rest of the flight went by without any further incident, my breath hissed out in relief when the wheels touched the French ground. When the illuminated sign went off above our heads, we unbuckled our seatbelts and got off the plane. My mother clung to Julian's arm as they descended the stairs. I followed on their heels.

Sweat beaded on my skin. Once inside the air-conditioned building, I wiped my forehead with the sleeve of my sweatshirt. Compared to the mild temperatures in Britain, France felt like a furnace.

At the luggage claim, we didn't have to wait long before our things came circling on the conveyer. Our baggage in tow, we exited the terminal to find a couple waiting for us by a dark gray SUV.

The tall man, dressed in beige shorts and a black shirt, had wrapped his arm around a smaller woman at his side. Long strawberry-blonde hair cascaded down her back. Her face lit up as she spotted us, and she came running. She greeted my mother and Julian in French, hugged and kissed them. Julian had to bend to receive a peck on both his cheeks. Releasing him, the woman turned to me, beaming like a hundred-watt bulb.

Instinct had me backing off, my hands raised in self-defense. "We better skip the kissing."

The lady held out her hand to me and said, "Hello, *chérie*, I am Marie Runné, your aunt."

She swallowed the H of *hello*, and I'd never heard someone pronounce the letter R in such a funny way. Fighting back a snicker, I shook her hand from two feet away. No need to run the risk of being pulled into an involuntary hug.

"This is my husband, Albert." She dragged out the last bit of his name like he was called *Al-bear*. The name fit. He was indeed as tall as a bear, though his silver-gray hair resembled the fur of a wolf's back.

"*Bonjour,* Jona. My wife and I are happy you decided to come and stay with us."

I shoved my hands deep into my pants' pockets and gazed straight into his green eyes. "I was given no choice."

Marie's voice remained soft as she spoke again. "It was very brave of you to travel so far to a place where you do not know anyone. But you will find we are family. Do not be afraid. We shall take good care of you."

Hello? Did I give the impression of being frightened? She could hardly hold the aversion to kissing strangers against me, could she? I narrowed my eyes and gritted my teeth. "I'm not scared of anything."

A train of fuzzy warmth spiraled down my neck the moment Julian leaned close to my left ear from behind. His voice was low as he said, "We both know at least one thing that scares you out of your wits, don't we?" Then the fiend picked up my backpack and chuckled all the way to the car's rear.

That boy got on my nerves.

The car was spacious enough to hold the three of us in the backseat without being squeezed in like sausages. With Julian separating me from my mother, I kept my back turned to him and stared out the window. It took a long, seventy-minute drive to get to the place at which I was supposed to do time until my birthday.

In spite of all the misery I had yet to face in this country, France was a beautiful place. In London, brick buildings and hectic traffic had closed in on me as soon as I'd stepped out of the orphanage. Here, trees lined the single-lane streets. Lakes, meadows, and hills with all kinds of slopes produced an enchanting landscape. It seemed as if the beauty of the country strived to calm everyone's stressed out day.

Unfortunately, my mother's company and the charity work I was bound to do cast an eerie shadow over the surreal peace. The strangers in the front seats tried to make friendly conversation with me, which I was so not interested in. But apart from all that, I might have even liked it here.

A soft poke in my ribs made me jump. Julian jerked his chin to the windshield. "We're almost there. This is—" He paused and pursed his lips. "The residence of your vacation."

"We might as well call a spade a spade." With one eyebrow cocked, I offered, "The place for slave labor?"

"Your temporary home."

"How very nice." Flashing my teeth in the parody of a smile, I dismissed him and read the sign next to the road.

Bienvenue à Fontvieille.

Albert steered through the narrow streets of the small town and a little farther until the line of houses and shops gave way to woods and stony paths. The car came to a halt in the driveway of an impressive property.

I climbed out of the car when the others did and gaped at the estate. To call it beautiful would have been a vast understatement. It looked like somebody had waved a wand and I'd arrived in a fairytale.

Surrounded by a caramel-brown picket fence, the house stood two stories. Front door, window frames, and the long balcony on one side adopted the color of the fence, while the sun reflected off the shiny white exterior and blinded my eyes.

I couldn't name the red, yellow, and violet flowers offering dwellings to butterflies and bees, but they hung profusely from the rectangular planters attached to each windowsill. A gentle wind fluttered the curtains like the twirling tutu of a ballerina. I couldn't wait to get inside to find out if the interior measured up with the fantasy façade.

Too amazed to even flinch, I stood rigid when my aunt rubbed both my upper arms with her soft hands. "Welcome home, Jona."

Home. The word lingered in my ears like the soft rustle on a midsummer's evening.

Marie let go of me, leaving my skin chilled in the unfamiliar French heat. She walked to the front door with my mother's arm looped around hers, followed by Albert, who carried our baggage.

I was set to fall into line with them, when a brown and white furry beast trotted around the corner of the mansion. I stopped dead. It came right for me with a murderous glint in its eyes, cutting me off from the safety of the house. Shit, it must have devoured a kid only minutes ago. The white shoelaces still hung from its jaws.

The pony-sized dog lifted its muzzle to my hand and sniffed. Afraid my wince might stir its appetite for dessert, I strangled the frightened sound in my throat.

The giant animal angled its head, gaping up at my face. A low grumble in its throat grew to the most blasé bark the world had ever heard. The laces tore away from its mouth and dropped as a puddle of dog-drool.

Julian's laugh made me jump. "And here I was thinking the

dog was mute."

I squeezed my eyes shut and bit my lower lip, hating how he caught my every moment of fear.

"Sit, Lou-Lou," he said. The mountain of fur lowered her butt to the ground. Her long tongue lolled out sideways between huge, but not very sharp canines. While her tail swished back and forth over the stone patio, Julian rubbed behind her wooly ear then dared to sling his arm casually over my shoulder and around my neck. "Shall we add dogs to the list of things that scare you senseless?"

The guy was seriously begging to be introduced to my great right hook. I challenged him with a pissed scowl as he dragged me toward the house. Before we reached the front steps, I managed to escape his grip and entered alone.

Hopefully, he would go to his own house soon, so I could be safe from his sneaky remarks and the bunch of butterflies he woke in my stomach each time he touched me. Actually, I couldn't wait for him to leave.

My newly discovered family members gathered in the wide hallway of the house, speaking to each other in fluent French. They quickly switched to clipped English, casting me a welcoming smile when I walked in.

The dragon tried to smile at me, too, but somehow the corners of her mouth wouldn't really lift. "It was a long and exhausting journey for me. I'll get some rest. Marie will help you make yourself at home."

At home, my arse. When would the bitch stop talking to me at last? I clamped down on my teeth, glowering at her until she disappeared into a room at the far end of the hall.

"I will make sure your mother is fine, then I shall give you a tour through the house if you like." Marie flashed an excited beam at me.

Pivoting on the spot, I marveled at the light-flooded interior. With a nonchalant shrug I accepted her offer, although I was more than eager to see the rest of the house.

The oval hall held nothing more than a wardrobe and a credenza with a blue and white patterned vase sitting next to an old-fashioned landline phone. Carved wood doors in off-white opened in either direction. When I was sure nobody would notice, I leaned slightly to one side, peeking around the corner of what seemed to be a study. Shelves filled with books and collectibles lined the walls of the small room.

To the right of the hall, a flight of semi-winding stairs led to the second floor. Only when I traced the staircase up to the balustrade did I understand the uncommon brightness inside. Part of the roof sloped down over the open space in a garret with a huge dormer window, providing the imitation of a real sky inside the house.

"It's a little bigger than your small room back in London, isn't it?"

At Julian's soft taunt I whirled about. He leaned against the doorjamb, his thumbs hooked through the belt loops of his jeans.

I straightened and put on my well-rehearsed girlie grin. "You're still here? Shouldn't you be heading home to your family by now?" The mocking edge to my voice did nothing to rattle his relaxed composure.

"No, dear. Julian is living with us," Marie said cheerfully as she exited my mother's room and grabbed my wrist. "Come with me. I will show you the kitchen while I put on the kettle for a cup of tea." She tugged on my arm until I followed her, but I couldn't hide my horror as I caught Julian's amused gaze.

As he winked, his beautiful blue eyes held the promise for a very special six weeks.

Cinderella

In a spacious kitchen, vanilla cupboards hugged white walls. The warm smell of freshly baked bread wafted through the room. The oak table sat eight, and with me the sole occupant at one end, the thing extended like the runway of a fashion show.

The island in the middle of the room reflected in the stainless steel fridge door as Marie rummaged through the shelves. The metallic giant should have come with a map. It was clear Marie was getting lost in there.

"I hope Albert did not eat it all. Ah, here it is." She emerged with a bundle enveloped in wax paper and grabbed a plate from one of the cupboards. She removed the wrapping, revealing a pastry of some kind, which she shoved in the microwave for a few seconds. Moments later, she placed the steaming snack in front of my folded arms.

With her elbows propped on the table, she lowered into the chair next to me. "Eat, *chérie.* You must be hungry."

"No, I'm not," I said. The same instant, my stomach gave a traitorous rumble.

Her laughter, like the peals of a tinkling bell, bounced off the walls and filled the room. "You are family, Jona, and very welcome in this house. Do not be shy to help yourself to anything." The soft shine in her eyes made me feel she meant every single word.

But why now? What drove this woman to play the good auntie today, when for almost eighteen years she hadn't even cared if I lived or died? This woman was a stranger to me. She'd never come to our small flat in Cambridge when I still lived with my mother, nor had Charlene ever mentioned a sister in France. I knew nothing about Marie and wondered how much more she knew of me.

Another rumble started in my gut. Embarrassed, I pressed my fist to my stomach and wished it would just shut up. My aunt flashed an understanding grin. I didn't care for it. But it would have been a shame to throw away the delicious smelling food now that she'd already heated it. I pinched the puff pastry from the plate and nibbled at one end. The flavors exploded in my mouth. It was a crime not to lick my lips free of any crumbs that remained.

Happy that I was eating, Marie nodded. When the kettle on the marble counter gave a short beep, she placed a palm to my cheek for the briefest moment. Her hand was gone too quickly for me to even think about flinching from her touch.

"I will take this cup to your mother." My aunt poured steaming water into a mug and dipped a tea bag in and out. "Then we can start with *la tour*."

I nodded while I took another small bite from the pastry. A couple minutes later, the snack was gone and I waited for Marie's return. Three minutes stretched into five. What kept her away so long? After all, my mother's room was just around the corner.

Tracing the geometrical line of triangles along the plate's brim kept me occupied for another minute or two. I chewed on my lower lip. How rude that she could forget about me in such a short time. No voices in the hallway or footfalls announced her return. The *tap-tap-tap* of my shoe against the warm terracotta tiles on the floor was the only sound cutting the eerie silence. Bored now, I pushed to my feet and carried the plate over to the sink; it took a minute to wash up.

"I see you are already making yourself useful," Aunt Marie chimed behind me.

I whipped around and met her delighted gaze in the doorway.

She took the plate from my hands to store the saucer away in a cupboard above my head. "Come. It is time to see your new home." Soft hands on my shoulders shoved me out through the door.

The living room on the opposite side of the hallway was partly walled with panes facing west. Gorgeous sunlight filtered through. A grand piano in front of the windowpane dominated the room. According to the set of sheet music on the stand, the glamorous instrument was actually used. My fingers brushed over the ivory keys chiming three dissonant notes as I walked by.

Next to an open fireplace, a big grandfather clock ticked in a hypnotic rhythm. It took me into a past, where the sound of a clock had provided my only comfort at night. My hand lifted to my left elbow, an injury that had long since healed. I pushed the memory away.

After I finished my walk around the room, Marie showed me their bedroom and my uncle's study, the one room I'd gotten a sneak peek into earlier.

When I stepped out into the hallway again, the front door tempted me as it stood ajar. A warm breeze beckoned me to take the chance and break free. Maybe, if I could catch Marie in an unaware moment and make a dash for the exit, I would get enough of a head-start to find a hiding place in the woods we had passed on the way here. In the dark I'd travel back to the airport and somehow manage to get a flight back to London.

Hands shoved into my empty pockets, I abandoned the idea of escape. With no money, the journey home would be more of an adventure than I cared for. A snort came over my lips as my mind worked hard on another solution.

"This is our bathroom. You can take a look as well if you like." Marie stepped in front of me and ruined my hope for freedom.

She knew what I was thinking.

For now it was best to follow her. Later, when I had a few minutes to myself, I'd make a detailed plan of my bid for freedom.

The only downstairs room I didn't get to see was my mother's. Fine with me. I'd be happy as long as the dragon remained inside her hole with the door shut. But to my annoyance the wooden door cracked open just as we headed back to the stairs.

Julian slipped out and silently closed the door, taking every care a parent would when leaving the nursery of his sleeping newborn.

"Is she asleep?" Marie's voice dropped to a whisper.

Julian nodded.

"Ah, the ever-present caretaker. Did you tuck her in like a toddler and kiss her goodnight at three o'clock in the afternoon?" I said.

He leaned closer and whispered, "I can do that with you tonight if you like."

My gulp echoed in the high hallway. I stepped back, fixing him with an unimpressed stare. A tingle in my stomach irritated me while shock and excitement pulsed through my veins.

Marie slapped his arm. "Oh, be nice, Julian," she scolded him, but he only laughed. Then my aunt turned toward me. "Your mother sleeps a lot these days. And the journey to London exhausted her even more." She snaked her arm around my waist and made me move forward. "Come, *chérie*. I believe you want to see your room next."

Upstairs, the corridor spread to both sides. I whirled around on the gallery, enjoying the sunny place. As I leaned over the balustrade, I saw Julian below, crossing the hallway with loose-limb strides, headed for the kitchen. Sunrays breaking through the dormer made the fair strands of his hair gleam. Being tucked in by him might make an interesting experience. My heart beat faster.

He stopped as if he could feel me watching him. His gaze lifted to me. His blue eyes twinkled.

Shit. I jerked back as embarrassment filled me. I whirled around to face Marie and let her show me to my room. His soft chuckles drifting to me from downstairs annoyed me to no end.

"We have a small library up here," Marie explained and pointed to the door around the corner to our right. "You can get yourself books whenever you like. Julian stays in the room on the far left. And this will be yours."

Great, Julian didn't only live in the same house, but also on the same floor. One foot of solid wall was all that separated us. I suppressed a snort.

Next to Julian's room, she opened the door to my private place, and I entered. As I crossed the threshold, I found myself in a fifteen-by-fifteen-foot piece of heaven. My breath caught in my throat, and I truly hoped my jaw wasn't hanging open.

Sunshine swamped in through wide windows on two connecting walls. The wind played with sheer curtains, pushing the white fabric in and out through the French door at the far wall that exposed a beautiful balcony.

The rubber soles of my boots made a squeaking sound on the light gray parquet floor as I crossed to the bed made of maple wood. A teddy bear was carved into the footboard and lured me to trace its outlines with my fingers. My hands skimmed over the floral design of the covers, and I enjoyed the luxurious feeling of the silken bedding. They were nothing like the stiff covers in the orphanage.

"I hope this room is not too childish for you." My aunt's worried voice broke my fascination. "Albert built the furniture with timber from our own woods. That was in the early days of our marriage when we hoped for children."

In the mirror of the wardrobe door, I caught a glimpse of her sad eyes as she rocked in a white rocking chair with a stuffed bear cradled in her arms. Although I hadn't paid much attention the night before, I remembered my mother mentioning that my aunt and uncle didn't have kids of their own.

If it had been anyone else, I would have asked straight away. But facing my aunt who had looked at me with those big warm eyes from the moment had I arrived, I considered it rude to ask for the reason they didn't have kids. However, my staring must have given me away.

"A genetic disease." She rose from the chair, placing the teddy back on the seat. Then she crossed the room in a stride that made it hard to back off. "I cannot get pregnant."

As she caressed my cheek, I was wondering if, over the years, she'd longed for a child as much as I had yearned for a caring mother. Everything might have gone differently if I had been born her daughter.

Marie would have loved me.

I bit down on the anger of this realization. After all, I wasn't supposed to like this stranger aunt of mine. But when she pulled her soft hand away, I almost reached for it to bring it back to my face. I covered the awkwardness by scratching my nose then marched toward a door standing ajar next to the wardrobe. "What's behind there?"

"A bathroom. Both upstairs rooms have one."

"You're shitting me. A bathroom for my private use?" With the door opened fully, I popped my head inside, then turned back at my aunt and cocked one brow. "Let me guess, you hoped for a girl?"

Marie laughed. "What gave me away? The pink and white tiles? Yes, I did hope for a girl. But also for a boy. Julian's bathroom is tiled all in white and blue."

Curiosity nagged at me; I wondered whether our rooms were totally identical. But I refused to ask. I didn't want her thinking I was in any way interested in the guy. Because I sure as hell was not.

"We will eat at seven," Aunt Marie informed me. "Take the time to refresh and make yourself at home. Albert brought up your backpack earlier and stored it in the wardrobe."

Some alone time sounded fantastic after this long day with people always surrounding me. I nodded, longing for the first shower in a private bathroom after more than twelve years.

"I will give you a shout when dinner is ready." As soon as the door closed behind her, I felt a bit lost. Of course she said this was my room now, but I had my doubts and refused to see it as such.

The bed, so nicely made, tempted me.

I eased onto the mattress. Not one bedspring gave so much as a peep. With my feet dangling from the edge, I sank into the pillow and started counting the small round spotlights dotting the ceiling. I could sneak out of the room and downstairs now. With any luck, no one would notice my disappearance within the next three hours, until it was time for dinner. A fantastic and maybe unique chance.

The curtains wafted over my face. A soft wind carried the scent of trees and freshly cut grass into my room. I took a deep breath.

And what if I stayed? Could I bear to live in this house for six weeks?

Tempting. But beyond all question.

The most I would do was delay my escape for one night. After all, it would have been a shame not to test this cozy bed just once.

I sat up with a jerk, kicked off my shoes so they'd not mess the beautiful bedding, and knelt on the mattress with my arms propped on the windowsill above the headboard. My head slipped under the thin fabric of the curtain. With the first glance outside, a stunned whistle escaped through my teeth.

A slim path led away from the house, about three hundred feet, to a giant garden that rolled out like an oversize vegetable patch. The whole vineyard was laid out in all its splendid glory in front of me.

Lush green shrubs rose side by side from the ground in several square yards. Broader paths separated them. The soft wind ruffled the fuzzy heads of the bushes. In the distance the misty rain from the sprinklers performed a dance of sparkles. Birds took a busy bath in it. I'd never seen such an enchanting place before. Not in reality, anyway.

I closed my eyes for a couple seconds, wondering how it might have felt as a child to run free and explore.

What would it feel like now?

The pounding of my heart in my ears, the wind in my hair—I hoped I'd get to roam the place soon.

What would Quinn say if he knew what a beautiful prison Abe had sent me to? He'd probably tell me to forget about my mother and enjoy the French way of life.

But I could never forget about that woman or pretend she wasn't there.

Or could I? *I might for one day.* A grin tugged on my lips. In high spirits, I bounced off the bed and went to inspect the bathroom.

The pink and white room was like walking into a fantasy. The sun peeked through frosty glass, gracing a spacious shower cubicle in the corner with warm light. Pulling one of the huge towels out, I rubbed the soft fabric to my face then wrapped it around my shoulders, drowning in the scent of peach. I could happily move into this small room for the rest of my stay.

A metal square built into the wall next to the credenza caught my eye. It resembled a cat flap. When I stood and pushed against the metal, it even moved back like one. I bent forward and slid my head into the hole in the wall to see where the shaft behind the flap would lead. Totally dark inside, I couldn't see anything. But my call echoed funnily in there. "Helllououou…"

Someone cleared his throat behind me.

I bumped my head as I jerked back. *Shit, that hurt.*

"That's a laundry chute. You drop your clothes in there when they need to be washed."

Glowering at Julian's amused face, I rubbed my skull. "Don't people ever knock in France?"

"Actually, I did knock. But when you didn't answer, I assumed you were having a shower and considered it safe to come in. I didn't know you were playing the terrycloth-princess in here."

I yanked the towel from my shoulders and shoved it behind my back. Heat rose fast to my cheeks. "And what is that?" I nodded my chin at the pile of clothes in his arms.

Julian ambled over to my bed where he dropped the entire load. "Marie had me bringing this to you. Apparently, these are things she no longer wears. Said to keep the stuff you like and burn your old ones."

"She said that?" I squeaked in disbelief.

"Well, not the *burning.*" He gave me a sheepish grin. "But I believe you can discard your shabby things now that you have a selection of nicer clothes."

The sound of my grinding teeth reverberated through my head. If I wasn't careful, I'd wear down my molars in this damn place. "My clothes are not shabby."

Julian pointed to my leg. "There's a hole in your knee."

"That hole is personal."

"Ooh, don't tell me. It's a special reminder of one of your reckless raids." He quirked one brow. "The pants got ripped during the dramatic escape, didn't they?"

Get bent and die.

I shrugged, lips tight. The pair of Doc Martens had totally been worth the sore knee and the damaged jeans.

His laughter as he walked out of my room haunted me. Only when I was undressed and standing under the warm spray of the shower did my irritation ease. This time I made sure the bathroom door was locked.

By the time I stepped out of the cubicle and wrapped myself into a soft white towel, the skin on my fingers and feet resembled prunes. But my hair smelled like a pool of rosewater, and my body soaked in the lotion of some gorgeous flowers. I figured Marie wouldn't mind if I used some of the stuff stored behind the mirror or else she wouldn't have placed it there. After all, she had told me to help myself to anything. I applied the creams generously.

On the credenza, several brushes and a hairdryer lay neatly arranged by size with the handles toward me. Marie could hardly have bought all these things for her possible future daughter the day she thought of getting pregnant. She must have stocked the credenza with ladies' utensils when she heard of my visit. The woman really made it hard for me not to like her.

When I was done with the difficult task of drying and brushing my hair at the same time, my usually dry, brittle strands had changed into a soft well of silk. Curtains of shiny auburn framed my face, and I had to double check the mirror to make sure it was really me.

Like a horse, I swayed my head from side to side as I galloped out of the bathroom, enjoying the sweet smell and the gentle caress of my hair on my cheeks. I leaped onto the bed and squealed, rolling on my back, feeling fresh like a newly plucked peach. Everything felt right in this brief, perfect moment.

But in the next, footfalls on the wood boards of the balcony stopped me in my gambol.

Clutching the towel to my naked body, I glared at the French door, but no one appeared in the frame. On tiptoes, I sneaked behind the curtains and peeked through. Outside was empty, but to the left, a silky white veil wafted in and out through a door just like mine.

Great. Marie had neglected to tell me the balcony connected Julian's room with mine. And unless I was totally mistaken, he'd just come to pay me another surprise visit. My heady romp probably scared him off—or maybe some sense of decency made him retreat.

Whatever the cause, it would be wise to get dressed. And fast. Last time a boy saw me naked, the oaf hopped out of the girls' shower room on one leg with a broken toe and a black eye, courtesy of my fist.

My body had sprouted curves since then, and Julian was the last person I intended to grant an exclusive look.

I dragged my backpack from the built-in closet and rummaged for a set of underwear. A faded gray t-shirt in my hands, I remembered the stack of clothes Marie sent me, which currently sat on my bed. Of course, I wouldn't do as that moron had suggested and burn my own clothes. But taking a look at what my aunt had given me wouldn't hurt. Maybe borrow a thing or two, just for today. Of course, the clothes would stay behind when I parted from the house and my family tomorrow.

Marie had been generous in her donation. This was the widest selection of clothes I had ever possessed. Several shirts with and without sleeves in different colors and patterns spread on the bedding. After wearing the same jeans and hoodies for so many years, this felt like diving headfirst into a pool of treasures.

I grabbed one piece after the other and held it to my chest in front of the mirror. Wow, what did people do with so much luxury? Folding the clothes carefully, I stored them in the wardrobe. For now, a black, snugly fitting tee with a V-neck would do.

There were also jeans and skirts. In this warm climate, I refrained from picking long pants. But not being the type to wear medieval gowns that reached my ankles, I chose one of the few pairs of shorts among the pile of cotton and linen. Hems fringed, it looked like someone had cut off the legs of a pair of jeans.

I had no trouble fitting into Marie's clothes. The shorts

enhanced my hips like they were made for me, although they covered little more than my bottom. The tee accentuated my breasts a tad too much, but long strands of my hair covered it nicely.

A whole new Jona stared back at me from the mirror. But most unfamiliar was the happy smile tugging on my lips.

Did I just think happy? *No, definitely not.* Marie and her family must have been out of their minds if they really thought they could bait me with a beautiful room and nice clothes. I didn't belong here and more importantly, I didn't *want* to live here. No one could make me, not even a bald judge with a wooden hammer.

Nothing wrong with enjoying one day in this place, but tomorrow I'd be off.

The little, round clock next to my bed said it was just shy of seven, and I decided not to wait for Aunt Marie to come and get me for dinner. I cast one last look out on the balcony, careful not to step on the boards, but only leaning my head out. The wood construction hovering fifteen feet above the ground made me aware of my vertigo all the more. Yet the balcony provided a priceless view of the vineyards.

Julian's door still stood open, but there was no sign of him outside. I took a deep breath, steeling my nerves for the coming dinner with family, including the dragon, then turned my back on the enchanting garden and headed for the door. As I pulled it open, I shrieked. Julian's fist came diving for my forehead.

"Whoa." He jerked his hand back just before he'd have bashed me flat on the ground. Shock or astonishment, I couldn't tell which, filled his face. Then his gaze dropped and lingered on my bare legs.

"Well, yeah, it's um…" Grimacing, I tried to tug my shorts and cover my legs. And failed miserably. "Short," I said, as if he couldn't see that.

He cleared his throat. "At least it doesn't leave much room to rip holes into it."

"Well if it isn't Prince Charming speaking."

That made him laugh. The sound ripped down the walls I had built around myself.

"Come on, Cinderella." He bowed. "The banquet is waiting."

"We better hurry before the clock strikes twelve and I turn into a pumpkin again." I loped down the stairs after him, grinning like a loon.

French climate

A warm, spicy smell clung to the air in the kitchen and made my mouth water. Ignoring my mother's attempts to greet me while she helped Marie with dinner, I slid into the corner seat. So the dragon had come out of her hole again. Admittedly, she looked a good deal better than a few hours before. But she got no more than a cold glare from me.

Julian stood behind one of the two high-back oak chairs, observing the drama going on. He shook his head, pulled the chair out, and sat down.

When Albert sauntered through the door, Marie ushered my mother to join the rest of us at the table. With six empty seats, the dragon chose the one right next to me. I rolled my eyes, turned and slid out. Disapproval reflected in the look Julian gave me. As I lowered into the chair next to him, his mouth opened. But before he could say one word, my mother cleared her throat a tad too loud to pass as a negligible cough. He drew in a deep breath and sighed.

Why the hell did he care about how I reacted to my mother? I sent him a dark glare, but for the moment, he ignored me.

Albert found a place at the head of the table, and Marie dished chicken with veggies onto his plate first. The smell of home-cooked food wafted from the serving dishes and promised a succulent meal. My stomach rumbled. I hoped no one heard it. Hastily, I gulped down some water from my glass then pierced a chopped carrot with my fork.

"Do you like your room?" Albert shoved a piece of bread into his mouth, his gaze focused on me.

I nodded, chewing on my chicken.

"The furniture might not match your taste," he continued, pouring himself a glass of wine. "Marie's teenage bedroom stuff must be stored somewhere in the cellar. We can change it if you like."

His offer surprised me, made me uncomfortable even. I frowned. Would he want a reward for his friendliness? In my almost eighteen years, only Quinn had ever helped me without expecting anything in return.

"That won't be necessary. I'll only be here for six weeks." The edge to my voice made me feel bad. In fact, I wouldn't want a single piece in the beautiful room changed for anything. It was perfect. And I'd only be staying for a single night, anyway.

Marie stroked her husband's arm. "See, I told you she likes the room."

When I met her gaze, her mouth curled into that sweet smile, which punched through my guard.

Argh.

My attention focused on the plate in front of me. I didn't want them to see how much Marie's care pleased me.

"Did you find Valentine and Henri in the vineyards?" she said.

Julian was the one to reply. "Yep."

"And will they come in later to meet Jona?"

"Actually, I asked them not to come until tomorrow. I didn't want to overwhelm Jona with new faces on her first day." His face remained expressionless as he glanced my way.

About to take a bite of the skewered asparagus on my fork, I set the silverware down. A hollow feeling spread in my belly. I didn't understand why he was being so nice after his earlier bantering.

"That was very thoughtful of you." Marie offered second helpings to Julian and Albert.

"Yes, very thoughtful indeed." Inwardly, I cringed at my own cynical words, when all I really wanted to say was *thank you*. I had no idea who this Valentine and Henri were, or why I was to meet them, but Marie and Albert were enough strangers to deal with for one day.

After dinner, the family moved to the parlor. Only Marie remained in the kitchen, and I stayed to help her tidy up the place.

"Just leave the cleaning to me," she said and took the plates out of my hands. "Why don't you go and take a drink with your mother and the others?"

"Uh, no." I had avoided my mother's gaze so well during the meal, I didn't want to ruin the evening with being shoved into a room together with her for any length of time.

My aunt took my face between her warm hands. "I understand it has been a long day for you. Get some rest. Tomorrow I will show you the vineyards." She kissed my forehead so quickly that I had no time to react other than close my eyes. "Sleep well, *chérie*."

Shock and confusion overpowered the comfort that her jasmine perfume and warm lips tried to raise inside me. My eyes blinked furiously as I concentrated on my boots. Spinning on my heels, I strode out of the kitchen. Then I stopped. Damn, I'd forgotten to say goodnight.

I rubbed the spot on my brow where Marie's lips had brushed against my skin. So I didn't bid them goodnight, big deal. They were not family. Marie and Albert were my jailers. No need to show them any pleasantries. Especially, when I *wasn't* happy in their presence.

Or was I?

Damn, what did they do to me? The French climate must have gotten into my head. I should have told Marie off for that unexpected caress and warned her never to kiss me again. The door to my room banged shut behind me, keeping out everyone—and those unwanted emotions.

In the fading light, I rummaged through my suitcase and found my notepad and a pen. I settled with the writing tools on the cloud-soft bed and piled the pillows behind my back.

As night fell, I filled eight pages with denials of my first impressions of this place and the people living here. By the time I came to ramble on about my aunt's kiss, the room had become too dark to distinguish the blue words from the white of the paper.

I lowered the pen and scanned the darkened room for a moment. Bile rose in my throat. I thought of this marvelous place and how I couldn't dare to stay.

It was like granting a hungry and freezing child a glimpse of a stuffed turkey through a window at Christmas. Only, I wasn't outside peeking through the glass. I sat inside the warm house, tasted a delicious meal. With two fingers, I massaged the spot between my eyes. The longer I stayed here, the harder it would be to leave.

The hoot of an owl carried through the open French door. A soft wind rustled the trees. The wood of the balcony creaked under someone's feet.

Julian.

My chest constricted, and I held my breath for an uncomfortable half-minute, straining to hear whether he'd come toward my room. But he wouldn't be so bold. With no light in my room, he must think I'd fallen asleep.

Apart from the wind and animals outside, the night remained silent. Tossing my notepad on the mattress, I rolled out of bed and sneaked to the door leading to the balcony. Carefully, I leaned only my head outside to peek around the corner.

Palms braced on the wood railing on his side of the balcony, Julian stared down at the vineyards. The faint shine of light from his room tinted his silhouette in soft gold. He hung his head, his shoulder blades flexing underneath his shirt. An invisible weight seemed to press down on his shoulders.

One had to be blind not to notice it was my mother's health that concerned him. The image of Quinn ruffling my hair when I was down or in trouble haunted me for a second. Maybe Julian needed a little comfort himself, and I could be the one offering it. God forbid, no ruffling, of course.

Teeth clenched, I fought against this urge. The story about him only being Charlene's caretaker struck me as a masquerade. Even if everyone else fell for it, I wouldn't.

What wouldn't I have given to find out about their uncommon relationship... Anything—but my pride. No way would I ask him about the matter. Leaning against the doorframe, I studied him silently.

"Can't you sleep?" His words, little more than a whisper, drifted to me.

My heart thudded in my ribcage, shocked he'd caught me staring at him. "I'm not tired." The answer came quick, yet my voice sounded like a stranger's in the dark.

"Come out, it's beautiful up here at night."

"Mm-mm." I shook my head.

For a brief moment, his eyes narrowed to slits. "You're scared." He said it with such conviction I wondered if he felt personally insulted by my refusal. Pushing away from the railing, he shoved his hands into his pockets and ambled toward me. "Hopefully, it's the height of the balcony that makes you nervous and not me."

"Why would you make me nervous?" The words shook slightly in my throat. I shifted against the doorframe as he drew nearer.

He halted before my room and leaned with his backside against the railing. "Why indeed?"

For an immeasurable moment, we stared into each other's eyes. If I hadn't known better I would have thought he actually *wanted* me to be nervous around him. Silly idea. I shoved it aside, clearing my throat. "Who are the two people Marie wants me to meet?"

"Valentine and Henri? They're nice people." Hands planted on the railing at either side of his hips, he hoisted himself up onto the edge.

"No, don't!" My warning echoed across the field as I let go of the doorframe and reached out in a helpless attempt to stop him from falling backwards over the balustrade. Yet fear kept my feet rooted to the floor inside.

His arms still braced against the wood, Julian cocked his head while one of his brows arched up. Not bothered by my concern, he eased onto the insecure railing, his gray sneakers dangling two feet above the floorboards.

His gaze mocked me like it suggested I come out of my room and make him get off the railing.

Oh, for the sake of my frazzled nerves, just get down! I tamped down the anger over his ignorance and kept to the safety of my room.

He cast me an amused glance from under his lashes then continued as though nothing had happened. "Henri and Valentine Dupres live down the road. They're an elderly couple working for your aunt and uncle in the yards. You will meet them tomorrow morning."

At his words, pictures of tonight's dinner rose before my eyes. Maybe now was the time to thank him for his concern, even though I cringed at the thought of letting him know how I really felt. I coughed slightly, tilting my head so the curtain muffled my voice. "It was actually kind of you to delay their introduction until tomorrow."

"Sorry, what did you say?" He smirked, and for an instant I considered tossing a pillow at him. But that might have caused him to fall backward off the balcony. I didn't want to take the responsibility in case he broke his neck.

"Thank you," I said more clearly, though through gritted teeth.

His teasing grin disappeared. "You are very welcome, Jona." His soft purr gave me chills. "Earlier, you seemed surprised I would care about you. Why was that?"

His serious words touched the spot of my mind responsible for lying or telling the truth.

"I thought you didn't like me." My croak clearly betrayed my unease. I dropped my gaze to the gaps between the boards of the balcony floor.

"You do your best to pretend not to like me either." His soft, smooth tone reminded me of sand running through an hourglass. "And yet you're worried I might fall off the balcony and get hurt."

"Hey, buddy, who says I'm pretending?" Looking up at his face, I found something in his stare that I couldn't quite place. It reminded me of Rottweiler Rusty when he'd ogled a bone.

My mouth was dry, a cloud of pleasant warmth expanded in my chest. A couple of seconds later, Julian slid down from the railing. A hundred tense muscles in my body relaxed, and a breath I didn't know I was holding whizzed from my lungs.

Damn him for making his point clear.

"Sleep tight, Jona," he said through a lopsided smile as he headed back to his side of the balcony.

"Goodnight," I whispered, hardly audible to myself.

Julian chuckled then disappeared through the floating curtains.

*

I woke snuggled in a sea of softness. The faint light of a breaking morning fell through the window above my bed. I yawned, my body completely relaxed. Something I'd never experienced before.

Still muzzy from sleep, I blinked, taking in the features of the room. Only then did I remember where I was. Alarm shot through me. Stupefying. How could I've slept so peacefully with my mother resting only one story below?

The floor felt cold against my bare feet as I got out of bed and shuffled into the bathroom. Warm water washed away the last bit of sleep from my eyes. In the mirror, I caught the face of an indecisive child. Chocolate or candy? Dream castle or freedom? If I wanted to leave, then now would be the perfect moment.

Yesterday, Marie had made me a fantastic dinner, and I had slept through the night on a bed of clouds. I'd tasted heaven, now I needed to go before I grew used to the comfort and wouldn't be able to part from it.

"The vineyard," the girl in the mirror whispered, her tone a suggestive tease. I couldn't leave before taking a walk through the vineyard. *Just once*, I promised myself. Tonight I'd certainly be off on my way back to England.

Five o'clock in the morning seemed a bit early to wander downstairs and wait for Marie to get up and show me the vineyards. I settled on the bed, tucked my feet under the blanket, and leaned on the windowsill. Chin resting in the crook of my folded arm, I gazed out on the vinery and mused about the breaking day.

The first and only day of my slave work.

What would my uncle expect me to do in the yards? I could hardly take a watering can and wet the entire field. It would take five hundred years or more.

Back straight, I narrowed my eyes to scan the little grapes on the bushes. Mid-August. They should still be too small for harvest. So, what else awaited me today?

With a little shock of anticipation, I couldn't wait to get out to the vine and do whatever tasks my aunt and uncle ordered me to do.

A shiver rattled my teeth as the morning wind blew around me. The blanket pulled up to my neck, I wrapped myself in it like a hotdog. The covers still bore the warmth from last night. I curled against the headboard and closed my eyes only for a second longer than a blink. But soon sleep sneaked up on me, and I dozed off.

Next time I woke, strong sunrays warmed my face and the chirping of a bunch of birds carried to me. A feather brushed the skin from my brow down to the tip of my nose. The purr of a happy cat pushed up my throat as the stroking continued. I blinked against the warm sun. Julian's blue eyes were level with mine.

My mind still drifting from chasing a sparrow in the vineyard, I wondered how Julian had found his way into my dreams. We gazed at each other. No one spoke in this unreal moment.

The corners of his lips twitched up and mine followed suit. What I had mistaken for a feather before was in fact a wisp of my hair caught between his fingers. He brushed down my nose one last time, then let go of the strand, and briefly knocked my chin with his knuckle. "Good morning."

"Hi." My voice matched the warmth of the sun.

"I hope you didn't sleep like this all night. Isn't a windowsill an uncomfortable excuse for a pillow?"

"Actually, I've slept in worse positions." The sereneness of our conversation and the peaceful morning embraced me like an extra layer of blankets. The mixture of mint, basil, and other herbal scents drifted on the breeze and filled my head. I snuggled deeper into the crook of my arm. "What are you doing here, anyway?"

"I came to wake you."

A mellow chuckle rocked my body. "With bunches of my hair?"

He shrugged. And he wasn't wearing a shirt. "Would you rather I poked you with a stick?"

The thought of being badgered with a piece of wood made me grimace. "Hair is fine."

My gaze followed the outlines of his naked shoulders and firm biceps. Strong pecs twitched underneath smooth, suntanned skin when Julian planted his elbows on his squatted knees. I could have watched him like that for hours.

"We're supposed to go out in a bit. If you'd like to have breakfast first, Marie would be happy to see you in the kitchen."

"Eat again?" I cringed. My stomach was still stuffed from the luxurious meal we'd had yesterday evening. "But aren't you going to have breakfast with them?"

"I don't usually eat breakfast." He rose to his full height, smoothing his blue jeans over his thighs. "So, are you getting up now or do I need to go looking for a stick after all?"

I tilted my head up to look at his face. "Please, no weapons. I'm coming of my own free will."

His sanguine expression changed to devious. "I'm trusting in that."

Neck stretched, I watched his taut butt as he walked to his room.

Teamwork

The very same moment I reached the bottom of the stairs, my mother emerged from her room, her bony body wrapped in a purple house dress. Stupefied for a moment, I trudged outside instead of into the kitchen and found a seat on a wooden bench on the stone patio. Better skip breakfast today.

Lou-Lou lay curled up under the bench and lifted her head to acknowledge me with a tired growl. I folded my legs underneath me—no need to take unnecessary risks with the black-eyed monster.

The morning sun warmed my face and bare arms. Marie appeared through the front door and approached the table with lazy steps. "Are you not hungry, *chérie?* I can make you a cup of tea or coffee if you like."

"No, thanks." I patted my still bursting stomach. "The yummy dinner last night should keep me going for a day or two."

The corners of her lips almost lifted as far as her ears. Oh my God. This woman had definitely touched my heart if I had just made a compliment about her cooking.

"All right then, shall we go?" she cheered.

I leaned sideways to peek around her. So far it was only the two of us. Wouldn't Albert and Julian come, too?

She tracked my gaze and then confronted me with a frown. "Are you expecting someone?"

"Where are the others? Are we going alone?"

"Oh, no." She waved a hand, then grabbed mine gently, and pulled me up. "Your uncle and Julian are in the field already. Albert can hardly wait until the cock crows before he leaves the house to tend to his beloved vine."

They left? How strange that Julian didn't take care of my mother before he went to work outside. Or maybe he'd popped into her room while I was getting washed and dressed. After all, I had taken nearly ten minutes to choose a pair of khaki pants and another dark t-shirt from Marie's donated stack of clothes.

Initially, I had intended to wear my own clothes. But they might have gotten dirty out on the field. I wanted them in nice shape for my escape tonight. Well, in as good condition as possible, overlooking the hole in the knee of my jeans and the tattered hem of my hoodie.

Marie tugged on my arm and started for the vineyard. "*Allez*, Lou-Lou," she ordered over her shoulder.

With a yawn, the giant dog emerged from under the bench to trot along beside me. I inched closer to Marie, but she assured me the Saint Bernard meant no harm. "In fact, a squirrel was the biggest thing she ever dared to get involved with."

A squirrel? Lou-Lou's back stood even with my hip as we walked along the footpath. I croaked out a hoarse laugh.

Her moist muzzle bumped into my hand. When she shoved her big head under my fingers, I figured she wanted me to pet her. Nervously, I skimmed my fingers through the soft curls on her meaty neck. It felt all right. Her head not twisting to bite off my hand seemed like a good sign.

The closer we got to the entrance of the yard, the more fidgety I became. The scent of young leaves wafted all around me. Everything smelled so…green. Juicy. Liberating. I picked up pace. Because Marie hadn't let go of my hand since we left the patio, it was me who dragged her along now. The yard spread out in front of us, longer than the runway of the French airport where we had landed. It must have stretched a mile in both directions, length and width.

Crushed stone crackled under my boots as I twirled along the path, drinking in the beauty of this place. Thousands of shrubs, tied to wires, stood like tin soldiers. They reached no farther than my chin.

"Wicked," I breathed.

"I am not surprised you like them." Marie grinned. "Some say, one either hates the vines, or loves them for a lifetime. In your case I would say, it is in your blood to feel close to the vineyards."

It was in my blood? What a strange choice of words. Yet, this little piece of earth connected with me in an instant. Invisible roots grew from my feet, dug through the stony surface, and anchored me to France. A warm vibration in my body tried to signal that I'd finally come home.

Get a grip, idiot. This is the land of the enemy.

I straightened my back, and the muscles in my face hardened. "What do you want me do?" My ice-cold voice detached me from my aunt as well as the vineyards.

Marie tapped a finger to her lips. "You can see if Julian needs help with the fertilizer."

I tracked the direction of her outstretched arm. Some eighty feet across the field, Julian scooped white powder out of a bucket and tossed it without much concern underneath the bushes. I could do that.

Lou-Lou's paws pounded on the dirt behind me as I jogged over to him. While I had trouble climbing through the two lines of wire ropes stretching along each row, the dog simply dodged them.

Seven rows of shrubs farther west, Julian greeted me with a laugh. "Seems like you made a new friend."

"Or maybe she just doesn't want to let her next meal out of sight," I muttered, eyeing the colossal dog sideways.

Julian set the bucket on the overturned soil and wrinkled his nose. "I really scared you with that silly story, didn't I?"

"No, you didn't." Unable to help myself, I stuck my tongue out at him. "But I think you owe me an apology for trying." Fists planted on my hips, I waited for him to say, *I'm sorry, Jona.*

A chuckle ripped from his chest instead. "Rrright."

My ego stomped an invisible foot on the ground. "That so didn't sound like an apology."

Bucket in hand again, he ignored my complaint and continued his work, with me fast on his heels. The smirk he cast over his shoulder irritated me like hell.

He'd better not dare think I followed him out of boredom. Or worse, interest. After all, I came over to work. "Marie said I should help you with, um, whatever you're trying to do here." I waved a hand at the powder he dropped to the ground in fistfuls every few feet.

"And here I thought you'd already taken a shine to me," he teased.

So says the guy who woke me this morning by tickling my nose. I snorted and fell back a few steps.

Julian jerked his head, motioning for me to follow him. "Come on, Jona. Of course, I know you came here to work." His laughter chimed out warm and fair and assured me he was just trying to wind me up again.

I paced up to match his stride. "Fine. What exactly am I supposed to do?"

He handed me the half-empty bucket. "For starters, you dust the roots along the path with this powder. I'll go fetch another bucket."

In a graceful jump, he took the two rows to our left and headed for some sort of square container. Lou-Lou chased him with a happy bark for twenty feet, then she angled off as a bird caught her eye.

While Julian filled an empty pail with the contents of a man-high box, I dug my hand into the fine powder and let it run through my fingers. What could a substance similar to flour do to the vine?

Following Julian's example, I dropped a handful to the ground, trying to draw a small white circle around the stem of a little bush.

"You don't have to be that precise," he said behind me, tossing a fistful to the ground on the other side of the path. "Rain will wash the powder in, so the roots can soak it up from the wet dirt."

Facing the clear sky, I squinted against the burning sun. "Doesn't look like it will rain any time soon."

"Then the sprinkler will do the job." He winked and continued to toss the floury matter.

Even after he'd turned away from me, I still stared at his back. I couldn't understand how such small moves set my heart beating like a jungle drum. He had me yearning for more of his attention. I flexed my shoulders, shook off the annoying feeling, then continued with the sprinkling.

The bottom of the bucket had already come into view when quick, heavy footfalls crushed the stone behind me. I jerked out of my monotonous work. Pail flying, I spun on my heel to gaze into the beaming face of a tiny woman who resembled a teapot. Her hair, no longer than my pinky, shone silvery gray in the morning light and curled like pig tails all over her head.

Her lips pulled back in an eerie, wide smile, revealing a set of healthy white, but uneven teeth. Stunned, I focused on her heavy eyelids that looked as if they yearned to close over her bright green eyes.

"Ah, Jona!" she cried out in delight, pronouncing my name *Shonáh*. Arms spread wide, she sang out in French, *"Je suis très heureuse de faire ta connaisance!"*

I had no idea what she'd said.

Then she pulled me into a tight hug. My body shaped against her round belly, she swayed me a couple of times from side to side. Her embrace knocked the air out of my lungs. Dumbstruck, I clung to her shoulders, so as not to tip over by her enthusiasm.

Only when she let go of me did I manage to croak, "Hello."

The teapot shot a few more words in French at me. I finally caught the name Valentine and figured she was trying to introduce herself. Obviously she knew my name, if not the right pronunciation, so I replied, "Ah, yes."

A moment later she hugged me again then shuffled away.

"Now, that was weird," I whispered after she was gone, trying to gather my composure. "French people seem to be a happy folks." Always friendly to strangers and blessed with a smile that they seemed to wear all day.

To my left, Julian chuckled low and deep. "Valentine was pleased to meet you. And she doesn't speak English."

Head angled, I mimicked his lopsided smile. "Really? I wouldn't have guessed."

His laughter shook us both as he wrapped one arm around my neck and pulled me forward. The warm ocean scent of his skin overlapped the intense smell of the young vine. I breathed in deeply then swallowed hard.

The small hairs on his forearm tickled my chin and made me aware of how close he really was. His side rubbed against mine, the warmth of his body seeping into my skin. I felt way too comfortable in his embrace. For a brief moment, I longed to rest my head on his shoulder. I tilted my chin to gaze at his cheerful eyes before I pushed out of his hold.

He wasn't my friend and shouldn't be so close. And most importantly, I shouldn't feel so good around him.

Julian studied me for a second. Though he didn't say a word, I could read the question clearly in his quiet, blue eyes. *Is it really so bad?*

It was too nice. And that was the problem.

His glance lowered to my chest. "Oh bugger, I smudged your shirt."

I pulled at my tee. The powder on his hand had left a white trace on the collar of my V-neck. Before I could dust it off, Julian was already brushing the fabric, giving me a quick start. But he only messed the mark of three fingers into one white blur.

"Stop it." I slapped his hand away and laughed. The powder wouldn't be padded off, not even with my clean hand. "You ruined my tee."

"And I had a nice time doing so." Julian smirked. "Don't worry, princess. A shirt isn't something that can't be washed." He tapped my nose with his powdered finger then returned to dusting the roots.

Hand shoved into the white material, I flounced before him. "You're right. It can be washed—" A big grin sat on my lips as I pressed my palm to his chest, leaving a white mark on his midnight blue shirt.

Julian didn't seem surprised, nor did he bother to wipe off the dirt. Instead he made one threatening step forward and leaned close to my ear. "I guess you would kill me if I did the same to you." His suggestive words set a bunch of butterflies loose in my stomach.

As he pulled me against him, his strong hand on my bottom made me suck in a breath. His whiskers rubbed against my cheek, playing havoc with my senses. With my front pressed against his, a weakness settled in my knees. I feared collapsing in his arms any moment.

"Don't worry, I'll have my revenge." His voice had dropped an entire octave.

If I wasn't out of my mind at that second, I would have sworn he nuzzled my temple. Before I could gather my thoughts, he let go of me and continued his walk.

My heart pounded like mad. I took a moment to steady my knees. Better stay a little farther behind, out of his reach.

We continued our task in silence. When it was time to refill our buckets, he got me set with a full pail but left his empty one by the container. "Can you continue alone for a while?"

"Sure." I frowned. "Where are you going?" I didn't want him to leave me.

"I won't be long. You just finish this line, and I'll do the other side when I come back." He strode off before I could agree to his order.

Headed toward the house, his pace increased while I watched him. Maybe he needed to pop to the loo. But he could have said so when I asked. I shook my head, returning to the task.

Without him, dusting the ground was a darn boring job. I'd covered about twenty yards when Marie found me. At her side walked a man with shocking red hair and a big bulbous nose.

"This is Henri," she said.

The man held out his hand, and my own got lost in the cup of his chunky fingers. With Valentine being a teapot and this man as tall and slim as a beanpole, they really were a mismatched couple.

"Hello, Henri." I tried to imitate the sound of his name the way Marie had said it. *Ou-ree.*

He flashed a chipped-toothed smile and squeezed my fingers. From his silence and nodding, I gathered he too didn't speak English. Cool, one more person I didn't have to talk to, although he and his wife seemed like nice people.

Attention dedicated to sprinkling again, I whirled around once more at my aunt's amused chuckle.

"Jona," she snorted. "What is that on your backside?"

"Huh? What do you mean?" I twisted my neck to catch a glimpse of my bum, first left, then right. A powdery handprint glimmered on my pants.

I growled, dusting my butt to get rid of the traitorous mark of Julian's hand. The bastard had gotten his revenge indeed. "This will cost him his head!"

Julian came back half an hour later. Too long for a loo break. Most of my anger had blown off by that time, too. And the bottle of mineral water he handed me vaporized the rest of my annoyance.

"Stay hydrated on hot days like this, or you'll end up with a headache." He took a swig from another bottle.

The wonderful liquid cooled my throat. Until the first swallow, I hadn't even realized how thirsty I was. I guzzled down half a liter within a few seconds. The rest we left in the shade beside the container.

The morning went by almost too fast, and soon Marie called us to come inside for lunch.

"Go with Marie, princess," Julian said. "I'll come in a few minutes. Your uncle needs help with the dirt scanner."

I knew what he was talking about. A small machine Albert had used all morning. A short cable connected a pen-like thing to a little box in his hand. Randomly, it seemed, Albert dug the pen into the earth under various shrubs and read information from the screen on the box. Winemakers used such funny equipment.

I rushed after Marie. My face red and heated from the sun, I appreciated the little break in the cool house. Since I'd refused to eat breakfast this morning, my stomach roared a starving rumble by the time I sat down at the oval table.

The dragon joined me, yet she was clever enough to choose the place farthest away from me. Dark rings shadowed her eyes, and her hand shook as she reached for a glass of water. Her fingers so bony and slim, it was a miracle she found the strength to lift the cup to her mouth.

While she drank, she gazed at me over the brim. Not to show any weakness, I held her stare with a grim expression. Looking away would have meant I cringed from her.

Unfortunately, eye contact brought her bad ideas such as speaking to me. "How did you like the vines? Julian said you were having a good time outside."

Julian said? Of course, he came to see her when he left me alone out on the field. Bloody hell, I should have guessed. A hint of jealousy mingled with rage at her boldness exploded in my stomach.

"The judge sent me here to work, and that's what I did. No more, no less." I rose from the chair to grab a drink. Sometimes backing off was the smarter way—whatever was necessary to make her stop talking to me.

While I filled a glass under the tap, Marie sneaked closer and wrapped one arm around my waist. "Really? No more than work?" she whispered. "I thought I heard you laughing."

I glared daggers at her, but she beamed. Jeez, I hated her for being so lovely.

When I lowered into the chair again, my mother averted her gaze to her folded hands. With her shoulders hunched, she looked like she couldn't hold her head up. I couldn't remember her being haggard like this in London. Actually, she'd made a rather steady appearance then, apart from her sunken eyes.

With my attention focused on her, she shocked me when her head suddenly snapped up. Her cheeks gaunt, the bones stood out even more as her face lit up.

My heart stopped for a second. Every muscle in my body tensed like wire. Bliss sparkled in her eyes. Her entire composure seemed at the ready to pull me into a bear hug.

Run for your life! Panic gripped me while my feet itched to take flight. Had she gone bananas? It took me only another moment to realize she actually stared *through* me and at the door. Still under shock, I turned my head, only to find the door closed. An instant later, the handle pushed down. Julian slipped in.

His stern features changed to happy when his gaze drifted to my mother. He dedicated the first smile to her. The second one was meant for me.

I couldn't explain what was happening in that room, but something was very wrong.

"Oh, you are here at last," Marie beamed as her husband followed after Julian. "So we can finally eat."

The two men took a seat, Julian next to me.

"Your face is a little sunburned," he said. His knuckles graced my cheek.

I flinched away, giving him a disgusted snort. His hand dropped to the tabletop. Definitely offended, he narrowed his eyes.

Marie's lasagna smelled delicious, but for some reason my appetite had disappeared. I poked bits of the meal with my fork, shoving it around the plate. No more than three mouthfuls would go down my throat. My stomach felt strangely full.

Aunt Marie placed her soft hand on my forearm. "What is the matter, *chérie?* Are you not hungry?"

The hair at my neck stood on end as I felt Julian's questioning look on me. Did he sense that he was the source of my queasy feeling?

Don't be ridiculous. How could he know? I couldn't even explain it to myself. To be jealous of his relationship with my mother felt totally wrong.

"I guess it's the heat that bothers me," I mumbled.

"Oh, of course, you are not used to the French climate. What was I thinking?" Marie patted my hand. "Maybe you should stay inside for the rest of the day."

And be alone with the dragon? Panic washed over me,

tightening my grip of the fork until my knuckles went white. No way. I wouldn't give her a chance to sneak around me, trying to engage me in chitchat. "I'm all right. I can go out with you in the afternoon."

Anyway, it was my last day around, and I wanted to spend some more time in the vineyard before I headed off to an uncertain destination after dark.

"Very well. Just let me know when it is getting too much for you," my aunt said in her ever so sweet French accent. She pulled back her hand after giving mine a short squeeze and returned to her food.

To evade Julian's glances, I loosened the strands hooked behind my ear and hid behind a curtain of hair.

When everyone had finished, Julian helped Charlene back to her room. This was a good moment to talk to Marie in the hallway.

"What were you doing with Valentine this morning?" I had seen the two women kneel on the ground a lot. "When you ripped out the bushes?"

She laughed. "We did not rip out the vine, but picked weeds. We need to keep the ground clean of pest plants which would soak up the minerals meant for the vines."

"Can I help you with that?"

"Of course you can. But would you not rather work with Julian. I thought you two had a nice time together. He enjoys your company."

And perhaps I enjoyed the time with him more than I liked to admit. But it was a bad idea to get too close to someone who was *allied* with a certain bitch. In fact, getting close to anyone in this house was a bad idea. A small twinge of regret already poked my chest when I thought of leaving without saying goodbye to my aunt.

Eyes fixed on my mother's door, I sighed. "I'd much rather work with you than with him."

Julian chose that exact moment to come out of the room. My mouth hung open. I froze under his stare, my shoulders tensed when he shut the door louder than necessary. A muscle in his jaw ticked.

Slowly, he came toward me. My strained expression hardened as I expected his pissed off remark. But he walked right past me and headed outside.

"Marie, make sure she applies sunscreen before she goes out again." His hard tone cut to my core.

Spying not intended

The leaves of the grapevine swayed before my eyes in the light summer breeze. Their luscious smell filled my head, while dirt crept under my nails. My hands were sore from pulling out wee plants by their roots. The muscles in my slouched back protested.

It took a lot of effort not to cry out in pain or quit digging and rest in the shade. I clenched my teeth as pride kept me going. Minutes stretched into hours, and my body screamed at me with the slightest move I made.

The aching seemed to lessen if I kept myself distracted, so I took the chance to make plans for my imminent departure. I'd pack my few belongings into my backpack before taking a nap until around midnight. By then, everyone else should be fast asleep.

The first few miles I could hike, or maybe even try to hitch a ride in a car. Without money, taking a bus was beyond question. To fund the flight, I was going to lift some money off people at the airport. This option I preferred to the alternative—taking money from Albert and Marie.

It wasn't only the promise to Quinn that kept me from stealing from my family's house, but my aunt's inevitable hurt and disappointment when she would find out.

A glance over at Marie had me thinking about a farewell letter to her. Although I didn't plan to take any of her clothes, I wanted to thank her for the nice meal she cooked me and her generosity.

The thought of her sad face when she noticed my disappearance tugged at my hidden conscience. I stopped thinking about her altogether and let the physical pain take control again. This sensation was easier to handle, if not for long. Finally, I sagged heavily on my bottom.

"This looks easier than it is, no?" Marie's soft chuckle charged the humid air. "You should take a break and get a drink."

I grabbed the water bottle from the ground right next to me and lifted it to my lips. Liquid heaven filled my Sahara-dry mouth and throat. Legs crossed, I rested for a few minutes and took the chance to study my aunt while she continued ripping weeds with admirable passion. Her love for the vines was almost tangible.

She had me wondering what would have become of me had I been raised by her patience and support. I might have been holding a high school degree just then and ready to go to college. My days as a criminal teenager probably would have never come. I hated how I had landed in the gutter instead of my aunt's care. But why hadn't she come for me?

Intrigued by this question since my arrival, I swallowed hard. Eventually, I said, "Marie?"

Her smudged hands stopped, and she turned her head to me. I cleared my throat, but words got stuck in it.

"What is it, Jona?" she prompted. The slight tremble of my hands certainly didn't escape her attention.

I swallowed past the lump that tried to keep me from finding out the truth. "You seem happy to have me here. And all the nice things you gave me—" I clasped my hands, lowering my gaze. "Why didn't you take me when my mother wasn't fit for the job and shoved me into the youth center?"

With a thrust, Marie embedded the small spade in the earth and wiped her fingers on her shirt. On her knees, she scooted over to me then cupped my face in her two dirty palms. "*Chérie*, I would have brought you to France that very instant. An orphanage is no place for a child." The warmth in her eyes showed all the love she had for me.

Then where had she been during the past twelve years? As a kid I would have loved to live in an enchanted place like these vineyards. Not quite a child anymore, I still loved it.

The heel of my boot dug into the pebbly ground. "Why didn't you come get me?"

"Because I did not know of you, *chérie*." She shook her head slowly, as though she couldn't believe the truth herself.

But what was she saying? She was Charlene's sister. Surely, my mother wouldn't have kept me a secret from her family.

Aunt Marie took my hand and squeezed it. "When your mother was about nineteen, she met that soldier from England. His name was Jake, or Jack. She never told me his last name. Charlene was determined to follow him to the island. Never-dying love—I think those were her words." Marie gave an exhausted gasp. "Poor Charlene."

From the disapproving frown on my aunt's face, I assumed my mother fell head over heels for a man who didn't return her love. An unexpected sting in my chest made me hunch a little more. I ground my teeth, confused as to why *I* would feel agitated that my mother wasn't loved by the man she wanted to be with.

"Our parents tried to talk sense into her. They argued a lot. But in the end, my sister left us one night. There was a little note of farewell which only told us not to go looking for her."

My mouth sagged open. Charlene ran away? To a foreign country? She was braver than I actually gave her credit for.

"Do you know what happened then?" The demand in my voice surprised me.

"After a month, I received the first letter from her. She told me she was all right, found work in a new country, and rented a small flat." Marie's features turned sad. "I think in total I received five or six of her letters over the years, but she never put an address on the envelope where I could have sent something back. It was terrible not to know where she was. But the worst thing was that my parents never forgave her for running away. They died four years ago without seeing their eldest daughter again."

I wondered if my mother felt sorry when she heard about her parents' deaths. "How come Charlene is living with you now?"

Marie sat on the ground, hugging her knees to her chest, legs crossed at the ankles. "A couple of months ago, she returned, broken and sick. She needed care."

And it was just like Marie to forgive her older sister on the spot and offer her a home. Like she did with me. I could do nothing but admire my aunt for her kindness. "Do you know about her life in

England?"

"I can only tell you what she told me." Marie's brows furrowed. "She was with child when she left. The soldier was your father, and she had to find him and tell him."

A silent moment gave me the chance to swallow my surprise. My aunt had spoken of the man who fathered me. Now, I understood why I felt sorry when I heard of this soldier toying with my mother. He hadn't only hurt her, he'd abandoned us. Abandoned me.

My chest constricted as I tried to breathe. In this big world, wasn't there one single person, who wanted me in his or her life?

"He was based in the United States for a few years. Your mother stayed in Britain, though, ashamed to return to her family unwed and with a baby in her arms after all the fights with our parents. She was certain they never would accept a child out of wedlock. So she hid you from us. Never let us know." Marie's sad eyes warmed when they intruded on mine. "The mentality never bothered me. I would have loved you all the same. You can imagine my surprise when I learned what a lovely niece I have."

Her loving words did little to soothe the anger that was brewing along with her story.

What was the point in bringing me here now, when my time of detention would have ended in a few weeks? Charlene had spoken of a home in France. Right, a home she'd denied me for seventeen years. Damn that woman! I'd go and wring her bony neck.

With a rush of energy, I rose to my feet and paced down the line of shrubs.

Marie followed me and grabbed me by my elbow. "What is wrong?"

"Because Charlene was ashamed of me, I had to pay for my

unworthy existence and spend my youth in a prison for kids!" I yelled, then yanked my arm free.

"Jona, wait!"

Her plea faded as my stride turned into a run. I was going to strangle my mother.

Burning rage constricted my lungs, made it hard to continue running. But I surged forward to the house. My breaths erupted like the puffs of an active volcano. I kicked at the ground hard. Stones shot in all directions as I let out some of the frustration that boiled in me.

Cancer was one way to get rid of the dragon, but today *I* would make sure her last hour finally came.

As I neared the house, I noticed that someone had beaten me there. Through the wide windowpane in the parlor, I could see the dragon resting on the couch with Julian seated right next to her. I kept to the low line of bushes in the garden. I even held my breath for a second then shook my head at my own silliness.

Drained of any healthy flush, Charlene looked close to death with her arms lying lifeless by her side. With a caring touch, Julian took my mother's hand. His other hand stroked first her fingers, then her forehead, wiping long, colorless strands of hair from her face.

To catch the two in an intimate moment ranked high on my *never-to-do* list. But for some reason, I couldn't tear my eyes away from the scene. Crossing to a weeping willow, I hid in the long overhanging branches and peeked around the trunk to catch another glimpse through the glass.

My mother's eyes remained closed, but her lips moved with an effort. I'd die to find out what she told him. The stroking continued for a couple of minutes. All of a sudden, Charlene's eyes opened and focused on Julian's face. Something she saw there must have caused her pure happiness, for that was what she radiated with both her face and body.

And then it occurred to me that it wasn't so much Julian's look, but what he did to her with his hands that stirred a certain change in my mother's composure. Hadn't I experienced a similar stimulation only yesterday?

Charlene propped on her elbows and waited until he helped her to a sitting position. The lively color of youth replaced her white face. Her eyes grew wider and lost their glassy sheen. A spine that had seemed broken only seconds before straightened. She beamed. Strong and content.

Oh my God! Julian was her personal brand of drug.

As my back sagged against the tree, a breath pushed out of my lungs. The scene I just witnessed seemed so very weird. Surreal. What was Julian's secret? There had to be one.

I peeked around the tree one last time to catch a glimpse of him talking to my mother while he held her chin cupped in his hand. Then he tilted his head to gaze through the window. His eyes caught mine in an instant.

Shock slammed into me. *Bloody hell!* I couldn't move.

Julian rose from the sofa, his expression blank. My nails dug into the bark of the willow, and my heart knocked against the base of my throat. I swallowed hard. As he held me with his penetrating stare, I completely forgot why I'd come there in the first place. The world spun around me. It needed to stop. Finally, I found the strength to tear my gaze away. I whirled around and marched back to the vineyard.

Marie cast me a troubled glance when I stormed past her and Valentine to find a place some fifty feet away. Knees digging into the ground, I ripped weeds with a whole new enthusiasm.

Secrets. Secrets. What was it about Julian that made everyone feel better around him? Calmer. Healthier. He could hardly cast a spell over people.

Capable of hypnosis? I shook my head. Dirt crumbled from the bundle of dandelion I just tore out of the ground and tossed to the side. With a smudgy arm, I wiped beads of sweat from my forehead, pushing an angry sigh through gritted teeth. Damn, there was something weird going on with that guy.

And Charlene? The dragon had awoken from the dead in the front room. All happy.

All his.

She shouldn't be his. She was my mother and about two hundred years too old to be *his*.

Someone laid a hand on my shoulder. At the touch, I jumped to my feet and shot around. "And why the hell do I care?" I bellowed before I even got a clear glimpse of who I was facing.

Julian gazed at me with a stunned expression. My outburst had made him back off a step. He shrugged, forlorn.

My nostrils flared as I pushed an angry breath out. A storm raged inside me. I didn't know what to do to keep myself from exploding.

Julian just stared at me. His silken hair glinted golden in the sun, his eyes shone like the surface of a calm sea. Inwardly, I whined. *How dare he look so sweet?*

Oh no, I wouldn't be fooled this time. A mental slap helped to tear me out of my passing fancy. His sweetness must in no way distract me now. He couldn't work this calming voodoo on me. I wouldn't let him. "Stop that!"

"Stop what?"

"Stop weaving your hocus-pocus around me."

The left side of his mouth twitched. "Jona, are you feeling all right?" One of his hands came up to touch my shoulder again.

A shrill siren shouted *suspicion* inside my head, and I slapped his hand away. "I feel perfectly fine." With my finger pointed at his face, I frowned. "I just won't let you infect me with your...your...happy feelings. You're like a drug."

He angled his head and questioned my sanity with an arched eyebrow. "You better put this on, girl." A straw hat dangled from his hand. "A sun stroke can be a nasty issue."

He stuck the hat on my head and tapped the top. Invisible roots tied me to the ground when he pivoted and walked away.

The hat shaded my face from the wretched glare of the sun and shielded my eyes. Julian brought it for me. I'd be damned if he wasn't concerned about me. My steely core turned liquid. He really cared.

But that was not an excuse for his relationship with my mother, and I sure didn't need him to care about me. I needed no one. Hand clenched around the brim, I tore the hat from my head. Like a flying saucer it shot at Julian's back. "I don't need a bloody hat! What I want is an answer!"

He stopped and turned around. "An answer?" After he picked up the straw hat from the dirty ground, he wiped off the dust with one hand. "And just what would you want to know, Jona?" he drawled.

One heartbeat. Two. I couldn't bring myself to mouth the question. Julian waited while seconds ticked by.

Ah hell, what was I afraid of? With a final deep inhale, I stalked the few feet to him and, on tiptoes, glowered at his face. "Are you, or are you not, my mother's lover?"

Julian cast a nervous glance over his shoulder like he was afraid someone could've heard me. His firm fingers curled around my upper arm. He pulled me farther away from where Marie worked the field.

"I'm a lot of things, but certainly not her lover," he hissed. "And if you stopped spying on people, you'd never come up with such stupid ideas."

"I wasn't spying," I snapped and yanked my arm from his hold. "Not intentionally, anyway."

He stopped in his tracks when I did and faced me. "What *then* were you doing in the garden while I checked on your mother?"

"That's none of your business."

"Oh, but what kind of relationship I have with her is *your* business, right?"

"Right! No. Argh!" I raked a hand through my hair.

It *was* my business. After all, we were talking about my goddamned mother. "What's your intention? To become my stepfather?" A gruesome shiver trailed down my spine. That could never happen—especially when I felt so annoyingly attracted to him.

Julian said nothing. Instead his brows pulled together. He studied me with penetrating eyes.

I retreated a step from his intense stare. But this little distance could barely block whatever channel he used to read me. I so hated to be an open book.

"Now, give me that damned hat," I growled. The woven straw crunched under my grip as I snatched the hat from his hand and put it on my head. I stormed away, headed for the fertilizer container. His amused chuckle bounced off my back in the heated air.

Done crawling on the ground for today, it was time to strew some powder again. The floury dust ran through my cupped hand

and bedecked the earth around the shrubs. Alone, the task was not the most entertaining of jobs but still preferable to the slouched work of weeding.

I had hardly made it down one row when shoes crunched the path behind me. I prayed it would be Marie or even Valentine, but I already knew it was neither of them. To suppress a pissed growl took some effort as I glanced over my shoulder. Julian had started tending to the other side of the path.

After a few more steps, he caught up with me but still avoided my glare. I couldn't resist casting a sideways glance at him every now and then.

The ripped hems of his blue jeans scuffed along the path as he moved. I traced up his long legs, concentrating a few moments on his lean hips, taking in the enticing sight. His blue t-shirt hugged his flat stomach and firm chest, the short sleeves flexed with his biceps. My fingers itched to trace a line from his neck down his back to the slight curve just above the waistband of his pants. Heat rushed to my cheeks at that thought.

While we walked with only about five feet of footpath between us, my annoyance with him flared off quickly. I tried to hold on to that anger—it felt more comfortable to be pissed with someone than discover an unwanted addiction to his smile.

Maybe I was mistaken. What if all the hocus-pocus around him was simply the way my subconscious was dealing with a very scary fact—that I was falling for this guy? And fast.

The comfortable feeling when I'd opened my eyes to him this morning surfaced in my mind. As if he was no ordinary man but my personal island of peace. I craved this man like nothing else. He said he wasn't Charlene's lover, but could he be trusted?

Every few steps, Julian wiped his dusty hand on his backside, just to dip his fingers anew into the bucket and retrieve another handful of powder. The right side of his bottom was soon covered in white—like mine had been that morning after he'd groped me.

To remember the feel of his hand on my butt brought a pack of hot coals to the center of my stomach. Dear God, I mustn't even think about it. I took off the hat to fan myself, then placed it back on, and tried to concentrate on the work.

"Is Quinn really your lover?"

Air whizzed out of my lungs. I shot a stunned glance at Julian's face. The question shimmered in his eyes.

Yeah right, you so want to know that, don't you? I didn't reply.

"I didn't think he was," Julian said, the satisfied tone unmistakable.

Even though we barely spoke during the following few hours, I enjoyed just being near him. Once, as I bent over and rolled up the hems of my pants to expose my pale calves to the warming sun, I caught Julian staring me. I tilted my head and met his gaze. He gave me a tight-lipped grin. Then he returned to work.

There were not many things I was going to miss when I took off tonight, but Julian's smile was definitely one of them.

We left the vineyard together with the others at about five in the afternoon. I was starved and welcomed the smell of food when we entered the kitchen. Marie had decked the table with cold cuts, vegetables, boiled eggs and bread.

To my great delight I learned that the dragon was fast asleep in the front room and Marie didn't dare wake her just yet. With only the four of us surrounding the table, I experienced what it must feel like to belong to a normal family.

My aunt spoke about a new boutique in town that she would love to visit on the weekend, while Julian playfully pierced a slice of cucumber on my plate before I could. He shoved it into his grinning mouth.

I'd just sucked in a breath to tell him off, when Albert disrupted my feigned anger. "Now, Jona, how do you feel after your first day out in the vineyard?"

To be fair, I had trouble keeping my eyes open, but I'd also hardly felt better in my life. "My back aches a bit," I admitted, stretching, and gave Marie a sheepish look. "Throwing that funny flour to the ground was the better idea after all."

"You mean the fertilizer?" my uncle corrected.

I nodded. "I only hope it won't turn into dough with the next rain."

Now he and his wife laughed while Julian shook his head.

"It sure won't," Albert said. "It is nothing like flour at all."

"What exactly is it?" I asked.

My uncle's eyes cut to Julian. "Boy, did you not tell her? You spent the entire day out there together."

And what a fine day it was.

Julian shrugged, swallowing a bite of bread. "She never asked."

While his nonchalant attitude made me and my aunt chuckle, Albert tsked at him. Then his glance returned to me. "What you and Julian did today was supply the plants with minerals and vitamins to grow healthy and strong. You could have dissolved the powder in water and poured it over the roots. But to carry a can is a lot more exhausting than to carry a bucket with powder. To the plants it makes no difference."

Excitement rode Albert's voice when he spoke about his vines. It made him happy to tell me all about the different types of grapes and how the geographical location affected the taste of the wine later.

That evening I found I could show the man a good time just by listening to him, even long after we'd finished our dinner.

"Tomorrow, when we are out again, I will show you how to operate the tester and you can do scans of the ground if you like." My uncle beamed at me.

I felt a painful sting in my chest, knowing there would be no tomorrow for me here. I'd already be gone and on my way back to England when my family woke the next morning.

The bird incident

The first light of a new day warmed my face. My nose itched and I rubbed my finger on the tip while forcing my eyes to open. Throbbing pain in my forehead reminded me of Julian's advice to wear a hat on a scorching day in the open field. A warm drop of drool rolled down my chin. I wiped it off with the back of my hand and raised my head from the hard surface. *What the hell...*

Where was I?

As I straightened my stiff back in the chair, a long yawn escaped me. My muscles rebelled but my joints clicked into place with a good stretch. When my arms sank back to the desk, I spotted my work from last night. A half-finished farewell letter addressed to

Marie, crumpled from my tired body resting on it all night.

"Bugger!" Yesterday's labor in the field had worn me out. The last thing I remembered was having to rest my head for one minute. I must have fallen asleep while writing the note.

My stuffed backpack waited in the corner next to the door. Damn, all I wanted was to get away from this place. But here I was, stuck in my aunt's house, trapped for another day with the dragon.

"No, no, no!" I banged my fist on the desk, sending the pen flying in a high arc to the floor.

My glance skated over the clock on my nightstand. I should have set the alarm. Falling asleep had ruined my chance at freedom for another day.

Tonight I'd be more careful, making no mistakes. I needed to get out of this place and fast.

Downstairs, I greeted everyone with a long face on my way to the door. Not even Marie's beaming smile could melt my ice-cold glare, and I shrugged off Julian's questioning tilt of the eyebrow with a sneer.

And then I bounced into *her.*

Charlene came in through the front door right as I wanted to walk outside. A big blue book slipped from her hands and dropped to the tiles. It flapped open somewhere in the middle. My hands fisted, and a grumble rolled from my chest, filling the hallway.

The dragon beamed. "Good morning, Jona."

Oh, get the hell out of my way or I'll put a stop to that happy grin with my bare hands.

I wanted to step over the book on the floor, which on second glance happened to be a photo album. The glimpse of one particular picture made me freeze.

The photo was of me—in front of this very house.

Sneaking up on me to take pictures? Damn her to hell.

Marie huddled next to us to gather the book for my mother. She rose with joyous surprise on her face. "Where did you find this?"

Charlene cut a glance to her sister. "It was one of the few things I took with me when I ran away. I must have thumbed through this book a thousand nights." Her sickly soft voice made me want to puke.

"Look, *chérie*." My aunt turned with the open album in her hands. "That is me and your mother when we still were young. Oh Charlene, you must have been Jona's age here."

My stomach dropped to the floor as I looked at the photo she pointed out. The faded color proved it was taken many years ago, but I would have sworn that was me standing outside the door smiling for the camera. The same dark red hair wafted around the girl's face, the same eyes stared at me. The yellow dress and white pumps looked stupid on me though.

"I cannot believe how much Jona resembles you in your younger days." Marie's words made me sick with repulsion.

"Come on, you two. Let's go to the front room and look at these pictures together."

Or, you could grab a gun instead and shoot me in the head.

I gave both women a wry look. "I don't think so." Bad enough that I looked exactly like the dragon in her younger days, but there was definitely no chance I would sit and reminisce with them about the "good old days" and notice every bloody detail of our resemblance. *No way in hell!*

Careful not to brush against my mother, I stepped past her and escaped into the morning breeze. Deep breaths calmed my anger only a little as I leaned against the wall.

Birds flew across the flawless sky. Another hot day in the

dragon's den. I really needed to get away from here. The farther I could get from my mother, the better. Did she honestly think she could just enter my life and expect us to be best friends? As if the past twelve years never happened?

Marie came out a little while after me, and together we walked to the field. I appreciated the silence between us.

Out in the vinery, my pacifying song crept to my mind, the one I didn't know the title of. I began humming, and the notes of this haunting melody stayed with me all morning.

As promised, Albert instructed me on how to use the cell phone-sized device to make scans of the dirt. For the simple purpose of distracting me from thinking about the unhappy meeting with my mother that morning, I wanted to get my hands on the gadget with the round keypad and a bright screen.

But my failed prison escape chewed me up inside. Pebbles bounced off my boot as I kicked the dirt. No matter what, I had to stay awake long enough tonight to pull off Houdini's grand disappearing act.

Since Julian was assigned to "cheer me up"—and I'd heard Marie use those particular words before she had sent him off with me—his short trips back and forth to the house and the field didn't escape my attention. If this was his way to perk me up, I could very well do without his help. What was he doing anyway? Serving the dragon another lamb for her to roast?

And yet, I found myself staring after him, every time he excused himself for a few minutes. I kept my face emotionless, but inside I screamed at him not to leave. Confusion and doubt were my permanent friends.

In the evening, I ate my gumbo extra fast. A headache provided a good excuse from the chitchat.

Aunt Marie bid me goodnight at the bottom of the stairs. "Too much work is not becoming you." She reached for my hand to squeeze it tight. "Tomorrow, you will not be going out to the vineyard."

Oh, how right you are.

Inwardly, I sneered. But at the same time, the loss of my new family slung a noose of barbwire around my heart.

"You need to recover, *chérie*," she went on. "And it is the weekend, so we will find something nice to do, just you and me." The corners of her mouth lifted. "How does this sound?"

It sounds great! Bile in my throat stopped me from slamming the lie right into her face. I pulled my hand away.

But it's not a lie, and you know that.

Damn that better part of me and its inclination to talk back.

I locked my confusion out and nodded once then turned on the spot to run up the stairs. Safely over the threshold of my room, I slammed the door shut and leaned against the cool wood. A sigh puffed through my half-parted lips. My gaze wandered heavenward. "God, let me get out of this house before I go insane and change my mind."

I rushed to the bathroom to shower off the sweat and dirt from today's work. Once clean and dressed in my ragged jeans and an old black tee, I sat at my desk to rewrite Marie's letter. The paper folded twice, I tucked the message into my notebook. Later, on my way out, I would leave the note on the kitchen table.

Light dimmed outside. So this was it, I was prepared to go. From my nightstand, I grabbed the alarm clock and set it for midnight. Strange, how such a simple task took me over three minutes. My throat tightened while I fumbled with the clock. I would also close the windows tonight, so the noise of the alarm wouldn't wake Julian.

Julian.

My focus blurred. I drew back to a part of my mind where I had saved his luscious scent. If only there was a chance to smell the warm wild wind on him again. Just once more, before I had to go.

My skin tickled at the memory of his touch. I stroked my fingers over my wrist, the spot where he'd wrapped his hand around me when he'd freed me from the cuffs outside Abe's office. An image of Julian's lopsided grin flickered before my eyes. The one that grew on me all too quickly.

I wished there was a way to say goodbye to him. A letter would never do.

Swiveling on the chair, I took in the beauty of my room one final time in the fading daylight. What a palace. And I was turning my back.

A dull thud, like someone had dropped a cutlet, snapped me out of my mulling. I walked to the open balcony door. The moment I pulled the curtains aside, a sparrow took off from the railing and gave me a start. It fluttered excitedly in circles then shot up to the roof and out of my view.

Crazy birds. The curtain slid from my hand, but upset chirruping drew my gaze to the boarded floor. My eyes grew wide, and my heart turned to pudding.

One step out on the balcony sat a young bird. Cocking its small head this way and that, it never let me out of focus. Its head was the only part moving, even when I squatted on the threshold.

"What are you doing on my balcony? Can't you fly?" Very slowly, I moved my hand forward, but the bird hopped back, its wings still folded at its sides.

"Don't touch it," my most favorite voice in the world said, and a spray of bliss washed over me.

Julian approached on a gentle step. "It must have fallen out of its nest. There is one right above your room. Underneath the eaves."

As he lowered to his knees, the bird retreated to the corner of the banister where it got trapped.

"Can you bring me a towel from your bathroom?" he asked.

"I don't think the bird needs to be rubbed dry. It needs a lift."

Julian's exhausted sigh came with an amused half-smile. "Off you go."

After a suspicious glance at him, I loped off to fetch the terrycloth he wanted. "So, what are you going to do with it?"

"I'm trying not to put my scent on the bird when I set it back in its nest. The mother bird won't accept her chick if she smells a human on it." He scooted forward and lowered his hands with the towel in them so the bird could clearly see his movements.

"Be careful," I whispered.

Julian moved so nimbly and gracefully, he would have been able to catch a wild horse out on the plains. All the while, I held my breath until he'd cupped the bird with the towel.

He turned and showed me the scared little fella in his hands. "Its heart is drumming like a machinegun."

I sighed, struggling against the impulse to stroke the tiny bird's fragile head. "What now?" My voice was barely louder than a whisper.

"Time for the little runaway to go home." Julian surprised me when he tilted his head up and bent his knees slightly. His stance suggested he was going to push from the ground and fly like superman.

Someone was definitely crazy out here, and it certainly wasn't me. I cocked a brow and bit my tongue, restraining from saying something stupid.

He straightened and avoided my stare, clearing his throat. "Well," he stammered with a sheepish expression. "Could you bring the stool from over there so I can climb to the nest?" He nodded his chin to his side of the balcony, where an old wooden stool sat in the corner.

Panic gripped me. I stepped from the threshold, back into my room, and clutched a hand to my chest. Shaking my head, I felt the color drain from my face.

"Oh, right." His gaze locked with mine, and he exhaled through his nose while his lips curled. He looked so cute when he searched for a solution. "Could you hold Tweety for a moment?"

I shifted my weight from one foot to the other. "I've never held a bird before." And yet I strangely wanted to.

"Don't worry. You can do it." He stepped into my room and handed over the small bundle.

Very carefully, I moved to take the bird from him. The tiny animal started rebelling and chirruped like I was after its life, and I shrank back. "Oh dear, I guess it wants back to you."

Julian laughed. "The bird wants back to its home. So we better hurry." At my reluctance to hold it, Julian shoved it toward me. "It's okay. Just don't squeeze."

His hands cupped mine, and he waited until the muscles in my clamped fingers relaxed. To be honest, it was hard to relax at all with him holding me so tenderly.

"Okay, you got it. And always remember, the bird fears you more." He winked.

I was afraid I'd crush the animal with the new rush of excitement swamping me.

While Julian slipped out to the balcony to retrieve the stool, joy filled my chest that he trusted me with the care of something as fragile as this bird. The sparrow's dark button eyes glinted. I felt the racing heartbeat Julian had mentioned. The powerful sense of a protector surged through me.

"Let's see if this works." Julian had placed the stool in front of my room and stepped on top. When he held out his hand, I placed the bird-package into his palm. My own hands trembled as I pulled them away from his.

He lifted the bundle over his head, growled low, and rolled his eyes. "Stools, my arse." In the next instant he stuck the chick in front of my face. "Take it again for a moment."

"What's the problem?" I said as I reached for the bird.

"The chair is too small, I can't reach the nest. And since I can't f—" He cut off and gave me a pointed look.

Don't even think about it.

Julian examined the square window right next to the door that led from my room to the balcony. "Do you think you can step onto the windowsill from inside your room?"

His encouraging gaze made me wonder if I actually could be brave enough, just for him.

"You don't have to lean out, just hold onto the window frame. When I reach down give me the bird."

"Reach down? From where?"

One swift move and Julian had hauled himself onto the railing. A breath caught in my throat, my spine stiffened with terror. "God, Julian, will you please get down?"

Not wavering an inch, he balanced along the narrow wood plank. "Don't worry. I won't fall."

I was too scared to lean outside and see what exactly he was about to do. Through the window, I glimpsed his feet lifting from the railing and figured that he'd pulled himself onto the roof somehow. Seconds later, footsteps sounded through the ceiling.

"Oh, this would all be so easy if..." he muttered on the roof.

"If what?" If he could fly? I snorted. *Well, buddy, if you could, I'd say you applied for the wrong job here in the vines.*

Julian's irritated grumbling surprised me. I knew he wasn't angry, but the slightly off tone was something that didn't fit him. It would rather come from someone moody—like me.

"Okay, hop onto the windowsill now." His order came from too far for me to feel comfortable.

I gathered every ounce of bravery stored within my shaking body and climbed over my bed onto the sill. My gaze focused on the task and the bird, but never outside. Not standing halfway steadily, I reached outside and lifted the bird.

"A little to the right," Julian said, and I obeyed, struggling to breathe. He laughed. "The other right, Jona!"

With a hot face, I steered my hand to the other side. The bird's tiny weight left my palm. Excited chirrups from more than one bird carried down to me and assuaged my tense nerves.

I dropped from the window ledge onto my mattress then stood and waited for Julian to climb down from the roof.

The white towel sailed to the floor. Next, his shoes and legs came into view, dangling outside my window for a second. Then he dropped to the balcony, and my heart skipped a beat. I took a jump backward into the room.

Julian landed softly like a cat. He straightened and rubbed his palms on his rear. "Job done."

"Jeez, you scared the hell out of me."

"Sorry about that. But you know," he took a step toward me into my room, "I'm majorly proud of you. Climbing up that ledge was very brave."

"You think?"

He nodded. For an awkward, long moment we stared at each other. When the silence became unbearable, I coughed. "So, what does it look like up there in the nest? Are there more young birds?"

"There are three. Why don't you come out and see yourself?"

An outraged laugh ripped from my throat. "Very funny."

"No, seriously. I think you should try to get over that fear." His face was stern, meaningful, but encouragement shone in his eyes. He grabbed my hand and tugged me. "Come on. Marie gave you the prettiest room in the house with this beautiful balcony, and you don't even appreciate it."

"I—that's not true." I wanted to defend myself, to protest—to his statement *and* to how his soft touch on my hand made me move. "I love the room."

Julian tugged a little harder. I stumbled one step forward, then another.

"Wait, I can't do this." My knees trembled when he tried to pull me out onto the porch engulfed by darkness.

"Of course you can. Just hold onto my hand and do as I say. I'm holding you."

I couldn't say what convinced me in the end, his gentle tone or his warm blue eyes. But before I could think straight again, my right foot shoved over the threshold and landed shakily on the dark painted boards. The wood felt warm against the bare sole of my foot, but it creaked eerily under my weight. *Please don't crack. Please don't crack.* My quavering left leg followed.

"Very good." Julian smiled. I drew encouragement from it. He tightened his hold of my hand then laced his fingers gently through mine. "Now turn around. No need to look over the railing right away."

"Huh?" My breathing went on high speed. I winced.

But he didn't give me time to think. With a soft shove, he directed me around until I faced the outside of my room.

"Oh my *God*, what are you doing?" I squeaked out in panic.

"I'll guide you. Trust me." Julian switched on the dim balcony light. Then he took my other hand, too, and pulled me away from the wall. "I won't let you fall." His voice held the seal of a promise.

With some reluctance, I made one step after another by his subtle pull. Hysteria blurred my vision. I closed my eyes and followed blind.

"Breathe, Jona."

Inhale. Exhale. Trembling breaths pushed out hard.

"You're doing great. We're almost there."

"There? Where? At the slide to hell?"

One more step, then Julian stopped and wrapped both his arms around my middle. He leaned against the railing, feet planted far apart for a better stance. He cradled my back against his chest. "You did it. Just look what a grand first step you made."

"Hopefully, it won't be my last." Reluctantly, I opened my eyes and faced the façade of the house tinted in soft porch light some seven feet away. My jaw dropped to my chest as amazement washed over me.

Oh *God*, all I wanted was to get back inside. But Julian's hold of me felt solid and secure. I knew he would keep his promise, and only for that reason I stood rooted.

"Now, eyes up there." With my hand wrapped in his, he lifted his arm and pointed one finger to the top of the roof.

I zoomed in on the small nest right under the eaves. Three tiny round heads popped over the edge, the mother bird towering watchfully over her spawn.

It was lovely. Not just the sight of the nest built under the eaves, but also how much care shone in the mother-bird's eyes when she hovered over her children.

"I always wished to have someone look at me that way," I whispered without thinking.

"Like the bird?" I felt Julian staring at me from the side. "You might not have noticed, but there is someone in this house who looks at you exactly like that."

I huffed and rolled my eyes. "Yeah, the dragon, right."

"I'm not speaking of your mother."

My brows knitted together, and I tilted my head to glance at him from only a few inches distance. "Who then?"

"It's Marie who tries to pull you into her embrace." Julian's thumb drew small circles on the back of my hand, sending little shivers up my arm. "She's pleading for permission, don't you see?"

"Permission to what?"

"To love you."

The truth tugged at my heart. Aunt Marie did everything possible to make me feel at home and welcome. But with so much hatred for my mother, I couldn't let anyone else's love intrude on me.

Hypocrite. There I stood, dreaming of someone who'd replace my loneliness, and yet I was about to break the heart of the only person who'd tried to make this dream come true. But I couldn't allow my aunt to break through my shield. Not when those who I opened up to tended to leave me in the end anyway.

"She offered to spend the day with me alone tomorrow." The reason I told him this eluded me, but suddenly Julian seemed like someone I could be honest with. Someone like Quinn. "And she gave me so many beautiful clothes."

"Sadly, you didn't put them on tonight." He tugged at the hem of my t-shirt to mock me. "But she knows how to welcome someone, doesn't she?"

"She does indeed." A low chuckle ripped through me. "Very much the opposite of you."

Out of the corner of my eye I caught him arch a brow. "What's that supposed to mean?"

By his voice I could tell he was smiling.

"Well, you weren't the most charming person in the world when we first met. With all the bantering and such, no wonder you don't have a girlfriend."

"Who says I don't have a girlfriend?"

"Well...you. I mean, you said you weren't my mother's lover. And I don't see any other girls around." I bit my lip. *Shit.* There was probably another woman waiting for him somewhere. Someone nice and young, not god-awful like the dragon. Suddenly an invisible boa slithered around my chest and did what it was supposed to do best. It constricted.

When I spoke next, I sounded anything but confident. "So...do you?"

"No." He dragged out the word and laughed softly.

No girlfriend! The snake evaporated and was replaced with a bunch of excited butterflies. I wanted to squash them with my fist. This really shouldn't have made me so happy. The pounding of my heart annoyed me something awful. Especially since he must have noticed it with my ribcage pressed so snugly against his warm chest.

Out of an insecure habit, I resorted to my snappy tone. "See, that might be different if you were a little nicer to girls to begin with."

"It might," he whispered. And then his lips brushed my ear as he spoke. "And yet, here I stand, holding you in my arms after only three days."

I sucked in a sharp breath and lowered my gaze to my bare feet. I shouldn't have been here, in this house. In his arms. And most of all, I shouldn't have enjoyed it as much as I did. Ready to rip out of his embrace, my spine stiffened as did every muscle in my body.

Julian's arms wrapped a little tighter around me. "Shh," he breathed. "You'll just scare the birds."

Midnight Talk

If someone had told me that one day I'd be sitting on a balcony fifteen feet above the ground and actually enjoying it, I'd have flipped him off. And yet, here I sat. The warmth of the wall seeped into my back while I watched the stars in the velvety night sky.

"Your knees stopped trembling. You aren't getting comfortable after all?" Julian glanced at me from the railing where he casually perched. For the past five minutes, he hadn't taken his eyes off my shaking body which he probably assumed was related to vertigo.

I hugged my knees tighter to my chest and nodded. "Strangely enough, it seems so." I wouldn't tell him that the rattle of my bones had actually set in with his tender hold and soft words and finally ceased when he'd guided me to the wall and released me. He didn't have to know everything.

"So, what's your plan for tomorrow? Will you and Marie paint each other's nails pink, lounge on the patio with your swim suits on, and sip from cocktails with fancy little umbrellas?" Blowing at his imaginarily polished nails like a real diva, he made me laugh.

"You'd like to see that, wouldn't you?"

The look he gave me from under his lashes would fit a hungry wolf. "I would so love to."

Sparkling electricity ran through me, raising gooseflesh along my arms.

"You cold?" He made the wrong connection again.

"Nothing ever escapes you, does it?"

Julian jumped off the banister and shrugged out of his gray hoodie. My eyes widened, and I tilted my head to keep him in focus when he stepped closer. He squatted, and I leaned forward so he could swing the sweatshirt around my shoulders, even though I wanted to protest.

"You don't need to do this. I can fetch my own from inside," I told him. "Keep it."

Without his hoodie, he sat back on the banister. "Nah, I'm not cold."

Neither was I.

But the smell that enveloped me the moment he placed the warm fabric on my shoulders kept me tongue-tied. It was like someone had popped open a can and a double dose of Julian's wild wind scent escaped. I breathed deep and shoved my arms through the too long sleeves.

With my arms folded on my knees, I buried my cheek in the cozy material and peered at him from the corner of my eye. Should I tell him that he was never going to get this sweatshirt back? The crook of my elbow hid my grin. But the dimple appearing in his left cheek and his slight frown had me wondering if he read my thoughts anyway.

He lifted one foot up to the railing and leaned his chin on his knee. Hand laced around his ankle, he held the leg in place. "It's the end of day three of your detention. How many more to go? Thirty-five?"

"Thirty-eight."

"Right." He chuckled, but I couldn't see how that was so funny. "What's your first impression of your new home?"

"It's not my home," I said in a voice gone cold, matter of fact. "But everyone is quite nice, and I like the house and the vineyard, if that's what you mean. Working is actually *okay*." I studied the stars for a moment. "This would be a good place to live if Charlene wasn't here."

"How so, Jona?" His intense tone pulled me back from the sky. He slid his leg down and leaned forward, resting his elbows on his thighs. The porch light played softly in his blond hair. "What exactly would be different if your mother wasn't in this house? I mean apart from you talking a lot more during meal times."

At his grin, I frowned. How dare he probe and poke his nose where it didn't belong? "Everything."

He cocked a brow. "Name *one*."

"Just one?" *I could allow myself to enjoy this place.* The sound of grinding teeth filled my ears, and my eyes narrowed. I hated being outsmarted.

"The stench of dragon wouldn't follow me everywhere I went." I grinned bitterly. "Come to think of it, do you believe Charlene would disown me if the smell of another human was on me?" To provoke him, I rubbed the sleeve of his sweatshirt on my cheek.

No answer came from Julian. Instead he eased off the railing and lowered to the floor opposite me. Burning blue eyes studied me for a long moment. "Do you always use sarcasm for protection?"

Yes.

It protected me from the world. From people who tried to get too close. If I hurt them first, they couldn't hurt me. Especially, when they planned to disappear from my life. "Why do you say that?"

"I haven't heard anything out of your mouth about your mother that wasn't dripping with sarcasm."

I shrugged. "Yeah, so what?"

"Just saying."

It bothers you like hell. "Well, I've got news for you, mister. That's just who I am, and if she'd cared at all the past twelve years she would have known me, and then she might not have forced me to come here after all."

"If that's really who you are, then why haven't I heard your lippy tone toward Marie?"

Lowering my gaze, my head sank back onto my bent arm and my voice dropped to little more than a whisper. "Marie is different. I find it hard to be myself around her." Only thinking of her calmed the emotional storm brewing inside me.

"Or, maybe it's just too *easy* to be yourself around her?"

I blinked twice then raked a glare over Julian. Was he accusing me of a soft personality? I was anything but.

The years in the orphanage and partly in the streets had taught me a hard lesson: be soft and you go down like a ship under cannon fire. Only the toughest kids kept their heads on in a place like the Lorna Monroe Children's Home, where teachers tried to get under your skirt, and bullies aimed to make you the poster child for losers.

"You don't understand," I muttered. "I don't even blame you. From your place in the world, everything must seem easy. Living in a palace with nice people around, and a good job in the vines, there's nothing to worry about. But things look a little different from the gutters of society."

Julian's lips curled as he scooted across the floor toward me. I watched his every move. His long legs sprawled out before him. When his left arm brushed my right, the nearness of him struck me once again. Excitement rose from my stomach to my chest and set my heart fluttering. Arms crossed over his chest, he tilted his head to regard the stars.

"What are you up to?" I murmured.

"Just trying to see the world from your point of view. If that's okay with you."

"Oh. Feel free."

He cast me a sideways glance, and the strangest thing happened. The expression in his face remained one of intrigue and friendliness, but his eyes seemed to live through a multitude of emotions in this extended moment.

What the hell did he see? For a second, I had the feeling he really had glimpsed the world through my eyes.

Scads of icicles stabbed a line from my neck to the bottom of my spine. My toes curled on the warm wood. The urge to crawl away from him—to safety—was overwhelming. But an even more powerful impulse kept me rooted. Like two opposite poles of a magnet, I was drawn toward this man with every cell of my body, with every breath of my soul. At this moment, I wouldn't have budged if someone had shocked me with a cattle prod.

Happiness invaded me and kept me paralyzed. If I'd been able to move at all, then it would have only been in one direction. Toward him. An invisible aura radiated around Julian that made me want to sling my arms around him and press my body against his as tight as a mountain climber would hold on to life.

"Knock it off!" Or else I was going to lick that peaceful aura off his very skin.

The sensation stopped. As fast as it had begun.

A final quiver started at the back of my neck and slithered down until it uncurled my toes. Julian crossed his legs, relaxed his hands at his sides, and gazed at the night sky. Everything returned to normal.

Apart from me. I sat rigid, but inwardly I panicked. *Bloody hell, what was that?* Had I gone mental? *Please not now.* Not so shortly before my escape into freedom.

Calm down, Jona. You're tired, that's all.

Shaking my head, I tried to get rid of the hysteria inside me. I clenched my hands to fists and buried them in my lap. An exhausted sigh lifted my chest. Calm enough to speak, I turned to him. "So, what does life look like from the gutter?"

Julian turned his head and studied me for a couple of seconds. "Can I ask you something very personal?"

Ugh. After what had just happened? I wasn't sure.

I shrugged one shoulder.

"If your mother was already dead, and Marie had offered to bring you to her home, would you have come?"

Of course was the answer I should have shot at him that very instant. But for a very strange reason I couldn't lie to him. Didn't want to. After a few seconds of deliberating, I slowly said, "No."

Julian nodded. "I thought so."

Swallowing hard, I tucked my hair behind my ears, let my

hands rest behind my neck, and dropped my head. One particular reason would have kept me from coming. I didn't want to get attached to anyone again in my life. *Ever.*

That was why I'd had no boyfriend yet. Why I'd had no real friends in the orphanage. And why I refused to let Marie get any closer than she had already managed in the past couple days. I had to protect myself from being abandoned, which was going to happen in the end.

To get my attention again, Julian tugged softly at one leg of my jeans. "It doesn't mean everyone will leave you just because your mother did."

My head snapped up with the feeling of being read like an open book once again. "Yes, it does. If my own mother could do that to me, what stops a total stranger from doing the same?"

My furious tone didn't affect his soft one. "You know, sometimes people are sorry for what they did and try to make up for it."

A warning light went off in my head. This conversation was going downhill and fast. Anger boiled and threatened to spill out. "And *you* know, sometimes they just make the same damn mistake twice."

A sad expression settled in Julian's face. Yep, he knew what I was talking about.

My voice took on a sickly sweet note. "I believe my mother told you that she came to the orphanage once before, when I was already twelve years old." I rolled my eyes. "Uttered incessant apologies. She promised to get me out of that hole in a few days when she'd arranged her new life." I paused, took a furious breath. "How stupid of me to finally believe her. The pain only cut deeper when she didn't show up a few days later as she'd promised. In fact, she didn't show up for another five years."

Until three days ago.

I feigned a smile. "She wouldn't have kept that part of her past a secret from you when you're *so* close, would she?"

"Maybe she had reasons not to come."

Oh yes, he knew.

I folded my arms over my chest. "What kind of reasons could that be? And why had she forgotten to inform me?"

"I don't know. Why don't you ask her?" A hint of innocence laced his voice, just enough to make me understand that he knew very well but wouldn't betray my mother and give the reasons away before she had a chance to explain.

A laugh escaped me at his ridiculous words. "Yeah, right. As if I really wanted to know. She can tell her lies to the reaper when he comes for her at the end of her goddamned life."

Julian's lips thinned to a line, and I went silent. He always seemed so hurt when I slagged my mother. I didn't want to hurt him. Not now. Not tonight.

A few minutes later, I cleared my throat and tried to steer the conversation in a different direction. "How long have you known Charlene?"

"A while."

"Oh, that says a lot." Behind closed lids, I rolled my eyes. "Was she already ill when you met her?"

Julian nodded. Of course, why would he know her before he started taking care of her?

A sudden curiosity kept me firing questions at him. "Does she pay you for your services?"

"I'm paid for the work I do for Albert in the vineyard."

"You didn't answer my question."

When Julian inclined his head to lock gazes with me, I could see that he chose his words very carefully. "I don't get any money from your mother. But she's paying a price to someone else. It's a high price, too."

"And that agency or whoever she's paying sent you to take care of her?"

His soft chuckle warmed the atmosphere around us. "Sort of."

Suddenly, Valentine's angry hiss cut through the night. She was underneath the balcony and cussed in French. Julian didn't bother to stifle a hearty laugh. He switched to the language that was all Greek to me when he replied to her.

When we heard her disappear down the path, I asked Julian, "What did she say?"

"She cursed the birds for pooping on her slippers and threatened to shoot them all with Henri's old shotgun."

The image of the teapot going berserk over a handful of birdies brought a grin to my face. "And what did you tell her?"

"To be careful not to shred the façade. The old, twisted gun backfires more often than it hits a target."

The laugh we share freed me like nothing before. When he didn't pester me about my mother, I actually really liked this man.

During the following half hour, Julian told me everything he knew about Valentine and Henri, how old they were, about their three grown up children who occasionally visited here, and what their main work in the vines was. But it was more the soothing sound of his voice that kept me intrigued than the actual information he gave me.

I studied his beautiful blue eyes as he spoke. The sight of his tongue whisking over his lips from time to time to wet them sent a shiver through my body. And I noticed how he would rub the back of his neck and stare into the distance when he tried to remember something in particular.

A yawn stretched my mouth. I tried to smother it in the crook of my arm.

Gentle fingers hooked strands of hair behind my ear. "Your day has been long enough. You better go to sleep now. I can tell you more about the people here tomorrow if you like."

"No," I said quickly. "Please, tell me now."

The shine in Julian's eyes seemed to intensify for a moment, then he continued.

Nothing could have stopped me from listening to him. Not even sleep as it crept over me. I still heard his mellow voice long after my eyes had closed, and my head rested heavily on my knees.

Half asleep, I barely noticed the strong arms that shoved under my bent legs and spine. As I was lifted from the floor, my head rolled to the side to rest on a comforting shoulder. My nose brushed against the warm skin of Julian's throat, and I buried deeper into the crook, savoring his enchanting scent of fresh wind wafting along a shore.

My hand wandered up his chest and cupped his neck for better hold. The cropped hair at the back of his head tickled my palm. If sleep hadn't captured me already, I would have started to explore the sensation and tangled my fingers in his soft tousled hair.

Holding on to him tight, I made him bend down with me when he lowered me onto my bed. His breath feathered against my face. I opened my eyes briefly. A smile that came mostly from his eyes bid me goodnight.

Please stay.

My knees dipped to one side as he let go of my legs. Gently, he removed my hands from his neck and placed them over my stomach.

"Sleep tight, princess," he whispered, brushing a wisp of hair from my forehead.

I blinked in slow motion, my cheek buried deeper into the soft pillow. Through a haze of sleep, I watched him turn away. His fingers swept over the clock on my nightstand. The hands on the clock spun madly.

"See you tomorrow," he crooned before he slipped out through the curtains.

Prolonging the stay

I stood next to Julian on the balcony, the little chick with the button eyes comfortably nestled on his palms.

Julian flashed a toothpaste commercial grin at me. "Are you ready?"

I nodded and he crouched. With his next stretch, he pushed off the ground, levitating toward the roof. All the while, I saluted and sang "God save the Queen," but the chirrups of the birds overhead overlapped my blaring. When I got to the part "long may she reign," I jolted upright in my bed, wide awake.

The sound of my gasp echoed through the otherwise silent room. I pressed a sweaty palm to my brow, trying to get a clear view.

"Crap, what a weird dream."

Bright daylight floated in through the windows. I snapped my head right and left, trying to figure out why I woke in this room again and not on an airplane to London.

Then memories of a glorious time on the balcony popped into my mind. Warmth filled me as I recalled being enclosed in Julian's arms. His scent still wafted all around me. A deep breath filled my head with a stunning sea breeze. Only when I wrapped my arms around me and my hands dug into soft cotton, did I realize the scent was coming from his hoodie that still shrouded me. I hadn't returned it to him last night.

And I never will.

But how had I gotten into bed? And why hadn't I taken off my jeans? The last thing I remembered clearly was his melodious laughter as he had told me of Valentine's landing on her broad behind while she tried to uproot an ill plant the other day.

I raked a hand through my bed hair and brushed the bangs off my face. My fingers skimmed over my right temple—*saluting?* There had been something…in my dream.

Then I whined. *Levitating.* Julian had become airborne.

And you hailed the Queen, silly. Weird things happen in dreams. Get a grip.

My eyes narrowed at the balcony door. The dream seemed so real. Julian had crouched before he took off, just like yesterday evening when he wanted to set the bird back in its nest. He prepared to—

To what? To fly?

Be serious. He wasn't a mutant, Superman, or anything like that. He was Julian, the ordinary guy next door. Lovely, but ordinary.

A sigh of frustration pushed through my nose as I dropped onto my pillow. A second later, the siren of an alarm clock blared next to me and gave me a jump-start out of bed. I beat the device with my flat hand. Three times, to make sure the blaring really stopped. With one hand clutched to my pounding heart, I sank into the swivel chair at my desk and let my head tilt over the backrest.

Boy, things were turning out really weird this morning. If I could judge the kind of day I was going to have by its beginning, I might do better to climb back into bed.

I snatched the clock from my nightstand to check why it had gone off in the morning when I had set it for—

"Midnight?"

My stomach dropped, my mouth sagged open. Both clock hands were aimed up.

A picture of Cogsworth, the living pendulum clock from *Beauty and the Beast*, sitting on my nightstand danced through my mind, the hands on his Disney face spinning madly. According to this overgrown pocket watch, it was twelve exactly.

I couldn't make any sense of it.

A frown pulled my brows together and I cut a glance to the French door, as if the answer to my confusion lay just outside. But what was there to see, other than the familiar scenery of a few trees in the garden and five hectares of vine?

Julian.

At the moment, a lot of things didn't make sense, but most of all him. Every time he came within an arm's reach, jittery feelings swamped me. And this went far beyond the average crazy. There was something very *not normal* about the guy.

Since I'd already missed my flight home—again—I thought maybe I should delay the escape for a little longer and instead do some detective work. Considering the nice time I'd had with him the previous night, I supposed I could survive a few more days in this place. Maybe a week even. Of course, it would be my first priority to stay out of the dragon's reach. But finding out more about Julian tempted me sorely. My stomach went all bloomy at the thought of spending a few more days around him.

From a drawer, I picked out a pencil and paper and started scribbling a list. After all, this was the first step Sherlock Holmes would take to resolve a case—take notes of anything unusual. It took only a couple of minutes to jot down everything weird about Julian.

There was the surreal happiness he infected me with every time he touched me. I stared at the wall in front of me for a moment. Was feeling happy so bad? *No, no. Stay focused.* I blinked and returned my attention to the list.

Next point was the revitalization of my mother when no one was watching—or when he *thought* no one was. The awkward incident last night, when he tried to see the world through my eyes and I almost turned into an aura-sucking vampire. And of course, his strange behavior when he put the chick back in its nest—the crouch before takeoff. Was there anything else?

Flying.

No, the dream was too weird to mention. Maybe the alarm clock? I pursed my lips. I could hardly blame it on him that the alarm went off at the wrong time. Grabbing the clock, I examined it from all sides. For the past five minutes, it had worked accurately; the minute hand was pointing at one.

Tapping the pencil against my pursed lips, I spun in the chair and thought of what else I could jot down about Julian. But a knock on the door made me jump right out of my seat. Rushed by panic, I shoved the list into the drawer and slammed it shut.

"Come on in!" My voice resonated with the awkward feeling of being caught.

Marie's friendly eyes peeked into my room. "Oh good, you are up. I was concerned when you did not come down for breakfast this morning."

"Yeah, sorry, I slept in. The alarm went a little crazy." I shrugged and held the clock out to her. "It didn't wake me at the right time." Which should have been hours ago.

"Do not worry. It is Saturday, you are allowed to sleep in. Are we still on for a girls' day out?"

Now that I had decided to stay for a little longer, the idea of spending a few hours with Marie alone appealed to me. It would be nice to get to know this friendly woman with her ever beaming face. Also it came to me that she had known Julian for a much longer time than I had, and she might come in handy on my expedition to discover his secret. The longer I thought about it, the more I believed he had one. So why not mix business with pleasure? Marie could at least answer some questions for me.

Step two of resolving a case: *investigate*.

A broad grin crept to my lips. "Sure. What did you have in mind?"

Marie stepped over the threshold, but didn't let go of the door handle. "Would you like to go to town? I have to stock the fridge for next week and I could use some help. Afterward we could go shopping for you, have lunch together, or get ice cream."

Shopping for me? *Lady, I've got no money. And you don't want to be seen with a criminal.* But ice cream sounded fabulous. We had never gotten any in the orphanage, and to run off with a cone in one hand had actually been a very bad idea. After I'd lost the entire load on a spectacular escape through Hyde Park a couple of years ago, I'd refrained from repeating that silly act just for one sweet lick.

"I'll get dressed and meet you downstairs in a minute."

The corners of her mouth tugged up. "But you are dressed, *chérie*."

"Oh, right."

Marie chuckled and left.

Swirling back to my desk, I shrugged out of Julian's hoodie and took a final deep breath of its scent. Mmm, this sea breeze cologne was the stuff that dreams were made of.

Downstairs, the remnants of a small breakfast Marie had served were visible, and she urged me to sit down at the neatly decked table with violets in a small pot in the middle. I'd barely swallowed the first draught of coffee, when Albert walked in and joined me at the table with a quirky look upon his face.

My gulp echoed through the room. Should I ask him why he was staring at me, or just pretend not to notice? From the plate in front of me, I stole a croissant and tore off a small piece, while my eyes remained on my uncle's face. Slowly, I shoved the bite into my mouth.

Albert nudged the glass of strawberry jam toward me then laced his fingers on the table. "How did you like your first two days in the vineyard?"

"It's okay, I guess. It's just work." I shrugged and dipped the knife into the jam, then smeared it on my pastry. "I really liked the dirt scanner," I said in between bites, and a grin slipped to my lips.

Albert unbuttoned the cuffs of his white shirt and rolled up the sleeves. "*Oui*, that is my favorite, too." His voice had dropped a notch and he mirrored my grin, which gave me a strange feeling of connection to this man.

With another sip from the hot drink, I washed the croissant

down. "Is there no one tending to the shrubs today?"

"Saturdays and Sundays we normally run shorter shifts. Today Valentine and Henri are working outside. Everyone else can take the day off. Although, I might take a look later and make sure everything is okay." He cast a sideways grin at my aunt, who snorted in response.

"Of course you will be out there later. When has there ever been a day in the past ten years that you have not?" Marie's loving tone didn't match her accusing words.

Albert pulled her to his side and planted a kiss on her palm. "But you knew that well when you married me." He chuckled. Then he turned his gaze back to me. "I watched you work, Jona."

"So?" If he intended to tell me off for not giving my best in the vines, I would have to enlighten him that this was, after all, slave labor and he should be happy I helped at all.

"It seems you had a good time out there," Marie teased as she eased into the corner seat next to me.

Taken by surprise, I arched a brow, but didn't find the right words to contradict her. Maybe because she was right.

"And you really were a great help," Albert continued. "You may not be too happy about the way you came to France." He curled his lip and scratched his head, appearing slightly uncomfortable. "But it seems like you are going to stay with us for a while."

A very short while. I licked a drop of jam from my middle finger, then leaned back and crossed my arms over my chest. My eyes darted from one to the other. What next?

"Your aunt and I do not want to force you into anything, but we could do with another pair of hands on the vineyard, especially in this busy season. So we wanted to ask you if you would like to do this as a real job. Just for as long as you will be our guest."

I liked how my uncle put it. Unlike everyone else, he understood this was only temporary quarters and not *my new home*.

"We will, of course, pay you for the work." Marie gave a reassuring nod which, together with her words, made my jaw drop to my chest. "How does two hundred euro a week sound to you?"

For about thirty seconds I said absolutely nothing but struggled to come back to my senses. "Did you just say two hundred? *Euro?*"

The dragon must have forgotten to mention I was bound by law to be their slave until my birthday. Old Abe definitely hadn't said anything about payment when we last met.

Albert nodded, pulled his wallet from the back pocket of his trousers and slipped out a one-hundred euro note. He placed it on the table then shoved it toward me, just like the jam before. "This is your salary for the past two days."

Or, as I liked to call it, my ticket back to England.

The little red devil on my left shoulder rubbed his hands while his horned head bobbed with conspiratorial snickers. If Albert meant what he'd said, and I could endure another week in this house, I might be able to walk off with three of those pretty green bills in my pocket.

To make sure none of them would go back on their offer, I gave both a daring glance before my hand slowly crept forward to snatch the money.

"You agree?" My uncle's mien did a good imitation of his wife's beam.

I nodded slowly, still unable to utter a single word.

"Great. Now, I wish you two a nice day." His gaze switched between me and my aunt. "I will be out in the vineyard and see if Henri needs a hand with the scans." He winked at me then turned to silence Marie with a kiss before she could tell him off in her sweet manner.

As he disappeared through the door, Aunt Marie sighed and planted her chin on her palm. "He is incorrigible." The devoted spark in her eyes had me wondering if she already missed him.

"If you are finished, can I get you to clear the table while I shove a load into the washer?"

"Sure." When she was gone, I hummed my little melody as I stored the butter and jam into the giant fridge then cleaned my plate. Water soaked into my shirt and, after rubbing the front dry, I bounced into Julian on the way out of the kitchen.

If he hadn't wrapped his arm around my middle so fast to prevent me from falling, I might have taken a vase from the waist-high credenza down with me. Marie certainly wouldn't have liked that, so I was happy to find myself in Julian's hug instead.

But this was definitely not the only reason.

"Whoa, sorry," he said, although his tightening grip revealed he was anything but. Also a smirk undermined his credibility a little too much.

I liked it when only one corner of his lips came up and he quirked his brows. All that was missing was the growl of a tiger that had claimed his victim.

For a fraction of a second, a very scary thought crossed my mind. What would happen if I took his face between my hands and pulled his head down for a kiss?

Are you nuts? You don't do kisses.

Right. A kiss meant giving up protection and showing affections. And this was something I could never let happen. When my stance was steady again, I shoved against Julian's chest, wrenched out of his embrace, and silenced the part of me that pleaded to stay in his arms just a little longer. "Get off. You're crushing me."

He tucked his hands into the pockets of his black pants and gave me a suggestive glance. "Sorry. I guess there's no immediate danger on the ground floor."

"None that would break my neck if I fell."

Ignoring my snappy tone, he leaned around the doorframe to survey the kitchen. "Is your aunt around?"

"Doing the laundry."

"I am here, Julian!" Marie climbed the stairs from the cellar and approached us, a basket full of freshly laundered clothes braced on her right hip while her hand clasped the brim. "What do you need, dear?"

"Can I borrow your car? I need to get something from town."

Marie's gaze darted to my eyes and back to him. Then her lips pursed. "Actually, Jona and I are going to town. You could come with us."

Julian frowned, luckily not at me but at my aunt. "I thought you two were going to have a ladies' day. I don't want to disturb."

Fingers laced behind my back, my mouth curved. "You're not disturbing." Oh my god, had I really just invited him? And with that silly sweet voice? Pivoting to Marie, I gave her an expectant look. "Right?"

Can someone slap me? Hard, please.

"Not at all."

Julian's eyes traveled to my side before his head inclined. "Okay," he agreed slowly. "I'll just check on your mother and then meet you two outside."

When he walked past me his eyes still fixed mine with a stare as though he doubted my good will and expected me to start laughing any second at his silliness to fall for my joke.

A sweet grin was all I granted him. "Hurry up."

"That was very nice of you, *chérie*," my aunt approved after Julian had disappeared in the dragon's hole.

Shrugging it off with one shoulder, I turned on my heel and sauntered outside. My grin spread wider and wider. Inwardly, I jubilated at the thought that Julian would be around us all day with no chance to run back to Charlene every half an hour. Oh, today was shaping up to be one fine day indeed.

The French menu

The backseat of Marie's SUV provided a good view at Julian, who'd climbed into the passenger seat. As far as the seatbelt allowed, I lounged in the corner with my legs pulled up and scanned every inch of his handsome face while the tires rolled over the unpaved country road. His straight nose perfected the harmony between his high cheekbones and intelligent eyes.

The corners of his lips twitched slightly when he cast me a knowing glance halfway over his shoulder. I probably turned red as a stop sign, but that didn't stop me from studying him. If at all, my gaze dropped for merely a second. The seawater blue of his shirt accentuated his midnight eyes. He blinked twice before he faced front again.

Outside, the beautiful French landscape rushed by on our ten-minute drive to town.

"I believe it best we start off with a little shopping," my aunt said while she steered the car onto the main road. "Afterward we can eat lunch together."

"Fine with me," Julian exclaimed, and I agreed with a low *um-hm* from the back.

After we passed the *Fontvieille* sign, Marie turned into a one-way street lined with colorful two story houses blending in perfectly with the mountains in the distance. In the city's public parking lot, she maneuvered the car between a green van and a convertible and cut the engine. As soon as we climbed out, the busy murmur of Saturday morning shoppers drifted to us and curiosity built high within me.

We rounded a corner, and then I halted mid-step, holding my breath. A whiff of home surrounded me, bringing with it memories of Friday raids in old Blighty.

"It looks like Oxford Street," I cheered, and spun on the spot to take in the neat marketplace, lined with fancy boutiques and shops.

Nudging my ribs with his elbow, Julian chuckled. "Just a wee bit smaller, I suppose."

"Much smaller." But it didn't matter. The sunny place was a good enough imitation.

We came past a stand where the reflection of the sun in silver caught my eye. A manifold of watches and filigree bracelets covered the velvety countertop, pendants in various shapes and all colors of the rainbow.

Seeing the fine jewelry, a tingle started in my fingers. Oh yeah, the *Dodger* was back. But my promise to Quinn virtually tied my hands. I shoved them deep into my pockets and swallowed hard at the temptation as I forced myself to walk on with the others.

Nevertheless, this crowded market presented another alluring opportunity. It'd be too easy to fall behind and take a wrong turn, then shake Marie and Julian off. Yesterday, I might have even considered a move like this to escape my punishment called *family*. But this morning, I'd come to a decision, and for now, I'd stick with it.

Julian startled me when he inched closer and said so low that only I could hear, "I didn't expect that a place like this would make you so happy. Should we keep a watch on you in case you get lost in the crowd?"

Had he gotten another sneak peek into my mind? I criticized him with a scowl. "If that is what's on your mind you should have brought Quinn's handcuffs."

Julian snaked his arm around my shoulders and pulled me close. "Maybe I did."

My focus zoomed in on the stainless steel loop he half-tugged out of the pocket of his pants; it glinted viciously in the sun.

Stunned, I pushed away from him. "Jeez, Julian! Who are you? Abe's twin brother? You're not going to use them on me."

His chest shook with another laugh. He shoved the cuffs back into his pocket. "Don't worry, I don't intend to." Hands raised in surrender, he moved closer with a smirk. "As long as you're staying near."

You keep your amazing smile on and I'll do whatever you say.

The little girl within me sighed in hopeless devotion to her Prince Charming. On the surface, I built a wall of protection with the only thing I knew always worked a hundred percent. "Okay, *Dad*. Do you want to hold my hand, too?"

His lips curled, and I could barely hold back an outraged laugh about him really contemplating this option.

"You can't be serious," I snarled before he could even insist on me taking his hand.

Julian raised a suggestive brow.

"I'm not going anywhere, okay?" My laugh softened, since this definitely was one of the most bizarre conversations I'd ever had. With a person anyway. Talking to the pigeons in the park didn't count.

We followed Marie, who'd walked a few steps down the street and peered through the window of a clothing shop. Julian nudged me again and offered me his bent elbow.

"Is this your insurance for me not to *fall behind?* An alternative to the shackles in your pocket?" In spite of my teasing tone, I wanted nothing more than to hold onto him and let him guide me through the maze of shoppers loaded with bags.

Julian blinked slowly. His arm didn't budge. "Come on, I won't wait forever."

"Oh, you're so pushy." I rolled my eyes at him, but then I happily looped my arm through his. My fingers curled around his firm biceps that flexed lightly when he tucked his hand into his pocket. With a firm squeeze of his arm against his body, he ensured my hand wouldn't slip away.

A few feet in front of us, Marie halted and took a step back to peek into another shop window. "Oh, this is just lovely," she cooed over a caramel colored blouse. Straightening, she pivoted to us and at the same instant caught our joined arms. Her mouth dropped open, her expression turned to an unambiguous *Oh.*

"It's not what you think," I whined. "He's just worried I might...get lost in the crowd."

"Oh." Now the word came from her mouth, but before she turned to walk on, she cut us both a joyful glance. She definitely approved of us being linked.

Oh glee.

Marie led us to another shop, and this time she intended to go inside instead of just gaze through the windows.

Julian stopped in front of the sliding glass door as we entered. "I'm sure you ladies don't need me for this. I'll head back to Paul's piano shop and see if he's got anything new. Back in ten." Then his eyes switched to me. "Have fun." The door shut when he stepped away and headed back in the direction we'd come from.

Marie's hand on my shoulder broke my staring after him. A warm shine lingered in her eyes. "The music store is only one block away. He will be back soon enough."

Yeah, right. And what do I care? I harrumphed and strode after her when she walked off with a chuckle.

Marie demonstrated then what a French woman in shopping mood was capable of. Within minutes, she'd rushed through the spacious store with dapperly dressed mannequins lounging at each end. It was hard to spot her face behind piled up shirts, dresses, and pants on her arm.

With her free hand, she tugged on my sleeve and dragged me toward one of the many changing cubicles lining the back of the shop. "Come, *chérie*. Let us try them on."

Shock slammed into me at her words, and I stopped in my tracks. With my abrupt halt, Marie whirled around because she still clasped my shirt. She struggled not to drop the entire load on the marble floor.

"What is wrong? I am sure I got your size right, and they are really lovely clothes." She held the rainbow colored pile out to me.

"Ma'am, I don't do lovely." And most of all, I didn't intend to spend a single cent of my traveling money in this shop. "Really, I don't want any new things. What you gave me the other day will do for a decade."

"Nonsense. You can never have too many clothes." She waved a hand, but then doubt rushed across her face. Her shiny green eyes narrowed. "Or are you worried about the money? Of course, you do not have to pay for any of these. Albert and I will cover the costs of everything you need."

This woman's and her husband's generosity went far beyond the levels of normal. An awkward fist clamped my stomach. "Why, thank you," I stammered, shifting my weight to one foot. "But you shouldn't. I really don't need anything."

Aunt Marie pouted. "All right then. But if you find something you would like to have, do not be shy to ask for it."

Knowing that would never happen, I nodded just to be free of her insisting.

While she vanished into the cubicle, I roamed the shop looking at things I'd never own. In front of a tall, slender mannequin that was modeled after an African woman, I halted and gaped at her short, bright red summer dress.

The halter neck top provided a stunning view of the upper bow of her breasts, and the waist of the dress was set high. The mannequin's bare legs were silhouetted against the three thin layers of laced fabric and her feet were clad in breakneck high heels. Though the design and style of the dress were simple, I'd barely seen a more beautiful thing in my life.

"You would look amazing in that dress."

I shot around to find Julian sprawled in a square leather chair across the way.

He was back. And I'd missed him in this—what? Eleven minutes?

Head on the low backrest, he'd laced his fingers on top of his stomach and eyed me through relaxed slits. His lips twitched.

I laughed low. "You're crazy. Me in this dress? Never."

"What's wrong with it?" He straightened, leaned forward, with his elbows on his thighs.

Stepping aside to grant him a better view of the dress, I motioned up and down the mannequin on the square pedestal. "It's bright red."

"So?" Smooth like a cat, Julian rose from the chair, and with his hands shoved into his pockets, he joined me by the dummy. "A little color would suit you. Why are you wearing black all the time? You aren't going to a funeral."

I shrugged. "Maybe I am." *Sooner or later.* "Actually, I like to stay invisible. Blend in."

"Which comes in handy when you're on the run from the police or a mad shop owner, I suppose." A tick in his jaw and a dimple—he was suppressing a grin.

Great. Anger ate at my insides that escapades of my old reality seemed to amuse the man I felt so strangely attracted to.

"Why miss out on all the action?" I crossed my arms over my chest. "The adrenalin rush from a close escape would bring some excitement even to your straight life."

"Diva," he drawled. "Do you bite, too?" Julian clicked his teeth twice, spun on his heel, and walked away, chuckling.

I flipped him the bird, but he didn't see it.

My attention returned to the dress. Me...in pomegranate red. The guy was nuts.

"I think I'll get these shirts and a pair of trousers." Marie's voice made me snap my head in her direction. She strolled toward me holding the clothes in front of her as if to examine them one last time before making her purchase.

Stopping next to me, she looked up. "Do you like that dress?"

"Not at all." I let the hem drop from my hand. "Just look at this hideous color. I would never wear anything like it."

"Really?" Marie scanned the mannequin from bottom to top. "I think it would look nice on you."

Oh no. Her, too? "I don't think so. Are you done here? I've seen a nice shop across the street. We could drop in there as well." The lie would distract her so she wouldn't make me try the gown on.

"Sorry." She scurried to the cash register with me in tow. "I got caught up with my shopping." Pulling her wallet out of her purse, she glanced around the store. "Is Julian back?"

"He's waiting outside."

The shop assistant scanned the price tags and shoved the clothes into a big plastic bag. The digital display on the counter flashed one hundred twenty-nine euro and seventy cents.

"Bloody hell, that much for a pair of pants and two shirts?" I blurted before I could think better of it.

The blonde woman stared hard at me, but my aunt didn't even blink at the total. She took my hand and led me toward the exit, where Julian waited, drinking from a small bottle of mineral water. He wiped the bottle's mouth then held it out to me.

I took a swig. "Thanks."

He nodded once.

The three of us made a tour through four more shops. The woman was insatiable, buying sweaters, blouses, skirts and shoes. Julian and I had to help her carry the bags or else she'd have been packed like a donkey in the veldt. She must have spent close to five hundred euro before we finally headed to a bistro with our stomachs rumbling.

We found seats at a table outside. Grabbing the menu, I scanned through the dishes, but they were all written in French. I flipped the card around to see if the other side would be in English. It only displayed a man slinging his arm around a man-shaped baguette. Brilliant.

Julian frowned at me over the edge of his card. "What's wrong?"

Leaning toward him, I whispered, "This is all French. I can't read the menu."

He smiled and rolled his eyes. "You're in France, girl. Of course it's in French." The legs of the metal chair scraped on the pavement as he scooted closer. "I'll translate for you."

He started reading the dishes out to me in the national language and gave me the appropriate English name for each. To hear the French words roll off his tongue set a sensual tingle on my skin. The temptation to ask him if he could read the menu again nudged me, but instead I settled for a pasta dish.

He ordered on my behalf when a man dressed like an oversized penguin appeared. "Would you like a Coke with it?" he asked me, and when I nodded he passed the order on.

Twenty minutes later, the waiter served our meals. "*Pour mademoiselle,*" he sang in a soft lilt when he set a nice heap of spaghetti in front of me.

"*Gracias.*" I cast the waiter a proud grin.

Julian shook his head, chuckled low, and started eating his chicken in wine sauce. I dug in, too, realizing I was starving.

"Are you ready for afters?" Marie rubbed the back of my hand on the table while the waiter came back for our empty plates.

I patted my bursting stomach. "I can't eat another bite."

"Oh come, you would not say no to ice cream, would you?"

My mouth watered.

Without waiting for my final answer, Marie spoke to the waiter, and he gave a nod. "Would you like some dessert, too?" she asked Julian.

"No more for me, thanks."

The penguin hurried to bring me and Marie each a cup the size of my foot, filled to the edge with chocolate and vanilla ice cream, topped with a mountain of whipped cream and two wafer rolls. My brain froze with every spoonful I shoved into my mouth. Three quarters down to the bottom, my stomach resigned, but I couldn't stand to waste any of this precious dessert.

"Please," I begged Julian. "Could you help me finish this monster sundae?"

Through with her dessert already, Marie offered him her spoon, and we took turns scooping the cream from the cup. Julian fished out the cherry that stuck on the bottom of the glass tub.

I was full to the brim, but this little cherry must have been the most appetizing thing in the world. Never having had any, I could only imagine how heavenly it would taste. My mouth watered anew with the mere sight of it on Julian's long-stemmed spoon.

He sneered at me as he lifted the fruit to his mouth. My heart sank. But then he gave me a wink and brought the spoon in front of my lips.

Uncertain, I chewed the inside of my cheek.

"Go on, it's yours," he urged.

I opened my mouth and he steered the cherry to its final destination, his eyes fixed on mine the entire time. I bit into the fruit. The sour taste was nothing close to what I had expected. I grimaced, swallowed the bite, but kept the pit in my mouth. It rolled along my teeth as we left the bistro and headed back to the car.

We made a stop at the local supermarket where Marie spent another small fortune on food and drinks, then she steered the SUV home.

My heart sank with each mile she drove. The day alone with her and Julian had been too beautiful. And too short. Already, in a few minutes, the horrible face of my mother would put a stop to my joy.

A song for Jona

Once back home, Julian and I lugged the heavy bags after Marie into the kitchen to help her put away the groceries.

As we walked through the door, the warm scent of chocolate took me on an immediate journey through time. A sudden impulse to twirl on the spot shot into my legs and, for the blink of an eye, left me light-footed. Without my knowing, soft giggles shook me. But catching a glimpse of my mother's rear when she was bent over the opened oven made me gain control.

"You came just in time for coffee and cake. I made your favorite, Jona," Charlene said as she pulled a steaming chocolate fudge cake out of the oven.

In spite of the delicious scent that wafted in my face, anger spiraled up inside me. Not just because of her talking to me, but most of all because it was a memory belonging to her and me alone that had made me smile right then. I fought to stay rooted in the present and leave things in the past alone.

"And just what makes you think you know anything about my favorites? It's not as if you've been to the orphanage lately to find out." My toxic voice earned me a poke from Julian. I didn't care. After all it wasn't half as painful as the twinge of my heart. With a heavy thump, the bag in my arm landed on the counter.

The blue cushions on the bench wrapped around the table flattened when we all took our seats while Marie brought the coffee pot and poured. Charlene dished out cake.

The devil may get me if I eat anything made by the dragon.

When she was about to hand me a piece, I stared straight at her, all memory shoved away. "No, thank you. I don't fancy your bloody cake."

My aunt exchanged an uneasy glance with my uncle, but neither reprimanded me. In fact, it was Julian's tender fingers that suddenly nudged my chin and tipped my head so I would look at his penetrating eyes.

"Did anyone ever tell you that you've the mouth of a snotty brat?" His thumb smoothed over my cheek, then he let go of me.

I was still gazing at him when he began sipping his coffee. The temperature around me dropped to an uncomfortable level. It was unbelievable, how he made me wish that, for once, I hadn't lipped off to my mother, all with this one reprobative glance of his. It scared the hell out of me to realize how much this man's opinion mattered to me. I had never cared what anyone thought of me, so why now?

I drank my coffee fast to quench the taste of bad conscience. And while everyone else still shoved bites of chocolate cake into their mouths, I excused myself from the next round of refills.

Some alone time was on the agenda. To have so many people around me all day had exhausted me. It surprised me when I realized I wanted to roam through the vinery instead of retreating to my room. Strange, how very much this place had grown on me in the last three days. Only now did I realize that I actually missed working out here today.

I paused from pounding the path in front of me and pinched the bridge of my nose. A glance back at the house and up to my open door on the balcony confirmed my suspicion. Damnit to hell—I was falling in love with this house and the grounds. I dragged two restless hands through my hair, pushing out a desperate sigh.

What would Quinn have said if he had seen me now? I missed my friend. I missed his scolding when I was dragged to the office and he had to take care of me as well as the saucy chats we'd had when he'd invited me to McDonald's for a Coke and a burger before he'd delivered me at the orphanage.

He would want me to be happy. *"If you can't change a situation, make the best of it."* His words surfaced in my mind. Maybe I should listen to him for once.

Kicking stones out of my way released some of my frustration, but the doubts and confusion remained. I'd run from so many places in the past after I nicked a little money or something shiny. I'd even run from the orphanage. Twice. But I'd never made it farther than Gatwick or Chelmsford by dodging the fare of the train before an official caught me and sent me back to the institution.

In fact, I'd grown tired of running.

Maybe, just for a little while, I could enjoy the pleasantries of having a nice place to stay put without worrying about what tomorrow would bring.

Surrounded by all the greenery, I tilted my head and gazed at the sky. "Damn, what's your bloody plan?" For a moment, I studied the clouds drifting by, knowing I wouldn't get an answer other than maybe a bird pooping on my face.

With my hands tucked deep into my pockets, I strolled back to the house. The kitchen was empty, but I heard people chatting in the front room. Muffled but desperate, Charlene's voice caught my attention.

It went against my nature to eavesdrop. After all, I didn't give a damn about what the dragon had to say. But as my foot hovered over the second stair, she mentioned my name and that was enough to change my mind.

I crept to the front room door and strained to listen.

"...will get over it eventually. Trust me."

I had a strange feeling of foreboding of the subject Julian was talking about.

Sounding close to tears, my mother replied, "But what if she just can't forgive me? It doesn't seem like she ever will."

Yup, my intuition was dead on. What struck me as weird was that the dragon confided in Julian with her doubts and sorrow, and not in someone who'd be a little closer to her. Like family. I'd have expected her to talk to Marie, instead of her caretaker.

"You have to give her some more time," Julian insisted in his familiar soft tone, the same one he used when he'd dragged me out onto the balcony last night.

"But you of all people know time is the only thing I don't have left!"

Hard as it was to admit, her grief sounded genuine. It gave my heart a twinge. The second within only an hour.

"Be patient, Charlene. Rest. Conserve your energy. I'll take care of everything else."

The room fell silent. What was going on? I urged to lean around the corner and peek inside, but I couldn't give away my advantage. The wall behind me cooled my back as I frowned at the ceiling, waiting for them to speak again.

Dissonant notes sounded from the piano, like someone hit random keys when walking by.

My mother cleared her throat. When she spoke her voice had dropped a few notches. "I've noticed a change about you."

A silent second ticked by.

"Have you?" The faintest hint of disapproval from Julian.

I hadn't observed anything different about Julian. But then she probably referred to a longer period than the few days I'd known him. My curiosity threatened to kill me, so could this woman be a bit more precise, please?

"I know that look," she said, and her off-key tone made the hair at the back of my neck stand up. "But you should be wise enough to see that there's no way."

"I don't know what you mean." Curt and precise. He knew what she meant, all right.

But should I know, too? What way did the dragon mean, and who was she to preach to him?

I silenced my thoughts to hear more, when my mother's harsh scolding of Julian drifted to me. "Of course, you know. Don't think I'm stupid just because you're that much older."

Oh boy, she must have forgotten to take her pills. Mental disorder. He could have hardly be older than twenty, and she must have been way over forty. In teenager reckoning this was like comparing Apollo to Medusa.

Her sigh dragged through the room. "You can never give her what she needs. All you will do is hurt her."

Her? A red-hot lance of jealousy stabbed my heart. Charlene was talking about another woman. No surprise, her mood had changed to snappy. From the very beginning, I suspected she wanted this man for her own, even if he played way beyond her age class.

But he couldn't be taken. He'd told me yesterday, and I would swear he hadn't lied to me. Just...*no*. I refused to picture him holding another girl like he had held me last night.

There...I...Oh, shut the hell up, Jona.

"I'm not intending to hurt her—or anyone. Don't worry, I do know my place. My first and foremost duty is to you. Your daughter," he said, pausing and then speaking with effort, "comes a close second."

Your daughter? That was *me*! I clapped my hands over my mouth to kill the sound of my happy, shocked inhale.

Footsteps approached the door. I swallowed the shock and quickly dashed up the stairs, taking the steps three at a time. At the top, I spun around and casually walked back down, pretending I hadn't heard any of their conversation. But my heart raced madly inside my chest.

Spotting me on the stairs, my mother paused. For the blink of an eye, the awkward feeling of being caught stopped me in my tracks as well. A purple shrug, wrapped around her skinny shoulders, made her ashen face appear more sallow. Without saying one word, she hurried on into her room and closed the door.

Stunned, I remained on the stairs and stared down the empty hallway, struggling to shake off this unnatural feeling of guilt. I would have never thought it possible, but her sorrow left a sore spot in my soul.

Dumping the thought, I spun on my heel, ready to ascend to my room. But music coming from the parlor froze me in place.

Julian was playing the piano.

Captivated by the sweet melody, I wondered if this was what he'd gotten from Paul's. I sneaked closer and peeked into the room. He wouldn't notice me with his back toward the entrance. Good, because after what I'd heard him say a minute ago, I didn't think I could look straight at his face. The feeling of confusion still wound around my throat, and words would have evaded me, anyway.

The beautiful chords he played filled both the room and me with calm. Clutching the doorframe, I pressed my cheek against the smooth wood, gazing dreamily out the window into the flaming red sunset.

It escaped me when the first piece of music ended and he started a new one. But at the familiar chords, I straightened with a start. He was playing *my* song. The one I so often hummed to myself, not knowing where I'd first heard it, or if I'd made it up by myself.

Only he didn't just play the single notes as I would have hummed them. His hands caressed the keyboard up and down as they flew over this little melody of mine. A minute later, Julian cast a glance at me over his shoulder. His eyes all smiles, he winked.

Argh, caught.

My heart thudded against my ribcage. If it had pounded a note louder, it might have served him as a metronome.

With a slight flick of his head, he invited me to come over and join him on the piano bench. Ever so slowly, I walked toward him, worried I had misinterpreted his gesture. But that doubt vaporized the moment I approached the piano and he slid over to the end to let me take a seat next to him.

He leaned in, and his familiar smell filled my head. "Could you turn the page for me?"

On the stand sat a pack of music sheets with lines and notes, but I couldn't begin to make sense of it. At this moment, though, I knew he'd gone to Paul's only to get this piece for me. That was the reason he'd come with us to town from the beginning.

My fingers cold, I fumbled with the page, turning it over, then I sat so still one might have mistaken me for furniture. His fingers never stopped moving over the ivory. Sometimes they just stroked the keys, the next moment they pushed them down with firm insistence. It almost felt like he made love to the piano with his very hands. For the briefest moment, I wondered what it would feel like if he stroked me the same way.

My eyes skipped to his face, and I bit my lower lip, not wanting to explore this thought any further.

Twice more, he nudged me with his elbow and said, "Next page, please," while he concentrated on the notes in front of him.

And then the piece ended, the final chords ebbing into silence. Hands clasped in my lap, I waited for him to turn to me.

"How did you know..." I uttered in a confused whisper. "This song. How did you know it's special to me?"

He sighed. "How could I not know when you hummed it all day yesterday in the field?" He tucked a stray wisp of hair behind my ear and brushed his fingertips across my cheek before he dropped his hand again. A sensuous shiver shook me, and I picked up my former thought once more.

An awkward silence fell between us. With my throat too dry, I had to swallow twice to find my voice again.

"What's it called?" I asked.

Julian smiled to himself as if this was a joke only he would understand. The next moment, his hand covered mine, and his warmth seeped into me. "It's called *Hallelujah*."

Hallelujah! My song had a name.

And what an irony the title was compared with my dreary life. It irritated me to no end that my hand wouldn't stop shaking under his. And to make matters worse, my breathing had noticeably picked up speed.

I couldn't allow him to see how nervous he really made me, so I cleared my throat something forceful and said, "Can you play it again?"

He wouldn't take his hand from mine. Not before he smoothed his thumb over my knuckles. Then he nodded and flipped to page one to read his way through the song once more.

My gaze switched back and forth between his concentrating face and his skilled fingers while he was performing this wonderful music for me. At his gentle shove I turned the pages, but eventually, I leaned my head on his shoulder and closed my eyes, soaking in the soothing sounds. Certain that his dancing fingers never stopped to turn the pages, I wondered how he could have learned this piece by heart so fast. But not enough to ask, or even to open my eyes.

When the song came to an end again, the final note lingering in the room, I didn't move. Neither did he. Only his head turned slightly, his cheek brushing my hair, and I felt his tender gaze searching my face.

"Again, please," I whispered, and without a comment Julian agreed. His steady, masculine shoulder told me I wasn't unwelcome, because if he had shoved me the tiniest bit, I would have backed away instantly.

He let me rest against him and listen for what felt like hours.

Each time the song ended, it took only a little nudge of my arm for him to play the beautiful melody again.

And again.

All evening long.

The almost kiss

I opened my eyes in my private castle the next day. The soft melody of "Hallelujah" still played through my mind. As they had every morning, the chirping of birds and a warm sun greeted me through my opened windows. Tucking the blanket up to my ears, I buried my cheek deeper into the soft pillow and reveled in the previous evening.

I lost count of how many times Julian had played my special song, or how many others he'd coaxed from the ivory keys on the piano. He must have played for hours. Just because I had asked him to.

Sometime after eleven, we'd finally ascended to our rooms and he'd bid me goodnight with a nudge of his knuckles to my chin.

Even though the story remained unclear, I knew Julian had entered my dreams again last night.

A sigh lifted my chest. I rolled on my back and put my arms behind my head. Soft light danced on the ceiling, reflecting off the opened window above my bed. Julian's confessing words to my mother filled me with joy. Of course, his foremost duty was to her, his charge, but he'd named me a close second. He would never find out how much that meant to me.

It was new that someone awoke this kind of feeling in me. My protective walls threatened to tumble. I could do nothing to stop the once solid defense from crumbling before Julian.

The idea to stay a bit longer played in my head.

I closed my eyes and rubbed my face. These thoughts were too weird and dangerous. However long I remained in this place, eventually the moment of parting would come. And I couldn't allow anyone, be it Aunt Marie, or Julian, to break through my circle of defense.

But just like this house and the vineyards, Julian had grown on me.

My attention fell on his gray hoodie hanging over the backrest of my swivel chair, and I swung my legs out of bed. My bare feet made no sound on the cold parquet as I ambled over to get it. The smell of warm, wild wind still clung to the fabric and wrapped me in a cloud of ocean breeze. Just how could any man smell this good?

No detergent or shower gel could bring on that irresistible scent. It seemed strangely natural, rolling off his very body and tinting everything in his vicinity with this sweet fragrance.

I slid my arms through the sleeves. Nearly three sizes too big, the hem of the hoodie hugged my thighs. The cuffs clasped in my palms, I brought my hands to my nose to get an extra shot of *Julian*.

At the same instant, footfalls on the balcony boards drifted into my room. Panic struck fast at the thought of getting caught reveling in his smell. I quickly locked my hands behind my back, presenting my most innocent grin, as a knock sounded on the glass of the open door and Julian shoved his head in through the curtains.

"Hi," I blurted, feeling my face turn red like a strawberry.

"Good morning." He swept the curtains aside and stepped into my room. On a small tray in his left hand, he balanced two steaming cups and a plate of toast with jam.

"You missed breakfast again. Since we skipped dinner last night, I thought you might be hungry. I saved this for you." He whisked the tray in front of my face.

The smell of hot chocolate drifting to my nose set my stomach to rumbling. But Julian withdrew the small breakfast and retreated to the balcony before I could make a grab for the cup. "I thought we could eat out here today."

Oh, you snake. Apparently, he hadn't grown tired of helping me get past my fear of heights.

"We?" I stopped by the door, watching him with hunger for both the man and the food, as he set the plate down on the railing. "I thought you normally don't eat breakfast."

"For you I'll make an exception." He picked up the hot chocolate and held it out to me, but from too far away for me to grab it.

"Know what?" I murmured. "I'm not hungry. I'll just wait until lunch. Yeah, that's what I'll do. It can't be too long until noon."

Twisting his wrist, Julian glanced at his watch. "It's nine thirty. Quite a while to go," he mocked. "Wouldn't a cup of sweet chocolate be nice now? And just look, I've brought you toast."

Yeah. And as if taking sides with Julian, my stomach chimed another annoying rumble. My frown ought to have told him he could shove the toast up his arse. Just because we spent this beautiful evening together, it didn't make him my personal instructor in overcoming vertigo. I pivoted and headed for the bathroom.

"Jona?"

I turned around.

Julian's arched eyebrow weakened my stance. "You still have my hoodie."

Don't even think about getting it back, buddy. This is mine. I might not have told you so yet, but that's a fact.

I crossed my arms over my chest and smirked. "So?"

"So?" he repeated with a disbelieving laugh. His sweet tone matched his look. "I'd say if you want to keep it you owe me."

He was willing to trade? That could be an interesting deal. "What do you want?"

Cup raised, he waggled his brows. "I want you to have breakfast with me."

"Okay, bring the food in and we can eat on my bed." My victorious grin said it all.

"Outside." This time it was as though his eyes spoke the word, and with a lustful growl. How could a girl ever resist him?

"Oh, for heaven's sake!" Arms raised, I stomped forward. "So gimme the bloody cup." All my strength was necessary to control the rising fear as I stepped out into the warm daylight. Panic gripped me harder with each stride. For a millisecond, an equally shocked expression flashed across Julian's face. There was barely time for him to shift the cup out of the way before I collided with him. His strong arm wrapped securely around my waist. A whine escaped me as I shut my eyes and buried my face in his shoulder where I hoped my deep breaths would steady my shaking nerves.

Julian's abs flexed against my body when he chuckled low. "Easy there, love."

In the next instant, he stiffened. We both did as his words sank in.

Aware of every inch of his body pressing against mine, a joyful song started to play in my mind and I tilted my head to meet his gaze. The tips of our noses almost touched when he dipped his head. I expected my heart to speed up. Instead it stopped beating all together.

His firm hold around me loosened. His hand came up slowly to shape against the side of my neck and face. His thumb brushed my cheekbone. Between his slow blinks, I stared into the deep blue of his warm eyes.

The balcony, the house, the entire world around me melted away. At this moment, I could have stood on top of the Eifel tower and would have felt utterly protected by Julian's embrace.

Heat seared me from the inside. My fingers trembled as they clenched the collar of his orange shirt. I forced my hands to uncurl and lay flat against his chest so as not to tear off his top button. When his face inched closer, I licked my lips. My breaths erupted like the puffs of a steam train.

I wanted to taste him. Feel the sensual curve of his lips. Trace it with my tongue. But the very instant they brushed against my bottom lip, he tensed and pulled away. A cold spot remained on my cheek when his hand dropped.

A dry cough made his throat twitch. He handed me the cup. "You better drink your hot chocolate while it's still warm."

The stern note in his voice dragged me back to reality. I double blinked. Grief caught me in a stranglehold when I saw the regret in his eyes.

Kiss. Fantastic idea.

What had gotten into me that caused me to let my control slip so badly? I took the cup from him, retreated to the wall, and sank to the floor. Sips of the hot drink warmed my stomach. But they could do nothing about the cold in my heart.

Julian stood rooted to the spot and studied me. Cursing the moment I bounced into his arms? I would've sworn he'd felt the same sparkle between us when he'd leaned down to kiss me.

Warming my fingers on the hot chocolate, I balanced the cup on my knees. The black smiley on the green mug presented a friendlier face than Julian.

"What changed your mind?" I croaked. "Didn't you say you were going to make an exception for me?"

"What?" In an awfully sweet manner his brows knitted together, and he stared at me, lost like a child in first grade who had no idea what the teacher wanted from him. Probably the very same look I gave him so often.

"Breakfast." Forcing a grin, I raised my cup. "You're supposed to sit down with me and eat."

Whatever had been on his mind before rushed from his face as he blinked slowly. Placing the plate with the delicious smelling toast between us, he lowered, too, and took a sip from his cup. Two of the slices covered with raspberry jam helped swallow my disappointment. Julian had none.

Neither of us spoke, and when I finished my drink, he grabbed the cup together with the plate and carried the tray to his room.

He didn't return.

Letting out the sigh that had tightened my chest during the previous ten minutes, I crawled into my room and jumped into the shower. It was time to wash off the confusion and drown my longing for this guy in the spray of water. After all, I should be happy we hadn't finished the kiss. It would have complicated my situation enormously.

The progressing Sunday made it clear that Julian was evading my presence. While I helped Marie prepare a pasta meal for lunch, he accompanied my uncle to the vinery. And when I joined them in the early afternoon simply because I was bored and would have loved to use Albert's dirt scanner some more, Julian excused himself and returned to the house.

Small needles of regret jabbed me in the chest and with every hour that separated us, the empty pit in my stomach grew. The needles had turned to lances by the time I went to bed, because this was also the first evening he didn't say goodnight.

On the plus side, my mother kept out of my way, too. She didn't stalk me, nor even talk to me during the remainder of the weekend.

The next couple of days, I gave my best in the vinery. But without Julian's company, the work wasn't even half as much fun. Chats with Valentine were the highlights.

They started on Tuesday afternoon. Together with Marie we knelt in the dirt and pulled weeds. Valentine rattled on in French for hours while my aunt replied with a few words every now and then. Apparently, the teapot-shaped chatterbox missed it when Marie rose from the ground and patted the dirt off her trousers then went back to the house to make us all a snack.

Helplessly, I stared after my aunt while Valentine continued her French monologue. It took her almost five minutes to realize no one answered her. Confused, she glanced to all sides. Her gaze focused on me. The grin of a happy farmer curved her mouth.

Very much to my surprise, she returned to her task and continued rambling. Just to make her happy, and maybe because I had no one else to talk to, I filled her brief gaps with *ahs* and *ohs*. Sometimes I would even ask, "Is that so?" or "Really?" But she understood me as little as I understood her.

The silence when she finally stopped talking actually felt weird. So in a funny mood, I told her about London in my language. I explained the location of the orphanage and detailed how Miss Mulligan had let us attend the celebrations in the street when Prince William and Kate married last April. Valentine's *ahs* and *ohs* filled my gaps now and made me chuckle, propelling me to continue my babbling.

Straightening once to ease the pain in my back, I caught a glimpse of Julian only a few feet away. A pair of sheers still clutched in his hand, he stood as if frozen in time and stared at us with narrowed eyes. Easy to imagine how our conversation must have intrigued him. City lass and countrywoman finding a way to communicate.

A weak smile pulled at the corners of my mouth. The first twitch of his lips after three days kick-started my heart into pounding with joy. His attention was little, though. With a sigh, he twisted and trudged off.

Wednesday, I sought his nearness purposefully, hoping he would say something at last if only I stood close enough for a while. Again, he wouldn't speak to me. But his returning glances didn't escape me.

Sometimes, he looked away quickly when I caught his gaze on me. Other times he would just fix me with his stare.

Needless to mention that his awkward behavior freaked me out. I decided to confront him later and set things straight between us once and for all.

In the late afternoon, a heavy downpour washed away our plans to work in the field and sent us inside sooner than usual. I showered and dressed in blue jeans and a dark blue tee from Marie's selection then peeked out on the balcony.

Tock-tock, fat drops tapped a romantic rhythm on the wood. Thick gray clouds hovered low. Not even seven o'clock, it was dark like bedtime. Light burned in Julian's room and illuminated the balcony through his opened door, but there was no sign of him outside.

"Julian?" I said, but he didn't hear me through the rain. If he did, however, he refused to appear on the balcony.

Crap. We really needed to get this straight. Now.

Back shoving against the doorframe, I slowly made a step outside. Fear slammed into me like a baseball bat from the shadows. The wood creaked under my weight and I sent a silent *Ave Maria* to heaven. My teeth crunched as I inhaled three times deeply through my nose. My eyes fluttered shut. Then I shoved my left leg in the direction of Julian's room. Dragging the right behind, I flattened my back and hands against the solid wall.

It would have been easier to take a walk down the corridor and knock on his door. But somehow it seemed important to approach him this way. Like I'd prove myself worthy by facing the danger on my conquest of his castle.

As I inched forward, the rough surface of the wall yanked hair from my scalp. Thin slits between the footboards allowed a glimpse of the pebbled ground underneath. If this weak illusion of a porch broke underneath my weight, I'd make a breakneck dive into death.

Just freaking wonderful.

"Julian," I whined. But when I angled my head to the left his empty doorway mocked me from miles away. "Lord, please let me survive this." I swallowed hard at the panic in my chest then shoved my foot another step to the left. And another.

Through the thick curtains of rain, I glimpsed a dark ball, growing as it shot toward me. I froze. As a big raven flapped its wings excitedly and landed on the railing of the balcony, my shriek ripped through the air.

"*Argh*! Gosh!" It took me several breaths to calm down enough to lower my arms from protecting my head. "You bloody...*filthy*...beast!"

The damn bird only cocked its wet head and fluffed up its dripping feathers. To my hoarse shooing sounds, the raven finally took off into the rain again, giving me another start as the wings fluttered like those of a bat.

I closed my eyes for a second. The image of Julian safely sprawled on his bed surfaced in my mind. "Oh, I so hope you know what risk I'm taking for you." Walking through my personal hell. Still, the thought of him filled me with encouragement.

I turned my head to the left to focus on my goal again.

And there he stood, like a dark knight in a circle of light.

Clad in a dark gray sweatshirt and even darker trousers, he leaned against the frame of his balcony door, arms crossed over his chest and eyes wide with wonder.

"Hi." Excitement replaced my initial panic, thudding my heart to a faster beat. He'd come and get me and everything would be okay.

But Julian remained motionless, watching my every move— which wasn't a darn lot at this moment. *Damn you to hell, wretch!* I almost breathed a hysteric laugh.

"What in the world are you doing out here?" he drawled

eventually.

"Coming. Talk." There wasn't enough air in my lungs for a longer answer.

"There's an easier way to my room."

"I know." I did sound desperate, all right.

His blond brow arched. "Why didn't you take that way?"

Questions, questions. Didn't I look tense enough? "I *don't* know."

"Would you like to come in?" He gestured a hand toward the room's interior.

"I guess." *Oh please, do I have to drop to my knees and plead for your help?* He could have that. My wobbly legs threatened to give way underneath me in a second.

He made a step toward me and reached out with one hand. It cost me quite an effort to let go of the wall behind me and lay my trembling fingers in his palm instead.

Instantly, his warm touch infused me with a strength I couldn't find only a minute ago. He pulled me into his protective arms and stared at me from an inch away. A second later, he ushered me through the door into his realm.

Julian's room

"Secrets" drifted from the iPod with the voices of OneRepublic. My boots sat lonely on the stone tiled floor while I hugged my knees to my chest, lounging on the center of Julian's queen-size bed. The lamp on his nightstand tinted the plain walls a soft yellow.

Pressing my chin to my bent knees, I eyed Julian half sitting on the corner of his maple desk, his hands gripping the edge. Raindrops slid down the window behind him in rhythm to the drumming on the roof.

"I'm impressed. You must have taken a ride through hell to see me here. So what did you want to talk about?" His eyes were warm, friendly, though his tone revealed a certain hint of impatience.

About why the bloody hell you're shoving me away.

I shrugged. My gaze wandered around, taking in the partly open door to the bathroom and the high wardrobe with sliding panes. "You've got a nice room."

"I guess it looks pretty similar to yours." He cast a glance over the room then at me. "But you certainly didn't take this terrifying walk to compliment my room, did you?"

I studied his face, which he kept expressionless. Okay, it was time to stop playing games and show my hand. "What happened last weekend that you now can't stand to have me near you anymore?" Incomprehension narrowed my eyes. "I mean, nothing *really* happened between us, did it?"

Lips compressed to a line, he puffed a sigh. "No, nothing really happened." His glance dropped briefly, a muscle in his jaw ticked.

"Then why are you staying away from me?"

Julian blinked slowly while he shook his head once. "It's complicated."

"Complicated?" *Wait one second; let me eat a bowl of alphabet soup and poop a better argument than that.* Loosening the hug of my knees, I crossed my legs and braced my elbows on my thighs, lacing my fingers.

He nodded, pushed away from the desk and paced the room, hands tucked into his pockets.

"Julian, I was shoved into an orphanage when I was five because my mother didn't want me. In the winter, I slept wearing all four pairs of socks I owned just to stop my teeth from rattling." My voice rose a few notches with every word. "Last week, I was caught stealing a bloody jacket, and a kid-loathing judge shipped me off to France where I now have to stay with people I hardly know and a mother I no longer care about. And you talk about complicated?"

The bloody wretch wouldn't even turn in my direction.

"Dammit, Julian, would you please look at me?"

First, only his eyes switched to mine, but then his head angled and he gazed at me directly. However, his lips remained sealed.

"Why don't we just pretend *that little nothing* which happened Sunday morning really *was* nothing and we go back to what we were before?" I rubbed my hands over my face. "I really could do with a friend here, you know."

As my words sunk in, his puzzled expression began to relax, as did the distance he'd put between us. Slowly, he skirted the bed to my right. He slumped down and leaned against the headboard. Arms crossed over his chest and legs stretched out on the mattress, he studied the far wall. "I didn't make it very easy for you to feel at home here, did I?" The socks on his feet swayed like a metronome.

I gazed at him over my shoulder. "You did brilliantly until Sunday morning."

"Is it too late to say I'm sorry?" His deep blue eyes reflected the honesty of his words.

A smile crept to my mouth faster than I could stop it. "I'd die to hear those words from you for once."

"Ah, God forbid I say them twice." His mocking laugh filled both the room and me with joy. Hand cupping my neck, he pulled me toward him. Astonished but without hesitation, I nestled on his chest and let his hand rest softly on my shoulder.

Oh. My. God.

Okay, he seemingly agreed to be friends again. And body contact between friends was absolutely fine. No need to go hysterical over it. *Deep breaths, Jona. And*—oh, he smelled so bloody delicious.

I went rigid in his arms, concentrating on staying calm. But with my fevered heart pounding in my ears it was hard to even hear the music coming from the iPod.

"Can I ask you something?" Whiskers tickled my skin when his chin rubbed against my forehead as he spoke.

"Shoot." My voice cracked at this one little word.

"What did you and Valentine talk about yesterday?" He emphasized each word separately.

"Oh, you don't want to know." Laughing, I twisted in his hold to gaze at his face.

From under his lashes, he regarded me with intrigued eyes. But he accepted my answer. The strong beat of his heart resonated in a calm rhythm against my palm. He must have been used to girls lying in his arms, because obviously I didn't make him nervous one bit. Unlike me, an agitated shooting star, he seemed the quiet center of my galaxy. And with just as many secrets.

I figured this was the right moment for some investigation. "Do I get a free question now?"

"Mm-hm." Underneath his hoodie, firm abs twitched with the word.

"Have you always cared for people like my mother?"

"Yes."

"And do you always stay with them until they die?"

Blinking twice, he seemed to contemplate his answer. "With some of them. Others I attended to for only a few weeks."

"Until they recovered from their illness?"

"Until they got on with their situations." Julian bent one knee and put one arm behind his head. "It's not always terminal care I do. In fact, cases like your mother are the exception."

Oh. So, my mother *was* a special case.

"What's your employing agency called?" Maybe I could find

some information about it on the Internet. On the ancient computer in the orphanage, I had learned how to Google things.

His lips curved on one side and he twitched his brows once as if to say, *you would so like to know that, wouldn't you*?

"So?" I pressed.

"So, it's not really an agency. It's more, let's say... an association. We like to call ourselves *Supporters*."

"*The Supporters Association*. I guess that name fits, considering how you're kind of playing angels for ill people."

The second half of his mouth curled up, too, and he rolled his eyes sweetly.

"Do you like your boss?" Somehow, I envisioned the head of the society like a nun, all in black-and-white penguin wear.

"He's a very charismatic guy."

"And is the headquarters here in France?"

"You have a lot of questions, young lady." His mocking tone of scolding ignited a sensual shiver down my back.

"Yeah, I know. Sorry." I flashed my cutest grin. "Now, is it?"

His chuckle shook me on his chest and reverberated through my head. "No. It's farther north."

My curiosity rose. "England?"

"Way farther up."

"That could be any of a million places, including the North Pole. So, where is it?"

"You never give up, do you?"

"And you never give a straight answer. Do *you?*" I liked how he laughed at that. But his evasion of my questions irritated me. What was so confidential about the location of this association? Maybe I would need to Google it after all. If an Internet connection existed in this house, anyway.

Because we both fell silent and I already missed the sound of him talking, I came up with a new question. "What did you do before you joined the group?"

Julian sniffed then cleared his throat. "The usual."

And that would be what? "Like school and college and stuff?"

"Yeah. And stuff."

Was I getting this wrong, or was he suddenly trying to stop me from prodding? An awkward annoyance gripped me as I strained to hear more about his life. "How old are you?"

"How old do you think I am?"

"Hm." I thoroughly studied his face. "Twenty-one?"

Julian held my gaze for a second, a grin coming to the surface that had little to do with amusement. "Good guess."

Taking this for a yes, I snuggled deeper into his hold and his arm tightened around me. "Was there ever a moment in your life where you felt utterly comfortable, with no thought about the rest of the world, or what life still held for you?"

"Many," he replied. "What about you? Have you ever had such a special moment?"

Apart from now? "There was only one time." The sound of waves rushing to the shore filled my mind while my toes curled in the memory of digging into the soft, warm sand. The wind that had wafted my hair around my shoulders had carried the cry of a seagull, drifting low above the ocean.

"Want to tell me about it?" Julian's whisper broke through to me like the echo of the waves.

"It was when I stared out at the infinite sea." I breathed a sigh. "Once, Miss Mulligan took us to the beach."

"Your warden?" he asked, only a notch louder than before.

"Yeah, the one with the mousy face. She was at the hearing last week."

"I didn't pay attention to *her* so much."

"No?" I teased.

"No." He laughed. "Your spectacular fight with the deputies captured me completely."

"Yeah, I can handle the cops," I said with a smug grin to myself. "It's just the handcuffs that irritate me sometimes."

He ruffled my hair. "You didn't seem all too happy when I came to spring you from the cuffs."

A cozy pink cloud of warmth settled around me at this particular memory. "You put a shitload of trust in me when you left me alone in the corridor. No one else would have done that."

"True." The muscles in his abdomen moved as he leaned his head closer to my ear and whispered, "But I guess no one else has ever been lying with you like this either, having an open conversation like we are."

Not that I would remember.

"You need to put some trust first into those who you want to trust you in return." His voice slightly trailed off. "Some people are like cats. You cannot train them to do anything. You just show them you mean no harm and wait until they come to you of their own free will."

"Oh, is that your tactic?" I shifted my gaze to his face, my chin deliberately digging between two of his ribs. "You think I can't be trained?"

Julian wiggled underneath me, exploding with laughter. "Nope, you're too stubborn. You know, if you pee on my floor I'll have to rub your face in it."

Eyes wide, my jaw dropped. "I beg your pardon?" I found more of his ticklish spots. To make him laugh was like playing a sweet melody on a human body.

"Will you please stop that?" His fingers curled around my wrists, gently but firm.

I stood no chance against his strength, even when he held me with only one hand. The other he planted on my neck and made me shift into the comfortable position of before. It was my pleasure to obey.

When his calm breathing together with the soothing music drifting from the iPod were the only sounds in the room again, I admitted in a whisper, "But it *was* nice of you to set me free in the courthouse."

"You had a strange way of showing your gratitude. If I remember it right, you damned me to hell."

Maybe because hell was the only place I knew and even back then I wanted him near me. With my eyes closed, I listened to his heartbeat.

Minutes ticked by.

The slow beat lulled me into a comfortable state of half dozing. And when Julian's fingers started to skim in circles over my shoulder, I was lost completely.

My tense muscles relaxed, my breaths slowed to deep satisfied intervals.

A little later, Julian said my name in his ever-soft voice and stirred beneath me. But I clasped his shirt and nestled a little tighter against him, wanting him to let me stay.

"Jona, you're pressing on my arm." His whisper caressed my ear. But I didn't care. I felt utterly comfortable and no way in hell was I going to move.

Eventually, he gave up and shoved slightly downward, so his head would sink into the pillow. I scooted down with him, but that was the most comfort I would grant him at the moment.

A blanket was pulled over my hips and the volume of the music turned down several notches. How he managed with the remote sitting on the desk, I didn't understand, but I was also too tired to think about it.

His wonderful smell carried me to the land of dreams.

I couldn't say what time of night it was when I woke, because the lamp was turned off. The little light the moon cast through the windows wouldn't be enough to decipher the face of my watch. It didn't matter, because my wristwatch was trapped underneath me together with my right hand, and I didn't dare move. If I had, Julian might have woken up—and pulled away his hand which covered mine on his chest. His left hand was shoved into my hair, creating a sensual tingle at the back of my neck.

I breathed in deeply, fighting a very content smile. No, I wouldn't have moved an inch for the life of me.

But the darkness irritated me slightly. Dead certain that Julian hadn't detangled from my clasp while I'd slept, I wondered how he'd switched off the lamp at my side of the bed. Come to think of it, the music had stopped playing as well. If Julian was one to fall asleep easily, he might've set those things on a timer. The iPod might have had that function, but the light? It seemed like a simple lamp.

Don't think so much. Enjoy. And as if on command, Julian's thumb started to smooth small circles around my knuckles. Every earlier thought dropped from my mind and, keeping still, I utterly surrendered to his touch. Hoping that this night would never end, I closed my eyes.

As a new sunny morning broke, I found myself shifted to the side, facing the French door and tucked softly under the blankets. Although completely snuggly and warm, I missed being held by gentle arms.

A stretch followed my yawn, and the blanket slipped away from my shoulders.

"You do like to sleep in, don't you?"

My head snapped around to find Julian lounging on a low sofa. A white t-shirt replaced the dark sweatshirt he wore last night and light blue jeans hugged his legs, which he'd planted fairly apart. Despite my wide eyes, his lips twitched to a friendly smirk. "Hi."

"I didn't notice you getting up."

"Ugh, yeah. I had to roll you to the side." His shiny teeth appeared as his grin spread wider. "I needed to check on your mother. And then I really, *really* needed to use the bathroom."

I scooted backward to lean against the headboard with the blanket wrapped around my middle. The fact that he would leave me alone in his room for the sake of my mother gnawed at me. But I absolutely understood the issue with the toilet when my bursting bladder reminded me of the urgency.

"Why didn't you wake me?" *I wouldn't have let you get out of bed then.*

"You were too sweet, lost in peaceful sleep."

With him running through my dreams, no wonder I didn't want to wake up. I narrowed my eyes and glanced at him from the side. "How long have you been sitting there and watching me?"

"Half an hour." His shoulder lifted with a shrug. "Maybe a little longer."

Please God, I hope I didn't snore. Warmth seared my face, and I lowered my gaze to my clenched hands on the blue comforter.

A fresh breeze coming through the open balcony door brushed my hair but did little to cool the heat in my cheeks. "What time is it?"

"Time to get up and hurry downstairs if you want to eat breakfast before we head out to the vineyard."

If Marie and Albert were still sitting in the kitchen sipping their morning coffees, it couldn't be later than seven. I swung my legs out of bed and slipped into my boots. Waving at him, I crossed to the balcony door.

Bad habit.

A blow of August wind slapped me in the face and fear stopped me in my tracks. I almost walked out onto the balcony like there wasn't an abyss waiting for me underneath. "Dear God, where are my thoughts?"

"Where indeed?" His purred jibe made the hairs on my neck stand on end.

I spun on my heel, stuck my tongue out at his amused face, and trudged to the door.

Smirking, he sank deeper into the couch and laced his fingers behind his neck. The small furniture creaked slightly. "See you outside, Jona."

A slamming door was my answer to his mocking me.

On Julian's advice, I hurtled down to grab the last croissant from the table and stuffed a big piece into my mouth. "Good morning," I mumbled with my mouth full. Too late, I realized my mother lodged next to Marie in the corner seat. Never would I have included her in my general greeting deliberately.

Forcing the croissant down, I filled a glass of orange juice and, standing with my back to her, I emptied it in one draught.

"*Chérie*, what put you in such haste? Come and sit down with us." My aunt's friendly invitation didn't sway me.

"I woke late again. Meet you outside." Before I could think better of it, I bent down and pressed a brief kiss to her cheek.

"Thanks for saving the last croissant for me."

Three pairs of mystified eyes turned to me. Oh no, what had I done? My spine stiffened. Like a fish on dry land, I opened and closed my mouth. But honestly, how could you take back a kiss?

Lips tight in a confused frown, I turned on the spot and rushed up to my room to change for the day—and to clear my head. *The aftermath of the happiness from your night in Julian's arms*, a small voice in my head chided. I couldn't contradict it.

Anticipation brewed in my chest as I loped down again, taking two stairs at a time. At the bottom, my aunt and uncle welcomed me with a parental look, and Marie pulled me into a hug on the way out to the vineyard. Her warmth captured me, and my arm snaked up to wrap around her waist.

The rich, deep smell of growing plants grabbed my senses. A V-formation of wild geese sailed high above our heads, and I gazed after them, feeling equally free.

Happy to see Julian already dusting the roots with fertilizer and next to him a bucket of powder waiting for me, I cut a pleading glance at Marie. "See you later?"

Her arm released me. "Off you go, *chérie*."

Untied boots pounded on the pebbled ground as I jogged down the path. My grin wouldn't stay hidden behind tight lips. Another day of hard work lay before me. But I didn't care. Not with this gorgeous and mysterious man by my side.

Bloody feathers

On Thursday, not a single cloud spoiled the metallic blue sky stretching as far as the eye could see. As the hours ticked away, the heat became more intense, and by late afternoon, sweat beaded on my forehead. Trudging behind Albert through the wide-open field, I mopped my face with the hem of my green and gray checkered shirt, while my uncle explained more about viniculture. I found it hard to concentrate, because my gaze kept drifting over to Julian in the distance.

Since last night, something had changed in his look. His brows pulled together, he had seemed to be chewing on a hard nut all day. But each time I'd asked what vexed him, he only shrugged and changed the subject.

Maybe for the best. A mist of uncertainty crept over me at the thought of how last night had changed *my* view of him. How the sweet moments together amplified my attraction to this man.

"Jona, are you listening?"

The French lilt of my uncle's voice tore my gaze away from Julian, and I blinked against the sun. "Sorry, what did you say?" In fact, I hadn't heard a word since he'd told me to listen carefully, for this was important.

Albert bestowed me with a sympathetic glance. "We better call it a day. It has been long enough for all of us, and I am sure your aunt has our dinner on the table."

I gladly followed him to the house after giving Julian a sign with a flick of my head to indicate work was done for today. A single slight nod was his response.

Since I was the first to come into the kitchen after scrubbing the dirt off my hands, I met Marie alone. The pork filets and vegetables added a spicy smell to the air.

"Albert said you struggled to pay attention to him in the afternoon because you were distracted…with Julian," Marie whispered behind me.

I gulped. "Did he?" My burning face was something I did not want her to see.

"I noticed it too this morning. You could hardly take your eyes off him." Her warm fingers hooked my hair behind my ear. "But he couldn't either. Is there something happening between the two of you?" Her green eyes glowed.

I choked on embarrassment. "No! Absolutely not."

The corners of her mouth pointed down, and she still couldn't ban the prodding tone from her voice. "Oh, that is a shame. You would make such a lovely couple."

The memory of me lying in his arms last night flashed before me, heating not only my face, but my entire body.

"Who would?" Julian's innocent question slammed into my back like a high-speed train.

I shot around and met his curious gaze. "No one would," I snapped. With the rest of the food in my hands, I wiggled past Marie and started to dish it out.

And what kind of silly idea was this anyway? Marie had obviously gone crazy. *Me and Julian? Hah.* I didn't need someone to fall in love with, just to be left alone again in the end.

Damn. I grimaced. *Did I just think about love?*

The dragon was hooked to Julian's arm and gave me a hard stare as he led her to the table. Yeah, and then there was her. My mother didn't approve of any of it. She'd made that clear last weekend when I had overheard her in the parlor.

Was she plagued by jealousy or simply the coldest person in the world?

That evening, I ate my meal in silence, my gaze primarily fixed on my plate. I killed off Julian's attempts to involve me in the conversation with a shrug or by stuffing more food into my mouth.

Marie's disappointed frown didn't escape me. Neither did my mother's stares. I only wished she would keep the painful expression from her face when gazing at me. After all, it wasn't *me* who'd hurt *her*, goddammit.

Ready for a reprieve, I was the first to leave the table. I stumped upstairs to take a relaxing shower. Marie's words about Julian and me still gnawed at me, and the picture of him nearly kissing me pushed to the front of my mind.

With it rose the question of what we would be now if he had

gone through with the kiss. Even that single slight brush of his mouth against mine had left my lips burning for his touch.

Water sprinkled my face. I rubbed my hands over my cheeks then slammed my fist on the faucet to cut off the spray.

Don't let him get under your skin. He'll only hurt you.

My crunched face reflected in the stainless steel of the faucet. I moaned, tipping backward, the tiles of the wall behind me cooling my skin.

Never before had I craved anyone's kiss—and then so badly. Damn him for turning me into a weak sissy. From the hanger next to the shower I snatched a towel and wrapped it around my dripping body. Wet spots on the floor dotted my trail out of the bathroom.

Maybe it was time to leave.

But, for the life of me, I couldn't get myself to pack. Too long I'd stayed in the land of plenty. The taste of it pulled me under like a vortex. I craved more.

Movement on the balcony set my belly flutter. I only had to step out and I would get what I wanted. But no. I forced myself to stay calm and slipped into a t-shirt and pants. Tonight, I wouldn't meet him outside. I couldn't risk running heedlessly into perdition.

Set with a copy of *The Lord of the Rings*, the first in the line of books on the shelf, I slumped into bed. The slatted frame squealed with the same frustration I felt. My head sank deep into the feathers. I made an effort to puff up the pillow around my ears, so the outside sounds wouldn't tempt me.

The opening of the novel kept me distracted well enough, but soon I passed out with my thumb between the pages, lost in the high and mystic mountains surrounding the Shire.

*

Not much happened on Friday and the minutes stretched like hours. Julian spent more time inside with my mother than outside helping us, and Marie drove Valentine to town for some shopping. Apparently, a small celebration would take place on the weekend, and they expected a few guests.

"Nothing special," Julian told me in the morning after they had left. "They do this every few months or so. A few of their friends get together and have a nice evening of dancing, eating, and sampling the wine they produced the previous year."

"When will the party take place?" My innocence covered my immediate scheming to escape attending.

"Tomorrow."

"Oh, so soon." But there was still time to come down with a headache by Saturday afternoon. I was certainly not attending a party where everyone would gawk at me—the recovered daughter from England. They would have to find some other party gossip.

"Yeah, but as I said, it's nothing big, so don't worry." He gave me a smile that stopped before it reached his eyes. And then he was gone. Without another word, Julian trudged back to the house, staying inside longer than usual.

Okay. Be gone. I don't care.

And I certainly wouldn't worry about the party. Didn't I feel a slight pressure in my forehead already? I sneered at the shrub to my right, caressing its fine leaves with dirty fingers, and said, "After all, I came here to work not celebrate, didn't I?"

In the evening, Albert startled me after dinner when he planted his big hand on my shoulder to stop me from retreating to my room too early.

"Are you not forgetting something?"

"What? No." With a peek around him, I checked whether I'd left a plate or a glass behind when I cleared the table. "Everything's in the dish washer."

A smirk deepened the laugh lines around his mouth. "Not the dishes, child. It is Friday, or payday for you."

He held two crisp green one-hundred-euro bills out to me. Heart pounding, I shook with excitement. Very slowly, my hand moved forward.

Suddenly, I felt a pinch on both sides of my waist and jumped with a shriek.

"It's just money, Jona." Julian laughed behind me. "It doesn't bite."

"But *I* might, if you do that again!" My scowl was meant to keep him off but it had no effect. The glint in his eyes indicated he was up to no good.

"What? You mean this?" He pinched me again, and I scrambled out of his reach.

"You're dead, boy!"

He only had a second to dash out of the kitchen and for his life before I started after him.

Bells of his laughter echoed through the entire house as he raced upstairs. "If you want to get me, you've to cross the balcony."

Taking the steps by twos, I darted after him. But he beat me to his room and slammed the door shut. I skittered to a halt, crashing into solid wood. Lips pressed together, I pounded a flat hand to the door. "You'll have to come out eventually. And then I'll get you."

"My balcony doors are always open." Muffled chuckles sounded from the other side. All right, he didn't take me serious.

The door rattled under my kick. I wouldn't give him the satisfaction and venture out on the porch again. No, I strode to my room and slumped into bed. Lying there for a quarter of an hour and counting the knotholes on the ceiling calmed me. Until I remembered that Albert still had my money.

"Crap." Shoving my boots aside, I walked down the stairs barefoot.

Voices drifted from the kitchen, Julian's among them. The perfect moment to get my revenge. Sneaking closer, I stopped in the shadows of the hallway.

"But don't you think it is mean to leave her unknowing?" my aunt said. Her concerned voice came from the direction of the table.

"You won't tell her." I took a slight jump back when I realized Julian was standing close to the door. Though his command sounded polite, friendly even, there was no mistaking he meant what he said. And if he'd asked this of me, I would have obeyed without further thought.

But what wasn't Marie supposed to tell? And to whom? The thought of revenge dropped from my mind. Stepping into the kitchen, I spoke in the most inconspicuous tone. "Are you talking about Charlene?"

Julian shot me a sharp glance. His knuckles turned white while he gripped the door handle, and a deep crease formed between his brows.

Shit. Could they have been talking about me?

Marie rose from her seat. Too quickly. "Good you came down. You forgot your money." She retrieved the bills from a drawer, which she slammed shut with a light bump of her hip. Her thumb smoothed over my cheek. "Now hurry to put the money away. It is quite a lot, and you better not carry this amount around in your pocket all day."

I nodded. "Thanks." But why would she want me out of the

kitchen so fast? This was totally not like her. Then again, who cared? I held two hundred euro in my hand! Turning to Julian, I flashed a grin. "See you upstairs?"

"Later. I promised your mother I'd take a walk with her through the vines." His mouth shifted funnily to one side. "But you could join us."

Bellowing a laugh, I put a distancing step between Julian and me. "Forget it."

He could act like her long lost son all he wanted, but he'd never succeed in reuniting the dragon and me. Disappointment stung my insides as I spun on my heel and headed upstairs.

I pulled the euro notes from my pocket. Shit, where could I hide the money? A book didn't seem the right place, too risky. Maybe somewhere in the bathroom? But there were only shelves and no drawers. Finally, I found the perfect place in my wardrobe underneath the pile of multicolored t-shirts. Content with my slyness, I rubbed my hands together. Not long before the bills would double in there.

Back leaning against the frame of the French door, my gaze traveled out to the vineyard. My mother's weak voice drifted to me from the garden and sent a shiver of aversion from my neck down to my toes. So they'd started their stroll, and I was left alone in my room. Julian should have asked *me* to join him and not the dragon.

Standing on tiptoes, I tried to catch a glimpse of them as they ambled out to the field. A scrape on my bedroom door drew my attention, but after a quick glance at the entrance, I peered outside again. The scraping became more insistent, and a dog's whine drifted through the slit under the door.

"All right, Lou-Lou!" My initial fear of her under control, I threw my hands in the air and crossed the floor to let her in. She'd never been up here in all the time that I'd occupied this room. Strange that she started visiting me now.

I pulled the door open. With the first glimpse of her blood-smeared muzzle and the thing hanging from it, I shrieked like hell itself had opened to swallow me.

The killer gaze from the dog's beastly eyes started an avalanche of horror-shivers raking over my body. With my hands pressed to my cheeks, I retreated into the room. The earsplitting screams continued to bounce off the walls.

Flap. Flap. A rumbling behind me. And then a pair of strong arms pulled me into a protective hold.

Julian must have come in over the balcony. He held me like he feared for my life. In his embrace, I turned to bury my face in his shoulder. A soothing wave carried me along, while his soft fingers brushed through my hair.

"What happened?" His chin rubbed against the side of my head as he spoke with insistence.

I pointed a hand at Lou-Lou. "She killed someone."

Julian gripped both my shoulders and shoved me away from him to look at my face. "What?" Shifting his glance past me, he seemed to notice the dog for the first time. "Oh, no."

He let go of me to kneel down. Lou-Lou sat still in front of him like she was waiting for the turmoil to cease so she could proudly present her catch. *A duck.* Julian took the slain fowl from her to cradle its lifeless body in his arms. Satisfied smacks drifted into the room as Lou-Lou licked the blood from her muzzle.

Tears of shock and also compassion for the dead duck blurred my vision. Through my misty eyes, I vaguely made out how Julian stroked the duck's feathers. Head dipped, he regarded the animal in his arm and walked past me toward the balcony. A torn sound came from the bundle he carried hidden from my view.

A quack?

No, couldn't be. The duck was dead.

The atmosphere in the room suddenly took on a sparkling charge that gently rubbed against my skin. Like a tub filled with cotton, the air bathed me in a feeling most similar to relief.

Frozen, I stood in the middle of the room as the quacking grew louder and fevered. Flapping wings and a clacking beak appeared over Julian's shoulder when he stepped out on the balcony. One second later, the duck, above Julian's powerful push, winged skyward.

What in the name of God—He had just resurrected a duck.

Like he'd done with my mother when he didn't know I was watching.

Disbelief choked me. Mouth dry, I struggled to put this puzzle together. But I was numb from shock, and nothing made sense. On wobbly knees, I stepped forward, gripped the backrest of my chair for support, and put it as a barrier between us as Julian returned.

"What did you do to that duck?" I croaked, passing the initial state of hysteria.

He shrugged. "I set it free."

"It was dead." I forced the words out, but they were barely audible.

"No, it wasn't." Intending to place a calming hand on my shoulder, he stepped around the chair. The casters on the wheeled chair squeaked on the floor as I retreated.

"Lou-Lou killed the duck before she brought it upstairs. I saw the blood. Your shirt is stained, and just look at her muzzle." I pointed to the door, and we both switched our gazes to the dog. But her face was clean again, her tongue lolling sideways in a contented way.

"Lou-Lou only shredded the duck...a little. The animal probably passed out from shock."

I inhaled. Deep and slow. "Okay." *Okay.* This might be a plausible explanation for the happy bird gliding into the sky again. Unconscious, all right. And Julian's stroking woke it.

Raised it from the dead. The thought turned my blood cold.

Now get a hold of yourself, he's no voodoo priest, common sense reasoned with me. *You passed out in the dining hall three years ago when Elisabeth Morgan accidentally slammed a door into your face. That's what happens when something gets hit.* Fine.

"Julian, is Jona all right?" My mother's anxious words carried to us from the garden. From the garden...where Julian should be right now.

My heart stopped. From three feet away, Julian stared into my eyes, his expression unreadable. My nails dug into the backrest so hard that I feared I'd rip the fabric.

"What are you doing in here?" Speaking deliberately slowly, I emphasized every single word with horror.

His expression did not change. He just stared at me with intense blue eyes, chin low and lips tight. "I came to your rescue when I heard you scream."

"No. I mean, *how in the world did you get here so fast?*"

Julian waited a second before he answered. "I...rushed."

Rrright. He would never have made it upstairs in less than two seconds. So for a change, he thought he'd jump the fifteen feet to the balcony.

He couldn't be here. And we both knew it.

Just friends

The chair swiveled on its casters between the two of us. I tried to stay steady, my shaky hands clutching the backrest. Silence hung in the room like a heavy curtain. Julian's eyes mellowed, his shoulders relaxed. But he still didn't speak. And neither did I.

Lou-Lou barked once then retreated from the doorway. Her large paws thumping as she trotted downstairs was the only sound. She'd left me alone with this mysterious man. I had no idea what to do next.

"You came in over the balcony. Not through that door." I moved my eyes to indicate the door where Lou-Lou was sitting a second ago.

My hands slipped from the backrest as Julian grabbed the chair and rolled it to the side. He approached with palms up, cradled my face, and forced me to meet his gaze. The shock of unexplainable events kept me rooted while I tried to gather my racing thoughts.

"I climbed the twine ladder Marie's plants grow on. Then I hiked over the railing. You scared me like hell. I guess I wasn't paying attention to details."

My breathing softened as I reveled in his touch. His tender hands on my skin swarmed me with ease. Abnormal, euphoric ease. Surreal for this world. Longing succeeded over confusion. I finally gave in as he gently pulled me to his chest.

His sigh brushed the top of my head. "I'm glad you're all right."

"I only hope Lou-Lou restrains herself from bringing me more dead animals." I slid my arms around his waist and let his earthy scent comfort me. The shock of the past five minutes shifted into an amazing state of tranquility.

He let out a soft chuckle. "You know, she brought you her prey to show that she likes you. Natural instinct."

"She scared the shit out of me." With a disbelieving frown, I glanced up at his warm eyes. "So if I ever find a man to love me, he might be bringing dead ducks to my bedroom?"

Julian's laugh conquered the eerily calm room. He ruffled my hair. "Somehow, I can't see that happening."

A cozy feeling spread through me as he fondled the back of my neck with his tender fingers. I wondered if Julian was the kind of man to give presents to show his affection. Definitely not a dead duck. So what—?

A hoodie.

I closed my eyes for a moment, pressing against him a little tighter, and reveled in his embrace. I allowed myself to daydream of him caring for me just a little more than for all the others. But I dismissed the notion with a snort.

After all, this caring stuff I experienced with Aunt Marie had left me messed up and vulnerable. For twelve-plus years, I'd lived in a loveless world and had adapted to it. I had to clear my head and return to that place, where no one could hurt me.

I jerked out of Julian's hold. "Charlene is waiting downstairs. You best hurry to her and go on with your walk." I couldn't keep the disgust and also a hint of jealousy from my low voice.

Gaze hardening, he nodded once. "Right." He kept his eyes focused on the floor as he walked out the door to the hallway this time. The door shut silently behind him.

Tracing my hands over my face where he'd touched me, I tried to recall the sensation of his soft fingers there. What was wrong with this man? And more important, what was he doing to me?

A feeling struck then. *I should be scared of this guy. Majorly so.* Was I the only one to see there was something different about him? And that *something different* was a far cry from the average kind of strange. Like almost paranormal. But something inside me refused to believe any of that shit. After all, my wits were still intact, so I should be able to separate reality from fantasy.

Pinching the bridge of my nose, I still had difficulty accepting his explanations. True, the duck might have not been dead after all. And he could have climbed the twine ladder. Julian wanted me to believe it. Why would he lie?

Slouched forward, I rummaged in the drawer to fish out the list I had started a week ago, titled *Julian's spooky dual life.* Reviving the duck and his jump fifteen feet up to the balcony added two more points to the data sheet. As I stared out of the window, my teeth sank into the top of the pencil and the taste of wood spread in my mouth.

Down in the vineyards, two small figures wandered along the path. My mother had looped her arm around Julian's bent elbow, and he turned his head toward her every now and then.

Damn, I wished I could hear what they were talking about. He seemed to revitalize my mother every day, so she must know about his secret. If there was one, anyway. After all, maybe he just served her stimulant drugs in a drink.

Flipping the pencil through my fingers and dragging a long sigh, I watched as darkness slowly set. This evening, I wouldn't wait for him to visit. The French door creaked on its hinges as I closed and locked it.

When I returned to my desk to hide the list in the drawer again, my gaze caught on my spidery handwriting.

"What's your secret?" My whisper echoed in the empty room.

Ah, bullcrap. I folded the paper and shoved it between the pages of *The Lord of the Rings.* Maybe I had read a bit too much last night, and the images had rubbed off on me.

That night, sleep didn't come fast. The clock's hands had only moved a few minutes each time I checked, and I predicted this was going to be one long night.

Lying on my back, I listened to the shuffling of footsteps on the tiles in the hallway. Julian had returned from his stroll with the dragon. Minutes later, the wood on the balcony floor creaked under his feet. The curtains banned the porch's soft light from my room, but the yearning to see him remained.

Close to climbing out of bed and dressing again, I tucked the blanket under my chin and turned on my side, facing the blank wall. The danger of these longings for him deepening loomed just around the corner. It was far too risky to fall into this particular trap. Hurt enough for a lifetime, I couldn't bear to be pushed away again. If I kept people outside the secure line of my self-protection, they wouldn't be able to hurt me.

In the morning, Julian and I were only going to be what I could afford the most to let happen. *Friends. Nothing more.* My growing fondness for him had to stay locked away in the depths of my heart. But those few precious moments I had spent in his embrace I would cherish forever.

Eyes squeezed shut, I willed the image of his warm smile to stop dancing before me.

When I blinked next, daylight broke through the slits in the curtains. A shiver gripped my entire body as cold enveloped my skin. The covers had slipped to the floor during the night. Dreams of a murderous Lou-Lou coming after me must have caused me to toss and turn.

I opened the balcony door, enjoyed the warm caress of the morning sun on my face and took a deep breath. The smell of Marie's hyacinths and freshly brewed coffee wafted on the breeze.

Ah, precious Saturday. No work for the next forty-eight hours. The muscles in my back would sure appreciate it. With a giant yawn, I stretched my limbs.

"Jona, is that you?" my aunt's voice drifted from the garden.

"Good morning," I said loud enough for her to hear. On my tiptoes, I tried to get a glimpse down, but the best I got was a glance at the entrance to the vineyard.

"Come down, we are having breakfast out here."

My stomach gave a rumble at the thought of toast with jam and orange juice. "Be down in a sec."

After I tucked a pair of shorts over my bottom and pulled the black V-neck tee from Marie's donated pile over my head, I jogged down the stairs and strolled out into the garden. Too warm to wear boots, I went barefoot, and the cool grass tickled my toes.

Everyone had already found a seat around a large table with a glass top where a colorful breakfast was laid out. Albert hurried to fetch another chair and placed it between him and Marie.

I met Julian's gaze and quickly dragged my fingers through my bed hair. Damn, I should have taken the time to run a comb through that mess.

"Good morning," I said again before I lowered into the chair. Steam rose from the pot when Marie poured coffee into my cup.

Julian lounged deep in the wooden lawn chair opposite me, with his fingers laced over his stomach. I raised my hand to give him a special greeting. A set of dimples perfected his smile.

Dear God, why did I lock the door last night?

Next to him sat my mother, but I didn't pay her the tiniest hint of attention. I'd trained myself in ignoring the dragon at mealtimes. It helped a lot that she didn't speak to me. She had stopped that habit when I had refused to eat her stinking cake.

An extra portion of milk and sugar toned down the bitterness of the coffee. I nicked a slice of toast and smeared butter and jam on it. Meanwhile, Marie scooped a spoonful of scrambled eggs from a ceramic bowl and dropped them on my plate.

Returning to her own cup and bun, she said, "Tonight, we will have a handful of guests for a little celebration, *chérie*."

"Yeah, I know. Julian said so yesterday." And I was most sorry that I couldn't attend the festivity, but a throbbing headache would without a doubt come on sometime this afternoon. Suppressing a grin, I bit the corner of the toast.

Julian fixed me with an intruding stare that I could hold no longer than a couple of seconds. He couldn't know what I was thinking, could he?

"Unfortunately, Albert and I are busy with party preparations, so we will not have much time for anything else," Marie explained.

"Can I help you with anything?" I offered.

"No, dear. You have worked enough for this week. You should take a look at the beautiful side of France while you are here."

I got a look at the most beautiful side of France when I glanced across the table.

Julian still held me captive with his gaze. His eyes sparked as though he knew what would come next and just waited patiently for my reaction.

"Luckily, Julian offered to show you around and to"—she paused and pursed her lips—"to entertain you."

Having just sipped from her coffee, my mother sputtered the entire load in a spray of drops over her plate then coughed as if her life had met an early end.

"Good gracious, Charlene!" My aunt clapped a hand to her chest. Then she fetched a napkin and, leaning over the table, wiped up the mess. "Are you feeling all right?"

"And I thought you'd only see that in films." Awash with disgust, I rolled my eyes. Nasty sprinkles of the dragon's spit had landed on my glass. With two fingers, I pushed the juice away from me.

My mother took the napkin out of Marie's hand. "I'm so sorry. Don't know what got into me." Her apology was an embarrassed mumble, matching the flaming red of her cheeks. She cast me a glance around the curtain of her hair, lowered into the chair, and ducked her head from Julian's disapproving look.

When everyone had calmed down, I glanced at my aunt and

Julian in turn. "There's really no need to entertain me. I'm used to spending time by myself."

"You are our guest, Jona. As long as you stay with us, I do not want you to feel bored, or worse, left behind." Marie placed her slim hand on my forearm. "And Julian insisted."

"Did he?" Not breaking gazes with Julian, my mocking grin mirrored his. "How *nice* of him."

He straightened, propped his elbows on the table and folded his arms. The amusement vaporized from his eyes and was replaced by a warm shine. "There's a place I'd like to show you. Marie said we can take her car. Today, I'll take care of you, if you're up for a little fun."

My mother's gaze snapped to her caretaker. The shock in her eyes was hard to miss.

Nonetheless, I ignored her. "We'll drive? Where is this place?"

"It's a surprise." The legs of his chair scraped on the patio as he shoved back and rose to his feet. "So if you're done with your breakfast, get ready and meet me in the garage. Oh, and Jona." He shot me a glance over his shoulder as he already headed to the house. "Bring a towel."

I frowned, totally intrigued now, but he said no more. A glance to my aunt and uncle in turn only got me a tight-lipped shrug from each. I refused to search for answers in my mother's face.

I licked my jam-sticky fingers and rose from the table. "I guess I better not be late then." I could hardly bear the anticipation.

Rushing back to the house, I came past the twine ladder underneath our balcony where Marie's hyacinth beans trailed up. Two fingers placed lightly on the skeleton structure were enough to pull it away from the wall. It confirmed my suspicion. Tacked to the façade, the construction of wood dowels and twine was hardly strong enough to support the growth of climbing plants. Never the weight of a grown man.

Lips pursed, I scratched my head. This was one fine lie he'd told me about the ladder. But one day alone with Julian would provide a lot of opportunities to draw out his secret.

After I retrieved a towel from the rack in my bathroom, I skittered back into my room to comb my hair. With my boots slipped on, I hurried to meet Julian in the garage.

Even before I rounded the corner, I noticed, with disgust, that he wasn't alone. The voice of the dragon carried to me and stopped me in my tracks.

"I really don't think this is a good idea, Julian."

The muscles in my jaw tightened. Had he lured me into a trap?

"But I didn't ask you for your opinion."

Oh boy, Julian's snappy tone had my hair standing on end. But he was out of his mind if he really believed I would go on a family day with Charlene.

Shoulders squared, my boots pounded on the tiles as I strode into the garage. An evil glare narrowed my eyes. "If she's coming with us, I'm cancelling."

Julian gave an exhausted sigh while his eyes rolled skyward. "No, she's not. And no, you don't. Your mother just came to wish you well today." He moved his gaze to her. "Right?"

My mother searched his face, almost pleaded with her eyes, but Julian remained motionless. Then she skirted the SUV's rear and stopped in front of me. "Have a beautiful day, Jona." Even if her saying this was so obviously imposed upon her, the smile she gave me appeared genuine. So much so that I had to fight the impulse to smile back.

Saying nothing, I watched her back as she trudged out of the garage.

"Are you ready?" Julian's enticing voice so close to my ear startled me. My head snapped around. His eyes were inches from mine, and I held my breath as one corner of his mouth twitched sweetly.

I raised the terry cloth. "Here's the towel."

"And I've got the rest." After lifting a picnic basket into the car's boot, he closed the door. "Get in. We've got a bit of a drive before us."

Excitement gripped my heart. I climbed into the passenger's seat. Simultaneously, we slammed our doors shut and fastened our seatbelts, then Julian reversed the SUV out of the garage.

For the first twenty minutes of the drive along paved country roads neither of us spoke. Lost in the romantic landscape, I peeked out through the window. With only little traffic, Julian sped south, concentrating on the highway ahead.

I feared he wouldn't talk to me at all, but he surprised me a little later when he cleared his throat and said my name.

"Hm?" I tilted my head to the left.

"Yesterday, you know, with Lou-Lou, the duck and everything... You seemed terrified for a moment." After the briefest glance at me, he stared in front again. "Did I scare you?"

Oh boy. And I had wondered how I would bring up the topic. All the better if he knew I felt something wasn't right. "You—" But my own sigh cut me off. "No," I finally drawled. "You didn't scare me. But I'll have you know I'm not buying your story with the twine ladder. I examined that thing. A bloody squirrel couldn't make it up there without breaking the wood."

Brows furrowed, his eyes snapped toward me. "You still don't believe me?"

"Shit, no. But I don't know why you're not telling me how you made it up to the balcony. Did you step on Charlene's shoulders?" I cringed at the thought. Under his weight her spine would have snapped just as easily as the wood.

Julian pulled a wry face. "Now you're being ridiculous."

"Then what?" I urged, shifting toward him.

He raised a suggestive brow. "What if I jumped and hung on to the railing?"

"What if you stopped finding excuses?"

"What if I get you some ice cream later and we don't speak of it again?"

"I can't believe you're trying to buy me off." But, damn, ice cream sounded tempting.

Although Julian didn't confess, I felt like I was one step closer to figuring him out. There was only one question burning in my mind now. *Should I be happy about my little victory, or scared as hell?*

He shifted his glance to me and, though his lips were tight, his eyes shone with warmth and care.

No, Julian didn't scare me. He never could.

"You better not forget about the ice cream." And with another sigh, I returned my attention outside, granting him peace for the moment. I glued my face to the passenger's window so he wouldn't notice my grin.

The ride took a little longer than an hour, and with the final miles the landscape changed from rolling hills to flat plains. Fidgeting in my seat, I couldn't wait to find out what kind of place he wanted to show me.

"How long until we get there?" I asked for the thousandth time.

"Be patient."

"Be patient, my arse. Patience is for OAPs. I'm seventeen!"

"You sure? Because right now you're acting like a three-year-old." He laughed.

Minutes later, he pulled the car to a curb and cut the engine.

I turned a beaming face on him. "Are we here now?"

He rolled his eyes. "Yes. Now get out, you little nag."

Surrounded by a line of conifer trees, several cars, and a souvenir shop, it was impossible to tell where he'd brought me. The road we'd come on wound to the right and kept going into the distance. This was an interesting place, peaceful, but strangely isolated.

Hands placed on my waist, I twisted from side to side, getting rid of the stiffness in my back. As soon as a fresh breeze wafted around me, I got lost in an oddly familiar smell. Eyes closed, I took a deep breath of...*Julian.*

The unique cry of a bird echoed in the distance. Even though I'd heard the sound only once in my life, I recognized it immediately and threw Julian an amazed glance across the hood.

Complicated begins now

The shade of the trees dusted my naked arms with goosebumps while Julian unloaded the boot of the SUV. With the basket and two towels in one hand, he offered me the bent elbow of his free arm to hang on. His smooth skin burned under my cold fingers. I couldn't help but skim them in circles over his biceps while we walked down a narrow path covered with small twigs and needles of conifers.

Julian laughed softly. "I probably shouldn't say anything...but this really tickles."

I lowered my flaming face and forced my fingers to lie still over his arm. I uttered an apology and was glad that he didn't pull his arm out of my hold.

During our walk of a few hundred feet, the cry of the birds grew louder, raising a fountain of anticipation in my gut. "Seagulls?" My eyes fixed on the impish smile that hovered at the corners of Julian's mouth.

"I guess this place wouldn't be the same without them," he replied the moment that the line of trees cleared and provided a view of the cliff before us.

It was crazy to ignore my trace of vertigo when I meandered toward the edge. But, shit, I had to take a look down. The marvelous sight of the Mediterranean Sea rolling to the beach eighty feet below caused my heart to stop for a moment.

Julian's tender nudge with his knuckles closed my dropped-open mouth. I turned to him and read the joy at my reaction in his face.

"I'm taking the basket and towels down first, and then I'll come up to help you down the slope. Just wait here," he said.

"Make it fast," I breathed happily, struggling to keep the boiling anticipation under control.

At his reassuring nod, I leaned against the nearest tree and watched him skitter down a gravel path that appeared dangerously steep. But his promise to help me make my way down banned all the expected fear from my chest.

"Ready?" he said, panting, when he came back and held his hand out to me.

To slide my fingers into his stirred a pleasant tremor in my belly. My free hand automatically rubbed over the tingly spot. Julian's warm gaze embraced me as his hand closed securely around mine.

The path being too narrow to let us walk side by side, he had me climb down behind him while he moved backward, facing me.

His left hand stretched forward and I clasped it for support, while he steadied himself on the rocky wall to his right. On a pebbled patch, my boots lost their grip, causing me to slide down as if on rollerblades. But Julian kept his balance as I bounced into him.

"Whoa." The squeal escaped me the third time I rushed down a foot or two and coaxed a low chuckle from my guard in front of me.

"Would you please stop laughing?" I scolded. "Why do we have to take this breakneck path anyway? Aren't there stairs somewhere, or at least a less life-threatening way?"

"There's an easier way to the public beach a couple hundred yards over there." He pointed to the left. "But this place here is...well, hardly anyone comes down here."

Rolling my eyes, I laughed. "I do wonder why that is."

His laugh came closer to my ear this time. He looped his arm around my waist to help me over a few rocks on our way. Scared of a fatal fall to the bottom of the cliff, I tensed, but enjoyed his firm body pressed to my side nonetheless.

He released me as soon as I'd successfully climbed over the difficult passage, but kept a strong hold on my hand. And by *successfully* I mean I only slipped halfway out of my shoe once and didn't break an arm, leg or my precious neck.

"Don't you ever tie your boots? It would help a lot, you know."

"I can't. One of the laces is ragged." I carefully scooted on. "Honestly, how stupid would I look with only one shoe tied?"

"Oh, you mean besides the hole in your jeans and the stained shirts you used to wear?"

Pebbles bounced down the path when I stopped abruptly to scowl at him. But Julian's tantalizing wink didn't fail to curve my lips. Shielding my eyes from the sun with my free hand, I slowly shoved forward until my soles sank securely into the sandy beach next to the basket Julian had brought down before.

A deep, relieved breath filled my head with a scent heavy with warm wind and sea.

So familiar.

My gaze snapped to him. Julian's eyes were closed. He sucked in a breath himself. Why would this man, who smelled like a gorgeous day on the beach, look like he'd just returned home?

His eyes slid open and he cast me a sideways look. "Come on, let's find a place over there."

The towels spread in the shade of two palm trees provided a place for us to sit. Kicking off my boots, I couldn't wait till the soft white sand touched my bare feet.

As I galloped toward the foaming waves, rolling laughter erupted from my chest. The first wave brushing my calves sent me leaping back out of the water. Strong arms wrapped around my waist when I bounced into Julian behind me.

I shuddered. "It's arse-cold."

"Once you get used to it, the cold isn't all that bad." He grabbed my hand. My hair danced in the wind as he pirouetted me in the sand like a ballerina. "Want to go for a walk?"

"Mm-hm."

Julian led the way. He was right about the cold water. My toes sinking into the soaking sand at each step created the illusion of walking on clouds. The seagulls above performed a concert of cries to accompany our stroll.

Drops of saltwater glinted in the sun as I shoved my feet against the oncoming waves. Julian flinched next to me as an unanticipated wave soaked into the hem of his knee-length shorts.

"It is cold, all right," he said through clenched teeth.

It didn't stop me from splashing water all around me. "These little sprinkles wouldn't hurt a tough guy like you, would they?" Scooping water in my cupped hands, I doused his entire front.

A menacing growl rumbled in his chest. It might have scared me, if his warm eyes hadn't raked me with something different than anger.

Mischief.

Uh-oh.

With one swift tug, he pulled his shirt over his head. Strong pecs twitched underneath his skin as he tossed it to the sand. He granted me a couple seconds to stare at his perfectly shaped body, my mouth watering for a feel of it. Then he charged toward me with a grin that meant no good and swept me up in his arms.

My girlish squeal and his cheerful laughter mixed in the soft wind.

With my hands in a death-grip at the back of his neck, he tromped farther into the sea. I pressed against him, dreading the moment he would let go and I'd drop into the cold water.

"Don't you dare!" I held on even tighter. A wave brushed my bum and drenched my shorts. "I have no change of clothes!"

"Then you better pray these aren't made of sugar," he chided and lowered me farther into the cold sea.

Chills ran wreaked havoc all over my body, and not only as a result of being dipped. His arms around me and his hands in places where he'd never touched me before ignited an unfamiliar heat in spite of the cold soaking through my clothes.

"You're dead, Julian!" The sound of the wild ocean muffled my cry. "My arse is totally wet. Now let me go, goddammit."

I regretted my words the moment I'd spoken them.

He grinned. "As you wish."

A wave swallowed me whole a second later.

Me and my bloody mouth.

Fighting to get on my feet again in the twirling water, I sputtered and wheezed as I broke through the surface. I rubbed the water from my face and caught a glimpse of Julian wading back to the shore, casting me a grin over his shoulder.

I shoved my soaked bangs from my forehead and laughed. "You just wait till I get you!"

Crystal clear water tempted me to stop on my way back and bend to retrieve one half of a shell from the sandy bed. Sunlight glistened inside it, playing out all the colors of the rainbow. Frozen, I ran my fingertip over the smooth texture, feeling every rise and fall of the beautiful shape.

Julian, who had already stepped out of the water, bent to pick up his shirt and returned to our makeshift oasis under the palms. Parallel to the shore, I strolled through the knee-deep water, collecting more of pretty shells in various shapes on the way.

Some looked like the wings of a butterfly, others resembled circular pyramids. Totally absorbed in the amusement, I waded up and down this private little piece of heaven while the sun dried my t-shirt and warmed my back.

In one sea shell that appeared amazingly similar to a cone, I even found an inhabitant. But as the small crab stuck its head out of the opening, I dropped the piece with a low shriek and it plummeted back into the ocean. An oncoming wave washed a layer of sand over it.

The bright white reflection of light on the surface hurt my eyes after a while. I peeked upward with my hand shading my face and found the sun had already moved a good deal across the sky. It had to be the middle of the afternoon.

Julian still rested in the shade with his back against the tree.

The sight of him sent little snakes of tickles down my arms and into my belly.

His left arm propped on his bent knee, he watched me.

Out of the water, I loped to him, more sand pasting onto my wet feet with every stride. Julian's eyes followed my moves as I drew nearer, but it was as if he didn't see me all. Like he gazed right through me.

Or rather, *into* me.

He appeared lost in thought. I'd have given an entire day of my life to get a sneak peek at those thoughts. It made me slow my pace and approach him with my head angled. In front of him, I dropped to my knees and sat on my heels with my hands braced on my thighs as I studied his face. "What's on your mind?"

His eyes twitched, and I knew now he'd gotten the first real glimpse of me. He caressed my cheek. "You," he breathed.

That one word blasted my mind blank. His fingers cupped my neck, his thumb brushing along my jaw. I swallowed against a dry throat. Staring deep into my eyes, he gave me a moment to recap the situation and make a decision. Pull back from his hold or face what would follow.

I didn't budge.

And then the world slowed down. Julian pulled me gently closer, my breath speeding up with anticipation.

Guided by his hold on my neck, my eyes fluttered shut, and I savored the moment with all my senses. As his mouth pressed against mine, it felt soft like cotton. A rush of ecstatic explosions inside me kept my skin tingling.

Bracing my hands on the sand, I leaned in without resistance. Julian angled his head, captured my lips time and again with feather soft kisses. His tongue delved into my mouth to start a playful game, while his fingers curled tenderly in my hair. Long, even breaths through his nose brushed my skin.

The rush of the waves toward the shore seemed to have eased into an unhurried stroll, the cry of the seagulls appeared uncommonly long and far away. Even the wind took it down a gear and tenderly caressed my skin. Time was not the same anymore.

I drowned in Julian's kiss.

When he gave my bottom lip a soft nip and eased the passion, I took the chance to draw back an inch and study his face. "What, does this mean we're past *complicated* now?"

"*Complicated...*" He paused to skim his fingers over my cheek. "Begins now."

I didn't understand the sadness in his eyes when he regarded me. But before I could ask what he'd meant, he delivered another tender kiss.

Then he took both my hands into his and looped my arms around myself so that I would twist and rest against his chest with my back, both our arms folded over my stomach. He held me so tight, I got the impression he feared someone or something was going to rip me out of his embrace any moment.

"I'm not running away. You can ease the grip," I teased him over my shoulder.

His dark sigh at my neck hurt my soul for no obvious reason. Nuzzling my temple, he spoke softly into my ear. "You promise?"

Yes, I do.

No place in the world could have lured me away from Julian. For the first time since I'd come to France and my aunt's house, I knew with an overwhelming clarity that I wanted to stay until the end.

The following four weeks I would enjoy living one room away

from him, spending as much time with him as possible. I could, hands down, no longer fight the feeling, and denying it only made me long for him more.

Even after my nod, it took another heartbeat until he relaxed. Our fingers laced, I gazed over the swaying sea. I should have gone rigid in his arms. Paralyzed with the excitement of finally being so close, so intimate with him. But I didn't. Nothing of the kind at all.

Calmness seeped into me through Julian's tender hug. Thinking of nothing but the beauty of this moment, I dipped my head to his shoulder and enjoyed his breaths brushing the hair on my forehead.

Julian protested when I slid my fingers out of his. But when I started exploring his hand, the tension in his wrist eased. Running my fingertips in circles, I felt every bit of his soft palm, stroked his slender fingers, bent and unrolled them in a tender game.

My palm pressed against Julian's, his fingers overlapped mine by an inch. There was something in them I couldn't grasp. My fingers tickled in his cupped hand like they were pleasantly electrified. Stimulated.

"I like your hands," I whispered.

"I noticed that." The tip of his nose caressed the side of my face. His breath tingled on the soft spot behind my ear where it ignited a spiral of shivers up and down my neck.

Threatening to get lost in this stunning sensation, I fought to stay focused. "They feel like they're charged, or loaded."

"Loaded?" Julian pressed a mellow kiss to my jawbone while he cupped my other cheek with his free hand. His fingers skimmed along the side of my throat. "With what?"

Energy.

"I don't know," I lied, since it felt insane to tell him. Instead, I surrendered to his touch. Butterflies took a ride on a roller coaster in my stomach at his continued stroking.

With his thumb under my jaw and his fingers splayed over my cheek, he tilted my head toward him. The flames of a sensual hunger licked at my skin through the depths of his demanding eyes.

Julian brought his mouth over mine to still this longing. The tip of his tongue traced my lips.

I half twisted in his arms and braced myself against his naked chest. The warmth of his skin seeping through my palms caused me to curl my fingers and skim my nails gently over his twitching pecs. He hugged me tighter, deepening the kiss.

The racing sensations in my chest barely gave me a chance to breathe. Carried away on a ship of affection, it felt as if I had melted into Julian—body and mind.

A hot, wet trail remained on my lips when he drew back. It took a couple of seconds until my eyes would open again. His crooked smile, which I deemed my favorite, adorned his face.

"You look like you're enjoying this," he teased and brushed a wisp of hair behind my ear.

He had no idea just how much.

"Kiss me again," I said dreamily, already dipping forward to catch his lips once more.

This time he took my mouth like a scoundrel, his hands stroking down my shoulders and arms. When he grabbed my middle and pulled me on top of him, I straddled his hips. My shirt no longer a barrier between his fingers and my skin, he caressed my back, my sides, the small crook right above my bottom. The roughish game of his tongue coaxed a moan from me, but he stilled it with his mouth.

His grip settled on my waist, tightening. "Jona, you need to get—" He got no chance to finish, not when I silenced him with a fierce kiss, dying for more of this sweet taste of him. I didn't know what it was about him, what drew me in so vehemently, but it felt like only through kissing him, I could get a taste of the stars in a beautiful midsummer night. Julian became my drug, and I his addict.

I reveled in his touch and scent. Although he gently shoved against my hips, trying to move me away from him, he met each of my claiming kisses.

"Could you sto—? Ah, please!" His croak sounded desperate, but I wouldn't hear him out.

The kiss broke, his abs twitched, and suddenly I was trapped underneath him. He'd rolled us both over so fast that I hardly had time to close my mouth before my back hit the sand.

Breathing hard, he staked me with a stare of relish from only a few inches above. "We really need to stop this before I do something—*stupid*."

Hands still resting on his chest, I rolled my head slightly to the side, gazing at him from the corner of my eye. "And that would make things more complicated."

The tip of Julian's nose nudged mine, then he planted a tender kiss to my neck. "Unspeakably so."

A call from the police

The midsummer wind rustled the palm leaves over my head, the warm air carried a note of sea and sand. I lay on my back and sighed, because Julian had left me alone.

The sensational tingle inside me took a while to cease, but finally my breaths calmed, and I got on my feet, dusting sand off my butt.

His hands tucked into his pockets, Julian gazed at the sea, seemingly lost in his thoughts. My feet sank into the soft sand as I ambled toward him. But I stopped a few steps behind, somehow not daring to interrupt him.

"Do you miss London?" he asked after a long moment, without breaking his gaze on the horizon. The light wind played with his hair.

Putting a reluctant foot in front, I closed the distance between us. "Right now? Not one bit." And with all of today's perfection, why would I? I was away from my mother's prying, with the loveliest man in the world, who'd kissed me amidst scenery that caused my heart to soar.

Bliss enclosed me in a bubble.

"Do you think you'll ever forgive your mother?"

Strange, why would he bring this up right now? But for once it seemed okay to speak about Charlene. "Honestly, I don't see it happening."

I traced the flight path of a seagull with my eyes, surprised how calm and disengaged I sounded. The usual anger when I thought or spoke of my mother had left me. "There is so much I don't understand about Charlene. She hurt me a great deal and she never cared what became of me. How could I ever get over something like that?"

The cold waves hardly brushed his toes when they crushed on the shore, yet a thin coating of gooseflesh covered his back. Skimming my fingers over his arm, I circled him. He kept staring out at the sea.

"Would you want me to forgive her?" Not that it mattered, because I never would, but his thoughts on the subject interested me.

His gaze moved to meet mine. "In moments like this one, I hope you never do." Deep affection laced his tone—and a hint of something else. A sorrow that made my throat burn and my body ache to hold him.

But his words were the last thing I'd expected. "I don't

understand."

He tucked my sun-dried locks behind my ear and cupped my cheek. "And you don't have to."

"But why—"

His thumb brushed across my bottom lip, cutting off my words. Julian shook his head slightly. He reached for my hand, placed it into the crook of his bent elbow, and walked me back to our picnic oasis. "Time to grab some food or we'll be taking the full basket back home with us."

It irritated me how he left me burning with intrigue, but my stomach also growled with hunger, so for once, I wasn't going to contradict him.

In the car on the way back, we hardly spoke, but once or twice Julian reached over to lace his fingers with mine for a while, until he needed to shift gears. I studied the fine features of his solemn face as he drove.

The corner of his lips tugged up. "Are you watching me?"

"Mm-hm. Do you mind?"

His sweet laughter made my heart jolt. "Not if you like what you see."

"I do."

"Then you're allowed to keep watching."

But somehow watching wasn't enough anymore. A longing to kiss him again gripped me, to feel his protective arms wrapped around me. That would be a better way to end our beautiful day together than to attend my aunt and uncle's party in the evening. *Come to think of it...*

"I think I'm getting a headache."

Julian glanced at me sideways. Playing my role perfectly, I rubbed my temples and pulled my brows deep into my eyes.

"If this is your attempt to wiggle out of attending the party, let me tell you, it's not working."

I dropped my hands from my forehead and straightened in the seat. "How do you do that?"

His grin grew wider. "Do what?"

"How do you snoop around my thoughts?" This was hardly the first time he'd read my mind, and it made me feel more than just uncomfortable. I felt exposed.

"I'm not snooping. You're just a lousy actor." Something in his calm voice told me he wasn't speaking the entire truth. "I think you'll have fun at the party if you just allow yourself to be happy."

"What's that supposed to mean?"

"That you shouldn't decide you won't have a good time before you give it a try. I've gotten to know you quite a bit the last couple weeks, Jona. And I can tell when you flip the switch inside your head that turns off the fun factor just because of your mother."

"That is not true!" I folded my arms over my stomach. And how in the world could he have figured me out so quickly?

"Is it not?" Mockery gleamed from his eyes as he glanced my way. "Then why would you pretend to have a headache and stay in your room, when you could spend the evening dancing with me?" He smiled my favorite lopsided smile.

That smile should be illegal. I threatened to melt next to him.

"I don't dance," I muttered, although I yearned to be held by him again. Dancing seemed the best possibility to reach that goal.

"Why not?"

Because I don't know how. "Because I don't like it."

"When have you ever been dancing?"

"Never." I puckered my lips and focused on my knees, which swayed slightly to the left as the car turned.

"See, you're flipping the switch off again." He grabbed my hand once more. This time he didn't release me when he shifted into a higher gear and sped along the road. His fingers dug into the back of my hand with his squeeze. "Would you consider granting me one dance if I said please?" He waggled his brows and made me laugh.

I swatted his shoulder. "Fine, I'm considering. Now leave me alone."

Julian nodded, satisfied.

He parked Marie's car in the garage, then unloaded the boot with the empty basket and the sandy, damp towels. When he reached for my hand next, I was reluctant to take his.

He angled his head. "What's wrong?"

I sucked in a long breath and released it slowly. "Nothing. I just don't want them to see—to know we're—you know."

Julian arched one brow and studied me. "And by *them* you mean—"

"The dragon." I harrumphed. She didn't approve of Julian and me getting closer, I knew that much. Probably because she still wanted him to herself and hated me like hell.

"I overheard you talking. Twice." When the scolding I expected from him didn't come, I continued. "I didn't mean to. But it was clear you were talking about me, so I couldn't just walk away. And I know what Charlene thinks of you looking at me."

His gaze lowered to the basket in his hand. "You heard that, did you?" He sounded more sorry than mad.

I nodded. "She doesn't like it."

His gaze met mine, his lips tightening. "Would you believe me if I told you she doesn't like it for a totally different reason than what you think?"

"I might if you explained," I suggested.

"I cannot explain."

Oh, why wasn't I surprised?

"Julian, you're one serious riddle to me. For now, I just want to act normal around them. Besides, I don't feel like answering my aunt's hopeful questions about whether we're getting together. Or listen to her romanticize how you and I would be such a lovely couple." I rolled my eyes.

Realization flashed in his eyes. "She was talking about us the other day?"

"I'm afraid so."

"Afraid?" His forehead creased. "So you don't want us to be—"

"A couple?" I cut him off. "God no!" The hurt shining in his eyes made me pause. "I don't think it's a good idea. I hardly know you. And you're linked to Charlene. And—and this is really not the right place to discuss it."

Especially not when a twinge of fear was spreading in my chest. Rubbing my throbbing temples, I whirled around and strode toward the door.

A couple—how could he even think that? Just because he kissed me? *And oh boy, he could kiss.* Butterflies still drifted in my stomach at the mere thought of it.

But that was no reason for a relationship. I wouldn't let Julian bind me to him. I was free, no ties to anyone. No *feelings* for anyone. This was the only way to keep safe from getting hurt.

I needed to clear my head and stop thinking about his lips on mine and his arms wrapped around me.

"Jona?"

Julian's soft voice made me stop before I reached for the door handle. I cast a glance over my shoulder.

He circled me to stand face to face then set the basket and the towels down to take my hands in his. "Don't waste a minute in your room, if you can be out here celebrating. Life isn't all that bad if you give it a chance."

"What makes you say that?" My voice almost cracked. I didn't understand the tears misting my eyes all of a sudden.

"Because I care about you. And today I saw how much happiness you're capable of if you allow it to break through your façade." His forehead touched against mine, and he skimmed tender fingers through my hair as he gazed into my eyes. "You withstood all the blasts in your life. I don't see why you refuse to take the chances life's offering now."

The soft scent emanating from him together with his touch soothed me the way it always did. Without my knowing my arms lifted and wrapped around him. I pressed my cheek against his chest. He hugged me tight and placed a soft kiss on my brow.

"I have a surprise for you if you promise me one dance tonight," he whispered.

I looked up at him. "What is it?"

"Uh-uh." He shook his head. "First, you promise."

I pulled back, staring at his face. It was full of anticipation. "Okay, I promise. Now, what's the surprise?"

"You'll find out later." He grabbed my hand, lifted the basket from the ground, and ignored my protest as he pulled me into the house.

Marie peeked out of the kitchen when the door shut. "You are finally back. Good. I just took the cake out of the oven, and the guests should be arriving soon." Her glance dropped to our joined hands. She paused, obviously puzzled. Then suddenly her mouth stretched wide.

I jerked my hand out of Julian's. There was no way I'd give her the chance to make this wrong conclusion in her mind. A hard stare made that point clear.

Marie remained silent while she regarded me with disappointment. Then she sighed and slipped a hand into her pocket. Out came a small yellow note. "There was a call for you today. A police officer."

My mouth dropped open. I twisted my head to catch Julian's narrowed gaze on me.

Lifting both hands as if being arrested, I took a defending step back. "I swear, I didn't do anything wrong! No stealing whatsoever. And how could I, without you noticing, when you've been with me all day?"

"Good point." His expression eased.

My aunt handed me the note. "He said his name was Officer Madison and that you might like to call him back."

"Quinn?" My friend hadn't forgotten about me. "He probably wanted to check on me." I beamed at Julian, who suddenly seemed irritated and shoved his hands into his pockets.

"You can use the phone here if you want to speak to this officer," Marie offered, although she didn't seem to quite understand why I was happy about hearing from the police.

"Yeah, thanks. I just want to shower off the salt and sand, and then I'll call him back."

With Marie gone, I turned to Julian. "You okay?"

He didn't seem angry, but my hearing from Quinn obviously bothered him more than I would have thought. *Jealous of my policeman friend in London?* Quinn was the best friend I could think of, but not once had I felt for him what I felt for Julian.

When Julian heaved a sigh, but remained silent, I rubbed his arm. "Back in London you seemed comfortable with Quinn. I thought you liked him."

"I do." He slowly drew nearer until the tip of his nose almost touched mine. "I just don't like the way you reacted to the news of him calling."

So he was jealous. I couldn't bite down a grin. "We're just friends." I planted a brief kiss on his cheek and rubbed the damp spot with my thumb. "See you later."

He strode toward my mother's room as I leaped up the stairs. With my hand on the rail, I halted and turned. "Julian?"

He pivoted, his brows lifted.

"We're still on for that dance, aren't we?" I suddenly felt anything but confident.

His lips curved, he nodded. My heart did a somersault of relief.

After the shower, I went back down to punch the number from Marie's note into the phone. With the receiver pressed to my ear, I paced the hallway as far as the cord would allow, waiting for Quinn to answer.

"Hello."

My heart lifted, and I drew in a breath to greet my friend.

"You've reached the voice mail of Quinn Madison. Please leave a message after the tone and I'll return your call."

In an instant, my shoulders sagged, my back thumping against the wall behind me. When the long beep rang in my ear, I said, "Hi, Quinn, this is Jona. I heard you called today and I'd have loved to talk to you, but obviously, you have other things—"

A crackling at the other end cut me off. Then Quinn blurted into the speaker. "Hi, Jona! Don't hang up. I'm here."

Cheerful warmth filled me. "Hi, Quinn."

"Hey." He sounded a lot softer and relieved as he drawled the word. "Sorry, I was just coming in. So, how're you doing, kiddo?"

"I'm just fine. Who would have ever believed that?" It was hard to speak normally with the broad smile stretching my mouth.

"I did. So, do you like it over there in France?"

"The house and the vineyards are beautiful. You've really got to see this. I've my own room on the second floor, overlooking the garden and vines. And everyone is really friendly."

"Sounds great. I knew you would get along well with your family."

I peeked around the hallway then lowered my voice. "Well, I do try to evade the dragon, but Aunt Marie and her husband are very nice people."

"That's good to hear. Now tell me, how often do you think of running away?"

"Never!" I said with feigned shock.

Quinn's laugh chimed through the line. "Really? And why don't I believe you?"

I chewed on the inside of my cheek. "Okay, maybe I thought about it once. Or twice. But the situation has changed. If you must know, I think I might even stay until my birthday."

"I hope you will!" His choice of tone made it clear I shouldn't even dare to consider otherwise. "But what's the situation you were talking about? What changed your mind?"

What? Or *who*? Thinking about Julian spilled the pack of butterflies in my gut once again. As if on cue, said man descended the stairs just then, hand sliding along the rail. My heart thudded against the base of my throat.

"To cut a long story short," I said into the phone, "I made a friend here."

"Jules?" A taunting note mixed with Quinn's cheerful tone.

Julian's eyes fixed on mine as he came toward me, his chin

tilted low. He leaned forward and whispered into my free ear. "Your surprise is in your room."

"Yes," I answered Quinn, but my eyes traced Julian walking away to the door. Before he slipped outside, he winked over his shoulder. For a moment, I covered the speaker with my hand, afraid Quinn might hear the hard pounding of my heart through the line.

"I knew you would like him if you gave him a chance," Quinn said. "He seems like a nice boy."

"Yeah. And he's helping me get past my vertigo, which comes in handy considering I do have a balcony attached to my room."

"Wow. You really seem to be living in a palace over there."

"Sometimes it feels like it," I confessed. "There's also a party on tonight, and I'm supposed to dance, can you believe it?" I snickered at the absurdity of the statement, but eagerly anticipated the moment I would be in Julian's arms again.

"I'm sure you'll have fun. I shouldn't keep you talking too long then. But it was very nice to hear from you." He paused. "Work has actually become quiet since my favorite criminal abandoned the country. London's streets aren't the same without you." His soft laugh sounded forced.

I swallowed against a tightening throat. "I miss you, too, Quinn. See you in a few weeks."

"Yeah. Pass my regards on to Jules and your family."

"Will do. And you say hi to Abe when you see him." We both laughed then said goodbye, and I hung up. Talking to Quinn made me a little homesick, but there was a good reason keeping me in this country a few weeks longer.

Julian.

And he'd said there was a surprise waiting for me in my room. I dashed upstairs, almost tripping over the last step. The door gave way to my eager push and slammed into the wall. Stumbling inside, I scanned the desk for a package or something out of place on my bed. There was nothing.

Had he just fooled me? Hands on my hips, I whirled on the spot while my narrowed gaze moved over the room.

And then my breath caught in my throat. I staggered a step backward, knocked against the bed, and slumped down on the mattress.

There, hanging on the outside of my wardrobe, was that blasted red dress.

Traitor

An awkward me stared back from the full-sized mirror looking like a rose from Marie's garden. According to the label on the inside, the bodice and three layers of skirt were Chinese silk. It floated around my knees as I swung my hips from side to side. This had to be the most beautiful piece of cloth in the world.

I couldn't remember what had been on the price tag in the shop, but I assumed Julian had paid a fortune for it. And for just that reason I decided to wear it that night. I didn't want him to think I was disrespectful or ungrateful. But I didn't feel wonderful in this dress.

The guests would all gape at me, and there'd be no way to hide in the shadows like I could have done if I wore my usual dark clothes.

Oh God! A shudder made me hug myself.

A deep breath forced my chin up. I could do this. I'd put on a nice smile and walk out into the garden dressed like a marigold. For Julian. And only for tonight.

A knock sounded on my door, and Marie popped her head inside a moment later. She gasped. "Good Lord, Jona. You look beautiful!" My aunt strode toward me to feel the fragile fabric between her fingers. "Is this not the dress we saw in town?"

"Yes. Julian bought it for me," I said quickly. I hoped she didn't think I'd stolen it from the shop while she was trying on clothes in the changing cubicle. "I guess he wants me to wear it for the party. But I don't feel comfortable in it."

"Oh, that was so nice of him. You absolutely need to wear it, *chérie*. It fits you perfectly."

Strangely enough, it did. He'd picked the right size. The dress hugged my body as though it was custom-made.

"And if it was a present from Julian, he might be very upset if you are not going to wear it."

I sighed. "I guess I have no choice then."

"Now, come quick. Most of the guests have arrived."

I looked out the open window. "They're here already? I don't hear anyone down in the garden."

"Because we decided to celebrate in the vineyard. There is more room for the band and the tables."

"Oh." *A band?* Just for a small get-together with a few friends? I directed a questioning glance at her. But she only waved her hand to hurry me on, so I slipped into my boots.

"Good Lord, no, Jona! You will not wear *those* with this

beautiful dress." Marie's accusing finger pointed at my raggedy Martens.

"I don't have any other shoes. And I can hardly walk barefoot, can I?"

"You wait here. I will be back in one second." As she swirled out of my room, I could only stare after her in wonder. She appeared again with a pair of white sandals clasped to her chest.

She presented them to me. The light in her eyes infected me with her enthusiasm. "Try these."

I took the shoes from her, sat on the edge of my bed, and buckled the straps around my ankles. Taking a few daring steps across the room, I realized they were the perfect size. Their short, broad heel clacked on the parquet, making me feel like I was running down a catwalk.

"Thank you," I said to Marie, who clapped her hands together without taking her eyes off my feet.

She ushered me out of the room and downstairs, where she fetched a cake covered with a plastic container. My ankles wobbled a bit on the stroll across the garden and down the rows of vines.

Some three hundred feet away, where the paths between the yards crossed, a handful of long tables were set up. People gathered in the clearing in the middle. Some were seated, others stood in groups of twos or threes. The sun was setting over the lush vineyards, but lanterns of various shapes and colors bathed the place with soft lights.

As we drew closer, I even made out what Marie had referred to as the band. It was Albert with an accordion strapped to his chest and two other men flanking him. One played the guitar and the other, with long dark hair, held an accordion with buttons instead of keys like a piano. Several couples boogied to their merry song on the square dance floor made of simple wooden boards.

A call from one of the guests nearby stopped Marie and me. We both turned in the direction of a tall man, who carried a toddler on his arm. The little girl wore green flap trousers and fixed me with her round, deep brown eyes. One arm wrapped around the neck of the man who carried her, she twisted a curl of her white-blonde hair around her small finger.

"*Bonsoir, Pasqual,*" my aunt greeted the man, who cast an intrigued glance at me. He only looked away when Marie stood on her toes to kiss him and the girl on their cheeks.

Holding the cake in one hand, Marie shoved me forward with the other. "*C'est ma niece. Jona. Elle est la fille de Charlene.*"

And it had begun already. Even though her words were Greek to me, I was sure I'd be shown around all night as the newly discovered daughter.

"This is my cousin, Pasqual, and his daughter, Claire," she then said to me.

Waving at the child, I gave in to my aunt's push and stepped toward them. "Hi."

Pasqual shook my hand with a firm grip. "*Bonsoir, Jona. Je suis heureux de vous recontrer.*"

Yeah, whatever. I smiled politely but kept my mouth sealed while Marie spoke. An awkward tension gripped me. I scanned the crowd for Julian, hoping I could use him as an excuse to leave Marie's side. Hands laced behind my back, I only tilted my head first, but when I couldn't find him, I pivoted on the spot.

My heart did a somersault as I caught a glimpse of the back of his head. His plain white shirt with short sleeves stood out against Valentine, who had stuffed her round body into a dress as dark as the wine Albert drank at dinner. The dragon was also in their company.

Charlene's astounded face was hilarious as she spotted me over Julian's shoulder. She clapped a hand to her mouth then quickly corrected the awkward move by smoothing the front of the brown blouse tucked into her black jeans. She appeared unusually healthy today, and the sheen of her hair suggested it was freshly dyed a darker shade of copper.

Following my mother's gaze, Julian glanced over his shoulder then back at her. It took him only a fraction of a second to whirl around again. This time, his perplexed gaze lingered on me for an amusingly long time. Not taking his eyes off me, he said something to the two women and strode my way.

With each of his steps, my heart pounded louder in my ears, soon drowning out the cheerful music from the band. I shifted my weight from one foot to the other.

Less than a foot away, Julian stopped and raked a stunned glance over me. From my toes peeping out of Marie's sandals, to the bare neck I presented.

"I was right," he breathed in my ear.

"About what?"

"You look amazing in this dress."

Clearing my throat, I tried to steady my voice before I spoke, not sure what I should be more embarrassed about. Being tucked into this light-beam of a dress, or the lustful glances Julian bestowed upon me while everyone seemed to be watching us. "Thank you for getting it for me, but you really shouldn't—"

"Shh." He held his hand out to me. "Are you ready?"

Before I dared take it, I gave him a wary glance. "What for?"

"Unless I'm totally mistaken, you owe me a dance."

"Ugh. Right." A dance in a dress that was a magnet for stares.

Julian grabbed my hand and pulled me along, pebbles crunching underneath my shoes. A fleeting glance around ascertained that every pair of eyes was set on me, and the guests started whispering.

I could just hear them in my mind: *Oh, look at the English girl.*

Great.

In the middle of the dance floor, Julian stopped and turned. His arms closed around my waist. The very moment his secure hold swallowed me and his sparkling blue eyes gazed into mine, every ounce of unease slid from me. Being in his embrace was like standing in our private little corner of paradise. I closed my eyes, inhaling his fresh, misty scent. The sound of waves rushing toward the shore claimed my memories.

The merry song Albert's band was playing stopped abruptly and turned into a slow, enticing melody. Julian wouldn't let me slip away. He pulled me tighter to his firm chest, swaying me softly to the rhythm.

The skimming of my fingers up his bare biceps left a line of gooseflesh in its trail. My arms sneaked around his neck. I enjoyed his hands tight on the small of my back. The tip of his nose brushed along my cheekbone, then he planted a mellow kiss behind my ear, triggering a fuzzy reaction inside my stomach.

"Everyone's staring at us," I hissed, though not really wanting him to stop.

"You're imagining things. Right now, there's only you and me." He reached for my right hand behind his neck. At his direction, I twirled in front of him and dived back into his embrace.

"Did you finally change your mind?" he said into my ear after another pirouette.

I followed his guide to the left and then two steps to the right with a turn. "What do you mean?"

"About dancing. You said you didn't like it much, but I can't remember you ever smiling so broadly."

"Well, it's not that bad," I said, struggling to keep my happy expression under control even for a second.

He put on a fake frown. "Not *that* bad?" With a swoosh, he waltzed with me then tipped me over backward, his arm always securely placed on my back.

Squealing with laughter, I held tightly on to his neck, so as not to drop to the hard floor. I surrendered. "Okay, okay, it's really nice."

Julian tilted over me, and I gaped into his beautiful blue eyes. He leaned farther down to press his lips on mine. The taste of his last drink lingered in his kiss. Coconut cream. I closed my eyes and kissed him back with the passion that had been rising in me all day.

Close by, the clangor of breaking glass was followed by feminine cursing. I grinned under Julian's lips. "I'll eat my hat if that wasn't my mother dropping her drink."

"Apparently, she has a dramatic streak." Julian chuckled, pulling me to a stand.

"You've chosen an interesting moment to expose *us*. She'll totally freak out."

"No, she won't. Not tonight."

"What's special about tonight?"

But before he could explain, Albert and his friends began strumming a new song behind us, one that was recognizable around the world and made me turn toward the band with confusion.

"Is it your birthday?" I asked Julian, but he said nothing. His hand wrapped tight around mine as he led me up to the longest table, where several people had already taken their seats.

Everyone joined in singing along with the band. Valentine and Henri scooted down the bench to make room for us, while my mother, at Marie's urging, lowered to the chair at the head of the table.

My aunt then rushed to the makeshift bar to retrieve the cake she'd brought. Only now it was lit with a sea of candles. She placed it in front of my mother's beaming face.

Shit.

My stomach slid to my feet. This must be an evil joke. They couldn't possibly have brought me to my mother's birthday party. "Why the hell didn't you tell me?"

Julian placed his hand on my thigh, trying to soothe me. And it almost worked like when he'd touched me before. But this time I wouldn't let it happen. I shoved his hand away.

"It was hard enough to make you agree to come when you didn't know," he said with a stern face. "If you'd suspected it was a party for your mom, you would have never even considered showing up."

"Damn right! And you shouldn't have tricked me into it." *Not today.* Not after the beautiful time we'd had together.

And suddenly, it clicked into place. He'd lured me away from the house so I wouldn't notice them preparing for the celebration. Hadn't I also overheard him forbid Marie and the others to talk to me about it? What a bloody betrayal!

As the birthday song ended, everyone applauded my mother. I folded my arms over my heaving chest.

Marie then insisted on her making a wish. Charlene's glance traveled to me, hope filling her features.

Even though her perfect make-up brought out a beauty I'd long since forgotten about, the evidence of her illness lay just underneath. Her eyes, sunken and troubled, and her cheekbones standing out reminded me of a starving woman. Although tonight, it felt as if she was starving for something other than food. She was starving for forgiveness. I realized then that I had a powerful instrument in my hand. It was like I could play God and decide whether this woman would be happy or suffer from immeasurable pain.

I didn't know what brought this on—spending too much time in Marie's love-filled house, or having found a place in Julian's heart at last—but in that moment, I hated having this power. Over Charlene. Over Marie. Over anyone who tried to get near me. All I wanted was to be left alone. For the first time in a long while, I didn't wish my mother anything bad, precisely. But I was also far from giving her what she wanted.

"I wouldn't waste a wish on that one," I said under my breath as she blew at the candles. It earned me a poke in the ribs from Julian, and I winced.

"Be nice," he said.

Rising from her seat, Charlene drew a deep breath then spoke loud enough for those in the last rows to hear. "Thanks to everyone for coming to celebrate with me tonight!"

Her glance lingered on me. The fact that she spoke in English and not in French, the language of most of the guests, left no room for interpretation. I narrowed my eyes to irritated slits and clamped down on my teeth. However, my rage was directed at someone else tonight.

When Charlene started to cut the cake, I seized the moment and rose from the table.

"Where are you going?" Julian's hand around my wrist caused me to slump back onto the bench.

"A walk. I need some fresh air," I hissed.

"We're outside. Where would you find air fresher than this?"

Leaning in a little closer, our gazes met from only three inches apart. Words came out in a sinister growl. "I'll find a place where I don't have to sit next to a traitor."

I jerked my hand out of his hold and stormed off into a part of the vineyard that wasn't illuminated by all those icky birthday lanterns.

Away from the lights and the crowd, a chill trailed down my arms. Heading for the house, I stumbled along the path between the vines, guided only by a soft beam of moonlight. Julian, calling my name, followed me. The entrance to the garden was still about fifty feet ahead when he caught up, grabbed my hand, and spun me around.

"Don't you dare touch me," I spat at his pleading face. There was no need to pull my hand away. My warning loosened his hold in an instant.

"Jona, please, I'm sor—"

"No! Just *no!* Don't even say it!" I whirled around and took a few steps toward the house with every intention of leaving him in the dark. But anger ate at me. If I didn't vent now, I might very well go break something instead.

The dress swayed ominously around my legs when I spun back toward him. "You betrayed me! How dare you play with my feelings?"

"I didn't mean to betray you. But she is your mother. And it's her birthday. Most likely the last she'll get to celebrate." His tone was so grave, it made my skin rise in goosebumps. "She wanted nothing more than for you to celebrate it with her. I know it's hard for you to forgive her. But you don't want your mother to die with a broken heart, do you?"

Didn't I?

Her hopeful look when she made her wish slammed painfully into my mind. What would it be like to run out of time? To know death was only a heartbeat away and there was no chance of getting your final request fulfilled?

Stop. Thinking. About it.

"Want to know what really hurts me? That you, of all people, lied to me. You could have asked me to join the celebration. Because for you, I think I would have come." I barely managed not to sob. "Now tell me one thing, Julian. Was all the kissing and the trip to the beach just part of your plan to trick me into going to my mother's party?"

A frown formed small lines at the sides of his mouth. "Don't be ridiculous. None of this was part of any plan." He reached for me.

But I jerked back. "I'll tell you what's ridiculous. This goddamn dress is! What were you thinking? That you could wrap me up like a birthday present? If it wasn't for the fact that I have nothing under it, I'd rip it off!" Fingers digging into the fabric of the bodice, I clenched my fists.

His right brow lifted, daring me to proceed. The urge to slap the stupid smirk from his face was hard to resist. I didn't move. Julian came closer and pried my hands loose with gentle fingers.

"This wasn't me wrapping you up as a gift," he said so softly it made my skin tickle like it was brushed with a feather. "I saw you staring at the dress in the shop. The gleam in your eyes. For once, I wanted you to see how lovely you are. Not for your mom, your aunt, me or the guests. But just for your beautiful self."

I forced a swallow through my dry mouth and throat. "I don't know what you saw that day, but I never said I liked this dress. And

I sure didn't think it would make me pretty."

"But you are pretty," he whispered, and at the same instant he pulled me closer to him. "The most beautiful girl I know. And I'm sorry I hurt you by tricking you into coming to the party tonight. But the kiss on the beach had nothing to do with any of this."

My fingers were splayed against his chest, the warmth of his breath caressing my face. I wanted to hold on to Julian, just for a second. To ensure this was not my imagination, that I had actually found someone who saw me for what I really was. He was someone who saw beyond all my sarcasm and knew when I needed a friend. "Then why did you kiss me?"

"Because I'm falling in love with you."

Can I get my list back?

Merry music from the three-man band and the singing of the jolly crowd attending my mother's birthday party drifted to me on the evening breeze. My feet had rooted at the entrance to the vineyards as Julian's words resonated in my mind.

He loved me.

A loud burst of cheer followed by clapping and laughter broke my bubble. At least I hadn't ruined the celebrating mood with my quick departure.

Julian's blue eyes shone in the dark. The sweet words of affection still hung on his lips, and my hands froze on his chest. By his expression I could tell he was waiting on my reply. What would I tell him? That I was falling in love with him too?

"I..." My voice was unrecognizable even to me. I couldn't finish the sentence.

What on earth was happening to me? I hadn't gotten attached to anyone over the past twelve years. *So why now?* It was a miracle even Quinn Madison had become such a close friend, when I had so carefully avoided any kind of relationship with anyone. But my well-built wall of protection had crumbled before Julian within days.

In fact, he'd blasted right through the instant he appeared outside Abe's office to free me from my cuffs. His touch, his look, the way he talked to me—it was all so different from anything I'd ever known.

And yet, I couldn't tell him. I had sworn not to get close to another person ever again, for the day that they shoved me away would inevitably come and the pain would be too much to bear.

My hands slipped from his chest, and I took a reluctant step backward. Emptiness swept through me, made me want to curl up in the grass and hug my knees to my chest, to ease the aching. I needed to get away. Put some distance between the two of us and reconstruct this solid wall of invisible brick around my heart.

I broke into a run. Crossing the last few feet to the house as fast as Marie's sandals allowed, I didn't stop or turn around to Julian's pleadings. Tears spilled from my eyes as the door gave way to my furious push, and I stumbled into my room. A thunder rolled through the empty house as the door slammed shut behind me.

I clamped down on my teeth and wiped the tears from my cheeks. I should have known better than to let my protection slip and to kiss him.

A glimpse of faint light on the vineyard caught my eye over the balcony's railing. I stopped in the frame of the open door, trying to get a clear view of the crowd. Julian must have returned there after I left him standing in the garden. But the celebration was too far away to single him out.

The veil curtains wafted after me as I spun around and stomped through the room in circles. *Damn Julian and my soft spot for him!* I missed life the way it was. The way *I* was—stone-cold and devoid of any feelings.

How could I ever return to my distanced self after the kiss he and I had shared? The taste of coconut still lingered on my tongue, making it easy for me to recall his lips pressed tenderly against mine.

Dragging my clawed fingers through my hair, I yanked on the strands and wished I could tear the memory out of my mind with it. But it wouldn't work. Every detail of his beautiful face drawing nearer, every soft touch of his tongue to mine was forever etched in my memory.

In a rush of frustration, I wiped the entire collection on my desk to the floor. Pens clattered on the parquet, books flapped open. And Julian's weird-things-list slid across the floor.

Kicking *The Lord of the Rings* aside, I bent to pick up the sheet and scanned the bullet points.

- *INFLICTS HAPPINESS BY TOUCH*
- *REVITALIZES THE DRAGON*
- *CAN JUMP 15 FEET HIGH*
- *RESURRECTED DUCK TODAY*

Oh come on, idiot, what kind of fairytale do you live in? All the sweet meddling he did with my mind had turned me into a complete imbecile. And why did I bother to keep records of his weird traits anyway? As if someone would ever believe that a flying healer lived next door to my room.

Angry breaths had my nostrils flaring. I scrunched the paper to the size of a ping-pong ball. "Bullshit!" Frustration powered my thrust as I tossed the ball at the wall over my desk.

Only it didn't fly in the direction I had intended.

"Yikes!" The paper ball shot right through the window and over the balcony. Both hands clapped to my cheeks, I grimaced.

Fantastic. Proof of my insanity had just landed in the middle of the garden.

I dashed out of my room and down the stairs. Aside from little bits of moonlight broken by the maples, the garden appeared as dark as hell's closet. Dew-covered grass, high enough to hide the rumpled paper, brushed my bare feet between the straps of Marie's sandals. Slow steps took me across the lawn. I scanned every bit of the ground in front of me. "Oh please, you bloody little thing, where are you?" I whispered.

"Looking for this?"

My sharp breath hissed through the air. Julian only narrowly avoided giving me a heart attack. I found him sitting in a lawn chair. It was too dark to make out the details of his features, but the sheet in his hands glinted evilly in the night.

Damn! He was supposed to be out in the vineyard celebrating with the others, not giving me a start in the pitch black of night.

I covered my mouth and coughed, glad he wouldn't be able to see my burning face. "This didn't by any chance fly from the balcony?"

"It did, indeed."

Shit. And it was unfolded, so he must have read it, too. Licking my dry lips, I shifted my weight from one foot to the other. "You shouldn't be picking up someone else's thrown away letters. That's impolite."

"It dropped directly into my lap. What does etiquette say about that?" His voice held no definable emotion, which for some reason freaked me out more than if he had vented his anger.

"Can I have it back, please?" My shy request was met with silence.

Julian rose from his chair then slowly walked toward me, his white shirt and blond hair the only parts of him visible in the night. He stopped some three feet away from me, clutching the paper with both hands. His lips curled in a way that made me want to lean forward and kiss him.

"Why do you want it back? Did you find another detail to add to the list?"

I swallowed hard.

"But I must give you credit for your creativity." He spoke very slowly, softly almost, as if my list didn't bother him at all. "*Julian's spooky dual life.* What a fancy title."

Gee, thanks. A hint of sarcasm at least.

"Listen," I croaked, clasping the skirt of my dress with sweaty hands. "This is something private, and I'd really rather have this list"—a cough gave me the chance to correct myself—"*paper* back."

He studied me for an infinite moment and again my lips itched to touch his.

"Jona, when you scribbled down all these things about me, what did you suppose I was? Some kind of sorcerer?"

No. Superman.

"I can't tell." *Yet.* "But there's definitely something wrong with you." This close to him, I could see his brow lift in a startled way, so I quickly added, "You do things to me and to others that seem...impossible."

"Like resurrecting a duck?" To accentuate the point, he flipped the list in his hands, displaying my handwriting.

I stood rigid, the shudder skittering down my spine tormenting me. "You have to admit all of the things listed did happen. You're capable of some special powers, and I don't see why you won't tell me the truth."

I would definitely get a chance to see a padded cell from the inside if I didn't stop this crazy rambling.

"The truth is there's nothing special about me. Why are you making things up?"

"Liar!" The word burst out without me thinking. Proof of his lying rang in his every word, reflected in his clenched jaw, his averted gaze, and in the way he took a small step backward. "It's not like you can fool me with your average clothes and your trying to act normal." I ripped the sheet out of his hands, not caring that it tore at the sides where he clasped it. "I'm not Lois Lane."

He frowned. "Lois who?"

"Never mind. The point is, I figured you out. You may as well tell me everything."

He chuckled, but there was no humor in his laugh. "Did someone spike your drink tonight?"

"*Argh!*" My teeth ground together; I restrained from speaking.

The same man who had claimed he loved me not ten minutes ago didn't trust me enough to let me in on his secret. And this was the most hurtful part of it all. Not the fact that there was actually something weird going on, like supernatural. I could handle that.

"It's late," I said, yearning for a break. "I'm tired, and you should keep Charlene company at the party. We can talk about this tomorrow." When I would be right in my mind again and wouldn't be thinking about kissing him every single moment.

"But there is nothing we need to talk about."

I sighed. "If you say so." I hung my head and returned to my room.

The chaos on the floor next to my desk would have to wait to be tidied. Tonight, a strange mental exhaustion overcame me. I slumped into bed fully dressed and with no thought of tomorrow.

Morning had already stretched into noon when I woke on Sunday.

The blanket was tucked nicely around me and Marie's sandals stood on the floor at the end of my bed. With the balcony door open, I assumed it had been Julian who tucked me in. It was difficult to tell what irritated me more. The fact that he entered my room anytime he wanted, or that he seemed to care for me one moment and then the next, he didn't trust me enough to tell me anything about himself.

After a shower, I dressed in my usual dark clothes. The red dress hung in the wardrobe as a reminder of a promising evening that had turned sour. Marie's sandals dangled from my fingers by the straps as I sauntered downstairs. I followed Marie's soft humming to the front room, where she was cleaning the wide windowpane. At the door, I coughed and she whirled around.

"Thanks for lending me your shoes," I said.

"You are welcome." Marie wrung a pink cloth over a bucket of water, then the glass squeaked as she wiped across it once more. "You can borrow them any time you want. I hope you didn't mind I took them off for you last night."

"You came to my room?"

"I wanted to make sure everything was all right with you, because I did not see you at the party for long. You slept so sound, though, I could not bring myself to wake you." Her concerned face reflected in the shining window. "There is a snack for you in the kitchen, *chérie*. We will be alone at home today, so I will not cook until the evening."

I put the sandals next to her other shoes under the coat rack. The kitchen was empty, but a sandwich sat on a plate next to a glass of orange juice. Taking a bite, I shouted with a mouthful, "Where is everyone?"

"Albert is in the vineyards, and Julian took your mother to the doctor," my aunt's call came from the front room.

Why would Charlene have to see a doctor? Was she getting worse? The expected spitefulness held off. Instead, unease stabbed my chest, accentuated by Julian's words last night. Surely she wasn't dying yet.

Was she?

With a swig of orange juice, I washed down the oppressive feeling in my chest. "Did she take a turn for the worse?" I shouted, cleaning my plate in the sink. Turning around, the sight of Marie leaning in the doorway made me jump. My hand flattened to my chest. "In God's name, you shouldn't sneak up on people like that!"

She studied me with a curious expression. "I do not think it is the cancer that troubles her. She was coughing a lot this morning, so she might have caught a cold last night." She inclined her head. "But I will let her know that you worried about her. It will make her very happy, I believe."

I grimaced. "I'd rather you didn't." It wasn't really a worry anyway, I was just curious. Yes. Curious. Nothing else.

After a moment of staring at each other, Marie took me by the hand and dragged me into the hallway, where she traded her house slippers for a pair of trainers. "Come on, *chérie*. It is time to show you something."

Reluctantly, I followed as she led me outside and down the narrow road. Occasionally, a car passed us, but otherwise the street was deserted.

"Where are we going?"

"You will see. It is not far." Her stern tone indicated it would be no use to ask again until we got there.

And we got there fast. After a five-minute walk we arrived at the local cemetery. Marie and I squeezed between the metal gates that stood ajar, then she led the way through a labyrinth of gravestones in a multitude of shapes.

A chill ran down my spine when I read some of the names craved into the marble blocks. *Isabelle Turmoire* had died last year after a life of only seven years. The blonde girl smiled at me from a picture placed next to the dates.

At the far end of the row, Marie pulled me to a stop in front of a wide double grave. I turned to read the words on the smooth surface of the creamy white marble stone.

Catharine & Joè Montiniere.

And next to a cross stood their date of death. *June 16th 2007.* I remembered Marie saying they had died in a car crash. The stone held no picture of my grandparents, but fresh red roses were neatly arranged in an urn matching the tombstone.

"Did you bring the flowers here earlier?" I whispered, somehow struggling with a dry throat.

"No. Since the day your mother returned to France, she has never let a day pass without visiting this place." Marie's arm sneaked around my shoulders, and she rubbed my upper arm. "Remember I told you she wasn't here when your grandparents died? She never made up with them, but she wishes she had. Every day."

In spite of the sun shining on our backs, a shiver turned my blood cold.

Aunt Marie twisted me toward her and cupped my face. "My

little darling. Soon, this will be the only place where you can talk to your mother. Don't make the same mistake like her. You will be the one living with the pain in the end." There was no anger or accusation. Only a deep sorrow.

Closing my eyes for a brief moment, I could already imagine Charlene's name carved into the stone under the names of her parents. And a little girl, no more than five years old, kneeling by the grave to replace wilted flowers with a fresh bouquet.

My throat constricted. For the first time in years, the part of me yearning for the love of not just any mother, but this particular caring mom I once knew, opened and sucked me into a deep hole of aching. A hole that I'd worked hard to fill up with sarcasm and rage. The pain Marie had released inside me threatened to eat me up.

I jerked out of her hold. "You shouldn't have brought me here!"

"Oh no, *chérie*. Now I see I should have brought you much sooner."

Burnt

Rays of a late afternoon sun reflected in the spotless glass that I'd just finished wiping. The labor had the effect of keeping me from musing over recent events, such as Julian's declaration of love and the visit to the cemetery. And also of those events soon to come.

My mother's death.

When we'd returned from the cemetery, I asked Marie which of the windows in the house she hadn't gotten to yet. Armed with cleanser and bucket, I set on a polishing frenzy. The window above the kitchen sink was the last on my tour from top to bottom.

The biting smell of cleaning solution hung in the room, pinching my nose, while the clinking of pots drifted from behind. At first, I thought Lou-Lou had knocked cooking utensils down to the floor with her tail. But the lazy dog still lay sprawled under the table. She watched me work with her sleepy eyes.

Marie was the one to break my serenity as she crawled into the credenza to retrieve a wide pan and a large pot. After returning the cleaning stuff to the mop closet, I helped peel a hive of potatoes and dropped them into the pot of boiling water. Meanwhile Marie breaded several fish filets for frying.

"You have become very quiet this afternoon," my aunt said, wiping her hands on her apron. "Is everything okay?"

I gave a quick nod, but didn't let her in on my thoughts. While I'd succeeded in keeping my mother out of my mind for most of the afternoon, I wasn't so lucky with Julian. Last night's argument kept haunting me.

He and my mother were gone for too long. No doctor would have such a long wait. It occurred to me that Julian was taking her somewhere else. Maybe to talk. Was he telling her what I'd noticed about him? About the list I wrote?

Irritated that he would put trust into my mother but not me, I washed my hands, slumped into a chair, and stared at Marie's back. "Can I ask you something about Julian?"

Salt shaker in hand, my aunt turned toward me with a grin. "Sure. I heard he kissed you last night."

My temperature rose, especially in my face. "Well, yeah." I wiped my sweating hands on my pants. "How long have you known him?"

"Not too long. He came here with your mother."

I propped my chin on my elbows on the table. "In that time, have you noticed anything unusual about him? Like not-quite-human-ish kind of unusual?"

"Certainly not." Her lips pursed as she came to sit with me. "Why would you ask such a question?"

Because he can resurrect the dead.

I shrugged one shoulder. "He just did a few things that made me wonder. Never mind."

"What is concerning you? I can see you struggle with something."

I chewed on my bottom lip. "Don't you think it strange that he's so close to my mother? It makes me wonder what kind of relationship the two of them have."

"He is her caretaker. As far as I know Julian, he definitely takes his job seriously." Her ever-kind tone proved to me that she wasn't in on Julian's secret, either. She had stomped on my hopes to find out more about him.

I had to find another source of information. "Is there a computer connected to the Internet that I could use?"

"Sure. In Albert's office. Feel free to use it whenever you like."

"Okay, thanks." The chair almost knocked backward as I jumped up and rushed to my uncle's study. It was hard to say how much longer Julian and Charlene would be out, and I wanted to get this done before they returned.

Halfway over the threshold, I skittered to a halt and spun around. "Marie?" I shouted across the hallway.

Her head appeared in the kitchen door across the hall.

"What's Julian's last name?"

Now she emerged fully, crossed her arms over her stomach, and pursed her lips. "How strange. He has been living here for so many weeks, and it never occurred to me to ask for his full name."

Weird.

Scratching her head, she disappeared into the kitchen again.

The smell of aged books whooshed into my face as I entered the office. The narrow room was rimmed with shelves on one side and a small desk at the far end. The window at my back when I sat in the big leather office chair overlooked the garden and reflected on the wide screen of the computer.

Unlike the single, tremendously slow computer we'd had in the orphanage, Albert's only took seconds to boot up. I connected to the web and typed *The Supporters Associates* into the search engine.

Biting my nails helped kill the tension as I scrolled to the bottom of the page with suitable matches. But apart from an advertisement for some social network and some books with either the word *supporters* or *associates* in the title, Google didn't come up with anything related.

While trying to think of another way to search for Julian's employer, I rocked back in the chair, my gaze traveling through the room. Alongside a few pictures of my aunt and uncle with Lou-Lou, two dueling guns hung on the wall. They looked ancient. Pushing up on the armrests, I rose from the chair and stepped closer to let my fingers glide carefully along one of the cold metal shafts.

"Be careful, that one is still loaded."

Spooked at my uncle's deep rumble, I jerked my hand away.

"The one who carried it never got a chance to shoot it. He did not survive *le duel*." Albert chuckled. "Your aunt told me you wanted to use the Internet. Can I help you with anything?"

"No, thanks." With a twinge of shock, I rushed back behind the desk to close the window on the screen before he could catch a glimpse of my research. "I just found"—*Nothing*—"what I needed."

The stubbly skin of his face lay in friendly wrinkles. "I do not mind you using my computer, so you do not have to be shy. Come in whenever you need to look up something."

Nodding, I scurried out of the room and back to the kitchen to see if Marie needed a hand.

A tea towel around the handle, she held the big pot's lid and poked inside the boiling water with a fork. "Can I have you drain these potatoes in a couple of minutes? The colander is in the sink."

A rattle of keys at the front door announced that Julian and my mother were home. A tickle of excitement stirred my stomach. Julian's lips twitched, and our gazes met as he spotted me leaning against the counter. My heart sped up. Even with the frustrating conversation of last night still ringing in my head, I couldn't help but smile back.

I'd missed him all day.

"Wonderful timing," Marie chimed out. "The fish will be ready in a moment."

Charlene glanced at me from the threshold then grimaced at her sister. "Don't be mad, Marie, but I'm not hungry. I'll just take one of these"—she pressed a small white pill out of the packing and grabbed a glass of water—"and then get some rest."

"Oh dear, you do look worse than this morning," Marie replied. "What did the doctor say?"

My mother took a long draught from her glass, so Julian answered instead. "Just a cold. But she's got a light fever. Since the cancer has already weakened her immune system, he ordered plenty of fluids and strict bed rest for the next couple of weeks."

"Shit, that's a long time to be bedridden." The words were out before I could snap my mouth shut.

Everybody turned to me. Biting the inside of my cheek, I hurried to drain the potatoes just to give myself something to do as their surprised gazes made me extremely uncomfortable.

A dishcloth wrapped around each handle of the pot prevented

the hot metal from touching my skin. Unfortunately, the bunches of cloth made it hard to get a good grip. When I lifted the heavy pot from the heat, the left handle slipped out of my hold. In a mad reflex, I pulled the right side higher and the boiling water poured over my left hand.

Everyone froze.

And then all hell broke loose. I screamed my head off. The pot dropped and clattered on the floor tiles sending hot water splashing all around. Frightened by my screaming, my mother and aunt cried in unison. Albert appeared in the door, terrified at what was causing the noise.

Hands touched me. Patted me. I was shoved, pushed, yanked, and dragged. The dog barked, fleeing from the room, knocking Marie over. Someone kicked the pot to the corner.

And then Julian was with me.

Grabbing my shoulders, he shook me once, forcing me to stare into his intense blue eyes. This alone stopped my screams, even with the excruciating pain searing up my arm. Next he closed his fingers gently around my burned hand.

And the pain eased.

My jaw dropped. But he didn't give me a single second to gather myself. Ushering me to the sink, he turned on the tap and held my hand underneath the stream to cool my burn. But it wasn't necessary. The pain had fully vanished, and with the way his fingers were wrapped around mine, the water didn't even touch my skin.

Breathing deep, I kept still in his hold but focused on his tense face. After a long moment, he switched his gaze to me.

"Marie, call an ambulance!" my mother cried.

"No," Julian commanded, without tearing his gaze from my eyes. "I'll drive her."

I sniffed, completely dumbstruck, as he wrapped a clean dishcloth around my hand, probably just to cover up the evidence of healthy which, by now, should have started to blister. I let him proceed and moved toward the door at his firm urging.

Grabbing Marie's car keys, which he'd previously placed on the credenza, Julian wrapped his arm around my middle and made me walk outside at a resolute stride. My head swarming, I had to carefully watch my step as he pushed me along. In the garage, he opened the passenger door, helped me climb into the seat, and leaned over to buckle me in.

Seconds later he pulled the car out. The tires squealed as he sped off toward town.

The spinning of my mind ceased. I gave my hand a test as I clenched it around the dishcloth. Nothing. No pain, no tickle, no soreness. How was this possible? What was there in Julian's touch that made a second-degree burn heal in the blink of an eye? As if it had never happened.

I gave him two minutes—precisely one hundred and twenty flicks of the second hand on my watch—to come up with a reasonable explanation.

But he remained silent.

I removed the cloth and tossed it into his lap. "You can stop now. We both know I don't need to see a doctor."

A couple of heartbeats went by without a change on his face. He just stared out the windshield. Then the car skidded to a halt at the side of the street. Pressed by the seatbelt, all air whizzed from my lungs. When I could breathe again, I waited for his reaction.

And he still said nothing. Gaze focused in front, his knuckles turned white.

"You're going to break the steering wheel." Slowly, I reached out to touch his clamped hand, but he hissed as if in deep pain and jerked it away. So did I.

"Julian, what is going on?" My voice cracked on the last word.

He inhaled deeply, swept his finger and thumb over his eyebrows, then pinched the bridge of his nose. All of a sudden, he yanked the door open and climbed out, faster than I could reach over to stop him.

After a long moment and a deep, encouraging breath, I eased out, too. Julian kept up his angry pacing, up and down the street, kicking at stones in his path.

Something held me back, rooted to the spot. But the moment he pivoted once more and I caught a glimpse of his torn face, I realized it wasn't wrath that drove him wild like this. It was frustration.

He stopped a few feet away from the car.

"Julian, I need to know what's going on."

"Then tell me what you want to hear!" he shouted, rounding toward me.

"The truth, for God's sake!" I yelled back, feeling cornered between the car at my back and his wild face in front of me. "How about your last name, for starters? Or where exactly the agency you apparently work for is located? And then, of course, how the hell you healed my hand?"

He braced himself against the roof of the car, hemming me in between his muscular arms. His head dropped between his shoulders. Silky blond strands fell over his forehead, begging me to run my fingers through them.

My hands fisted at my sides. "Why won't you tell me?"

"I can't." He spoke through gritted teeth.

He couldn't answer any of my questions? Rage soared from my

gut to my tightening chest. "You can't, or you don't want to?"

Suddenly, his eyes turned from their usual brilliant blue to a misty gray. I sucked in a breath, and he quickly shut his eyes.

"What are you?" I whispered, tears of tension trying to battle out of my eyes. But I fought hard to keep them at bay, because however alien Julian seemed to me at this moment, I still wouldn't cave to my qualms. I wouldn't be scared of him.

There was a long pause in which his lips compressed to a thin line. "Please, Jona, don't do this to me." The softness of his tone failed to cover the torture he was obviously going through. His forehead lay in wrinkles; his eyes were squeezed shut. Short breaths erupted fast from his chest.

Cupping his face, I made him look at me again. To see so much torture in his gaze was hard to bear. I swallowed hard at the light in his eyes that I had gotten so used to since the first day we had met; it was fading. "Why don't you trust me?"

"I do."

"But not enough." I leaned forward to brush my lips against his. "You broke through to me so easily. Now let me know what I can do to get through to you." Pressing my lips to the corner of his mouth, I inhaled the scent of warm, wild wind and ocean, feeling the need to get closer to him. Not physically. But to reach the part of him that he fought so hard to keep locked away from me.

His stiff reaction told me he didn't want me to proceed with the kiss, but he didn't pull away either. A deep moan tore from him as he finally gave in to my urge. His hands slid from the roof of the car to lock behind my waist. I cupped his neck, stood on tiptoes and pressed hard against his chest. His tongue swept over my lips, delved in between the seam, and began a slow game of give and take.

With a sigh, I broke the kiss and gazed into his eyes. The blue was shining through again. "You taught me how to trust you. It's time to return the trust, don't you think?"

He shook his head. "This isn't like me helping you step out onto the balcony."

"Then what is it like? Me jumping off a cliff?"

His soft lips pressed against my brow, infecting me with a new rush of relief and serenity. For the flash of a second, I knew it would be wise to jerk out of his hold now. To keep my mind clear and stop whatever magic he was trying to weave around me. Because—

Not again.

Tension eased from my body and mind. I didn't react fast enough, and it took him only a heartbeat to make me surrender. I sank into his embrace, reveled in his scent and touch.

"In your case," he whispered, and his lips brushed my hair, "it would be like sky diving."

In spite of the unusual sleepiness that crept over me, I heard myself say, "I would sky dive with you." And it was nothing but the truth.

It had to be the shock of my burn and the argument with Julian that exhausted me. My eyes refused to stay open, yawns kept breaking my train of thought.

"And yet, you wouldn't trust me enough to love me." His voice came from far away as darkness closed in around me.

A missing chapter

I awoke to the monotonous drone of the engine in Marie's car. My temple was pressed against the cool glass of the passenger side window. My head throbbed as the car rolled over the cobble stone driveway and into the garage. A low moan of pain escaped me as I turned toward the driver.

The sight of Julian confused me. I searched my mind for the reason why we'd been out this late. It was already dark, and no one was with us. In what little light the dashboard provided, Julian's face appeared tense.

"Did I fall asleep?" I rubbed my eyes and noticed something was wrapped around my left hand, preventing my fingers from spreading. *A bandage.* "What's going on?"

Julian cut the engine, leaving us in the dark, and turned to me. "You fainted." His ominous tone made my toes curl inside my boots.

"I fainted? Why? And where have we been?" I tried to go through the events of the day. Marie had taken me to the cemetery. I cleaned windows all afternoon. Albert tried to shoot me with an ancient pistol because I couldn't find any useful information about Julian's employer. And a huge potato knocked me over.

Okay, something was seriously wrong with my head.

"You burned your hand with boiling water when you were helping Marie in the kitchen. Don't you remember?"

No. And what was with that testy edge to his voice?

I shook my head. The fog in my mind irritated me to no end. It was like an entire chapter of today had gone astray.

"I drove you to the local clinic to get your hand examined," he said.

I shook my head again; nothing of what he said made sense.

"They applied antibacterial ointment and bandaged your wounds. You need to leave the gauze on for the next forty-eight hours. Then your skin should be fine again. They said there shouldn't be any scarring."

"Ah, okay." If my hand was burned so badly, I probably wouldn't want to see it anyway. "And when exactly did I pass out?"

"You collapsed on the way home. Aftermath of the shock most likely." He pulled the key from the ignition and grabbed a dish towel that lay in a bunch on the middle console. What it was doing in the car was, like the rest of his story, a riddle to me.

"It's normal that you wouldn't remember what happened in the hours before you passed out." Julian grimaced. "The missing information might never come back." The resoluteness in his tone was hard to understand. I followed him when he climbed out of the car.

He waited for me at the entrance to the house. "They gave you some medication, so at least you shouldn't feel any pain."

He was right. My hand felt totally normal. Just the pull of the bandage annoyed me a little bit. It might have been easier to accept the gauze if my skin hurt, but then again I was better off with feeling nothing.

Julian unlocked the front door, pushed it open, and let me enter first. All three members of my family stormed toward us as soon as we crossed the threshold. Gathered around me, Marie and Albert took turns firing off questions. "Are you all right? Is your hand all right? What did the doctors say?" It was touching how much they cared.

But one person looked the most worried of all. My mother stood next to her sister, not daring to touch me like Marie did, but her terrified eyes captured me from three feet away.

The vague memory of her and Julian entering the kitchen this afternoon swam in my mind. I also recalled she'd been seeing a doctor today. Strange how I could gaze at her face and, for once, feel no hatred.

The cemetery.

Images of her name carved into white marble danced up and lanced my heart. I shoved the disturbing thought aside and focused on her pale face again. She looked like shit and shouldn't have been up. But like my aunt and uncle, she'd been staying awake for my return. In a way I was grateful.

"I'm fine," I said before turning away from her. "But it seems I passed out. Julian can fill you in on the details. If you don't mind, I'd rather go to bed now."

Everyone stepped aside to let me ascend the stairs. Julian's words, as he retold the story I'd heard a few minutes ago, chased me upstairs. It still felt like he was talking about someone else.

*

The blanket wrapped around my shoulders kept me warm while sitting on the threshold of the open French door in the late night hours. At my last check, it had been eleven fifteen. The nagging feeling of having lost a part of the day, however small, left me anxious for a chat with Julian. But he hadn't come upstairs yet.

My hand itched underneath the bandage. Since I felt no pain at all, I played with the thought of taking the white gauze off in spite of the doctor's warning. But not being a fan of blood or wounds, I restrained and decided to go looking for Julian instead.

My tailbone hurt from sitting on the floor for so long. Rubbing my bum with one hand, I tossed the blanket onto the bed and sneaked out into the dark hallway. No sounds drifted from the ground floor. Most likely everyone had gone to bed already. Why hadn't Julian?

On my tiptoes, I descended the flight of stairs, sliding my hand along the rail. I turned left to peek into the parlor. It was dark and empty, and so was the kitchen. The door to Albert's study was closed, no light shone underneath. My trip down here had been in vain.

Then the sudden sound of Julian speaking made me spin on my heel, kick-starting my heart into high gear. *Of course.* I slapped my brow. Where else would he be than in my mother's room?

I drew closer, staying to the side and away from the door in case one of them came out. Unlike the last times I'd accidentally eavesdropped on their conversations, this time I deliberately chose to stay and listen. If Julian spoke to her about my misfortune today, it was my bloody right to hear it.

And then there was the slight chance he would talk to her about his little secret...his dual life. I might have forgotten part of today, but last night's conversation with him rang in my ears clear as Christmas bells. He wouldn't get away with *there's nothing we need to talk about*.

"I had no choice." Self-reproach pealed in Julian's tone.

"You did the right thing," my mother said, farther away than him.

"Then why does it feel so wrong to push her away every time she brings it up?" And with *she* he meant me, right? Oh, it seemed I'd jumped in at the perfect moment.

"Julian." Charlene paused, maybe for a sigh. "I know how you feel about Jona. But you of all people must understand that there is no chance for a future together."

Wait. Who was talking about a future together? Was that what Julian was aiming at? My insides warmed. I leaned back against the wall.

"She's suffered so much already," my mother continued. "And now...don't look at me like that. I'm well aware that most of it was my fault. But don't you see that you'll break her if you commit to her? You know you cannot stay."

I didn't have the slightest clue where he might have to go, but it squeezed my heart to think of not being able to see Julian every day. Why did she think he couldn't stay in France?

"Maybe I can."

"What do you mean *you can?*"

"I mean, there is a way. But she's not ready to accept it yet. It'll take time to make her understand." Julian's voice changed from low to loud in short intervals as his footsteps approached the door then faded away.

"Is that why you're reluctant to help me all of a sudden? Are you playing for time?"

A hard thud on the door made me jump. Julian must have slumped with his back against it. His voice was extremely close when he said, "Is that so wrong? What's a few more days? A couple more weeks."

What kind of game was he playing? I didn't understand what he expected to happen in that time. And most of all, I didn't understand why my mother needed him to help her.

"Would you please look at me, Julian? My time is up. It's been up for a while now. You can't keep this charade going forever. As much as I wish it was different, as much as I long to watch Jona become a grown woman, I feel I have to go."

She was dying. I heard the resolution in her tone.

Hands clapped over my mouth and nose, I struggled to breathe. My mother expected her death. She faced it so calmly. Why in the world would this bother me, after hating this woman for most of my life? My chest shouldn't be aching the way it did.

And then there was the part Julian played in this game. Was he the one responsible for her still being alive when she knew better? My heart and throat constricted with fright. I couldn't stop the cold shiver running over my body.

"And my daughter must be happy again. If you refuse to leave her alone, I'll put a stop to it. I won't let you continue your care of me."

"You asked for help, Charlene. And here I am. Now do not interfere with my plans."

"Your interest has changed. That revokes my deal with your

boss." My mother's voice toned down a notch, growing almost humble. "Does *he* know about your plans?"

Julian's exhausted laugh grew fainter as he walked away from the door. "Do you honestly think there is one tiny thing in this world he doesn't know about? In fact, I had no idea there was a possibility for me to stay until he told me so a short while ago."

"But it's wrong!" Charlene exclaimed. "You don't belong here."

"Love can never be wrong. And that is what both of you have to learn."

The intense serenity of Julian's lecture and the softness of his tone invaded me like hot chocolate running down my throat on a cold winter's day.

"Love can be wrong, if it's going to be taken away in the end." My mother spoke in a suppressed way, yet the anger and frustration were clearly audible. "I want the best for Jona. And if this means I have to die without finding forgiveness first, then I'll pay that price."

Swallowing hard, I tried to recap. They had a deal. With me as its focus. And Julian was keeping my mother alive against nature.

Oh. My. God. Realization struck me. He was some sort of alien. With powers beyond belief.

Panic surged though me, climaxing in a mental scream. All the new information swimming in my head made my brain spin like a mad carousel. Stumbling sideways then backward, I staggered through the hallway, trying to get a hold of something solid. Of myself. The screeching in my mind got more intense as I trembled.

"Seems like you got what you wanted," Julian's resolute statement drifted through the door. "Your daughter is outside. I suppose she's been listening all along."

How did he know? I hadn't made a sound, other than my breathing and even that I was finding difficult with the hysteria screaming in my mind.

I jerked around just in time to see him coming out of the room. A dim shine fell on the tiles in the hallway. Behind Julian, on the far end of the room, Charlene sat on her bed, wrapped in a green bathrobe, her look one of horror. But Julian closed the door fast and cut her off from my view.

Darkness swallowed the hallway once more. But this time an alien was with me.

He stared at me for the length of a breath, maybe giving me time to make an escape. But when I gazed at his blue eyes that sparkled even in the dark, there was no chance I could run away. In fact, there was only one direction I could move. Toward him.

It was like getting hooked by a fishing rod and being reeled in. Mentally, I fought against the urge, but my body wouldn't obey. The most I could do was stay where I was.

And then he came for me.

Even though his demanding stride scared me, I stood rooted until he grabbed my hand. He pulled me with him, upstairs. The alien found his way easily in the dark.

To my very surprise, Julian led me into my room, but didn't stop when the door shut behind us. Without pausing, he proceeded to the balcony.

"Julian, wait. Don't—" My plea bounced off his back. His hand curled tighter around my good one, and I stood no chance against his pull.

A cool wind brushed my face. The night sky was illuminated with a million stars and a harvest moon hanging low. Julian stopped and turned. He closed the little space between us and gazed into my eyes, cupped my face, and pressed his lips to mine.

Together with time, my heart stopped. For an infinite moment,

Julian and I melted into each other. His kiss was fierce and demanding, and still, I had yet to come across something equally as tender in my life. It felt as if he'd poured his very soul into this kiss.

And my heart opened for him to enter fully.

I didn't know how long we stood entangled. But when he pulled back, the pain of being ripped apart soared through me. I yearned to stay with him as one being. Forever.

"I love you, Jona," he whispered with no one but me and the stars to hear.

And deep inside me, I felt I loved him, too, no matter who or *what* he was. I was devoted to this man with my mind, body, and soul. But I've never said those words to anyone before. And however long he waited on my reply, the words wouldn't come through my dry, tight throat.

With a long sigh, Julian closed his eyes and touched his lips to mine for another tender moment. Then he stepped back, turned, and walked across the balcony toward his room. A heavy burden seemed to press on his shoulders, urging me to run after him. Or to call him back at least. But tongue-tied and frozen, I watched him disappear through the floating curtains.

So many bottles

"*Seventy-six bottles of wine in the box. Seventy-six bottles of wine. Take one out and dip it into water, seventy-five bottles of wine in the box...*" I sang.

Warm water ran from the faucet into the kitchen sink. For the past couple of hours I had performed the monotonous task of rinsing one empty bottle after the other. This annoying song had crept into my mind, and I couldn't get it out but kept singing under my breath.

I turned the bottles upside down on a wide towel spread on the table where they could dry.

Because of my injured left hand, which still felt just fine, Marie had forbidden me to go out with them to work in the field today.

Afraid the dirt would make my wound worse, she gave me an easy task to fill the boring morning hours. Rinsing a stack of bottles that Albert had retrieved from the cellar; single-handedly.

The bottles were covered with more dust than Captain Blackbeard's rum bottle. Soon they'd be refilled with new wine from this season's crop.

About forty more waited in the box, but my bursting bladder urged me to rush upstairs. I didn't stop when the door to my mother's room opened and she popped her head out.

"Julian, is that you?" she asked hoarsely.

"No!" I shouted down, then slammed the door to my room shut and went into the bathroom.

What did she need that alien for today? Did she want to discuss *me* again? If she wanted to talk to him, she would have to wait until he came back or take a stroll out to the vinery. I sure as hell wasn't going to get him for her. Not after he'd left the house without a glance at me this morning.

A few minutes later, I was on my way back downstairs but whirled about once more. Leaning over the sink and rinsing the bottles had drenched my t-shirt. The fabric stuck to my skin and irritated me, so I went back and changed my clothes.

Downstairs, a door opened, and my mother's panicked voice echoed in the house. "Marie?"

"Oh, give it a break. You know she's not here," I muttered to myself. Buttoning my fresh shirt, I went out into the hallway and leaned over the banister. "Marie's out! Everyone is!"

I cringed at the shrieking sound of glass breaking. If Charlene had knocked over the bottles in the kitchen, I was going to make her clean up the mess by herself.

A wave of anger washed over me as I stormed down the

winding staircase and strode toward the kitchen. The first thing that came into view was a sea of green shards spread all over the floor.

"Shit, what have you done?" Glass crunched under the soles of my boots as I entered. But at first sight, my mother wasn't around. Maybe Lou-Lou had come in and—

My gaze fell on a limp body on the floor. Covered with fragments of glass and blood. My heart stopped. I spun on the spot, cut a glance at the door and then back at Charlene. I dragged a clawed hand through my hair and pressed the other over my mouth. An eerie silence numbed my ears. What in the world was I to do now?

Get back to your room.

Close the door.

Pretend nothing has happened.

I could ignore her. Wait until the rest of the family came home. Julian would know what to do. He'd coddle her as always. His regular check on her was overdue, anyway.

Seconds ticked away, and hysteria gripped me around the throat. Where was he?

And what if he didn't come?

This is it. She's dead. It's over. You can breathe.

With the first long breath, tears sprang to my eyes. Figuring out how to make my mind and tongue function together was hard. I had her name in my head and wanted to speak it out loud, to get a reaction from her. But when I opened my mouth I couldn't produce any real sound.

The passing moments seemed like an eternity as I stared at the lifeless body in front of me. It was like I was staring into an open grave at the cemetery. My skin went ice-cold. I hated Marie for bringing me there yesterday.

"*Do you really want her to die with a broken heart?*"

I shot around to see who'd said that. No one stood behind me. Then I realized it was Julian's words ringing in my ears. And suddenly, the first memory from my early childhood flashed in my mind. I remembered happy moments in my mother's arms as she hugged and loved me, twirled me around in the kitchen when her violent boyfriend was out and it was only the two of us in the flat.

I remembered chocolate fudge cakes. A lullaby and goodnight kisses. Even the red velvet dress she had sewn for my first day in nursery school surfaced in my mind. It had taken a whole long week of my pleading until she had bought me the matching patent-leather shoes.

This woman was my mom.

She was the one who gave me life. A good deal of it might have been miserable, but she'd tried to make up for it by bringing me to Marie's wonderful place with people around who seemed to love me for no other reason than that I was part of their family. And I loved them in return.

I didn't want her to die. Or to suffer from cancer and be in so much pain. And most of all, I didn't want to feel angry at her any longer. All I wished for in that moment was peace for me and for this woman who I'd loved unconditionally so many years ago.

Dragging my boots through the shards, I stumbled to her side.

"Charlene?" My voice broke and I tried again. "Charlene! Can you hear me? Mom?"

I skimmed the hair off her face. An acrid smell wafting toward me made me wince. There were traces of vomit around her mouth, stains on her shirt. Two scarlet streams of blood ran from her nose over her top lip, and angled to the left, dripping to the floor. Cuts dotted her face and hands.

Carefully, I wiped all the tiny pieces of glass off of her then pressed my palm to her cheek. She was hot. But at least her chest lifted slowly with steady breaths. I took her face in my hands and said once more, "Mom? Look at me. If you can hear me, please say something."

She was silent.

I struggled to lift her from the hard stone floor. Her upper body cradled in my arms, she finally opened her eyes.

I freed her of any remaining shards of glass, then gathered all my reserved strength, and heaved my mother up from the floor. Half dragging and half carrying, I took her to her room, where I lowered her to the bed and began stripping off her shirt.

"Don't—"

Her weak objection didn't make me stop. This wasn't the moment for an argument. When her body lay undressed before me, I gasped. Beneath her clothes, Charlene was nothing but skin and bones. If I hadn't seen her moving around the past couple of weeks, I would have believed she was already dead.

On her nightstand sat a glass of water, which I held to her lips so she could rinse her mouth and get rid of the awful taste of vomit. The first mouthful she spewed into the bucket next to her bed. Then she drank in slow sips.

From the closet, I grabbed a new shirt, opening the window on my way. Fresh air drove the nauseating smell out of the room.

I helped my mother into the sleeves, pulled the quilt over her legs, and cleaned the blood from her face with a wet cloth.

She gaped up at me and reached out one shaky hand.

Too exhausted to stifle the sigh in my throat, I sat on the edge of the bed. Her hand felt cold, sweaty. This was our first touch in over twelve years. Nothing was left of the soft, warm fingers she used to run through my hair when I was little.

Her mouth opened, but she couldn't bring up the strength to speak.

"Don't worry," I hushed her. "Everything will be fine. In a little while." As soon as Julian came back. I cast a longing glance at the empty doorway.

The squeeze she gave my hand wouldn't have been hard enough to crush an ant. A single tear ran down her cheek as she made a weak attempt to smile.

"Try to get some sleep now," I said. "I'll clean up and be back in a bit."

Glad to have a reason to get out of the room, I left her to rest, struggling to keep my own tears at bay. I couldn't allow them to spill over in front of her.

Emptying the bucket into the toilet made my stomach roll. I sucked in a breath through my mouth then held it until I was out of the room. With an old broom from the closet, I started sweeping the kitchen floor. It felt good to have something to do at this moment. The only other option was to walk back into my mother's room. But my mind was spiraling, and it needed to calm first.

With all the memories that had come back in a rush earlier, and with the panic I had felt, I found I could open the door to forgiveness. Even if it was only cracked open. Now that I didn't have to see her sorrowful eyes, I wasn't so sure if I fully wanted to walk through it.

It wasn't like she could undo the past twelve years in which she'd completely kept out of my life. In which there hadn't passed a single day that I hadn't brooded over why she'd abandoned me.

But this was probably my last chance to find an answer to those nagging questions. If I closed the door now, she might die before she could ever tell me. And before I could tell her how much I had missed her in those lonely years.

I realized I'd stopped sweeping and was instead gazing at the blank wall. Heaving a long sigh, I pinched the bridge of my nose. I knew I needed to talk to her eventually, and it might as well be today. But first I needed to finish cleaning up the mess.

In the cupboard under the sink, I found a dustpan for the shards. I knelt on the floor and was wiping the broken glass onto the dustpan when the gauze around my hand snagged on the broom. Since there was no pain in the injured hand, I tugged one end loose and began un-wrapping the bandage. First slowly, and then faster as I noticed no sign of a burn underneath.

The gauze landed in a heap on the counter. I examined my hand, turned it in the light, and stroked it with my good fingers. *Amazing.* Julian said I had poured boiling water over it only yesterday. But my skin was completely intact. No blisters, no soreness. It was like nothing had happened to my hand at all.

Think.

The story he had told me last night seemed totally unfamiliar. So there was the off chance that none of it had, in fact, happened. But then again, everyone had been worried and bombarded me with questions when we had come home. My family had definitely seen me burn my hand before Julian took off to the hospital with me.

Once again it all came down to Julian. Something must have happened that he had refused to reveal. Oh boy, would he ever make sense to me? And when the hell was he going to come inside, goddammit? He should have checked on my mother over an hour ago. If he had performed his spooky alien healing on her, she would probably not have collapsed. A weird chagrin budded inside me, and I braced myself to give him a mouthful the minute he walked through the door.

Vigorously twisting the bandage into a tight bundle, I tossed it into the bin underneath the sink together with the shards of glass bottles. If Julian wouldn't tell me his secret, it might be time to ask someone else. I leaned the broom against the credenza and strode back to my mother's room.

But she was sound asleep. Her chest lifted and sank in a steady rhythm. I stopped three feet into the room, weighing my options. Leave and wait outside, or sit by her bedside and watch her sleep. After all, she might get sick again and need my help.

I tried to make no sound as I crossed to her bed and settled on the mattress. She heaved a sigh but didn't wake up.

Hard to say how long I sat there, watching as she slept. But with a soft melody on my lips—the song she used to lull me to sleep with ages ago and which Julian had played for me on the piano—my head dipped forward, and I drifted off to sleep, too.

The feeling of someone's eyes on me woke me a little later. But my mother's eyes were still peacefully closed. Pain shot through my cramped neck as I raised my head to scan the silent room.

Julian stood in the doorway, thumbs hooked through the belt loops of his jeans. The way his shoulder and head rested against the frame made me believe he'd been watching for a while.

Should I be grateful that he was finally here or angry that he hadn't shown up sooner? I tilted my head back to the wall, deliberating, and eyed him through drowsy slits. My bottom lip stuck between my teeth, a sigh rolled off my chest.

The longing in his eyes was transparent. It made me wish he'd come closer, so I could wrap my arms around him and bury my face against his chest.

"Why didn't you come to check on her this morning? What

have you been doing for so long?"

"Giving you time." His soft voice floated in the room.

As my mother stirred slightly, I turned to gaze at her. She probably felt his presence, too. Who wouldn't? It was as if his aura penetrated me in waves with each breath I took. He might have been doing the same to her. Maybe she was afraid of him after their conversation last night. After all, she'd said her time was up.

"Is she going to die?" I asked him.

"Not today."

So life and death really were in his hands. I took a shaky breath, steeling my nerves for the unbelievable. It was time to get a few answers. But I couldn't find the courage or the right words to begin.

After a long pause, Julian straightened. He nudged his chin at my hands. "You removed the bandages."

I inspected my hand from all sides then dropped it to my lap. "Yeah. Seems like it's healed. That wouldn't have anything to do with you, would it?"

The weak smile he gave me made my heart flutter. He held out his hand to me. "Come on. Let's take a walk."

So the alien was ready to talk at last. As silently as possible, I rose and moved toward Julian. Warmth surged through me as he closed his hand around mine. But before we left, I cast a concerned look over my shoulder. "Will she wake up while we're gone?"

"Don't worry. She'll be sleeping until I call her back."

Ah, right. Master of minds.

The calm serenity he emitted enveloped me completely. And suddenly, I had the feeling of being a small child holding on to the hand of an older and much wiser being than I could grasp. A person who could decide between life and death, sleep and awake. Who could heal wounds, inflict happiness with a single touch, and for all I knew, might even be able to fly.

If it wasn't for the immense amount of kindness rolling off him in waves, I would have been scared as hell. But right now, I looked at him with adoring eyes.

Julian led me outside and past the field. On the way he waved at Marie and let her know we were taking a little stroll but would be back in time for dinner.

Behind the vineyards, we crossed a line of trees into a wooded area. In the shade of all the firs and spruces, a chill slid down my arms, reminding me that I was about to leave civilization behind and head to a place unknown with an alien by my side.

Julian surveyed me from the corner of his eye. "Are you cold?"

"Just a little."

Heat ignited where our palms touched. The unusual warmth slowly soared up my arm. With each pound of my heart, it spread further through my body.

"How do you do that?" To my own amazement, my whisper didn't reflect fear, only fascination. It also occurred to me that he might be doing some alien hocus pocus to keep me at ease.

Julian didn't reply. But when we left the broad strip of woods and stepped into a wide meadow, his grip tightened. "Jona, can I ask you something?"

Shuffling through the ankle-high grass, I nodded, hoping to get my questions answered afterward as well.

"When you overheard your mother and me talking last night, and of course with the list you already started a few days ago, what have you concluded I am?"

Wariness settled in my sideways glance and tone. "Will you have to kill me if I'm right? Because if so, I'd rather not say."

He rolled his eyes. "Of course not, silly." Lifting the hand that held mine, he wrapped his arm around my shoulders and pulled me closer as we strolled.

"Okay," I drawled. "I think you're an alien. Like Superman from Krypton. Just with different powers, you know."

He frowned at me. "That's your best guess?"

"I'm wrong?"

"Totally!"

A little ashamed of my assumption, I thought of the only other theory I had about him. "Apparently you can resurrect the dead. So, are you into voodoo?"

"No." Now he seemed almost offended, but not in an angry way. "I thought you'd figured me out already."

I frowned, my lips tight. Any normal person would have been freaked out by all this. At that point, I was pretty damn sure he was weaving his magic around me to keep me calm, or else I wouldn't have been able to have this conversation. "Then stop playing games and just tell me where you're from."

He pulled me to a halt in the middle of the meadow. Apart from the woods behind us and an occasional tree every few hundred feet, nothing but grass and flowers spread as far as the eye could see.

With my hand still in his, I gaped into the face of this devilishly good-looking man. His eyes a bright blue, he seemed to smile, even when his lips remained straight. And suddenly it dawned on me. His defined features, the way he performed magic, his boss my mother made a deal with, it all pointed to—

"Oh. My. God," I breathed. "You're working for the devil." It definitely was the most absurd thing that ever came out of my mouth. But it seemed to be the only logical explanation.

Julian's mouth dropped open then closed. He continued to

study me with a new interest. "Would you be scared if the answer was yes?"

I'd never before crossed myself, but at this moment I came terribly close. Only I thought that might offend him. So I stood rigid, staring at him with eyes so wide it hurt.

However, the answer to his counter question was a definite, "No."

I'd seen him do too much good to think he could be a bad entity, no matter who he was working for. Nothing could take away my feelings for this man, not even the depths of hell.

The left corner of Julian's mouth lifted. "In fact, I'm working for the other side."

"The other side of what?" *Of hell?* I frowned. "That would be Heaven... But, no." I laughed at myself for going the wrong way again. "You're certainly not an angel."

A spark in his eyes came with his grin.

My fingers slid from his. "Shit. You're serious."

And then he stopped time

A warm wind ruffled the leaves of the nearest lilac and sent their rich, exotic smell down to us. A platoon of fluffy clouds marched like sheep across the sky. They created a lulling interplay of sun and shadow on my face. Sprawled out on the long grass, I enjoyed Julian playfully teasing my jaw with the petals of a daisy. His head was supported by his hand as he lay next to me.

"You're taking it quite well."

If he was referring to me being silent since he told me he was an angel, he was right. I knew I should be totally freaked out, but I wasn't. "Are you keeping me calm with your angelic powers?"

"Would you mind if I did?"

I sniffed when he tickled my nose with the flower. "As long as you don't tamper with my mind so I can't make my own decisions, I think I'm fine."

"No tampering," he said solemnly. "It happens on an emotional base only. All I do is expand my aura a little and include you in my circle of—" He broke off, narrowing his eyes. A second later, he smirked. "Of heavenly coolness."

It made me laugh. But I could definitely live with that.

I sat up, crossed my legs, and braced myself on my hands behind my back, gazing at the sky. The drifting clouds were beginning to clear, leaving nothing but blue above. Hard to imagine how an institution like Heaven fit there.

My eyes leveled with his. "What does it look like? Heaven. Is it a city in the clouds? A palace where more angels like you hang out?"

Julian rolled onto his back and propped on his elbows. "The human mind can't grasp the true image of Heaven. No offence, but you simply lack the imagination and language to describe it."

His words didn't offend me, yet I yearned for a visual. Disappointed, I lowered my gaze.

He sat up and cupped my chin with his gentle fingers. "Heaven is not one particular place, or town, or house. It would be best described as—" His lips pursed. "It's a feeling. Deep inside you, as well as all around you. Something absolutely peaceful. And harmonious. Like the love of an innocent child."

"Those are mighty words," I whispered, awed.

"You asked for them."

And yet they were hard to comprehend. A place inside me where only love existed, without doubts or anger? Heaven definitely didn't reside within me. And what about fear? Could an angel be afraid of something?

"You look like you have a lot of questions," Julian said.

"Only a million. Or two."

Laughing, he tucked a wisp of hair behind my ear. "Why don't we try to get some of them answered?"

"Is that possible?" It seemed completely unacceptable for an angel to spill secrets to a meagerly developed human. But Julian's nod assured me.

If only I knew where to start. Everything that came to me seemed equally interesting and important.

"How many angels are there? Do they all look like you? Do you know God—personally?" The smile on his face grew wider with each question I shot at him. "How old are you? Is Julian your real name?"

"Easy there." He raised his palms and cut me short. "We do have more than two minutes to talk about it all."

I sucked in a breath, calming my spinning mind, waiting for him to get started.

"Okay, so how many of us are there?" he repeated my first question deliberately slow. "There'd be twelve for each human soul. Then there are the Supporters, who aren't assigned to a particular soul yet. They are about as many as the assigned ones. The healers, the guardians—"

My jaw dropped as he counted them on his fingers.

"The escorts, the muses, the keepers, and the counsels. I'm sure I left someone out, but in total there would be...let's just say countless. And I'm grateful they all do *not* look like me."

My mouth hung open. Ignoring it, he went on. "I do know God. We all do. And Julian is my name. Well, at least it is when I travel down to Earth. My angel name is a bit of a tongue-twister in human language."

I frowned. "How so?"

Julian rubbed his neck. Then his lips curled and his eyes lit up. "Come closer." But he didn't give me time to scoot forward as he leaned toward me, placing both hands to my temples.

A confused laugh escaped me. "What are you going to—" I fell silent. A choir sang out in my mind. Only they didn't sing particular words, but rather hummed various chords as beautiful as the sound of winter bells.

"Now, that's a mouthful," I murmured.

"You see why it's hard to say my name out loud. And to answer your last question, I would like you to take a guess at my age first." He grinned.

"But the other day you said you were twenty-one."

"No. You said it. I didn't say yes or no. Remember?"

I actually did. When he'd called it a good guess, I'd automatically assumed he was confirming it. *Tricky devil. Or angel...*

"Okay, do you go by human years?"

"Actually, we don't, but I can convert it for you. So, what's your guess?"

I scratched my head, uncertain of what to say. "You look twenty-ish to me."

He dragged his mouth awkwardly to one side and made a snorting sound. "You're not even close, honey."

"All right then thirty?" But even I knew that would be stretching it.

Julian cut a bored glance skyward. "In fact, I'm sixty-five."

"Bloody hell, what's your secret? Sixty-five years old and not a single gray hair on you." I clapped my hands together, feigning dramatic surprise, when I actually almost tipped backward in honest amazement.

With a rascally spark in his eyes, he leaned forward to whisper into my ear. "It's sixty-five *millennia*."

That left me breathless. "You're shitting me."

"No shit." Julian raised his right hand as if to swear and kept his face straight. But in the next second, he ruffled my hair. "Don't make a face. Compared to as long as I will exist, the last sixty millennia were only the blink of an eye. And you mustn't forget, I only spent a bit of that time on Earth in human form."

Trying to comprehend would only make my head spin. But honestly, sixty-five thousand years? He must have met quite a few people in that time.

Quite a few women. I could do nothing about the stab of jealousy that came with that thought.

"In all that time, how many girlfriends did you have?"

He studied me. After half a minute, I started to feel really uncomfortable. But finally he said, "As an angel, you feel love for everyone and everything. Different to the way *you* feel it. We enjoy the company of others. We watch people be born, grow up, live their lives. And during all this time, we love each of them. Yet, no angel ever feels the need to be *with* someone. With anyone. *I* never felt it. Until I met you."

He let go of a sigh, brushing his thumb over my cheekbone. "It seems like with every move and every word you say you pull me in, and I can't turn away. Every bit of your mind intrigues me like nothing else ever has. You come close to me, and I can't resist touching you. Your hair. Your skin." He laughed softly. "Your rebellious heart."

"Why is that?" I whispered.

"I don't know. It just *is*."

This was so hard to believe. After all, I was nothing but a

bedraggled teenager, who'd spent more time hiding from the police in public toilets than in school.

We both fell silent for what seemed like minutes. I wished I could find the right words to tell him, in as beautiful a way, what he was to me. My life might not have been as long as Julian's, but it seemed I'd always saved this exclusive little spot in my heart for him. However, my mouth stood sealed, and I could only hope he understood what I failed to speak out loud.

I let another couple of minutes pass, in which he tenderly stroked my arm, or skimmed his fingers through my hair. When the opportunity for me to open up to him had completely disappeared, I came up with something else that had been burning on my mind for the last few days. "Can you fly? And if you're a real angel, why don't you have wings?"

"I *am* a real angel. And I certainly can fly."

"So you do have wings? But where do you keep them? You sure can't take them off and hide them in your pockets, right?"

The rolling of his eyes and the soft *tsk* made him look sweet. "Just where do you get your imagination from? I can't take them off. But I can let them vanish."

"How?"

Julian rubbed his chin, pursing his lips. "How can I explain? It's like, I can manipulate their molecules. Slow them down or speed them up. They're always there, but you wouldn't see them."

I had always been a slouch in physics, so his elaboration made little sense to me. "It sounds like you're able to control matter and time. Somehow. Right? Can you also travel through time?"

One corner of his mouth tugged up. "Let's put it this way: I can bend time to my advantage. No one can jump back to an earlier moment, but through immense control, I can reduce the speed at which the molecules move. Thus I can sort of...hover."

"Hover?"

"Between moments." He held out his right hand with his index finger stretched. From a bush nearby, a sparrow took off, gliding toward us. About a foot away from Julian's hand, the bird's flight suddenly slowed. Each flap of its wings was carried out with incredible slowness. What would normally happen in the fraction of a millisecond, now took longer than half a minute.

Its thin claws stretched wide before they curled around Julian's finger, slowly, like a flower withdrawing its blossom after dark.

Settled on my haunches, I inspected the bird from all sides. "Epic."

The sparrow blinked once in some fifteen seconds. Then it spread its wings again and left Julian's finger, no faster than it had landed.

My curiosity got the best of me. "How slow can you go?"

Julian grinned and flicked his eyes at the bird that now hovered in midair, not moving at all. It was like the world had stopped around us, and Julian and I were the only beings in motion.

"And you can hold this for how long?"

He shrugged. "Like, forever."

"One moment stretching to eternity? That must be an awfully long time." My glance switched between the bird frozen in mid-air and Julian's face. Then a realization struck me. "You do this when we kiss."

Julian slid his knuckles along my jaw. "I like to savor the moment."

The bird broke free and fluttered excitedly away. Watching the sparrow land in another tree, I leaned into Julian's palm. "So, can I get stuck between moments, like you?"

He nodded. "If you're with me."

"So you can show me your wings, too?"

Without a word, Julian began unbuttoning his shirt. He shrugged it off and dropped it to the grass. The sight of his firm, smooth chest made my mouth water. His abs twitched, his pecs bulged as he flexed his neck, closing his eyes for a second. A vertical beam of white light appeared behind him and reached about two feet above his head.

After what he'd shown me with the bird a minute ago, this shouldn't have surprised me at all. And yet, I held my breath, palming my cheeks.

The column of light parted when Julian opened his eyes again. A set of marble white wings unfolded as wide as his height, layered with a thousand downy feathers.

Sunlight reflected off the wings, dipping his shape in a mist of halo, which made it hard to look away. But at the same time, the light blinded me. I swallowed hard against my bafflement. "Can I touch them?"

For the first time since we came out here, Julian seemed the tiniest bit uncertain. "No one has ever touched them before."

"I promise to be extra gentle," I teased, already crawling toward him. Kneeling, I reached out. Julian's sudden tension didn't escape me, but it also couldn't make me stop. As soon as I traced the curve of his left wing, the limb twitched away. A visible shiver raked over his naked torso.

"Sensitive, are we?"

"You have no idea," he drawled on a deep rumble.

I gasped when he grabbed me around the waist and pulled me into his lap. Dipping his head, he purred into my ear. "But I can show you a spot or two on your body, which are just as sensitive."

He took my earlobe into his mouth, nibbling gently.

The whisk of his tongue coaxed a surprisingly loud moan from me. He continued to nibble a path along my jaw, and I surrendered to his embrace.

His wings flapped to the front. They closed around me, enveloping me in total protection. His tongue trailed down my chin and neck in the most enticing way, aiming at the hollow in the base of my throat. I angled my head to give him access to that sensitive part of my skin. Above, a swarm of swallows hovered motionless in the sky.

"You froze time again?" I breathed, running my fingers through his silky golden hair.

Julian skimmed the tip of his nose across my cheek. When his eyes were level with mine, he gave me a determined look. "I told you, I like to savor."

He cupped my face, brushed my lips with his thumb, and took my mouth with a ferociously slow kiss. Pleasant tickles raked down my front to center in my belly. I shivered in his arms. But he only held me tighter, supporting part of my weight.

His hands trailed down my sides then moved up again. With them came my shirt. I lifted my arms to let him strip it off and toss it aside.

"You're so beautiful, I could eat you up."

"So says the shiny angel," I replied.

Feeling his soft hair and warm skin, I skimmed my fingers down his neck and over his shoulder blades. My hands found the roots of his wings. I traced the edge winding around me. Warm and soft, his wings trembled under my touch, but he didn't pull away this time. Instead, he dipped his head to the crook of my neck. His breath as he moaned was hot and moist on my skin.

His feathers brushed down my spine, the sensation more than I could bear. Without thinking, I shifted in his lap, straddled him, and cupped his face. He welcomed my burning kisses and pulled me down with him. At his sides, his wings spread and lowered, flattening the high grass.

A wonderful shiver stole through me as his hands stroked down my back, skimming over the curves of my bottom and trailing further along my kneeling legs. But the intensity of his kissing abated, filling me with unease.

The fire had vanished from his eyes as his hands came to rest on my thighs, and he stilled.

I pushed out a sad sigh. "Let me guess. Complicated again?"

Slowly, the angel nodded, his eyes so full of pain that my chest constricted. "Jona, this is wrong."

My heart sank. "How can it be wrong?" It felt perfect.

Julian held my piercing gaze. "It wouldn't be fair to you."

"What do you mean, not fair?" Bracing my hands on his chest, I straightened my back.

His long silence filled me with foreboding. "I can't be with you, Jona."

"But you are with me." A testing glance upward confirmed the flock of birds still hovered above us. "You dragged me into this moment. I'm here, and the world stopped turning."

"That's what I'm afraid of." His fingers caressed my burning skin down my arms to wrap around my hands. "It would only be for a moment."

My glance moved to our joined hands. One moment, where the world stood still. I knew he was right, had known it all along. Ever since last night when I heard my mother accusing him of having to leave in the end. Leave with her. Leave me behind.

Alone.

"How could I forget about that?" I whispered to myself. Then my gaze switched back to his eyes. "You have to go, don't you? Back to Heaven." The hesitant nod he gave me cut deep into my heart. "How long do I get to keep you?" But even as I croaked the question, I knew he wouldn't answer.

And it wasn't necessary, because I already got the answer last night. Her deal with God was about forgiveness. *My* forgiveness.

Today I turned my back on the past and let my mother into my heart again. She got what she wanted. The deal was fulfilled.

"You said she won't die today. But she will soon. She's getting worse as we speak, isn't she?" A small part of me still hoped he'd shake his head. But Julian only kept staring at me with sadness in his eyes. "I found back to her just today, and now I'm going to lose you both?"

"Jona—" His voice, as he reached up to cup my cheek, carried all the sorrow I tried to hide by biting back my tears.

Squeezing my eyes shut, I soaked in the longing and gentleness of his touch. "But you're an angel. You can heal her. Make her feel better. You did it before, I know it."

Julian pulled me down and cradled my head to his chest. His heart beat slowly, but loudly. "I'm not a healer, Jona. From today on, my powers are bound. I can't help her other than ease her pain while she's getting weaker." He stroked my hair, and I surrendered to his hold. "She made a deal. And the rules must be obeyed."

"Fuck your damn rules!" I nestled tighter against his chest, my fingers digging into his hard muscles. "I don't care about your bloody deal. I want you to stay."

Julian remained silent for a long while. When he spoke next, it was nothing more than a whisper in my mind. "Yesterday you said you would sky dive with me. Was that the truth?"

What he said didn't ring a bell, so I sniffed then lifted my head to him. "When did I say that?"

His eyes tilted back to regard the sky. "A moment before I wiped your memory."

What was he saying? He made me forget? A loop of barbwire tightened around my heart. "You meddled with my mind?"

"I had to. You came too close to discovering my secret." Julian pressed his palm briefly to my forehead, and all of a sudden, a heavy fog, that had clouded my mind for the past twenty four hours, lifted. All the events of yesterday returned with such clarity that it knocked me breathless.

But I couldn't be mad at him. He'd risked exposure to everyone only to heal my burned hand. His torn face when he'd begged me not to push him into revealing it flashed before me. *I'd sky dive with you.* My own promise rang in my mind.

It took him no more than a blink to take all those little memories from me. And what about today? My throat constricted, making it painful to swallow. "Now that I know you're an angel, will you have to wipe my memory again? Will we go back in an hour, with me not being able to remember any of these precious moments with you?"

"Eventually, I will."

"What?" I was nothing short of hysteric.

Julian said nothing. But he lifted me gently, to place me next to him, then he sat up. His wings started to tremor, getting to a very high frequency until they finally disappeared. Feeling bereft of his true beauty, I ran my hand up and down his back, but there was nothing to be felt.

I put on my shirt when he buttoned up his. Taking my hand,

he rose from the grass and pulled me with him. I followed with a sinking heart as I realized he was heading home.

And then he spoke. "Jona, the day that I return to Heaven—" He paused to gaze at me with somber eyes. "When your mother dies, I will take away all your memories of me. And not only from you. From everyone I came into contact with."

From the past

With the woods before us, I kept my eyes on my feet threading through the knee-high grass. Julian's hand on mine felt warm, faking that the world was still all right. A calm wind swayed the green blades, proof that he'd released his freezing grip on time. The moments rushed by once more like wild rapids.

The horror of losing the most important memory of my life anchored deep in my bones.

We returned home. In the middle of the afternoon everyone was still on the field. Except my mother. She slept peacefully in her room when I entered on silent steps, Julian behind me. He brushed his palm over her forehead. Her soft moans the only sound, she woke from this unusually deep sleep.

It was one thing to know that Julian could do magic to others, but a totally different thing to see it happen. I couldn't decide who to look at first. Julian's beautiful face when he concentrated on his powers, or my mother's happy eyes when she caught me standing in the middle of the room.

Welcome back to life, Mom.

Julian sat on the edge of the bed and took her bony hand into his. Color returned to her cheeks, her huge liquid pupils reduced to a normal size.

"Is it already time to go?" A frightful shiver came with that question.

Julian shook his head. "The deal is fulfilled, but *He* is no fiend. The two of you do have time to talk." He rose from the bed and held out his hand to her. "It's a beautiful day. Would you like to sit outside?"

"Of course," my mother replied, accepting his help when she climbed out of bed, and forced a smile. "After all, it might be my last chance to see the sky and the vines."

My chest suddenly seemed too tight for my heart, and I had to cough against the lump in my throat.

Julian helped her to the bench on the patio then left us alone to make tea. Seated facing my mother, I studied her features, that already bore the stamp of death. How long until God would take her away from me? Another day? Two?

"Why the deal with God, Mom?" There was no way to ban the tremor from my tone. "Why didn't you seek the doctors' help instead?"

"So he finally told you." She shook her head slowly, but then a soft laugh rocked her bony shoulders. Her hand crawled across the table and landed over mine. "I'd been on medications for months, darling. But it's cancer of the pancreas. It's incurable."

I'd heard about the incurable detail before. Only, now I refused to believe it. "There must be a way. What about one of those chemotherapies? Or a surgery. Do you really need a pancreas anyway? They could take it out, or maybe part of it."

She grimaced. "Whatever modern medicine can do, it would only prolong the suffering."

I saw pain in her eyes, which had nothing to do with her own misfortune. Her discomfort was due to my horrified expression and her inability to comfort her daughter with a better prognosis than she could give me.

"So how did God get into the game?" Fighting not to whimper, it still felt strange to talk to her. And about such an off-the-wall topic, too. "I mean it's not every day you hear He sends down an angel to fulfill people's wishes." At least He'd never sent someone my way in the twelve years I'd prayed for help.

A grateful shine lit up my mother's eyes, and she cast a glance toward the sky. "No, I guess it's not. He must have taken great pity on me that evening." When she looked at me again, I lifted one eyebrow, urging her to explain. "You see, it was the evening after I returned from hospital with the news that they couldn't help me anymore. I was advised to get my affairs in order."

"Another way of saying your time was up."

She nodded. "They gave me half a year, if that. My thoughts kept coming back to one topic only. You." My mother searched my face while her hand closed around mine. Firmly. The angel power Julian had filled her with strengthened her.

"I had made a mess of my life and in the process hurt you so badly. You, the only good thing that ever happened to me. On my knees, I begged for a chance to fix my screw ups. I asked for a possibility to set a few things straight before my days were up. It already killed me to think of dying without ever talking to you again. Without the chance to ever hold you—" Her bottom lip trembled. She reached for a tissue in her pocket, wiped her nose, and dabbed at the tears in her eyes.

My heart as tight as my throat, I reached toward her, placing my hand on her forearm. "You can hold me now, Mom."

Her mouth quirked as though she wanted to smile. Instead, more tears spilled over.

The next moment, Julian stepped out with a tray carrying three steaming mugs. He put them down and planted a hand on my mother's shoulder. She sucked in a breath, which I didn't realize she was running out of, and her torn face relaxed a little.

With the strength he gave her, she continued. "That night, I offered to trade the rest of my life for one peaceful moment with you."

My mouth fell open.

"I do confess I didn't put much faith into a happy ending then. But shortly after I'd finished my prayers, a strange white light brightened the room, and Julian appeared. He said he was sent to help."

When Julian withdrew his hand and sat next to me, she gave him a sheepish smile. "You had a hard time making me believe, didn't you?"

He chuckled as he wrapped his arm around me but still looked at my mother. "You were definitely one of the harder nuts."

I reached for my cup, blew on the steam, and took a small sip. My eyes snapped toward him. "So your plan was to keep her going until the day we would meet again and I would miraculously forgive her?"

"Not quite." His grip on my shoulder tightened. "I made preparations. Went looking for you and found out what you usually did at what time of the day."

"You stalked me?" My eyes grew wide.

"Stalking is such a harsh word. I did proper research of an individual. Studied you," he drawled. His gaze lingering on me, he leaned back and skimmed his fingers over the back of my neck. "At the same time, your mother made sure you'd have a home here in France with your aunt once things worked out well. Eventually, I set the course. When the police caught you at Camden Market, it wasn't coincidence."

"No, it was freaking bad luck." Or was it? A lot of nice things had happened ever since.

"I kind of planted stones in your way. People, who shoved you in the right direction."

My thoughts returned to my flight from the cops that particular afternoon. "The man with the hat," I remembered half aloud. "The kid. And the lady, who almost beat me with her bloody crutches. That was all your work?"

He nodded. Of course, for someone, who could hover between moments, this was like a waltz.

"I can't believe it. You manipulated me. How rude." And yet, when I gazed into his shiny blue eyes, I wanted to kiss him for all his sneaky behavior.

"It was easy enough to convince your friend, Quinn, and the judge of our intentions to bring you to France," he said. "And well, you know the rest."

Shivers ran over me. I breathed deep, crossing my legs at the ankles under the bench. "That morning in Abe's office, I saw you wearing a shiny white robe. Why?"

He ruffled my hair. "You've always been exceptionally observant. Or maybe I was just too easygoing around you, I don't know. I had a hard time hiding from you from the beginning." He sounded as if he knew the deeper truth behind this, but didn't let me in on it.

I liked to think it had to do with his strong feelings for me. There was this slight chance that he'd wanted me to see who he really was all along. To be honest with me.

The thought of honesty caused me to glance at my mother again. Julian had said there was time to talk, and I had so many questions that only my mother could answer. "Why did you give me away, Mom?"

The moment stretched in silence as she clasped her hands and shifted in her seat.

Julian pressed a kiss to my brow and whispered, "I'll see if Albert needs a hand in the vineyard." Although I would have been thankful for his assistance and the soothing effect he had on me, I appreciated his retreat.

With him gone, I gripped the warm mug a little tighter for an alternative source of comfort. When I spoke, my voice sounded too calm for my agitation. "Why the orphanage and not this place? Why wasn't I entrusted to Marie's care instead?"

My mother held my gaze, but all color had disappeared from her face. A hint that she'd dreaded this question for a very long time.

She inhaled deeply. "My family didn't know of you. I never told them, because I was ashamed of the situation I was in—pregnant by a man I hardly knew and who left me even before our child was born. I had nothing at that time but a shabby one-bedroom flat, a handful of pounds in my pocket, and a pile of overdue bills that kept mounting."

She swallowed hard, gazing at the distance. "When John came into our life, I thought things would change for the better. I loved him. And I thought he loved me back. But soon I learned a hard lesson. John was a drug addict, and all he needed me for was the money for his next fix. He was a violent person." Her gaze shifted back at my face. "But I'm sure you remember that."

I gave a quick nod with my lips pressed together.

When her pause stretched on, I wondered if she was envisioning the many times John had hurt me in his rage. Or the countless nights when she tried to soothe me with her soft humming after he'd beat the shit out of me. All of it must have reflected in my eyes at that moment.

Her hand closed tighter around mine. "One morning, you wouldn't stop crying after his beating. I begged him to let me take you to the emergency room. He refused, afraid the staff would find out about the abuse going on. But I didn't give up until he agreed."

I remembered that day. My left arm was on fire. John must have broken something when his hard slap at my face knocked me off my feet and into the wall. Perched in the backseat, I'd watched his murderous face in the rearview mirror all the way to the hospital. In those few minutes, both of them had drilled into me what I had to say to the doctor.

I fell off the swing on the playground. I fell off the swing...

"And then the nurse in the hospital reappeared alone after examining you." My mom's voice cut through my memories. "My heart felt like it was being crushed inside my chest. I knew I had lost you. I couldn't get you back. But I was also relieved, because I realized that John couldn't get near you ever again."

Now that I had opened my heart to my mother after all the

years of anger, I felt the pain she must have gone through. She had been torn apart between relief that I was safe and the grief of her loss.

"What happened to you and John?"

Her gaze dropped. She turned her head away from me. Her hand came up to her mouth, and she squeezed her eyes shut, probably willing the tears to go away. "John went to prison for child abuse. I was sentenced to six years for not doing anything about it. I wasn't allowed to see you, not even to tell you goodbye."

"I missed you so much. No one would tell me why I had to stay in that place." I half expected this to come out as a mere whisper but found that my voice was steady after all.

"I missed you, too, baby." Her misty eyes rested on my face again, and she reached out to touch my cheek. "I was determined to endure that time and then get you back home. Back to me, where you belonged. I couldn't send you to Marie and risk that you'd never want to return to me after you'd lived for years in a good place like this. That's why I denied having any family members willing to take you on. I was stupid and selfish."

As much as this information hurt, I was glad to find out that she hadn't intended to abandon me completely. "So when you got out, you came to see me in the orphanage. I was ready to go home with you. What kept you from coming like you promised?"

She fingered her tissue for a moment. "I sorted out my life and made preparations for the two of us to be together again. But the day I decided to bring you home, John returned. He was released about the same time as me, and he sneaked back into my life so easily. He promised he'd changed in jail. That he was clean now and wanted to start all over again. But that evening he nearly killed me in his drunkenness. By no means could I allow you to be near that man again."

She wiped her nose. "I tried to run from him, but he kept finding me wherever I went. Then, one day, he didn't show up, and I read in a discarded newspaper that the police had found the body of John Malton. He was killed in a drug deal gone bad. Two months before I found out about my illness."

Finally, I had my answers. Neither of us had had an easy life. When she had tucked the tissue back into the pocket of her house coat, she hung her head and exhaled a long sigh.

Silently, I rose from the bench and skirted the table to sit next to her. With my head resting on her shoulder, I wrapped my arms lightly around her breakable body.

Immediately and with a suppressed cry, she hugged me hard, her tears seeping into my hair. "I thank God for this moment."

I didn't.

God didn't know what it meant for me to hold my mother like this and at the same time know it might be the last time ever. The burden pressed down on me and cut off the steady stream of air into my lungs.

Even if she had come to terms with the way things had played out, I couldn't accept this end. I wouldn't allow God to take my mother away from me again, and with her, the only other person I loved just as much. There had to be a way, and I would find it.

A warm feeling surrounded me, taking away a lot of the pain that had centered in my chest. My mother seemed to feel it, too, because she suddenly tilted her head upward with a faint smile and a relieved sigh.

The angel was near.

I let go of my mom and shifted to look over my shoulder. Julian leaned against the wall with his hands tucked into his pockets.

His peaceful expression failed to cover the sadness in his eyes.

"Can I get *a moment* with you?" I asked.

"Anytime." With a soft twitch of his lips, he came forward. "But let's take your mother back to bed first. She looks worn out."

Mom gladly accepted his bent elbow, and I followed as he led her back to her room. I promised to look in on her in a bit, but right now I had to find a way to keep her.

With my mother drifting off to oblivion, Julian silently closed the door. "Where do you want to go?"

I shrugged, not really caring, as long as I was with him. But then I reached for his hand and led him upstairs, through my room, toward the balcony.

He stopped me in front of the balcony door. "You sure you want to go out there? We can stay inside."

Fear already gripped me around the neck, but it seemed important to get past that fright and proceed outside. "Just don't let go of me, and I'll be okay."

Julian nodded. He followed me with his hand securely wrapped around mine. Next to each other, we lowered to the floorboards, and with the wall behind us, I leaned my head on his shoulder. The clouds that sailed across the sky on a steady breeze slowed. Then they stood still.

Julian pulled my hand into his lap and began to play with my fingers. "This is your moment. What's up, Jona?"

I heaved a deep breath. "What does it take to trade? My life for my mother's."

His skimming of my palm ceased, and his head snapped up to meet my gaze. "That's impossible. And you shouldn't even think about it." The severity in his tone made me cringe. "Life is the greatest gift in the world. You should not be trifling with it."

"It is my life, and I can do with it what I want." I hardly found the strength to hold his glare. "I don't have a reason to live with both of you gone. What kind of justice is that? I find my mother after half a lifetime without her, and in the next moment I have to let go of her again." I paused. "And you."

"Accept what she did for you. From this point on, you can start your life anew. Marie and Albert will be more than happy to give you a good home." He let go of my hand to tuck a strand of hair behind my ear. "As for me, I should have listened to your mother when she warned me. She told me I'd cause you too much pain. But I was too selfish to see it. I thought what you needed was someone to show you what love can do. I refused to think of the consequences, didn't see the pain I was going to put the both of us through."

The pain he spoke about was tangible. The fear of loss, the longing, it all reflected in his face. It was impossible to even think of surviving one day without him. Or my mother.

"Can't you call on one of those healers you mentioned? Someone must be able to help her. Give us more time. Just a little. And if she stays, you can, too, right?"

He shook his head. "No healer can help her now. She knows that. And you need to accept it."

Sitting cross-legged, I braced my elbows on my knees and supported my aching head. "You know I heard you talking to her last night. You said there was a way." A few minutes ago I had believed taking my mother's place in death was the only way to be with Julian. Now a new flicker of hope kindled in me. "Tell me about it."

Julian didn't confirm, nor did he deny there was a possibility. He just said, "I cannot."

"Then what does it take to find out?" I demanded, loud enough to make him wince. "Do I have to randomly guess ? Is there a trial of courage required? You said something about sky diving." I jumped to my feet, standing firmly in the middle of the balcony, and pressed my hands to my hips. "If that's it, come on. Fetch your wings, and I'll prove I'm ready to sky dive with you."

He stood, reached around my waist through my bent arms, and pulled me closer. "You're a brave one, aren't you?" His lips brushed my hair as he spoke, then he pressed them tenderly against my temple. "This is one of the many reasons why I love you."

This was the third time he'd said it, and I longed to surrender to the words. But an immediate rush of white-hot anger flooded me, propelled me out of his arms. "How can you speak of love, when you won't move a finger to stop things from happening? If you really meant it, you wouldn't sit and watch my mother decay."

Not giving him a chance to hold me again, I whirled past him and dashed through my room and downstairs. The bolt clicked inside the lock of my mother's room as I turned the key, even though I wasn't sure if that could keep an angel out.

My mother didn't wake at my noisy entrance, so I perched next to her on the mattress and caressed her burning skin. I watched over her steady breathing for what seemed like hours. And in that time, I made a plan.

If God decided to take both of them, he would have to deal with one more.

*

Mom woke up at the same time my aunt and uncle returned from the field. Delighted to see me in her room, she immediately pulled me into an embrace. It felt so very unfamiliar to be held by Charlene, but at the same time unspeakably pleasant. I breathed in the cherry blossom scent of her body lotion, the one she hadn't stopped wearing since the days she'd tucked me in as a child. The memory of loving her flooded me in a warm rush of comfort.

We didn't talk much, but I helped her get to the kitchen. Julian sat at the table with his chin cupped in his hand. I cast him a long glance, letting him know that I was no longer mad at him.

Marie and Albert greeted my mom and me with eyes so wide they threatened to pop out, gaping at us with open mouths.

I waved at both of them then caught a glimpse of the box with the dirty bottles. "Sorry, I didn't finish cleaning those." I grimaced. "And on that note, I'm also sorry for the broken bottles."

"Oh, do not worry about it, *chérie*," my aunt said. "I am so very happy you and your mother finally made peace. It was about time."

I glanced at Julian, who seemed just as unhappy about it as I was. And for the same simple reason: We were going to lose each other soon.

"Oh, what is this? You took off the bandage?" My aunt interrupted my staring. "Is your hand fine again?"

In all the turmoil going on, I had completely forgotten to cover up Julian's miraculous healing demonstration. My hands disappeared into my pockets. "Yeah. Well, it tingles a little, but the pain is actually gone."

"That is good news. But still, you will not be going to work in the vinery this week. I want your hand to be healed completely before you handle dirty roots and fertilizer."

I nodded, trying not to think of tomorrow. I had a plan to carry out.

That night, Julian and I stayed long in my mother's room. I intended to savor every moment I had with the both of them, while Julian's supportive embrace kept me calm enough to face the inevitable.

Shortly before midnight, he led me away from my sleeping mother. "It's late. You should go upstairs and get some rest."

Heavy lids pushed over my eyes. I forced them open and shook my head. I didn't speak in order to suppress a yawn with a clenched jaw.

His fingers brushed my too-long bangs from my forehead. "She's going to wake up again tomorrow. I promise."

My lips trembled as I pressed a goodnight kiss to my mom's cheek. Shoulders hunched, I followed Julian upstairs.

In the hallway at the top of the staircase, I pivoted to glance at his face one last time. The way he tilted his head had me wondering if he sensed I was brooding over something. But I didn't give him time to question the matter. Instead, I cupped his face and, standing on my tiptoes, I pressed my lips against his.

His mouth opened, welcoming the kiss, while his arms encircled me. The aching in my chest almost broke me when I let go of him and hurried into my room.

The door clicked shut behind me, sounding like the signal of my intention. Slouching on my bed in the dark, I waited a quarter of an hour, reveling in the taste of Julian on my mouth. Then I rose and sneaked out into the empty hallway.

To carry out my plan, I needed a weapon. And I knew exactly where to find one.

Angel Tears

Albert's office was dark and silent. I didn't dare switch on the light, but I pulled back the curtains Marie closed every night, and soft moonlight streamed through the window.

From the wall, I picked up one of the dueling guns. The right one. The one Albert had told me was still loaded. I wasn't sure what this medieval weapon was loaded with. A bullet, lead shot, whatever. It should suffice to kill me if shot into my head.

Walking slowly around the desk to stand in front of the window, I wondered if I should have written a letter of farewell after all. One to Marie and Albert, who came so close to being like parents in the past couple weeks. And one to my mother to tell her

I'd tried to take her place, but wasn't allowed. A letter to Julian wouldn't be necessary. He'd know why I did it. And he could tell me off for it once we were reunited after death. In Heaven.

I took a long, deep breath, steeling my nerves. Then I lifted the gun to my right temple.

"*Jona, don't!*"

The shock of Julian's voice behind me almost caused me to release the shot that instant. My already tense body now prickled with the addition of his presence.

I turned around. "Go away."

Julian didn't budge an inch.

I didn't lower the gun, but raked the hammer back, determined to go through with it, whether he watched or not.

His hands were fisted at his sides, but he remained in the doorway. He probably feared what I'd do if he rushed me. "What are you trying to achieve with this?"

"If I can't take my mom's place, then I will go with the both of you." My voice had an unnaturally calm note that surprised me here, at the edge of life and death.

"Please, put it away." With lowered palms, he gestured for me to set the gun down.

"No." I gave a desperate laugh. "No, you can't leave me here all alone. You can't just walk out of my life tonight or tomorrow and think I'll take it just like that." I snapped the fingers of my free hand on the last word. "You can't! I won't let you. I want to come with you. And if this is the only way, then it's fine with me." The mouth of the pistol had lowered while I spoke and now I pressed it back into place. "I'm not going to let go of you."

"Jona, will you please put the gun down? This is not an option. Suicide never is."

He didn't understand. To me, this had nothing to do with suicide. Not in the usual way. I didn't want to end a lousy life. If that had been my wish, I'd have done so a long time ago. This was about him. And about being with him. In the afterlife.

I love you, I thought so hard I hoped he could understand.

"If you kill yourself, Heaven will be denied to you. You'll go to a different place, worse than anything you've ever known." The fear in his face seemed real. "There's no way for me to follow. Now put it down, in Heaven's name. Please!"

I hesitated. Suddenly, I felt completely insecure. What if he was right? What if I got this wrong, and he wouldn't be there, at the other side? And then a much worse thought haunted me: What if he didn't want to have me on the other side at all? He seemed fine with the way things were turning out. He wasn't fighting it, like I was. As an angel, he must've had means, ways to fix this. But he was just waiting patiently until all was over. Until he could return to his sunshiny place with no thought of me, or how much he'd hurt me the day he left.

The day he would take my mother with him instead of me.

I squeezed my eyes shut for a second. My hand slowly sagged down, and I shook my head in utter despair.

Julian must have thought he'd broken through to me, talked me down. He started forward, but at his first movement, I raised both my hands with the gun clasped between them. This time I pointed it right at the center of his chest.

"Fine," I whispered. "If you don't want to take me with you, then you won't take my mom either. Go to hell, Julian."

For the count of a heartbeat, Julian seemed more hurt by my words than the prospect of being hit by a bullet. But he gathered himself quickly. "You can shoot me if you want. It won't help you one bit. And after today, you should have realized a bullet would never be fast enough to hit me."

He took a step forward, a bit uncertain it seemed. He didn't yet trust that I wouldn't shoot after all. And a good thing he didn't. Because I had every intention to stop him from reaching me.

"Stay where you are." My finger trembled on the trigger.

But I didn't shoot at his next step. Or the next.

As he skirted the desk, our gazes locked at all times, I tracked his every step with the gun's mouth. The final blow never came.

We stood face to face for the length of a breath. Then he slowly reached for the weapon. "Give it to me."

I had run out of options. Realizing I couldn't shoot either him or myself, there was only one possible way to get where I wanted: to take one step forward and proceed into his arms.

Eventually, I surrendered and let go of the gun. Julian placed it on the desk, never taking his eyes off me. He closed the remaining distance between us with one last step and took me in his arms. I shoved my hands up his chest and locked them around the back of his neck in a clinging embrace, burying my face in his shoulder.

Julian rested his chin on the top of my head and hugged me tighter.

"Love you," he whispered, but I couldn't tell if I'd really heard it, or if the sound of it only played in my mind.

I wished I could tell him the same, just once, so he'd know before he disappeared forever. But sobs rocked me in his arms, and I couldn't bring myself to speak. Never before had I felt so helpless.

*

The darkness in Julian's room matched the grief inside me. My cheek against his chest, the tear-soaked cotton of his shirt stuck to my skin. Aftermath chills of what had happened in my uncle's study raced through my body. But warmth emanating from the angel I embraced soothed the nerves that were on the edge of breaking.

I closed my eyes, trying to find some peace before I paid my mother another visit. Maybe the last one.

At Julian's stir underneath me, I jerked upward, wide awake. "Mom?" I glanced around the room. Daylight had swapped the darkness in the room already.

Julian brushed tender fingers over my forehead and cheek. He pressed a kiss to my brow. Looking at his calm and beautiful face helped me catch my breath. "Everything's all right. Your aunt is just a little worried because your mother's still asleep. I can sense her fear. I better go down and let Charlene wake up."

The lump in my throat eased with a swallow. I sat on my legs. "Okay, I'll just pop to the bathroom and then come down with you."

His lips pressed together and his brows pulled to a frown, giving me the impression he was about to contradict.

"Don't you dare leave me behind!" I held his gaze for the length of a breath, eyes narrowed.

"I better not let you out of my sight, anyway. Who can say what reckless idea you'll come up with next?" A sense of honesty shadowed his taunting.

He waited while I used the bathroom. Cold water revived my tired eyes. My hand back in his, we headed downstairs. Marie's anxious whisper to Albert in the hallway drifted to us.

"Something wrong?" Julian said as we approached them. His perfectly innocent tone gave me more chills.

"It is Charlene. She did not wake up this morning when I walked into her room to help her get dressed. She looks like she is asleep, but what if she fell into a coma?" My aunt sounded close to cracking as she clasped her hands together. Fear flashed clearly in her eyes. "I was just saying to Albert that we better call an ambulance."

Julian stepped toward her and touched his hand to her forearm. "Jona and I kept her awake long last night. She's probably just exhausted. Let her rest for a few more minutes. I'm sure she's fine."

I was already heading into my mother's room, but even with my back to him, I felt the lie in his words. She wasn't going to be fine. Today very well might be her last. Maybe someone should tell Marie. She would want to say her goodbyes, too.

But how to break the news? *Sorry Marie, but you know Julian—the angel—was taking care of my mother while I was still furious with her. Now that everything is fine between us, God is going to collect her soul.* Not quite the words someone wanted to hear when they were expecting "Good morning, did you sleep well?"

My mom lay on her side, facing the door when I entered. Although her eyes remained motionless behind closed lids, her breathing seemed steady enough for someone sleeping. *Not dead.* Yet a hint of uncertainty stopped me in the middle of the room. Regarding her for a long moment, the aching in my chest welled, and my breathing hitched to staccato sighs.

Gentle hands wrapped around my shoulders. "You can wake her. She'll hear you," Julian said into my ear.

Dragging a deep breath, I crossed to her bed and settled down. My first touch to her arm coaxed out a moan.

My mother rolled to her back, her lids slowly opening. "Good morning, sunshine."

I clapped a hand over my mouth, trying to strangle the tears burning to the surface of my eyes. There was nothing good about this morning. My mom was going to leave me. Again. Without a word, I collapsed beside her and let the pain come out in hard sobs.

She scooted backward to lean on the headboard, dragging me with her. Then she hugged me so tightly I could hardly believe she had the strength for it. "Don't cry, my baby. Everything will be good—you'll see. I've lived my life and found a happy ending with you. I'm not grieving."

She sounded bright and sober-minded. Neither fear nor sorrow rang in her words. "And I don't want you to be sad either. You're young and have a good life to live. Promise me you'll stay with Marie and Albert. They can be the parents you always wished for."

"I never wished for anything but for you to come back. How can I not be sad when *He*'s going to take you away from me?" The words ripped from my clamped chest as if they tore my throat bloody. This time not even Julian's loving hand on my neck could soothe me.

"*Mon Dieu*, what happened?" My aunt whirled into the room as though she expected the worst, her face horror-stricken. At the sight of my mother sitting upright Marie's gaze lit up. She pressed a hand to her chest, breathing a sigh of relief. "*Dieu merci!* You are awake. I was so worried this morning when you kept sleeping though I shook you."

She lowered next to me on the mattress and skimmed her fingers through my hair. "But why are you crying, *chérie*?"

The bile rushing up my throat kept me from answering. Marie turned her head toward Julian when he planted his hand on her shoulder and urged her with a flick of his head to follow him outside. "Can I have a word with you?"

Confusion creased her forehead. "Yes, of course." Her movements when she rose from my mother's bed were reluctant, as if she already sensed Julian had bad news.

As the door clicked closed, I sank deeper into my mom's embrace.

It didn't take Julian long to return with a sobbing Marie in tow. One look between the sisters seemed enough to confirm what Julian must have told her. My aunt knelt next to the bed and grabbed my mother's hand. She kissed her palm and squeezed it. "You should have told me sooner."

I caught my mother's questioning glance. Julian cleared his throat. "I told her what the doctor said on Saturday. That you might not recover from the cold."

Wondering whether the doctor had really said this, or if Julian made it up to cover the truth, I rose from the bed and crossed to him on slow steps. He wrapped his arm around my shoulders and pressed me tenderly against him.

"It would be unfair not to give your aunt a chance to say goodbye to her sister," he whispered. "She doesn't have to know everything, just this much."

I agreed silently, his calming scent comforting me.

While Marie and her husband talked to my mom, encouraging her that everything was going to be fine and the doctor must have been mistaken, Julian ushered me into the kitchen to have breakfast. But apart from a few sips of tea, nothing would go down. My stomach churned.

With the warm cups in our hands, we just stared at each other across the table. It was a hard fight against the tears wanting to spill over, but I remained strong. And so did Julian. His blank face revealed nothing, but his heavy sighs cut the silence. He rubbed his hands over his face, then reached for my hand and brought it to his lips. Warm breaths coming through his nose caressed my fingers.

"Will you remember me?" I said with a hardly audible whisper.

Instead of answering, he furrowed his brows in a puzzled way.

I forced a hard swallow before I could speak again. "You said you will make me forget everything about you. So I wondered if you would remember me once you've returned to Heaven."

Julian coughed. His throat must have hurt him as much as mine did. "Of course, I will remember you. I'll treasure our moments together. Forever."

Each breath I took filled my chest with rocks. A small part of me anticipated the time when I would forget, for the pain wouldn't be so excruciating anymore. But it was easy to silence and bury that part of me under more heavy stones.

Marie came in a few minutes later, her eyes glistening and her nose red. "Henri just called and said one of the modules of the sprinkler broke. Water is flooding the vines. I will go with Albert to help them fix it. It won't take long." She waited for us to nod then scurried to the door with her gaze focused on the floor. In the threshold, she stopped and looked over her shoulder. "If anything happens, if your mother's condition gets worse, call me in immediately."

We both nodded again and returned to my mother's room.

"Is there anything I can get you?" I asked her. A wet cloth lay on the nightstand, and I patted her burning forehead with it.

"No, dear. Just stay with me while I rest for a moment." Her eyes had already closed, so I remained silent and kept caressing her hot face.

Julian knelt on the floor, his chin supported on his bent arm that rested on my lap. There was no way to say whether losing him or my mother would hurt more. But the aching coupled together was too much for one person to bear. I yearned to close my eyes like my mother and escape the pain.

After a half hour in which my legs went numb and my back started to ache, Julian stood and steered me to the wide chair in front of the window. He slumped down first, pulled me onto his lap, and cradled me against him.

"You know, as an angel," he said softly, with the weight of honesty in his voice, "I've seen many beautiful things and experienced thousands of wonders. But the most beautiful thing I've ever seen is you. And with you I've had the best moments of my life."

Knowing he spoke of sixty-odd thousand years, his words filled me with warmth. "You certainly are the best thing in my life, too."

His breathing stopped, his body tensed. Almost as if he expected something important to happen.

"What?" I demanded.

He relaxed—on the surface. But his hollow eyes and his tight grip on my hand told me he struggled to hide deep disappointment. He buried his face in my hair. "Nothing, love. It's nothing."

With my cheek nestled against his chest, minutes ticked by like seconds. The rhythmical skimming of his fingers on my neck lulled me to a state of half sleep. The warm scent of wild wind was all I noticed as his chest rose and fell steadily. I would have fallen asleep if my mother hadn't woken with a gurgling cough.

Before I knew what had happened, I sprang to her side and grabbed her hand. "Mom, I'm here." Unfortunately, the worry I tried to hide from her echoed clearly in my voice.

The strong squeeze of her hand gave me some confidence. "I need a sip of water. Can you get me a fresh glass?"

Her lips were dry like sandpaper, and it didn't help that she licked them with a tongue just as parched. I made it to the kitchen and back in less than ten seconds, although I left a trail of water after me. My hand placed behind my mother's head, I helped her drink in slow sips.

When she'd had enough, she opened her arms for me. Happily, I dived into her embrace.

"Thank you so much, baby."

Fear gripped me as I realized she wasn't speaking about me getting her a drink. My head on her shoulder, she asked me to summon my aunt.

Fear changed to panic. I shot up. "Why? Are you feeling worse?"

"No, dear." She gave me a strong and confident smile. "I forgot to tell her where my life insurance is, and now would be a good moment to talk to her. I'm feeling just fine."

Did she really, or was this Julian's angel powers giving her strength? Her hand on my cheek felt warmer than before. But with the color returning to her cheeks, she looked a whole lot better.

"I would send Julian," she said, "but I'm afraid I need his help in here. So could you get Marie for me?"

To my questioning glance, Julian replied with a nod and walked toward me. I stood, uncertain if I really should leave my mother.

Strands of my hair ran through his fingers. He pulled my head against his chest and planted a gentle kiss on my brow. "It's okay," he promised.

So I slipped into my boots and hurried toward the vineyard. A few hundred feet ahead, I spotted Marie and Albert, both bent over the small sprinkler that stuck out from the ground. They were too far to shout, so I scurried on, my thoughts lingering in my mother's room.

What were she and Julian talking about now that I was outside? Mom didn't seem scared at all today, although we both felt it was going to be over soon. Maybe she was asking Julian about life on the other side. Getting prepared.

I stopped dead, and with my feet, my heart stopped, too. The world spun around me in an endless carousel. Eerie underwater noises bubbled in my ears.

How could I have been so stupid? My mom wanted me out of the room so I wouldn't have to see what was going to happen. She could have sent Julian, but she needed him with her. To escort her to the other side.

God, no!

"Jona?" Marie blurted. "Is your mother feeling worse?"

But I had no time to reply. I whirled around, needing to get back inside as quickly as possible. But invisible cords slowed my movements. The first few steps seemed to take an eternity while my breaths erupted in painful spasms.

"Julian, don't!" I croaked, although I wasn't sure if I even said it out loud. In my mind I yelled his name over and over. He had to hear me! *Please.* God couldn't take my mother today. Not now, when I wasn't with her. When I hadn't said goodbye.

"Jona! What is it?" The shouts from behind me couldn't make me wait.

The house suddenly appeared as if it was a mile away. It would take me hours to get there at this rate.

And then I broke into a run. My loose boots pounded on the path, kicking pebbles to all sides. Marie's cry grew fainter.

My heart pounded a frantic beat in my ears when I finally reached the house. It was a long way through the hallway to my mother's room. The door stood ajar, and I slammed against it.

"Don't! Please, don't!" I choked. My mind swarmed with panic. I gasped for air, stumbling farther into the room.

Caught by strong hands, I glanced up at Julian. I sucked in a breath at the sight of him. His eyes were the only thing I recognized about him. His casual clothes gone, he was dressed in white light, a long cloak swaying around his legs. The pair of wings sprouting from his shoulder blades hovered two feet above the ground, spreading so wide they almost brushed opposite walls.

The angel took me into his arms and leaned his forehead against mine. His wings enclosed our embrace into a ball of white light.

My nose dripped. The first rush of tears burned like hellfire. Salty streams ran over my lips. "Please wait!" My voice hoarse and shaky, I clutched the front of his cloak as I begged. Stopping him from taking my mother was all I could think of. "Let her stay with me. Let her live. I don't want to lose both of you. Give me a few more hours. A few more days. Don't leave me, Julian!"

A trail of vapor traced the movement of his hands as he reached up to brush back my hair. "It's impossible." His tone was soft, yet it left no room for negotiations. "Look at her. She's ready. It's time."

His wings lowered to grant me a glance at my mother, her eyes wide and happy. She gazed in our direction, but she only focused on Julian. The angel in white light.

A part of my heart splintered and remained with him as I broke free from his hold and inched toward my mother.

I was right beside her as she finally tilted her head toward me and smiled. "Jona, you came back?" She sounded far away and surprised.

"Yes, Mom. I came to stop you."

The warmth of her hand seeped into my palm. "To stop me? From what?"

"From leaving," I sobbed, wiping my nose with the back of my free hand.

"Why would you do that?" Her innocent, confused gaze matched her childlike tone.

"Can't you see the beautiful place over there?" she crooned. "They are calling me. It's an invitation. I would be a fool not to go."

"She's already glimpsing Heaven." A shiver skittered along my arms at Julian's announcement behind me. "It's time to let go."

But I wasn't ready. Unable to make myself speak, I cradled my mother's defenseless body against my chest. Lungs tight, I shook with fear.

Her gaze cleared, warmed even. "Let me go, dear child."

"No. No! Never!" Over the crook of my arm wrapped around my mother's shoulders, I glowered at Julian who was coming closer. "You won't take her anywhere!"

One silver tear glistened in his eye, shining with the light of a star. He blinked, and it was gone. "I wish I didn't have to, but it's not up to me."

Half of the room glowed with his presence as he sank to my side. He pressed his palm to my brow. His touch dragged a storm of memories out of my mind. Each of them flashed before me then vaporized into a void.

I fought against the pull, jerked my head from side to side. I screamed at him. "Please, Julian! Don't do this. Leave me this one precious thing!"

But just like my heart, my mind was left empty. And in the next instant, the spell was over. I slouched alone in the room, holding my dead mother.

Delusions

The birds chirped an unearthly happy song in the crown of the maple tree next to the patio. Between the new green leaves, the sun struggled to shine through. It played a befuddling game of light and shadow on my closed eyes. A fresh peachy smell emanated from the cushion of the deck chair. The fact that the patio furniture was out of winter storage and Marie had laundered the cushions gave further proof that spring was winning over the cold winter months.

With the skirt of the dress tugged over my bent legs, I hugged my knees, pressing my cheek on them. *Red.* Marie had smiled and said the color would be good for my depression when she had seen me coming downstairs that Sunday morning.

But I didn't see how it changed anything. I might as well have worn my usual black cloths that went so well with my mental state.

After my mother's death, the world had not been the same vivid place for me. Like a vortex, sadness had drawn me under with no intention of setting me free. Her funeral seemed to have closed a chapter in my life. A very painful one, with many twists and an unexpected turn at the end. But I couldn't find the will and strength to start a new one.

Quinn had come to attend the sad ceremony. He'd just finished reading a passage from the bible for me when I had finally choked into sobs in the church.

After a long conversation with Aunt Marie and Uncle Albert, Quinn had offered to take me back to England with him when all the formalities of the death were settled. Albert even promised that he and Marie would pay the rent of a flat and the tuition should I choose to study at the University of London.

But I'd declined their generous offer.

Under tears, I'd begged them to let me stay in their house instead. How else would I be able to bring fresh lilies and roses to my mother at her grave every few days?

There was no discussion necessary, no further pleading. Marie had folded me into her loving arms and welcomed me as the member of their family that I had been in their hearts from the very day of my arrival.

So I stayed.

From the window in my room, I'd watched the summer give way to a colorful fall and snow cover the vineyards with a thick white blanket. Permanently red from crying too much, my nose burned at the slightest touch. And when my eyes finally dried and not a single tear would come anymore, my mind seemed to shut down, too.

Once, Marie had tried to talk me into seeing a psychotherapist. *You are walking around the house like a zombie.* But I wouldn't go see the shrink. Not for the grief inside me. Nor for the delusions when those set in.

It had started with dreams. Dreams of a face I couldn't get a clear view of. Night after night, I saw the same shining blue eyes, and each morning when I woke, I yearned to find them, searching the crowded market like a lost child each time we went to town.

Over the weeks, the fine features of a boyish face formed around the eyes and became clearer. But I couldn't recall the face from my memories. So why would I keep dreaming of a man I didn't know?

Unfortunately, my artistic skills were nonexistent, or else I would have captured the face in a drawing. In fact, I had tried, but what came out was more like a cartoon Garfield than the fine lines of a gorgeous man. Not someone Marie or Albert could help me identify when I showed them the messy sketch.

Thinking of their perplexed gazes as they doubtlessly questioned my sanity, I winced and shifted in the deck chair. Marie came over with a glass of lemonade and placed the drink on the table.

"Here, *chérie*," she said to me in French. "If you don't want to eat breakfast again, then you should at least drink some juice."

During the last half year I'd made good progress in learning the language. And how could I not, when my aunt and uncle refused to talk to me in English? They'd decided the best way for me to learn was to hear French frequently, more often than just once a week in the course they had signed me up for.

"*Merci,*" I replied, accepting the drink.

She sat down on my lounge chair in front of my legs and touched the seam of the three layers of my skirt. "That dress suits you so well. You should wear it more often."

"I don't feel good in it," I said. The dress placed on a hanger outside my wardrobe had really startled me this morning. Especially since Marie never walked into my room uninvited. A habit of both my aunt and uncle that I appreciated. "You shouldn't have picked it out for me today," I added.

A confused smile tugged on her lips, and she glanced at me from the corner of her eye. "What are you talking about? I never pick outfits for you to wear, you know that."

"But you placed the hanger on my wardrobe door," I replied, suddenly not so sure. "How else could it have gotten there?"

How indeed?

"Maybe you put it there before you went to bed last night?"

"When have I ever chosen to wear a color like this?" I arched a brow and lifted the top layer of the skirt demonstratively. "I don't even know why this is still in my wardrobe. I thought I'd given all the fancy clothes back to you ages ago."

Marie cupped my chin, searching my face with compassionate eyes. For the flash of a second her mind was transparent. I dreaded her next words.

"Is this like the piano playing in the middle of the night?"

Hell yeah, it was. And just because none of them had heard the music at night, it didn't mean that no one had played the damn piano. My song. "Hallelujah." The melody that had been stuck in my head since I was a child.

After I found the parlor empty that first night and screamed my head off, Marie had made me a cup of warm milk with honey and tucked me back into bed. "So soon after your mother's death, it's only natural that your mind plays tricks on you sometimes. Everything will get better in time," she'd assured me.

If only.

The music kept playing in my mind. And I knew it could only be *there*—in my mind—because I started to lock the lid over the piano keys in the evening and took the small brass key up to my room. The metal felt hot in my palm when I lay in bed, tense and anxious that something was seriously wrong with my brain, while the softest melody played downstairs.

But as so many things in life, I got used to it over the months.

I lowered my gaze from Marie's questioning eyes, but snuggled deeper into her soft hands, soaking in the tender feeling of being held. In all the months I had been living with her and Uncle Albert, she had grown to be like a second mother. At times, I found it hard to return her love with the sadness eating away at me, but I was still grateful beyond words.

Pressing a kiss onto her palm, I cleared my throat. "I'll go pay a visit to my mom. Do you want me to bring something from the baker?"

"Thank you, dear, but I've already been there this morning." She rose from the lounge chair and went to break a red rose from the bush next to the patio. "But you may want to bring your mother this."

"Sure." I took the flower and kissed her cheek.

The trip down to the cemetery only took me five minutes, and I could have walked it blindfolded by now. I knew the exact step count and also every patch of roughness on the street where puddles would form on a rainy day.

As usual the big iron gate at the entrance to the graveyard was closed and creaked eerily at my push. The pebbled ground sank softly underneath my steps. One of the tiny sharp stones slid through the straps of my left sandal and pinched my sole. I shook my foot, but the pebble wouldn't come out, so I leaned against my mother's tombstone and worked it out of my shoe.

When the stone dropped to the ground, I placed Marie's flower in the copper vessel with the bunch of white roses. Then I traced the inscription on the marble underneath her name with my finger.

May your angels take care of you, always.

I never understood why, but when the chiseler had taken the order from my aunt before the burial, I'd asked him to carve those words into the stone. Marie found this a lovely way to say goodbye to my mom, but for an unknown reason the line had a deeper meaning to me. One more of the many mysteries my life seemed to be filled with. A deep sigh expanded my chest, containing a lot of the confusion and longing that wearing this pomegranate red dress had brought on today.

"God, Mom, I'm not going mental, am I?" *I mean other than talking to stone at a cemetery.*

Movement to my right caught my eye. I whirled about, expecting to face the old lady with the gray chignon. She came here regularly to tend the grave of her recently departed son. The tiny woman used to gawk at me like I was a dead fly in her glass of wine whenever she caught me talking to myself.

But there was no one there. I pressed my palms to my eyes and groaned. "Who's doing all this to me?" Through my splayed fingers, I peeked at the small square picture of my mother on the white marble. "Are you still hanging around, Mom?"

Girl, you better stop thinking such nonsense, I scolded myself. And if I had to think it, then I could at least keep it to myself. The long argument over the shrink still loomed in the back of my mind.

But I knew something unnatural was going on around me. Something no one else seemed to notice. And why in the world did I keep dreaming of a man whose beauty took my breath away every morning when I woke up?

Because you're bat-shit crazy.

Yes, that must be it. I arranged the flowers in the vase, brushed the curve of the stone and said a silent goodbye to my mother. "See you tomorrow."

After dinner, where I'd mostly stared at my food, a strange impulse sent me out onto the balcony. Annoyed with my fear of heights, I had started to train myself to overcome the vertigo that had bothered me my entire life.

At the beginning, my bones had shaken like the tail of a rattle snake each time I stepped onto the fragile structure, but by now I could lean over the railing to talk to Marie or Albert below without going into hysteria.

The guestroom next to mine had a French door that led to the balcony, too. On warm days, Marie would open the door to air out the completely furnished room, like someone was going to move in any day.

I liked the dark blue bedding. On some evenings, I just sat on the center of the queen-size bed and rocked back and forth in a trance-like rhythm with my legs hugged to my chest.

Peeking into the room through the gently swaying curtains now filled me with a longing I couldn't understand. With my mother gone, I often felt alone—like the days when I had lived in the orphanage. But there came moments when I felt even lonelier.

I closed my eyes. In my mind, I saw a pair of gorgeous blue eyes staring back at me from inside the room.

"Who are you?" I whispered as the rays of the setting sun

touched the side of my face. If only I could plug my mind into a printer and get the picture of this man on paper. A photograph I could stare at when I was by myself, like now.

Tired from another day filled with thoughts, I stripped off the red dress and hung it inside the wardrobe. The fluffy pillow welcomed me, and I drifted off to sleep within minutes.

The dream returned.

I saw nothing but a beautiful face with glowing blue eyes. When I lifted my hand to touch it, the person inched back just out of my reach. In an eerie dreamlike way, I knew I would again be chasing the smiling man all night until I woke with a sigh in the morning.

But this time something was different. Although he wouldn't allow me to touch his face, I felt a soft caress on my skin. Fingers curled around my hand, warm and smooth. Tender. The sensation seemed so real that in my dream, I struggled to wake. To see who was holding me.

It was a long and hard fight against the numbness of my mind, but finally I managed to open my eyes to slits. Dawn filled my room like a sea of gray fog. Nothing seemed changed inside, but a soft squeeze of my hand dragged my glance down to the side of my bed.

A man knelt on the floor.

The beauty of his face took my breath away just like every time I woke after my dreams. But this time a shadow of him still lingered in front of me. He slouched over the edge of my bed, with his chin resting in the crook of his elbow. He gazed at me with his intense blue eyes. The golden strands of his hair falling over his forehead entangled with his long lashes and twitched at each of his slow blinks.

He was clad in a white robe, and a set of giant wings sprouted from his shoulder blades, covered with soft feathers everywhere. They lay like a blanket over the floor. Warmth seeped into me from the hands that held mine.

"I know you," I breathed, surprisingly calm. "You've been there. In my dreams."

The angel nodded.

"Am I dying?" *Maybe I should be afraid.*

A smile played around his sensual lips. "No."

"Then I'm dreaming?" Or hallucinating like the last eight months that I'd been hearing music when no one played it.

He lifted his chin from his arm and shook his head slowly. "Not quite. But I can only stay as long as you haven't fully broken out of the dream." His whisper was as soft as the wing beat of a dove.

"But you look like an angel. What are you doing in my room? On the floor?"

"I came to return something to you. Something that I'd stolen from you a while ago." He cupped my hand with both of his, then brought it to his lips and planted the softest kiss on my curled fist.

I squinted, struggling to fully awake and make sense of what was going on. But I should have heeded his warning. One heartbeat later, the figure tinted in a misty white light wavered before my eyes and disappeared.

"Don't go away. Please stay! Tell me your name!"

As I reached for the vanishing angel in a useless attempt to hold him back, a small paper ball slipped from my fingers and dropped to the floor.

Finally

As the sun rose above the trees, warm rays danced on the cream-colored walls. The comforter tucked around my waist, I sat up in my bed and scanned the room for any sign of the illuminated angel. The experience had seemed so real, it had left me with the impression I'd been fully awake.

Holy crap, what had Marie put in the meal yesterday? Magic Mushrooms? I rubbed the bridge of my nose, squeezing my eyes shut. If the hallucinations got any stranger, I might have to reconsider seeing the shrink.

But hadn't there been something left behind in my vision? A small, balled paper had dropped to the floor. Scooting to the edge of the mattress, I peeked under my bed. *Nothing.*

But wait, there was a crumpled paper ball under my nightstand! The angel had really left a souvenir. Anticipation sped up my breathing as I unfolded the sheet. I recognized my own handwriting, but not the note itself. The headline read *Julian's spooky dual life.*

"Julian..." Was that his name? The man from my dream—the angel?

"Inflicts happiness by touch," I whispered the first line. A tingle started in my stomach, wringing my insides into a tight knot. The sensation spread fast through my body up to my head.

Revitalizes the dragon. Can jump 15 feet high. Resurrected duck today. Reading each line pulled me into what seemed like a roller coaster ride back in time.

I recalled the day my mother had brought me to France, only this time a young man sat between us on the plane. His hand covering my clenched fist had sent waves of happiness into me.

The same happiness that swamped me now.

Julian. It was him who had come out of Abe's office the day of my hearing and freed me from the steel cuffs. The memory of how he'd sat in my room in the orphanage when it was time to leave for the airport flooded me. I reveled in the sensation of his protective arms wrapped around me, keeping me safe, when he'd dragged me onto the balcony.

The vision was as clear as one of Marie's freshly polished crystal glasses.

Breathing fast, my eyes skimmed over the lines in the list again and again. Each time a new wave of memories washed over my mind. Eventually, I was filled with three weeks of memories that must have been the best time of my life. For I'd spent them with *Julian.*

The angel.

"Oh my God. How could I forget?" But that part wasn't a secret any longer, either. The moment my mother had died, he'd pressed his palm to my brow and pulled out all my memories of him. Every single one. He'd left me hollow and unknowing. Empty.

"What have you done to me?" My lips trembled. The past eight months I had gone through a depression that had consumed me, causing me to doubt my sanity. But it must have been him who had played the piano for me at night. And of course he would have placed the dress on the door of the wardrobe. Had it not been a present from him the day that he'd first kissed me out on the beach?

I covered my mouth with my hand, struggling not to wince with a mix of happiness and despair. My gaze moved to the bottom of the paper. Another line had been scribbled onto the list of Julian's extraordinary behavior, but in a different handwriting than mine.

Loves you more than he can possibly understand.

My heart exploded. An unstrained smile stretched my lips. He'd never really left me, and with the subtle actions that only I would notice, he'd made sure that a small part of me remembered him. Even if it was only the shadow of a face in my dreams.

Flipping the comforter to the side, I jumped out of bed, slipped into my jeans, and tugged on a t-shirt. Barefoot, I strode out the door, crossed to his room, and stopped in the threshold with his name on my lips. But he wasn't there; the room was empty.

My heart sank.

Reluctant steps carried me further into the room. My gaze wandered over the furniture that no one had used for so long. But Julian had stayed here for many weeks. His aura had left its imprint—it closed in, enveloping me.

In front of his bed, I stopped as I glimpsed something that had long been wiped from my mind. A gray hoodie lay sprawled on the blanket. *He gave this back to me, too?* And I had never even noticed he'd taken it from me along with all the precious memories of him.

Sinking onto the mattress, I pulled the sweatshirt into my lap. Uncertain what rush of emotions and longing the scent would evoke, I hesitated to bring it to my face and sniff. But the joy filling me as the fog lifted from my mind was too great. I buried my face in the hoodie.

Ocean. Sun. Warm, wild wind. Happy day. A kiss. I drowned in the wonderful flood of remembrance. In his arms, the world had stopped turning. He'd taken me to a place between times. To live in a special moment.

"I miss you so much." The words hurt in my tight throat. And now it was all clear why I had never seemed to recover from the loss of my mother. Because the day that she died, I had also lost the love of my life.

It was hard not to break out into tears, but by pressing my lips together I managed to stay strong. I slipped my arms into the sleeves of the hoodie, which was a few sizes too big for me, and brought the cuffs to my nose to draw in another deep breath of him.

I would have given everything to hold him again, just once more. Julian was the best thing that had ever happened to me.

"I love you," I croaked into the fabric. "I've always loved you. From the moment you broke through my protection and walked straight into my heart."

"It's about time you realized that."

A breath caught in my throat. I snapped my head toward the French door where the chuckle had come from. Julian sat on the railing of the balcony, his feet dangling. It was a good thing I was already sitting, or I would have collapsed on the spot.

There you go. Craziness is taking over.

Julian returned my intense glare. Then he lifted one suggestive brow. "Don't want to come join me out here?"

Slowly, I shook my head. "I'm hallucinating. I'm hallucinating..."

Then why the hell bother to shake your head at a mirage? Why was no one around to slap me when I was so obviously going insane?

Julian drew his brows together, the corners of his mouth turning downward. "Come on, Jona. You didn't make me wait for you this long just to call me a fantasy in the end."

His voice sounded so real. And his body seemed solid, not ghostlike as I had seen him half an hour ago. He also appeared without his wings, dressed in his usual outfit of blue jeans and a shirt.

But, jeez, what would happen if I fell for my own delusions?

Better make it a good one!

My gulp echoed through the room as I rose from his bed. Knees wobbly, I crossed to the door, but stopped with a hand to the frame for support.

"What brought you back?" My voice had abandoned me completely. In order for him to answer, he would have to be able to read lips.

"You. Because you finally accepted what you felt all along. You've learned to trust. And by speaking it out loud you opened the portal for me to return."

"Fully? Return?" My sandpaper-dry tongue stuck to the roof of my mouth. It made me stammer. "I—I mean, did you come back as the man or the angel?"

His shoes thudded on the floorboards as he hopped down. The

boxes planted with bright red flowers shook, releasing drops of dew. His thumbs dipped into his pockets, and he leaned against the railing.

"Fully," he confirmed. "I'm here to stay."

I struggled to grasp what he'd said. I'd endured so long without him, and now he'd come back. I was tempted to run into his embrace. But the small chance that he would vaporize into thin air the instant I wrapped my arms around him kept me rooted. How much craziness was one mind capable of?

"*Bonjour*, Jona," my aunt shouted with her usual cheerful tone from the garden below. "Hi, Julian. Will you stay for breakfast?"

I held my breath. Leaning slightly to the side, I gazed past Julian and spotted Marie carrying a scalding pot of coffee and a tray of buns to the table under the willow tree.

"Yeah, I think I will," Julian replied with a grin but without turning away from me.

"She just invited you to eat with us." As though it was the most natural thing in the world to have an angel sitting at the breakfast table. "How come she remembers you?"

"You opened the gate." He shrugged. "Everyone affected will accept me as part of their life again."

Mind swimming, I gave him a pointed stare. "My aunt doesn't wonder where you came from all of a sudden?"

"She knows me as her sister's caretaker. As far as she remembers, I left shortly after the funeral on another assignment. She doesn't doubt I'm real." He walked toward me at a seductive pace, his chin low and fire sparkling in his eyes. "So why do you?"

I reached out, almost expecting him to draw back like he had done so many times in my dreams. But he moved closer and let me feel the smooth skin of his face. I skimmed my fingers over his cheeks, his lips, down his neck and shoulders.

"You feel so real. Totally alive. I think even though I couldn't remember, I was waiting for this moment all these months." Feeling his firm biceps, I ran my hands lower and finally laced them with his. "And now you're here, and I can't dare to trust my eyes."

"You'd better believe it, baby. Because it makes *this* feel so much better." And the next instant his lips took mine in a slow, thrilling kiss. My palms pressed against the wall as I surrendered to him. His tongue delved into my mouth, whirling ravenously around mine. My knees gave way, but he steadied me with his body pushing against mine.

Kissing a path along my jaw, he purred into my ear. "Until the sun sets tonight I will still be an angel. It is up to you to decide before then whether you want me to stay—or leave again."

Huh? Stop kidding me, angel! "Can I make that decision now? I want you to *stay!*"

One corner of his mouth lifted in my favorite lopsided smile. "I hoped you would say that. So after sundown, I'll lose my angel powers and spend this life with you as *ordinary Julian*." He nibbled my earlobe. "But before that happens, there is something I've wanted to do with you for a very long time." His fingers found the first button of his shirt.

"What?" I rasped a joke, pressing harder against the wall behind me. "Make love to me?"

His fingers went down from one button to the next, revealing his strong chest to my gaping eyes. "That, too." A rascally grin flashed across his face. "But it will have to wait another *moment.*"

Over his shoulder, I spotted Marie pouring coffee into a cup, only the stream didn't reach the cup. She seemed suddenly frozen in time. My unbelieving gaze moved back to Julian, who had dropped his shirt to the floor. Behind him the air wavered until a jet of light emerged. Two marvelous, wide wings appeared and hovered at his sides.

Their sight robbed the air from my lungs.

One arm behind my knees and the other planted firmly on my back, Julian swept me up. Mischief sparked in his deep blue eyes. His warm breath brushed my face. "Are you ready to sky dive?"

Head tilted back, I laughed out loud. "Bring it on, angel."

The End

Playlist

OneRepublic – Secrets
(On the run through London)

Jervy Hou – A Short Beautiful Piano Piece - Improv
(Saying goodbye to Quinn)

Lord of the Rings – The Fellowship of the ring
(The vineyards)

OneRepublic – Good Life
(Teamwork with Julian)

British Anthem; God Save the Queen
(A weird dream)

Owl City - Fireflies
(Balconies, birds, town, ice cream. He's impossible. And then there's that dress...)

Guillaume Robbe – Hallelujah (piano cover)
(A special song for Jona)

Wall.E Soundtrack – Define Dancing
(The wingbeat of a bird stretched to eternity)

Jervy Hou – A Breathtaking Piano Piece
(Truths, lies, confessions, loss)

Lindsey Stirling – Elements
(Run. Before it's too late. He'll leave.)

Miley Cyrus – When I look at you
(No memory of the angel, but he's still around)

The Piano Guys – Over the rainbow
(Return of the angel)

Find another enchanting romance in
Anna Katmore's
A PRINCE FOR LITTLE RED RIDING HOOD

A Prince for little Red Riding Hood

or

When Red Riding Hood decided to catch herself a royal.

Every time someone opens a storybook and reads the four magical words "Once upon a time," my granny gets eaten a few hours later. Boy, it sucks! I wish my tale had a cool ending, like Cindy and Briar-Rose got. Along with a castle and a dashing prince to marry.

Did you ever kiss a frog? No prince pops out of that. Trust me, I've tried. Seventeen frogs, and nearly one warty toad—for nothing.

What I get is Jack. Alas, he's unsuitable for a romantic ending. The Wolf simply lacks the manners for that. And obviously, a crown. Because, off the record: love only happens among royals in Fairyland.

Since royalty doesn't just rain from the sky, I'm going to build a prince trap tomorrow, and then I'll write my new ever after. It'll be so good...

cough Hi, I'm Jack Wolf—yes, if Riley gets to say something here, so do I.
And she better forget about this harebrained idea to elope with a royal. We're not going to rewrite anything. If she wants to make out with somebody, she can do it with me or no one.
Oh, and...it *will* be good.

GROVER BEACH TEAM

Play With Me

Ryan Hunter

T Is For...

Dating Trouble

The Trouble with Dating Sue

FALL FOR ME

The Impossible Bet

Taming Chloe Summers

CRUSHED HEARTS

Unfair Love

Broken Dawn

Awaking Trust

ADVENTURES IN NEVERLAND

Neverland

Pan's Revenge

GRIMM WAS A BASTARD

A Prince for little Red Riding Hood

A Wolf in her Way

Seventeen Butterflies

My Secret Vampire

Julian

"I'm writing stories because I can't breathe without."

Anna Katmore lives in an enchanting world of her own, which allows only those to pass who are ready to hand in logic and rationalism. But beware, if you dare to step through this door, you'll never want to leave again...

Disney is her attitude towards life, and if she could, she'd save the world from itself. Her patronus is a wolf, her wand the broken twig of an apple tree, 10 inches long, but it does the job. Glitter on her shoes is a must, though she doesn't care for Cinderella's glass slippers. Too risky that something might break...

For more information, please visit *annakatmore.com*

Printed in Great Britain
by Amazon